The Heirloom

Books by Beverly Lewis

The Heirloom • *The Orchard*
The Beginning • *The Stone Wall*
The Tinderbox • *The Timepiece*

The First Love • *The Road Home*
The Proving • *The Ebb Tide*
The Wish • *The Atonement*
The Photograph • *The Love
Letters* • *The River*

HOME TO HICKORY HOLLOW
The Fiddler • *The Bridesmaid*
The Guardian • *The Secret
Keeper* • *The Last Bride*

THE ROSE TRILOGY
The Thorn • *The Judgment*
The Mercy

ABRAM'S DAUGHTERS
The Covenant • *The Betrayal*
The Sacrifice • *The Prodigal*
The Revelation

THE HERITAGE
OF LANCASTER COUNTY
The Shunning • *The Confession*
The Reckoning

ANNIE'S PEOPLE
The Preacher's Daughter
The Englisher • *The Brethren*

THE COURTSHIP OF
NELLIE FISHER
The Parting • *The Forbidden*
The Longing

SEASONS OF GRACE
The Secret • *The Missing*
The Telling

The Postcard • *The Crossroad*

The Redemption of Sarah Cain
Sanctuary (with David Lewis)
Child of Mine (with David Lewis)
The Sunroom • *October Song*
*Beverly Lewis Amish
Romance Collection*

Amish Prayers
*The Beverly Lewis Amish
Heritage Cookbook*

www.beverlylewis.com

The HEIRLOOM

BEVERLY LEWIS

a division of Baker Publishing Group
Minneapolis, Minnesota

© 2023 by Beverly M. Lewis, Inc.

Published by Bethany House Publishers
Minneapolis, Minnesota
www.bethanyhouse.com

Bethany House Publishers is a division of
Baker Publishing Group, Grand Rapids, Michigan

Printed in the United States of America

All rights reserved. No part of this publication may be reproduced, stored in a retrieval system, or transmitted in any form or by any means—for example, electronic, photocopy, recording—without the prior written permission of the publisher. The only exception is brief quotations in printed reviews.

Library of Congress Cataloging-in-Publication Data
Names: Lewis, Beverly, author.
Title: The heirloom / Beverly Lewis.
Description: Minneapolis, Minnesota : Bethany House, a division of Baker Publishing Group. [2023]
Identifiers: LCCN 2023009159 | ISBN 9780764237560 (paperback) | ISBN 9780764237577 (cloth) | ISBN 9780764237584 (large print) | ISBN 9781493443659 (ebook)
Subjects: LCSH: Amish—Fiction. | LCGFT: Romance fiction. | Christian fiction. | Novels.
Classification: LCC PS3562.E9383 H45 2023 | DDC 813/.54—dc23/eng/20230227
LC record available at https://lccn.loc.gov/2023009159

Unless otherwise indicated, Scripture quotations are from the King James Version of the Bible.

Scripture quotations identified NKJV are from the New King James Version®. Copyright © 1982 by Thomas Nelson. Used by permission. All rights reserved.

This story is a work of fiction. Names, characters, incidents, and dialogues are products of the author's imagination and are not to be construed as real. Any resemblance to any person, living or dead, is purely coincidental.

Baker Publishing Group publications use paper produced from sustainable forestry practices and post-consumer waste whenever possible.

23 24 25 26 27 28 29   7 6 5 4 3 2 1

To
longtime friends
Martha, Charity, and Johnnie,
dear sisters three.

Blessed are all those who
put their trust in Him.
Psalm 2:12 NKJV

My mouth shall speak wisdom,
and the meditation of my heart
shall give understanding.
Psalm 49:3 NKJV

Prologue

JUNE 1994

Mamma always said we should never waste a speck of time, "since that's what life's made up of." So with that in mind, I finally sat down at her oak desk. *Dat* had made it back when they were first married, and after Mamma's passing a year ago, he gave it to me. He'd also asked me to discard its contents for him as I saw fit, urging me not to spend too much time on the task.

Now there in my sunny upstairs bedroom, I ran my hand across the desk's smooth surface. I'd purposely delayed this effort, thinking reading Mamma's personal mail and all would only make me sadder. Yet I cherished having anything of hers, dear as she'd been to me.

Jah, life's made up of segments of time,

but no matter how long or short our lifespan, wasn't it what we did with our years that counted? Surely Dat must have felt the same way. After all, he'd gotten himself married to the widow Eva Graber two months earlier . . . a mere ten months after Mamma went to Glory.

I'd grown closer to my father after Mamma's passing, but when Eva entered his life, everything changed. *Nee*, I didn't deny that my step-*Mamm* should hold a special place in Dat's heart, but while continuing to grieve the loss of precious Mamma, I was still getting used to Eva's presence. And although I understood the necessity of such change in my father's life, I recognized I'd have to leave home at some point to have a fulfilling life of my own.

I just didn't know when . . . or how.

Opening the top left drawer of the desk, I stared at the cards, notes, and letters neatly stacked all the way to the back.

"If I could just have one more day with Mamma," I whispered, recalling how I'd tried to be strong right up till the end. But after my mother drew her last breath, the realization that she was gone had felt ever so weighty.

Turning my attention back to the correspondence bundled in every drawer, I refused to get bogged down with memories. I quickly scanned the missives from friends and family and then dropped most of them in my wastepaper basket.

But I couldn't help noticing one person's name and address turned up more frequently than all the others—Ella Mae Zook from Hickory Hollow, Pennsylvania. I shouldn't have been surprised, I guess. Mamma had often talked about her aunt by marriage—nearly like a big sister to her. Ella Mae was her uncle Joseph's wife. He'd died a few months after Mamma.

Out of curiosity, I set aside all the letters from Ella Mae. Then, nearly finished with my task, I started reading the one she'd written six weeks before Mamma died.

My dear Lillian,

I'm thinking of you as I sit here with your recent letter in my lap. How I wish we could speak face-to-face.

My heart is so heavy. Your suffering is mine to bear, too, because in our hearts we carry closest those we love most dearly. I pray each and every day that the Lord himself will minister His healing and comfort as you try to rest.

And, my oh my, your youngest daughter, Clara, must surely be the hands and feet of Jesus to you. What a compassionate young woman she sounds like, and I thank God for her every time I think of you. She is in my near-constant prayers, as well.

I had to stop reading for a moment, the words stirring up a longing for Mamma. And gratitude, too, for this most wonderful relationship she'd enjoyed with her aunt.

Through the window, I could see Dat outside hitching up Mack, one of our two road horses, the slump in my father's posture gone since marrying Eva. I couldn't help but wonder if he'd known how close Mamma and Ella Mae had been—a godsend for my dear mother not just while she suffered with her illness but through all the years she'd lived here in Indiana.

As it turned out, I ended up reading all of Ella Mae's letters, riveted by her thoughtful words of friendship and caring. By the time I'd finished, I simply could not throw away this collection of treasures connecting two hearts across the miles. Just by reading them, I, too, was deeply touched and felt uplifted in spirit.

I bundled up the dozens of letters, placed them on my dresser at the other end of the room, and then returned to wipe out each of the drawers with the cloth I'd brought up from the kitchen. Glad to have completed this task for Dat, I was also thankful I'd stumbled upon Great-*Aendi* Ella Mae's letters of tenderest care.

I must meet this woman someday!

The following day, after I'd gathered the quilted oven mitts and pot holders I'd made for Saturday market, I invited my *Schtiefmammi* to go along, just as I had each week since Dat married her and moved her into the house.

Eva shook her head. "Need to bake a batch of pies," she replied.

There was always an excuse not to go.

"All right," I said, not pressing her. Still, I wondered if my father had any idea how hard I'd tried to make even the smallest connection with Eva. *And she takes no interest in quilting*, I mused, missing the close bond I'd had with Mamma and our shared love of quilt-making. *What do Eva and I have in common besides Dat?*

"I'll be gone most of the day," I told her. Not that Eva needed to know, but I wanted to be considerate.

"Have yourself a nice time." She turned from the gas range, looking rather bright in her turquoise dress, cape, and matching apron. For a woman in her fifties, Eva seemed drawn to wearing loud colors. "Supper'll be ready at five-thirty," she said in a reminding tone. "You'll be hungry by then."

"*Jah*, I'm always hungrier on market day. Must be all the goodies there," I said, smoothing the gray dress and black apron I still wore in mourning. With that, I picked up my purse and headed out to the horse and carriage, where Dat had already placed my box of wares to sell this beautiful day.

After my father and Eva retired that evening, I sat out on the back porch, newly painted white with a dark gray ceiling. Mamma's two wind chimes still hung in the far corner.

Feeling underfoot in my father's house, I stared at the deepening sky, knowing I wasn't really needed here. Eva was the one cooking and keeping house for Dat now, like I'd done after Mamma passed. I had to get on with my own life somehow, so I considered what opportunities a young, single, baptized woman had here in First Light, Indiana.

All my friends were seriously courting or engaged, but unfortunately, finding a new beau for myself wouldn't be easy. Not in this small community with no suitable fellows my age available. And the recent calamity with Wollie Lehman, my first-ever serious beau, had set me back. Sure, I'd enjoyed the time we spent together, but our friendship and eventual courting had only led to a sudden tearing apart I never saw coming. One day we were planning our future and sharing our dreams, and the next day, those dreams lay shattered around us.

Had she been alive, Mamma would have comforted me, helped see me through the pain and disappointment somehow.

I thought again of the letters from her aunt Ella Mae and all the appealing descriptions of Hickory Hollow in Lancaster County. Mamma had lived there till age thirteen, when her parents and most of their siblings and families moved out here.

At that moment, an idea began to flit around in my head. What if I could visit there, see where Mamma grew up—and get to know Ella Mae?

I fairly leaped out of my wicker chair, then quietly hurried into the house and up the stairs to my room at the far end of the hall. I lit the gas lamp and sat down at Mamma's gleaming desk to compose a letter, the small circle of light my companion as I wrote to the woman who'd devotedly carried my dying mother in her heart.

And who'd cared enough to pray for me.

CHAPTER
One

Ella Mae carried her round yellow teapot with its padded tea cozy to the trestle table in her sunny kitchen and placed it in the center. She'd just finished steeping her favorite peppermint tea this lovely Wednesday, the eighth day of June, expecting a visit from her eldest daughter. Last Sunday, Mattie had made a point of telling her she planned to drop by today. Mattie's husband, David, was the older brother of their newly ordained young bishop, John Beiler, but Ella Mae doubted this visit had anything to do with church.

No, she was quite sure of Mattie's reason for coming. *There's a bee in her bonnet.*

Eyeing her placemats, where two small yellow-and-white plates matched the teacups and saucers, Ella Mae was ready to hear Mattie out and then politely set her straight. And the freshly baked maple-syrup-and-sour-cream muffins might just help her cause.

She'd risen early to redd up the house, mopping all the floors on the main level as well as sweeping the long and deep back porch adorned by hanging baskets of Boston ferns. But now she was glad for a rest. Since her husband's passing five months earlier, she hadn't felt nearly as peppy. Yet according to her widowed cousins and other womenfolk, this was to be expected.

Still, she yearned for her departed husband. Despite her advanced age of seventy-seven, she'd been his caretaker. Joseph's smile and gentle spirit, no matter his ailing, had brightened her days. Devoted to him since their marriage over five decades ago, she was still attempting to create new daily patterns. But it was as hard as trying to change the design of a finished quilt.

Near impossible.

Just this morning, she'd caught her breath at the sight of the oval rug she'd braided specifically for Joseph's side of the bed, so his bare feet wouldn't touch the cold floor if his slippers weren't handy. It was that way with other insignificant things, too, nearly every time she turned around—so many reminders of their shared past. Yet she kept this to herself, not wanting her family and others to fret over her.

Truth be known, she still slid her hand across the bedsheet at night, missing Joseph, whose weakened heart had simply given out. Sometimes she even called to him while making breakfast, for the moment forgetting he wasn't over in the corner of the kitchen reading *Die Botschaft*. Or sitting out on the porch to watch the lively hummingbirds at the feeders or their young great-grandsons swinging double on the tire swing in the side yard, not far from the rustic rose arbor.

She sighed, tears welling up. *How long before I feel a smidgen normal, O Father?*

Sunshine spilled across the kitchen floor as Ella Mae poured tea into her daughter's teacup, then into her own. "Muffins are right out of the oven," she told Mattie, who sat across the table from her. Uncovering a small basket, Ella Mae sniffed the familiar aroma. She knew how moist and delicious these muffins were because she'd pinched off a piece before Mattie arrived—and then another before wrapping that muffin for later.

"Smells *wunnerbaar-gut*, but ya didn't have to bother making these." Mattie set a muffin on her plate, then sipped from her cup before setting it down with a faint clink.

"Ain't a bother a'tall. Be sure an' take home what we don't eat, dear."

Mattie smiled. "David'll be happy 'bout that."

Ella Mae broke her muffin in half and spread butter on it, the warmth melting it quickly. Mattie did the same, glancing at her a couple of times without speaking, like she wasn't sure how to start.

"Somethin' on your mind, dear?" Ella Mae asked.

Mattie finished chewing, then swallowed before pushing her white *Kapp* strings over her shoulders and noticeably drawing a breath. "*Mamm*, I've been thinkin'—well, we *all* have, really."

"*We?*"

Giving a little nod, Mattie replied, "The family." She looked suddenly serious, hesitating a bit, like she was expecting an argument. "We think it's time to move ya in with David and me . . . till we can build a *Dawdi Haus* for ya."

Thought this was coming. It was expected of a widow her age to move in with family.

Ella Mae took her time drinking her tea, then said, "That's considerate, but this is still my home, Mattie." She glanced around the large kitchen. "Everything I built with your Dat is here," she added more softly. "Right here."

Her daughter's face collapsed. "I didn't want to be the one to tell ya, but at some point, you'll have to make some changes. It's unavoidable."

Ella Mae offered to pour more tea, but Mattie shook her head. So she poured more for herself. "I can take care of myself, as you can see," she said.

"Well, Dat was worried 'bout ya keepin' up this big house after he passed, remember? It was a big concern of his. He was thinkin' of ya, Mamm."

"Honestly, I do a little cleanin' every day . . . ain't a problem. And yous have already taken the care of the livestock and the farm off me, which I appreciate." Ella Mae shook her head emphatically. "Surely you can understand. This here house is a comfort to me—all the memories."

Mattie frowned. "But ya can't stay here forever."

Ella Mae wrapped her hand around her teacup, comforted by its warmth. "I wouldn't mind that, really."

Mattie sighed. "You don't know it, but Jake promised Dat we'd get ya moved in with one of us."

Ella Mae groaned at hearing this.

"Dat was adamant, Mamm. He worried 'bout your future without him."

"He needn't have."

"*Ach*, you're makin' this harder than necessary," Mattie said, concern on her pretty face. "You know how determined Jake can be. So maybe you could start packin' in a couple of weeks. We'll all help, ya know."

Ella Mae's heart sank. Her eldest son *could* be mighty stubborn. "*Ach*, that's awful short notice, for pity's sake!"

"Well, Dat would turn over in his grave if he knew you were livin' here alone."

Ella Mae drew a breath. Joseph had been in the process of dying, yet apparently, he'd been thinking more of her than of himself.

"We want to honor Dat's wishes, Mamm. He wanted this for you more than you're willing to admit."

"Truth be told, I'm just not ready." *Not ready to say good-bye.*

"The family cares 'bout your wishes, too. We really do, but . . ."

After an awkward pause, during which Mattie finished her muffin, leaving only a few crumbs on her plate, she perked up a little. "I have somethin' else to tell ya—more pleasant."

"I should hope so," Ella Mae said.

"Rebecca has the wedding quilt that belonged to your parents, an' she wonders if you might like to have it. It's threadbare in places, though. How'd ya feel 'bout tryin' to restore it? After all, 'tis an heirloom by now."

"I'll have a look-see. I've wondered where that quilt disappeared to."

"It was in a batch of things from Aendi Essie. Rebecca said she could try an' repair it, but she doesn't think she can do it justice."

Ella Mae should have assumed the quilt to be in her now-deceased twin's possession, then in her niece Rebecca's. Essie had passed well before Joseph. *Another hard loss.* "Maybe I can work on it little by little."

Mattie lifted her teacup. "Rebecca says that quilt has a unique story behind it."

"Indeed it does." Ella Mae's mother had talked fondly of the wedding quilt back when her twin daughters were only young teens, not even courting age yet.

Mattie glanced toward the kitchen window. "Whenever you're ready for it, I can bring it over. Or once you've moved over to our place."

"*Abselutt.* I'll see what I can do with it . . . before or after my family forces me out of *mei Haus.*"

"Mamm, for goodness' sake." Mattie rolled her eyes and said no more as she finished her tea. When she was ready to leave, she excused herself from the table to head for home.

So I have only a few weeks, Ella Mae thought miserably. *If Jake's behind this, I'll have no further say.*

That afternoon, following a noon meal of leftover meatloaf, half a baked potato, and green beans with ham bits, Ella Mae bowed her head and beseeched God to make it possible for her to remain in her beloved farmhouse awhile longer.

Please, dear Lord. Whatever it takes.

Still stewing about her circumstances two days later, Ella Mae stepped out on her front porch and found her mailbox brimming with letters. Most envelopes were thick with circle letters from her grown children in Big Valley's Belleville, Pennsylvania—her younger son Abe and married daughters Emmie and Faye—and from cousins in Sugarcreek, Ohio. A flatter letter was postmarked First Light, Indiana.

How about that. A letter from Lillian Bender's youngest daughter.

Glancing down the lane, she squinted into the sunlight at the picturesque rose arbor with its trailing pink roses. How she missed hearing from her lovely niece Lillian—and such a shame for her to be struck down by cancer at only fifty-five. The silent kind that surprised everyone.

Back in the house, Ella Mae closed the screen door behind her and sat herself down in the front room rocker nearby, enjoying the breeze coming through. She placed all the other mail on the small table next to her and reached for her reading glasses, then opened the letter from Clara. She'd never met her, but she certainly knew a lot about the young woman from Lillian's thoughtful letters throughout the years.

Clara was delighted when her older sister, Bertha, dropped by with a quart of fresh strawberries from her berry patch. Bertie offered to wash and stem them for Eva, but their stepmother insisted on doing it herself.

"We could make quick work of it together," Clara spoke up.

"Ah, yous just enjoy your visit," Eva said with a smile.

"If you're sure," Bertie said, then motioned Clara toward the back door.

As they walked along the road near Dat's cornfield, Clara expressed her frustration. "When I offer to help, like I did with Mamm, Eva sorta shoos me away."

"S'pose she's just independent," Bertie said, walking briskly.

"But not around Dat."

Bertie laughed softly. "Well, she's obviously in *love* with him. And still prob'ly getting adjusted to being married again—and havin' a stepfamily."

"And a stepdaughter she leaves at home alone when she and Dat go to visit her children and grandchildren."

"No wonder ya feel left out. I'm sorry to hear this, Clara. But these things do take time."

Clara tried to put herself in Eva's shoes, but she couldn't imagine stepping into a home where another woman had loved and cared for a man and his family the way Mamma had.

"Say, I've been mullin' something for a while now," Bertie said. "What would ya think about goin' to the youth conference in Lancaster County come fall? Would that interest you?"

"Hadn't thought 'bout it."

"Well, if you'd like to go, Peter and I'd be happy to help with the cost."

Clara smiled. "Are ya hopin' I'll meet a new fella there?"

"It's crossed my mind." Bertie glanced at Clara. "Our community is so small . . . as you know all too well."

"That's nice of ya to offer, but I might have some plans of my own. I'm waitin' to hear back from Mamma's aunt Ella Mae in Hickory Hollow."

"You wrote her?"

"*Jah*, about a week and a half ago." She would explain about the letters she'd found another time. "Dat said it was okay. The mail can be slow sometimes, but surely it won't be much longer before I get a letter in return."

Bertie's blue eyes widened as she swept a stray wisp of dark
hair, a deeper brown than Clara's, behind her ear. "Do ya hope to visit there?"

"Lord willin'. Just a week." Clara walked faster to keep up with Bertie, who was taller and had longer legs. *Tall like Mamma was.* Clara recalled her mother's eagerness to take walks, as well. "Mamma loved growin' up there, and I thought I might feel closer to her, maybe."

"That was a long time ago, though." The hem of Bertie's dark green skirt swooshed as they walked. "I'm sure a lot's changed since then."

"Well, a lot's changed *here* since Mamma died . . . and in a short time, too."

Bertie slowed her pace. "I'm sure you've noticed it more than the rest of us . . . livin' at home an' all."

"*Ach*, I didn't say it for sympathy." Clara shook her head.

"But it has to be harder for you, sister." Bertie wiped her brow with the back of her hand. "Goodness, it's so hot and sticky for only mid-June."

The sultry air's getting to her, Clara thought briefly before her mind returned to Ella Mae and the hope of visiting Hickory Hollow.

CHAPTER

Two

After Bertie left in her spring wagon, Clara made her way to the barn, hoping to find her father there. She slid open the heavy door and walked over the newly swept cement floor, past the two horse stalls on either side and the watering trough in the center. The sweet scent of hay was in the air, and motes hung suspended in streams of light from windows high overhead.

Dat was in the corner, sharpening the blade on his gas-powered riding mower, which was minus a seat. Unlike more traditional Amish church districts she'd heard about, here they were permitted to have power mowers and rototillers, and they stood to ride on the back of the lawn mower instead of sitting.

Dat was stooped over, his straw hat pushed

back from his forehead enough to make his graying brown bangs visible.

"Can I help ya with anything?" she asked, hoping to spend some time with him.

"Once this chore's done, I'll be headin' over to talk to our deacon. Besides, you've got indoor chores, ain't?" He glanced at her, then returned to his sharpening.

"I'm all caught up." Clara stepped closer. "I haven't heard back from Great-Aendi Ella Mae yet."

"Oh, but ya will." Dat chuckled. "That woman loved your Mamma, and she undoubtedly knows all 'bout ya. And all of us, too, fast as the letters flew back an' forth 'tween there and here."

Clara recalled the dozens of letters she'd saved from Mamma's desk. "I'll try to be patient," she replied.

Dat's gaze met hers again, and after pausing a moment, he said quietly, "Listen, daughter, I hope ya don't feel ya have to take a break from me . . . and from Eva."

She shook her head. "I'd like to see where Mamma grew up . . . and get to know Ella Mae."

"Are those the only reasons?"

She looked down, the cement cool against her bare feet. "I really need some time away, Dat."

He nodded, taking it in. "Just keep in mind Hickory Hollow's Amish church is known to have a low church ordinance, much more traditional than ours. They follow excommunication and shunning practices, for instance. And there's more emphasis on rules and regulations than on God's grace." He sighed loudly. "And, Clara . . . it's important that ya meet a young man who shares your strong faith . . . and your relationship with Christ."

She remembered Mamma mentioning that district's tendency toward theological hairsplitting some years ago. "You must be concerned that I want to visit there."

Dat was slow to reply, but when he did, he spoke with confidence. "Like I said, big differences exist between the two church districts. Your Mamm and I discussed this often durin' her years of writin' to Ella Mae."

"I read Ella Mae's letters to Mamm, and she seems as certain of her close relationship with the Lord as we do here. Even Mamma told me that."

Dat nodded. "Ella Mae's quite unique for Hickory Hollow, I'll just say that much."

"So maybe I'll fit in with *her* durin' a visit."

He groaned a little. "I'm just glad ya won't be there for very long, daughter."

She couldn't help but notice how attentive

her father was just now. And before she could think the better of it, she told him what she felt up to saying. "One of the reasons I want to go there is that my beau and I broke up . . . after bein' close to a betrothal."

Her father's thick eyebrows rose. "Oh?"

Clara nodded, surprised at herself for revealing even this, but she didn't intend to explain why she and Wollie were no longer together.

"I knew ya'd been goin' out near every weekend for a while there." He looked rather quizzical. "But not lately."

"*Nee.*" She stopped to breathe. "Honestly, part of me walked out the door with him."

Dat's eyes locked with hers. "It must feel thataway, Clara. Mighty sorry."

She pressed her lips together lest the lump in her throat turn to tears. "Our courtship came to nothin'—*futsch.*"

"Well now, a nice young woman like you won't have trouble findin' another beau."

Blushing at the rare compliment, she shrugged. "Only the Lord can see into the future."

"I'll say," Dat said softly.

In that moment, Clara understood he must not be thinking about her but rather about Mamm's death and his new wife.

The barn door opened and closed, and

there was Eva carrying a thermos and coming their way. "Would ya like something cold to drink, Vernon?" she asked, beaming. Then glancing at Clara, she said, "*Ach*, didn't see ya, Clara. Goodness, if I'd known, I would've brought you some, too."

"It's okay. I'll get something back at the house."

Clara politely excused herself, heading toward the barn door, leaving the two of them alone. As she pushed the door open, daylight rushed in, blinding her briefly before she pulled it shut, all the while pondering what she'd just done, spilling out a few pieces of her heart.

Her father had no idea what had happened with Wollie Lehman—and she prayed he never would.

After breakfast the next morning, Clara walked the half mile to Bertie's to help pick strawberries while her two school-age nephews were with their Dat at a farm sale up the road. When she and Bertie finished picking, they started washing the main-level windows in preparation for hosting Preaching at Bertie and Peter's house this Sunday. At each one, Bertie worked on the outside while Clara worked inside.

"I'm thinking of not goin' to the next Singing," Clara confided in her sister. "I'd rather be in Hickory Hollow."

"Well, Ella Mae's getting up in years, so ya don't know if she's ailin' or even up to havin' overnight company, let alone a week's visit."

"You're right." Clara stepped back to scrutinize the front room's north-facing window. "I sure hope she's okay, though." *Would hate to miss out on meeting her.* "I didn't tell ya why I decided to ask her 'bout a visit. Dat wanted me to clear out Mamma's desk, and when I did, I found dozens of *wunnerbaar* letters from Ella Mae."

"Must've been too hard for him to do it himself."

"*Jah*, and at first it was hard for me, too, but I'm happy to have the desk and the letters from Ella Mae. Our brothers out in Missouri wouldn't have wanted either one—" A thought suddenly occurred to her. "Would you have wanted the desk, Bertie? As Mamma's oldest daughter? I wouldn't want to—"

"*Nee.* I'm glad for ya, sister. I have some other things of hers."

Bertie headed around the house to the next window, and Clara met her there.

"I hope it's okay that I kept Ella Mae's letters," Clara said as she removed the screen inside, then reached high to wash the windowpane.

"Why wouldn't it be?"

"That's what I thought, but I didn't tell Dat."

"*Ach*, no need to. His mind's on Eva now. 'Tis for the best."

Clara smiled. It was just like Bertie to take the lead like that. "I couldn't bear to discard them. I mean, the tender way our great-aunt shared with Mamma 'bout her care for her was truly special."

"So then, it's *gut* ya kept 'em." Bertie grinned at her through the newly cleaned window. "And if ya *do* get to go visit her, I'll want to hear all about it when you're back home."

"If I go, I'd like to be a big help to Ella Mae."

Bertie laughed. "Knowin' you, I have no doubt."

That afternoon, Clara received a letter from Ella Mae. She hurried to sit in the porch swing facing the road and began to read.

Dear Clara,
I was delighted to receive your letter. And, my goodness, I can't wait for your visit!

> *Jot me a note and let me know when you'll arrive. Meanwhile, the spare room is ready and waiting for you. We'll have us a right good time.*
>
> *With much love,*
> *Great-Aendi Ella Mae*

"*Wunnerbaar!*" Clara said, hopping off the swing and twirling around just as the bishop and his grandson rode past in their market wagon. The bishop waved, looking quite astonished, and Clara quickly headed inside.

Upstairs in her room, she wrote a note to Ella Mae, letting her know she'd plan to arrive a week from this Saturday afternoon, Lord willing. That done, she squeezed her eyes shut and thanked God for this most delightful reply indeed.

CHAPTER
Three

After the noon meal the Monday after Clara should have received her letter, Ella Mae wandered through the large front room of her farmhouse for the third time since redding up the kitchen. She stepped out the front door to check the black mailbox attached to the gray stone exterior of her home. Hoping for a reply from Clara, she wondered if their longtime carrier had come but forgotten to move the flag.

Wouldn't be the first time.

But no, the circle letters to her children in Belleville were still waiting to be picked up. "Charlie must be runnin' late," she murmured, moving across the porch and looking up the road to the north, then south through the willow tree.

Sitting herself down on one of the porch's two oak rockers, she fanned her face with the hem of her long black apron. She kept her eyes peeled toward the road as she rocked, enjoying the familiar sight of swaying cornstalks in the field over yonder. In a few short weeks, the sweet corn would be ready for harvest. She could almost taste that first bite of corn on the cob, butter running down on all sides.

A flock of purple martins congregated across the road near a row of honeysuckle bushes, and she closed her eyes, listening to their burbling, chatty song. On many early summer evenings, she'd sat in that very spot with Joseph once their chores were done, leisurely commenting about the weather, or which of their younger grandchildren might be getting married next, or who they planned to visit on the off-Sunday from Preaching. The delightful east-facing location was the one they most preferred, sheltered as it was from the sun's late-afternoon rays.

And after Joseph turned ill, they would often sit out here waiting for the mail to arrive together. Sometimes it was the highlight of her husband's day.

Dear man. Everything I do reminds me of Joseph.

Just then, from a near distance, she heard

what was surely the mail truck, and when she got up and walked to the porch banister to lean on it and look, she smiled.

Spotting Charlie Kline stopping at the end of her lane, she returned to sit in her rocker lest she look too eager, like a schoolgirl waiting for a love letter.

When the middle-aged man came up the steps, smiling, he handed her the mail. "Warm enough for ya, Mrs. Zook?"

"A breeze would help." She smiled back, noticing the dots of perspiration on his brow. "Say, Charlie, would ya like a glass of my meadow tea? It'll be nice and cold." And before he could answer, she added, "Won't ya sit down while I get some?"

"Please, don't go out of your way," he said, lifting the mailbox lid and removing her letters.

"It won't take but a minute."

Ella Mae made her way to the kitchen, carrying the mail and immediately spying her grandniece's letter on top of the stack. She poured the mint tea over ice and brought the tumbler out to the front porch, just itching to read Clara's letter.

But Charlie came first.

"This'll wet your whistle," she said, handing the glass to the kindly mail carrier, then sitting down in the other rocker.

"Of all the people on my route, you're the one who spoils me," Charlie said.

"How's that possible with only a cold drink?"

Charlie hooted, his broad shoulders heaving up and down.

"Last I read in the Good Book," she added, "the Lord himself recommended a cup of cold water."

Glancing at her, he said, "You should have poured some for yourself."

"I daresay I'd be tea-tipsy if I drank a drop more after two tumblers full durin' the noon meal."

Charlie took another long drink. "So besides mint and cold water, what *else* is in this tea?" He was smiling again.

"That's my secret."

"It must be sweetened with something."

She laughed softly. "Ever hear of honey?"

While Charlie finished his tea, she mentioned that her niece's daughter from Indiana was likely coming for a visit. "I'm s'posed to be packin' up soon to move in with my daughter Mattie and her husband, so I daresay Clara's comin' at just the right time. I'm in no hurry to go."

She couldn't help but grin.

"Well, if I know you, Mrs. Zook, she'll enjoy her visit here."

"I've never met the girl, but I feel like I've known her all her life 'cause of her Mamm's many letters 'bout the family."

"She must have enjoyed keeping in touch with you," he said. "Lots of folk do, ya know." Charlie set the empty tumbler on the small wooden table between them. "I've even heard some refer to you in rather reverent tones."

Ella Mae waved that off and shook her head. "Considerin' the unwise choices I made in my youth, I could hardly agree with that."

Charlie's brown eyes got bigger. "You, unwise?"

"'Twas mighty true. Sorry to say." She paused, eager to change the subject. "Folk haven't been comin' to see me for tea like they used to. It's been a long time since I've had the opportunity to lift someone's spirits by listenin' and then prayin' for them."

"Could be they were respectful while you were looking after Mr. Zook."

"But now that I have all this time on my hands, they still don't come," she replied, sighing.

"Well, you're still in mourning. That might be the reason."

He was undoubtedly right.

Charlie leaned forward in the rocker and said, "I suspect the mail won't deliver itself." He rose and stood near the porch steps.

"Thanks for your kind hospitality, as always." With that, he waved and headed for the walkway.

"Have yourself a *gut* week!" she called after him, then rose to go inside, where Clara's letter was waiting.

Ella Mae removed her reading glasses to look at the day clock on the kitchen wall, smiling after reading Clara's letter. *Around this time Saturday, she'll be here.*

She moved to the gas-powered fridge to check that it was well stocked, then down the hall to the spare room across from her own bedroom. It was quite tidy, rarely in use nowadays. This week, she'd dust and mop it thoroughly and bake something special, too, recalling from Lillian's letters that Clara had always enjoyed her mother's chocolate mousse cake.

Won't Clara be surprised!

Ella Mae caught herself laughing lightly as she walked outside to check on the clothes hanging on the line, her heart ever so full.

An hour or so later, she heard a horse coming up the lane and looked to see her tall, burly son Jake sitting at the reins in his spring wagon. She couldn't help but notice the pile of flattened boxes in the back.

Jake leaped out of the wagon, tied his driving horse to the hitching post, and then hurried up the walkway to the back stoop, where Ella Mae stood waiting for him. "Hullo, Mamm!" He wiped his sweaty forehead with the back of his forearm, then removed his straw hat and fanned his already tanned face. So much about him reminded her of dear Joseph when he was a young man.

"Just droppin' off some boxes and packing material for your dishes and other breakables."

Ella Mae eyed the wagon bed again. "I won't be getting to any of that for a *gut* while yet," she told him. "I've got company comin' from Indiana this weekend."

Jake frowned. "Mattie didn't say a peep about this."

"Well, Mattie didn't know."

"What's goin' on?" Jake scratched the back of his blond head.

"My niece Lillian Bender's young daughter, Clara, wants to visit."

"Why's she seekin' *you* out? Couldn't she visit other kinfolk, considerin' everything?"

Ella Mae explained that Lillian had passed away a year ago and Clara likely needed solace or simply a change of scenery. She didn't tell Jake the young woman planned to stay only a week. And maybe . . .

"She might be stayin' all summer," she added.

Groaning, Jake shook his head. "*Puh!* Terrible timing."

"So you'll just have to wait awhile longer to move me. Besides, what can it hurt?"

"We need to get ya resettled before it's a hardship for ya, Mamm."

"Listen, son, I doubt I'll fall apart in a few months' time. Besides, it'll take all summer, if not longer, to build the *Dawdi Haus* over at David and Mattie's, so since I ain't ailin', I could just as easily stay put here till it's built."

Jake grimaced. "Mamm . . ."

"I'm at peace here, son."

He shook his head as if unable to comprehend what she meant.

"Chust go an' unload the boxes and things in the barn for now," she told him.

Jake drew an audible breath and raised his hands, palms facing her in surrender. "Guess we'll have to do it your way, Mamm."

"I guess you're right."

CHAPTER

Four

The gravel lane leading to Ella Mae's gray stone farmhouse curved to the right alongside an arching rose arbor with numerous pink trailing roses and a wrought-iron bench. Several giant beech trees graced the lane as well, dappling sunlight over neatly trimmed hedges on the other side. Setting her suitcase on the ground, Clara stopped to take in her lovely surroundings as the taxi cab pulled away.

Mamma never spoke of this house, but she must've come here sometimes as a girl.

Except for the captivating landscape, which she'd tried to imagine earlier while on the train, Clara had never expected to see such a grand and beautiful place. The wide front lawn was immaculate with its edging and dark, rich mulch spread around each tree. One tree even had dazzling yellow and purple pansies ringing its base. She felt suddenly overcome with longing, not only for her mother but for a time years before she was born. A time Clara knew very little about.

This all felt ever so strange.

She tilted her head back, squinting up at two dormer windows. The image of a dusty attic with old trunks and such things came to mind, items that might tell secrets from the past. Then she lifted her suitcase and headed toward the front porch made comfortable by two large rocking chairs and a chain swing at one end. Bright red geraniums in clay pots sat on the left side of the wide porch steps.

Which door do they commonly use here— front or back? she wondered, then decided to take the pebbled pathway to the front entrance. Once there, she knocked on the door and stood straight like Mamm had taught her.

In an instant, a dimpled-faced elderly woman wearing a dark green dress and black cape and apron opened the screen door. "You must be Clara," she said in a husky little voice.

"I'm glad to finally meet ya, Aendi." Clara followed her inside, then set down the suitcase and on top of it, her shoulder purse.

Ella Mae flung her arms wide to her. "*Willkumm,* dearie. I'm happy you're here."

Her aunt smelled like lilies of the valley as Clara stepped back from a hug to smile at her, noticing her soft blue eyes and her gray hair pulled back into a low bun beneath a white *Kapp*.

"How was your trip?" Ella Mae asked.

"Well, I made friends with a young woman on the train who had an infant and a toddler in tow. I helped as much as she'd let me, and it passed the hours."

"You're a lot like your Mamma, ever so caring." Ella Mae drew a breath. "She was truly special to me."

"I miss her every day. And I thought I might feel closer to her here than I do at home . . . now anyway." Clara didn't know what had come over her, but she felt surprisingly free to share her heart. "With Dat's new wife takin' Mamma's place, well . . . it's just so different there."

Ella Mae nodded slowly, her wrinkled face forming a thoughtful smile. "I understand why you'd feel thataway."

Standing there, Clara felt thoroughly wrapped in acceptance. "*Denki*, Aendi."

"If ya like, chust call me Ella Mae."

Clara smiled politely. "Well, I think Mamma'd want me to call ya Aendi."

"That's fine, too." Ella Mae nodded, then motioned for Clara to follow her. "*Kumme*, let's get ya to your room, only a few steps down this hallway. I moved all my things down here after Joseph took sick," she explained, "and after he passed, I disliked the idea of huffin' and puffin' up the stairs every day."

"Must be cooler for ya on the main level this time of year," Clara mentioned as she carried her suitcase and purse.

"*Jah*, for sure."

Ella Mae hung back at the doorway leading to the spare room, where, as she stepped inside, Clara saw a white quilted coverlet and small matching pillows adorning the double bed.

Clara set her suitcase on the floor near a tall chest of drawers.

"Unpack to your heart's content," Ella Mae said as she joined her in the room. "All the drawers are empty. Feel free to use the closet, too. Just make yourself at home."

"*Denki*. That's so thoughtful."

"Well, honey-girl, I've been lookin' forward to getting acquainted ever since your first letter arrived." Ella Mae paused, looking at Clara kindly. "Ya know, I believe I see some of your mother in your face."

Clara's cheeks warmed. "Mamma always said the nicest things 'bout you."

"Then I s'pose we've got ourselves a shared

admiration." Ella Mae chuckled demurely, her little eyes shining. "I'll leave ya be to get settled."

Once Ella Mae left the room, Clara sat on the cane-back chair next to the bookcase, gazing at the surroundings—the pretty embroidered sampler wall hanging and the blanket chest at the foot of the bed. The room was bigger than hers back home. Airier and brighter, too.

Stepping to the windows, she saw a green meadow where two horses grazed near a row of trees. Over on the side lawn stood a tall birdhouse for purple martins, and in the barnyard, two men were standing near the fence posts. Clara guessed they were Ella Mae's relatives.

The landscape was similar to her father's back home, yet she felt transported to a more peaceful place. Over near a carriage shed was a flourishing grape arbor, and Clara noticed a berry patch farther beyond, as well as a hen house.

I can be of some good help while I'm here.

During a supper of crispy fried chicken, cold macaroni salad, and buttered peas, Clara asked Ella Mae how long she'd lived in this house.

"Let's see, now. Joseph an' I moved here six months after our wedding. He and his father and brothers—and a Mennonite uncle, a stonemason—worked together to build it while we were stayin' with my parents."

Ella Mae explained it was customary for a newlywed couple to travel on weekends for the first six weeks of married life, staying overnight with different relatives to receive their wedding gifts. "Is that what's done in Indiana?"

"In some communities, but in others, the kinfolk come to the bride's parents' home to visit and bring gifts."

"Seems I remember your mother tellin' me that years ago. Our community is more tied to the Old Ways of doin' things than yours."

Clara remembered what her Dat had said about that.

Ella Mae picked up the platter with the chicken and offered her more. "Eat yourself full."

"Actually, I snacked quite a bit on the train," Clara said, declining politely. "Eva, my step-Mamm, sent along a lot of goodies."

"'Twas nice of her, but I hope ya have room for some chocolate mousse cake." Ella Mae had a twinkle in her eye.

"Why, that's my most favorite dessert. How'd ya know?"

"I read your mother's letters," Ella Mae replied, smiling. "But I understand if you're too full now. We can always eat some of my cake later."

Clara could see the joy on her aunt's face. "Sounds *gut*."

Ella Mae reached for her tumbler of cold water. "It'll give us somethin' to look forward to after Bible reading and prayers later on."

Clara agreed. *To think she made a cake just to please me!*

"By the way, we have Preachin' tomorrow, and the hosting family lives just two farms down from here. So we'll go to church on foot."

"I brought along two for-*gut* dresses, capes, and aprons," Clara told her. "But both are dark in color since I'm still grievin' Mamma."

"You'll always miss her, dearie. It's natural when ya love someone so much. We never get over such great losses, but we eventually get *through* them with the Lord's help."

"Do ya think I'm wearin' dark clothing for too long, though?"

Ella Mae shook her head, smoothing her own dark dress. "You'll know when it's time to start wearin' colors again."

The comforting way her aunt said it made Clara feel heartened. On the other hand, she hadn't actually commented on her drab dress, but certainly she'd eyed it.

"I appreciate what ya said." Then Clara added, "Are ya sure you don't mind me stayin' a whole week? I don't want to be a burden."

"Ah, no worries about that. For now, why don't ya just relax and catch your breath from your travels? Then after some rest tomorrow afternoon, maybe you'd like to take a ride round the area."

Clara smiled. "I'll look forward to it."

"Also, if you're interested, tomorrow *die Youngie* are gatherin' with a Singing after supper. I'm sure ya'd be welcome."

Clara shrugged, uncertain. Not knowing any of the youth, she might feel self-conscious. On the other hand, she *was* curious—especially about the young men.

"You can always decide later," Ella Mae said.

After the blessing at the end of the meal, which her aunt surprisingly prayed aloud, Clara helped clear the table and dried the dishes. Ella Mae glanced at her now and then as they talked and sweetly said her coming to visit was a true answer to prayer. Clara felt so pleased but also curious why she'd say that. Still, one thing was certain—she hadn't felt this cared for since before Mamma died.

After Bible reading and prayer, followed

by some chocolate mousse cake with Aendi Ella Mae, Clara settled into her room early, tired from the trip. But she could scarcely wait to see her Aendi Ella Mae at breakfast tomorrow and then attend church together. *Mamma was right. Our aunt is a delight.*

CHAPTER

Five

Birds warbled their melodious morning song high in the beech trees as Clara and Ella Mae headed for church in their Sunday best, both wearing black dresses. Ella Mae walked tall and straight for her age, wearing a rather pretty heart-shaped white *Kapp*. Clara thought of her mother as a girl, wearing a similar head covering on a Sunday like this, walking with her parents and siblings to attend church at one of the nearby Amish farms.

What sights caught Mamma's attention back then? Clara wondered as she took in the landscape—neighbors' well-kept yards and flower beds, a freshly painted white fence, and a family of five just ahead of them on their way to Preaching, too. The father was pulling a wagon with a small boy in it. The mother and the older girls wore dresses nearly to their ankles, causing Clara to glance down at her mid-calf hemline.

Soon a carriage with two teenagers in the second seat came up from behind them. The parents called a greeting, and the son and daughter smiled and waved, too.

"That's Adam and Leona Ebersol and their oldest two, Rosanna and her big *Bruder*, Aaron," Ella Mae told Clara after the buggy moved past them. "The younger children go with Adam's widowed father, who lives in their *Dawdi Haus*. Mighty *gut* folk." She paused, then said, "I hope you'll meet Rosanna and Aaron soon."

Slowing her stride to match her aunt's, Clara remembered Ella Mae's comment about the youth get-together and Singing later that day. She also enjoyed the woman's cheerful outlook despite being a rather new widow.

As they turned into the narrow driveway, Clara noticed several horses at a round watering trough, and in the side yard, a considerable group of enclosed gray carriages neatly lined up in two rows. *I've never seen so many at a Preaching or even a wedding*, she thought, realizing Hickory Hollow was far more populated with Amish than First Light was. And even though she surely had a few distant blood kin living round here, she was coming to church as a visitor.

Wearing visitors' clothing, too. Her outsider status must surely be obvious to others—the deep-cup style of her white head covering, for instance?

Now she unexpectedly felt out of place even though she was with Ella Mae. *I'll stay right with her as much as I can*, Clara thought as they walked past a birdhouse high on a post, then around to the backyard, where lines were already forming near the back of the farmhouse—one for the men and one for the women.

Ella Mae stopped repeatedly to talk with several women, introducing Clara to each one. Then she said, "Oh, there's Rebecca Lapp, my twin's daughter. *Kumme*, let's talk with her."

Clara recalled reading about Essie's passing in one of Ella Mae's letters.

Rebecca was stout and looked hardy, like most of the farmers' wives there. *Dat always said a good wife oughta be at least a little plump. Just like Mamma . . . and Eva, too.*

After Clara was introduced, Rebecca asked Ella Mae if Mattie had told her about the heirloom quilt she'd uncovered.

"*Jah*, she did."

Clara asked, "How old's the quilt?"

"Close to eighty years, I s'pect." Rebecca looked at Ella Mae for confirmation.

"Eighty-three, to be exact," Ella Mae said, adding that it was crafted as a wedding gift for her mother, who'd married in 1911. "She'd just turned eighteen. Might seem kinda young to wed nowadays, but it wasn't back then."

Clara was itching to ask more about the quilt, but she patiently waited while Ella Mae and her niece talked about other things. Ella Mae did say she'd stop by Rebecca's soon for the quilt, though.

After they'd visited with several other women, it was time for everyone to line up before going inside the house. Ella Mae instructed Clara to take a place at the end of the women's line with the youth and visitors from other districts. Clara had expected to sit with that group, and she gave her aunt a nod and watched as she walked toward the front with the oldest women in the church district.

This is what we do back home, she thought, feeling suddenly alone.

As she made her way, she noticed a tall dark-haired fellow hurrying across the backyard with another young man who was surely his brother or cousin. The taller fellow looked at her, bobbed his head, and grinned. Clara quickly looked away, conscious of his fetching smile, as if he wanted her to know he'd seen her and wanted her to feel welcome. Or had her out-of-town attire caught his attention?

Whatever the reason, when several teenage girls had taken their place in line, Clara stepped in behind them, the memory of that full-faced smile lingering as she made her way inside the temporary house of worship. Then, picking up an *Ausbund* hymnal, she took her seat on the backless bench in the very last row.

As was usual, Ella Mae sat next to Ruth Stoltzfus, one of the other older women. Then she lowered her head in reverence and prepared her heart for the day's two sermons. But it was hard to remain focused. The look in Clara's gray-blue eyes had made it clear she would rather stay with her, even though they both knew this was their way both here and in Indiana. All the same, Ella Mae wished some of the old traditions were more agreeable, especially in a case like this. Truth be told, she'd had some difficulty with *Gelassenheit*—letting go and not trying to figure out everything related to the Old Ways.

Hopefully, Clara would get acquainted with some of the girls—even shy Rosanna Ebersol, who'd be sitting in the back with other younger youth.

Ella Mae squeezed her eyes shut in an attempt to concentrate on the service ahead.

The wall partitions had been removed, Clara could see, making it possible for so many people to fit into the house, the meeting place for this solemn gathering.

The Scripture readings and first sermon were in High German, so Clara didn't understand them. But thankfully, the second sermon was given in English. Back home most everything was in English.

Though she knew it was frowned on by the more traditional Amish communities even in Indiana, she wondered if they ever had Bible studies here like some of the young married folk did in First Light. *How might that be viewed in Hickory Hollow?*

Following the benediction and closing hymn, the bishop called a meeting for members only. So Clara filed out through the kitchen to the back door with the other youth her age and younger, as well as eight or nine little girls. She waited for the other teens to move ahead of her, then followed them out to cluster near a darling little playhouse with a shingled roof and bright blue morning glories growing on either side of the small front door. The little girls made a beeline for the structure, and after they closed the door, Clara could hear soft giggles erupting from inside.

As for the teen girls Clara had followed, three were dressed in royal blue with white organdy aprons. The other three wore violet-colored dresses, and Clara wondered if they might be sisters or cousins who'd shared a large quantity of the same fabric. Clara and her own sister had often done that. Seeing their lovely colors, she figured she looked as drab as a stormy sky.

The girl who introduced herself first was cheerful and a bit chubby, with deep dimples and big brown eyes. "I'm Lettie Zook," she told Clara. When Clara gave her own name, Lettie said, "Oh, I heard you were coming!" Then she said to the others, "Clara is my *Grememm*'s grandniece."

So this is Ella Mae's granddaughter.

"Indiana's quite a distance away, *jah*?" asked a pretty, round-faced girl who introduced herself as Mary Stoltzfus.

Clara nodded. "And a long train ride, for sure."

"I've never been on a train." Mary paused, then asked, "Is Indiana anything like it is here?"

Clara explained that she'd just arrived yesterday. "I haven't seen enough of the area to tell yet, but my town is very small—only sixteen families in the church district."

"Well, a lot of Amish live round here." Mary glanced at her red-haired friend, who had yet to introduce herself.

"Does it ever rain so hard here that it floods the fields?" Clara asked. At least they could talk about the weather.

"Not that I remember," Mary said. "Does it out there?"

"It can be real stormy. Sometimes we even have tornadoes."

Mary and the other girls exchanged worried glances. "Tornadoes frighten me. They're so unpredictable," Mary said, blue eyes troubled.

Clara agreed. "We've had several close calls, but my Dat always says if our corn and hay crops are destroyed, the Lord will supply what we need."

The girls all nodded in unison, and Clara suddenly felt included. And none of them had looked twice at her black dress, which both surprised and pleased her.

Mary asked, "Say, I'm curious 'bout your recipe for shoofly pie out there in Indiana. Do ya prefer yours or ours here—the wet-bottom kind?"

"Well, I've never had yours, so I guess I'll have to try it," Clara replied.

"Oh, ya must. I think you'll like it *much* better." Mary's eyelids fluttered, as if she realized she'd boasted. "*Ach,* you should decide that, sorry."

Just then Mary's auburn-haired friend spoke up. "It's nice you're visitin', Clara. I'm Katie Lapp, Samuel and Rebecca Lapp's daughter."

"I met your Mamm before the service." Clara mentioned the talk of an heirloom wedding quilt. "Have ya seen it?"

"*Jah.* It's worn and nearly comin' apart in places, but it must've been real perty at one time."

Now Clara was all the more curious.

"I hope you'll come to the youth's outdoor supper later," Katie said, smiling. "It'll be right here on the back lawn."

"We'll save a seat for ya," Lettie chimed in.

Clara delighted at their sincere welcome. "*Denki,* I'll think 'bout it."

"Believe me, you'll have a nice time," Katie said as she looked across the yard to an area near the stable. A group of young men stood there, all dressed in black trousers, suit coats, and white shirts.

"And if ya get asked out by one of the fellas, ya won't have to walk back to Ella Mae's in the dark," Mary said, grinning.

"Well, Aendi Ella Mae surely has a big flashlight I can use."

The girls grinned, and Lettie said, "Oh, I doubt *you'll* be needin' one."

Clara was relieved to learn there were at least a few girls she could get to know. And if the fellows were this friendly, maybe she'd meet someone special. After all, it was slim pickings back home, for sure.

The wind picked up after the fellowship meal, and the sky clouded over with only a few streaks of blue showing. Ella Mae suggested they head home "lest it starts makin' down soon."

"I hope the picnic supper won't get rained out," Clara said as they walked up the road. Several groups of other Amish walked ahead of them, and two women had already discreetly removed their shoes and dark hose.

"They'll use the barn if the rain comes." Ella Mae glanced at Clara. "Are ya thinkin' of goin'?"

"Not sure." Clara told her she'd met her granddaughter Lettie and named the other girls. Some had looked almost too young to be in *Rumschpringe*—the time when teens started socializing and pairing up at activities. Mary Stoltzfus, especially, looked very young—younger than Katie—and almost angelic. "Lettie was exceptionally friendly."

"She's always been the life of the party, at home and elsewhere."

"She was so kind to break the ice for me."

"That's our Jake's daughter, all right. And if ya decide to go, I daresay she'll take ya round to meet *all* her friends—both girls and fellas."

"I'd like that," Clara said, thinking how nice it would be to get acquainted with new people and, hopefully, let herself enjoy this visit to the fullest.

CHAPTER

Six

Before they left for their afternoon ride around Hickory Hollow, Clara sat at the kitchen table writing a letter to her father while Ella Mae read from her German *Biewel* in the front room. Clara let her Dat know she had arrived safely and mentioned the few differences she'd already noticed between their district and this one, assuring him he didn't have to worry about any of it. *Nothing here will influence me to go backward in my faith*, she wrote. *Besides, I'll be home soon.*

She also shared about meeting several girls following the Preaching service today and enjoying getting to know them. *Thanks for letting me visit here, Dat.*

Staring at the address she'd written on the envelope, she felt almost relieved not to be spending the Lord's Day back home. Everything about Dat's farmhouse was now a strange blend of Mamma and Eva—familiar yet ever so different.

But here she felt more alive, like her life was about to turn to a new page.

Early this morning, she'd slipped out of the house and explored the cottage-style greenhouse in the backyard, about the size of the spare room where she was staying. She'd poked her head inside the Dutch door to see shelves running lengthwise on either side of the structure, where clay pots, gardening tools, and seed envelopes were stored. She'd assumed the sunny space was used to start flowers from seed and as a potting shed, though it was much prettier than any she'd ever seen with its knotty pine wood, skylights, and windows. And dahlias surrounded the cottage in pink, peach, lavender, and orange.

Aendi's place is perfect, she decided.

Once they were ready to leave, Aendi wedged a note in the back screen door. "In case some of my family comes to visit, they'll know where I am."

"Do they come often?"

"Well, the married ones have their in-laws—and their own married children, in some cases. But *jah*, they all visit from time to time, takin' turns. Not like it used to be when my children were first married, though. And it's harder for my family in the Big Valley area, expensive as it is to travel by train or bus."

Clara's brothers, Calvin and Harley, rarely came home with their spouses and children, either. She hadn't seen them since Mamma's funeral, and Dat had made it known he wasn't happy about that. But it was too challenging for them to come all the way from Missouri.

Clara went out to hitch up for their ride. Aendi had suggested they stay in their for-good clothes. "That way, we're ready to visit somewheres if we want to. Chust never know on a Sunday afternoon."

She liked her aunt's spontaneity, reminding her again of Mamma, who was always eager for visitors. She'd consistently had baked goods set out, ready to offer them nearly any hour of the day, especially following church and on the between Sundays.

Aendi got into the driver's seat of the waiting carriage. The short rest had obviously revitalized her, because she talked a blue streak as they rode, pointing out one neighbor's farm after another. "There's our deacon's place. They have one of the oldest barns in the county."

Clara noticed how dark and weathered the wood looked. "Do they worry 'bout fire from lightning?"

"Do they ever. And their woodshed's even older and more susceptible to burning down after a strike."

"My Dat had to level ours several years ago. But he built a new one—had it framed in the space of an afternoon."

"A quick fix, I'll say. Always helpful to have a handy father round . . . or husband."

Aendi looked a little sad just then.

After they came over a rise in the road, a covered bridge came into view. Another half mile and Aendi pointed toward a large white clapboard farmhouse. "There's the farm where your Mamma lived with her parents and six siblings."

Clara felt nearly breathless seeing the main house and its three attached *Dawdi Heiser*. "Could we pull over and stop?" she asked.

Aendi directed her mare Firefly to the dirt shoulder and halted. "Take your time lookin'." She turned in her seat a little. "Five family generations live there now, but none of these smaller homes were built when your mother was here. They were constructed after your grandparents moved to Indiana."

Captured by curiosity, Clara asked, "Why did my Dawdi and Mammi Zook move away?

Do ya know? They died when I was young, and Mamma never said—if she even knew."

After a slight hesitation, Aendi told her, "Your Dawdi and his married siblings—my Joseph wasn't one of them, of course—had developed an interest in the First Light settlement, newly founded though it was."

"I wonder why that would be."

"Well, this here hollow's been known for decades to be extra strict with *die Youngie*. And what with four teenagers round that time, including your Mamma, maybe your Dawdi wanted more freedom for them."

Clara wondered if this might be what her father meant when he told her this community was more old-style. "More freedom than even other Plain communities?"

"Oh *jah*. I'd say so."

Clara pondered that, wondering why Aendi had hesitated to answer her question. All the same, she drank in the beauty of the white horse fences enclosing great square paddocks, the hen house not far from the large bank barn, and the hog pen she could see only partially from her vantage point. "Did my Dawdi raise hogs?"

"*Nee*, but they had hundreds of laying hens and many goats, which was unusual for the time since most Amish round here were dairy farmers. They managed to sell all their livestock—in fact, before even movin', which just showed how important relocating was to them."

Clara closed her eyes for a moment, trying to picture her strawberry blond Mamma as a little girl tossing feed to the chickens, gathering eggs, and milking goats. She could also imagine her dashing outside with a broom and sweeping the porch and walkways, pinning clothes to the line on washdays, and using the push mower that was customary here. Mamma always did her best to "do her part," which she'd instructed her children to do growing up.

"Long before your Mamma lived here, one of my own cousins rented this place. Come to think of it, my mother's wedding present from all the womenfolk was quilted on a large frame in this *Haus*."

"The quilt your niece Rebecca talked 'bout?"

Aendi laughed softly. "The very one."

Clara stared with longing at the sweeping yard surrounding the large farmhouse and its additions. When she was ready, she said, "Okay, we can go on now."

Aendi clicked her tongue and directed Firefly back onto the road. "Would ya like to see where your Mamma's schoolhouse used to be?"

"Sure."

"It was torn down years ago after lightning struck *it*, but you'll smile when ya see what's there now."

"*Wunnerbaar*," Clara replied, enjoying this ride around the hollow, as Aendi referred to the area. Her gaze remained on the farmhouse and grounds for as long as they were visible, and she wished her siblings could see this place sometime, too, missing Mamma as they all still were.

Farther up the way, she noticed the wall of cornstalks on either side of the road and the green pastureland eventually appearing, as well as more Amish farms with their tall silos. The gray cloud banks sailed on the winds, and within a few minutes, the sun burst out of hiding. Clara squinted at the now glaringly bright sky.

In another mile or so, Aendi slowed the mare and pointed. "There's the plot of land where the old schoolhouse stood for so long."

Clara gazed upon a drive-through ice cream stand and bake shop there, surrounded by a mown lawn and flower beds plentiful with yellow roses.

"Our deacon's brother and his wife own it," Aendi told her. "The courtin' couples like to come out here on Saturday evenings."

Clara grinned. "Who doesn't love ice cream and baked goods?"

"Some folks come a-strollin' or on their scooters on a nice night."

Hearing her aunt talk so stirred something in Clara. Or perhaps seeing the sunshine and the wind chasing the rain clouds away prompted her to decide to go to the picnic supper and Singing. She wanted to spend time with Lettie Zook again, and she even hoped to be introduced to the handsome fellow who'd looked her way before filing into church.

Almost the minute Clara arrived for the picnic supper, Lettie rushed across the back lawn to greet her. "I'm glad ya came," she said, leading Clara to where tables and benches had been set up.

A large group of young people were already interacting with one another, some standing and others seated. Lettie stood with Clara, asking what she'd done that afternoon.

"Aendi Ella Mae gave me a tour of the hollow," Clara told her, happy to be welcomed so.

Lettie smiled, her deep dimples making an appearance. "You sound like one of us already."

"'Cause I said 'hollow'?"

Nodding, Lettie asked, "What stood out most to ya? I've lived here all my life, so it's impossible to see it with fresh eyes."

Clara mentioned stopping by where her mother had lived. "I wish I could go inside and look around sometime."

"All you'd have to do is walk up to the door and tell them your Mamma once lived there. Oh, and say that Ella Mae Zook's related to you."

"Really? They wouldn't mind?"

Lettie shook her head. "In fact, if you'd like, I'll go with ya."

"All right." Clara loved how friendly Lettie was.

"*Kumme*," Lettie said. "I have some friends who wanna meet ya."

Clara was introduced to one fellow or girl after another, surprised, even heartened, by their warm reception. She quickly discovered that Zook, Stoltzfus, Fisher, King, Ebersol, Lapp, and Beiler were the names of many of the youth there—last names uncommon to the Indiana Amish she knew. Clara took notice that Katie Lapp came over about the time Lettie introduced her to Daniel Fisher, as well as to Katie's older brothers, Elam, Eli, and Benjamin. And if Clara wasn't mistaken, a noticeable sparkle came to Daniel Fisher's eyes when Katie joined them.

After Clara and Lettie were seated, the tall fellow who'd looked Clara's way that morning arrived and walked across the lawn toward their table, his gaze fixed on her. "You're Ella Mae's grandniece, *jah*?"

Clara nodded.

"I'm Thomas Glick, but Tom's okay, too." He extended his hand.

Clara shook it. "I haven't heard the name Glick yet today."

"Well, there's plenty of us here in Lancaster County." He smiled. "What's *your* name?"

"Clara Bender."

"From Indiana, right?"

"*Jah*. Ever hear of the town there called First Light?"

Perhaps not wanting to listen in, Lettie looked away.

"Interesting name for a town, *ain't*?" Tom replied. "Could've called it Daybreak instead." He chuckled, then surprised her by sitting down next to her when Lettie rose to walk toward the house.

Tom leaned his elbow on the table. "How long are ya here for, Clara?"

"A week."

He nodded slowly, as though contemplating that. "So even though it might seem forward, I'd better ask ya out ridin' *tonight*. That is, if ya'd like to."

Clara had never met such a confident fellow. And one who seemed so eager to get acquainted with her. As nice-looking and congenial as he was, she was surprised he didn't have a girlfriend.

"I don't bite," he said, joking. "Really."

She was still astonished at being asked out so quickly. But thinking, *What could it hurt?*, she said, "All right."

The host and his wife were coming down the walkway now, and Tom excused himself to head to one of the tables surrounded by young men. Ike King, the host, introduced himself and his wife, Ada Ruth, and then welcomed *die Youngie*, singling out Clara.

That was definitely embarrassing yet very nice, too. Lettie hurried over and sat back down with Clara as Ike announced that a cornhusking contest was planned for this coming Saturday afternoon at the deacon's farm. Then he asked everyone to bow their heads for the blessing over their meal.

Following the silent prayer, Ada Ruth numbered off the tables for an orderly approach to visiting the food table, where a big spread awaited.

Several of Lettie's girlfriends Clara had

met that morning came and sat with them, including Mary Stoltzfus and Katie Lapp. They talked together for a while, and then when discussion amongst them had quieted down, Lettie turned to whisper to Clara. "Just so ya know, Tom's friendly with a *lot* of the girls."

Clara listened. "But not dating anyone steadily?"

Lettie shook her head. "*Nee.*"

"*Denki,*" Clara whispered back politely.

CHAPTER

Seven

Leaving the barn with Tom Glick after Singing, Clara was glad to know what Lettie had shared about him. *He must enjoy casual dating,* she assumed, which made her more comfortable with agreeing to ride with him.

Tom slipped on his black vest as they walked across the yard to his waiting horse and courting carriage, then offered his hand to help her in before hurrying around to the front to untie the horse from the hitching post. Right away Clara noticed the carpeted buggy floor and a fancy-looking console with extra buttons, perhaps one for a battery-operated heater. Was this permitted here, given all the strict rules? Back home, lots of fellows had courting carriages just like this inside.

The evening was still hot and sultry, and an almost full moon was rising, noticeable now through the lowest tree branches. A crickets' chorus was constant as Tom's horse trotted up the road. Soon they approached a farmhouse where a picturesque stone wall bedecked with ivy lined the vast front yard. A middle-aged Amishman waved at them near the roadside mailbox.

Tom called, "*Wie geht's*, Popcorn Gid!"

"Hullo there, Tom!" the man called back, grinning.

After they'd passed, Tom explained, "That's my Mamm's cousin. Friendliest fella in the hollow."

"Does he grow popcorn or just like to eat it?"

Tom chuckled. "Both. His older brother gave him the nickname when Gid was little, and it's stuck all these years."

"Sounds like he grew into it, then."

She noticed the covered bridge ahead and realized they must be on the road leading to the farm where her mother had lived. And farther up, the field where the old schoolhouse had been.

As they rode past the farm, Tom mentioned, "It's too bad the ice cream shop and bakery ain't open on Sundays."

"Aren't all the Amish businesses closed

on the Lord's Day here? They are where I live."

"Sure, but a body's gotta eat every day of the week." Tom grinned.

Clara didn't know what to say. Was he just trying to be funny?

She changed the subject. "Aendi Ella Mae told me that's the spot where the schoolhouse was. My mother went there till they moved to Indiana after she finished seventh grade."

"My Dat attended that school, too. Did ya know he was sweet on your Mamm? He was a class grade ahead of her."

Clara had never heard her mother talk about anyone by the name of Glick, but then, she'd never talked about *any* male friends other than Dat. "Small world, for sure."

"When he heard you were comin', Dat told me no one back then understood why your Mamm's parents up and left for Indiana."

Clara recalled what Ella Mae shared with her. "Maybe just lookin' for greener pastures."

"Hard to imagine anything greener than round here."

She shook her head. "I mean, maybe they wanted to follow a different kind of *Ordnung*."

"So ya don't think your Dawdi Zook was happy raisin' his family here?"

"I don't really know."

"Well, my Dat did say the bishop at that time was mighty strict with the youth, 'specially after somethin' unspeakable happened."

"Unspeakable?"

Tom shrugged. "Dat didn't explain when I asked what he meant. But whatever happened, I'm sure it's long forgotten."

In a community this small, nothing's ever forgotten, Clara thought, curious.

"But things must've loosened up since then," Tom continued. "Fewer chaperones at youth outings and no rules against buttons and gadgets in buggies . . . things like that."

"Could it be your bishop now trusts the youth more?"

"Guess so." Tom sped up the horse.

Clara didn't have to ask him to take her home when she thought Ella Mae might expect her. Tom returned her at a respectable time, and he even walked her to the back door. There was a certain dignity about him, she decided as he reached for the screen door and held it open for her. *So self-assured.*

"Wish ya didn't have to leave at the end of the week, Clara."

"Well, we had a nice time tonight, *jah*?" She smiled.

He nodded. "Maybe I'll see ya again before ya head home."

She hoped so. "*Gut Nacht*, Tom."

Inside the house, Clara found Aendi sitting in the rocking chair in the kitchen reading her Bible, her glasses perched on the end of her nose. She was barefoot and wearing a gray housecoat.

Did she wait up for me?

Peering over her small spectacles, the older woman smiled when she saw Clara. "*Die Youngie* must've been right friendly to ya," she said. "I heard a carriage comin' up my lane."

"I was surprised, *jah*," Clara said, then told her about the delicious food and gospel music. Clara was still amazed at some of the things both her parents had shared about the Hickory Hollow church's strict *Ordnung*. For one thing, any songs other than the old *Ausbund* hymns were forbidden to be sung or even hummed, except at Singings for the youth.

Why would that be? she wondered.

"I learned some songs I'd never heard before. And I met all of Lettie's friends, like ya said. *Denki* for encouragin' me to go."

Aendi placed a black ribboned bookmark in the spot where she'd been reading and slowly closed the Good Book. "Tomorrow, once the washing's on the line and we've had a nice breakfast, would ya like to go with me to pick up the wedding quilt from Rebecca?"

"That'd be fun. And before we go, I'll get out early and pick all the ripe berries for ya," Clara said, happy to offer all the help she could. "And gather the eggs."

"Well, the laying hens were sold to Samuel Lapp after Joseph died, so that's one less thing to think 'bout." Aendi smiled. "Besides, you're on vacation, remember?"

"Only from my life back home. But while I'm here, I want to help. I also want to give ya grocery money. Don't wanna eat ya out of house and home."

"That's awful kind, Clara, but there's plenty-a canned goods down cellar from last summer yet." Ella Mae rose and set the Bible and her glasses on the table. "We're also getting a bumper crop of strawberries, so you an' I can put up some jam while you're here."

"I'd like that," Clara said, noting Aendi's big yawn. "Well, s'pose it's bedtime."

Aendi nodded. "I had company while ya were gone. Two sets of married grandsons and their wives. We had us a nice visit, their little tykes runnin' round and jabberin' to beat the band."

"Sorry I missed them."

"Oh, maybe you'll see them round the hollow this week. Well, so glad ya had yourself a nice time with *die Youngie*. I'll say *Gut Nacht* now, honey-girl. Have sweet dreams."

"You too, Aendi."

And with that, Clara left for her room, slowly making her way to the hallway.

Glad Clara was home safe, Ella Mae outened the gas lamp in the kitchen, then moved down the hall to her bedroom, shadows flickering from the kerosene lamp on the hallway table.

Inside, she closed the door and leaned back against it, where Joseph's long house robe still hung on a hook. She sighed, missing him all the more at night.

Turning, she moved to the dresser Joseph had built when they were first married and removed a white cotton nightdress from her drawer and placed it on the bed. Joseph's pajamas—all of them washed after his passing—were still neatly folded in the bottom drawer, as were his socks. His hanging clothes were still on the row of wooden pegs on the wall. Even his two sets of suspenders—for work and for good.

Having his belongings near was a comfort to her, though it was customary among the People to give away or discard a deceased spouse's clothing within days after the funeral.

I'm an odd duck, she thought, taking the

hairpins out of her bun, then sitting on the edge of the bed to brush her long gray tresses. Through all the years of their marriage, Joseph had enjoyed watching her do this, commenting on her beautiful hair. The last weeks of his life, though, his eyes were closed in repose or sleep most of the time. Still, he'd loved stroking her hair while thanking her for being so caring toward him when he could no longer look after himself.

Joseph's suffering is over, she reminded herself, though his presence seemed ever so near at times. *Just my imagination—or wishful thinking—after so many decades together.*

Clara read from her New Testament after preparing for bed, the windows wide open to let in the sweet night air. A breeze rustled the dark green shades, different from the white blinds and homemade curtains in her room back home. Then she outened the small gas lamp at her bedside and slipped beneath the lightweight quilt before closing her eyes and silently reciting her bedtime prayers. She added her gratitude to God for a lovely first full day here.

Rolling over, she let her mind wander back to her casual date with Tom Glick, recalling what he'd said about his father's crush on her mother when they were in school. It struck her that Tom must have known more about her than he'd let on when he first introduced himself. *Strange that he asked my name if he already knew it.*

She yawned, also baffled about something else Tom said. *Would Aendi know about the unspeakable thing that happened so long ago?*

CHAPTER

Eight

Monday morning's weather, already quite sunny and breezy at a little before seven o'clock, was ideal for drying clothes on the line. Clara helped Aendi with that chore, having already picked several quarts of plump, ripe strawberries from the patch.

"We'll have strawberry pancakes for breakfast," Aendi announced as they walked back toward the house, Clara carrying the empty wicker wash basket.

"I'll clean the berries and remove the stems." Clara's mouth watered at the thought of those pancakes.

"We'll have us a little celebration each day you're here." Aendi gripped the porch railing as she made her way up the steps.

"Just bein' with ya is a celebration," Clara told her when they were back in the house.

"Ain't that nice." Aendi washed her hands at the kitchen sink; then it was Clara's turn.

When they sat down to eat, Aendi led out in a spoken prayer over the food, which caught Clara off guard again. But then she remembered Mamma telling her Ella Mae was known to do this sometimes—praying aloud like Mennonites and other Christians did, even though it wasn't encouraged here in the hollow.

Nor back home, either.

"Amen," Clara repeated after Aendi, wanting to know how it felt, the reverent word falling off her lips.

"Ya look a little startled, dear."

Clara explained she'd rarely heard anyone pray out loud.

"'Tis all right, even though some say it's prideful. But I believe it's somethin' our heavenly Father welcomes, even treasures. After all, He taught His disciples to *say* the Lord's Prayer. So I frequently speak my prayers, even for mealtime blessings." She waved her hand. "Even my Joseph didn't mind much, 'specially after he prayed a sinner's prayer just weeks before his passing. Tellin' the truth, I feel all the closer to my Savior when beseeching His name aloud. It fills up my heart."

Clara listened, quite surprised that Aendi's husband hadn't really known the Lord as Savior throughout his life. Maybe he'd been more concerned with following the rules and traditions of the community here.

"Just so ya know, I ain't cut from the same cloth as most Amish round the hollow," Aendi added.

Clara recalled Mamma saying something like this about Ella Mae from time to time, and how Dat had called her "unique" the day they'd discussed her trip in the barn. "You want to be who you're meant to be, *jah*?"

"Well, who the *Lord* made me to be. No matter what folk might think." She reached for the maple syrup and drizzled it over her pancakes, then cut into them with her fork and took her first taste. "*Ach, des gut.*" Her face was almost glowing.

Clara did the same, only she put more than a drizzle on hers. And oh, was that first bite scrumptious!

After they'd had their fill of pancakes, long bacon strips, fresh fruit, and coffee, they bowed their heads, and Aendi asked the second blessing after the meal. And for a moment after the "amen," Aendi sat quietly, looking at Clara with soft eyes. "Ya may not know it, but your visit has kept me in *mei Haus*, at least for a little longer. A *gut* thing, indeed."

"Oh?"

Aendi explained that she'd felt pressed by her children—particularly her son Jake and her daughter Mattie—to move to Mattie's place till a *Dawdi Haus* could be built. "They don't want me to be alone here, so your comin' has been a godsend."

Clara's heart was warmed by this news. "Honestly, it is for me, too."

Aendi's eyes grew misty. "I know you're missin' your Mamma."

"Bein' here seems to help," Clara said, looking forward to spending the next few days with her aunt. "I can't explain it."

"Well, that's my hope and prayer."

After Aendi read aloud from Psalms, Clara cleared the table and then washed the dishes while her aunt wiped them dry. "I'm curious 'bout something," Clara told her as she placed a rinsed plate on the drying rack.

"Don't be shy." Aendi smiled, her little eyes squinting nearly shut.

"All right, then." Clara paused, not wanting to go too far into what was on her mind. "I'm sure ya know many of the womenfolk's maiden names round here, *jah*?"

"S'pect I do."

"What 'bout Thomas Glick's mother's? Do ya happen to know hers?"

"'Twas Mast," Aendi replied casually, like she was trying not to show her interest.

Mast, Clara thought as she pulled the plug in the sink to let the dishwater run down the drain. "Hmm."

Aendi tilted her head, studying her. "Somethin' else on your mind, dear?"

Shrugging it off, Clara rinsed out the bubbles. "I best not say."

Hanging up her tea towel, Aendi said, "Whatever you're a-ponderin', remember, it's safe with me."

Clara took a deep breath, then asked what her aunt knew about a long-ago happening. "It was supposedly something unspeakable that caused the bishop to get very strict with the youth back then."

Aendi's mouth instantly gaped. "*Ach*, where'd ya hear this?"

"Last evening. From one of my new friends."

Her aunt turned to put away the dishes she'd just dried.

"I was told it was long forgotten," Clara added, feeling like she'd put her aunt on the spot.

"Well, that may just be."

Clara waited for her to say more, as shocked

as she'd looked, but it was obvious she didn't want to discuss it.

Like Tom said about his father.

While Aendi was busy watering her dahlias outside the little greenhouse, Clara hoed the kitchen garden plot. It looked like the weeding had been done rather recently, though. *Aendi's not one to get behind on things,* Clara thought, guessing Lettie Zook and her family or other close relatives might have come by to redd up the garden. *Likely so.* She also recalled Lettie's kind offer to go with her to knock on the door of the house where Mamma had lived.

When the hoeing was done and Aendi was finished watering, Clara hitched Firefly to the buggy so they could visit Rebecca Lapp and pick up the heirloom quilt. On the ride, Aendi pointed out the General Store and the Hickory Hollow Post Office, as well as other locations Clara's Mamma would have walked past from time to time.

Seeing these places, Clara suddenly had a lump in her throat. She even felt like crying but managed to hold back the tears.

"Clara?" Aendi said, glancing at her.

"I'm sorry. . . ."

"Grievin's nothin' to be ashamed of, dear."

Clara nodded slowly, wanting to share

what was on her heart. "When my Mamma died, I was just sure I'd never be happy again," she said, her voice throaty with sadness.

"That's understandable. Truly, 'tis. I'm sorry you're goin' through this." Aendi sighed. "When my Mamm's mother died in her sleep at just fifty-seven, my life seemed to come to a halt. I'd felt as close to her as to my own sweet Mamm, but I never told that to a soul 'cept my sister Essie . . . till now."

Clara's lower lip trembled. "I know that kind of sorrow well."

"Seems we both grieve deeply." Aendi sniffled.

"Because we love so deeply?" Clara whispered.

Her aunt gave her a small smile. "I should say."

"Sometimes I wonder if I'll ever bounce back to the way I felt before she passed."

"You'll always miss your Mamm."

"But will I ever be happy again?"

"Grievin' takes time, but there'll come a day when the pain isn't as intense or constantly on your mind, more like a dull ache. 'Least that's how it was for me after my twin, Essie, died." Aendi paused, glancing at her with tender eyes. "Everyone sorrows differently, though."

"*Jah*, I've wondered how my Dat could fall in love again in the midst of his great loss."

It was Aendi's turn to nod slowly. "Well, I'm certain your father still misses your Mamma. But Eva's presence may help soothe his sadness."

Clara considered that; then Aendi went on.

"Honestly, I was shocked—and saddened, too—when my Dawdi got himself remarried less than a year after Mammi Esther died. It knocked the wind out of me. I felt such anger toward him for a long while."

"Seems too quick," Clara said, tearing up again. "Like with my Dat, 'cept I'm more numb than angry at him 'bout it."

"The anger may come later."

Clara paid close attention to that. Far as she could remember, she'd never been that frustrated with anyone. Would she really feel anger toward her own father?

A few minutes later, a large stone house similar to Ella Mae's own came into view. Clara wondered if it might be where Rebecca lived.

"Here we are," Aendi said, making the turn into the lane leading to the farmhouse.

Clara brushed tears from her cheeks. "I'm eager to see that old quilt."

"It's been years since I've seen it." Aendi

halted the horse, then sat silently as she held the reins.

Clara looked over at her aunt and felt honored to have been entrusted with Aendi's close childhood connection to her deceased Mammi. Already the growing bond between them was ever so dear.

CHAPTER

Nine

Ella Mae rapped on the back screen door, and through it, she could see her niece leaning over her black metal woodstove in the center of the large kitchen. Not waiting to be invited in, since none of the womenfolk ever did, Ella Mae motioned for Clara to follow her inside.

The house smelled like shortcake, and she called "Hullo" as Rebecca removed a round cake pan from the oven. "Smells mighty *gut*," Ella Mae said, making her way to the counter where Rebecca set the white cake on a cooling rack. "We should'a brought ya some of our fresh strawberries."

Rebecca smiled, her round face pink from the heat of the stove. "Katie was out pickin' a batch this mornin' before she left to visit

Mary Stoltzfus. They're studyin' together for their baptismal classes this summer," she replied, looking now at Clara. "*Ach*, I'm so happy to see ya again, Clara."

"You too," Clara said.

"Don't mean to take up your time on a Monday morning," Ella Mae said, glancing at the day clock on the wall. "We chust came for the old quilt, if it's handy."

Rebecca nodded. "No bother a'tall. But since you're here, why not have yourselves a seat? Coffee's already a-brewin', and there's sticky buns, too."

Always glad to sit with Rebecca at her sawbuck table, Ella Mae eased down onto the wooden bench that stretched across the whole length of one side. Clara sat next to her, glancing up at the gas lamp hanging over the table's center.

"Katie'll be sorry she missed yous," Rebecca said as she wiped her perspiring brow.

"Tell her hi for me," Clara replied, crossing her legs at the knees and bouncing her bare foot repeatedly.

She must be itching to see the quilt, Ella Mae thought, remembering all the years the lovely quilt had adorned her parents' bed.

Rebecca brought over a tray of sticky buns and set it down. Then, busy as she liked to be, she brought over her coffeepot and poured the brew into three of the clean mugs already in the middle of the table. "I hope ya ain't discouraged when ya see how badly worn the quilt is."

Ella Mae sighed. Too bad the years had altered it so. "Aging's hard, and not just on fabric," she murmured.

"Katie said it must've been real perty once," Clara spoke up, as if sensing what she was thinking.

"*Ach*, was it ever," Ella Mae replied, glad Clara was along. "My sister Essie was so eager to have it when things were divided between all the siblings after our Mamm passed."

Rebecca joined them at the table, bright-eyed as she reached for her coffee mug. "I'm glad for your company, what with Samuel and the boys out hayin' and Katie gone for the day. I thought it'd just be me and the clothesline today."

Ella Mae smiled. "Ya must've gotten an early start to hang up so much washin'. Clara and I got mine out of the way 'fore breakfast."

"Well, same here. Quite a while before." Rebecca had always been a little proud about how early she got her washing on the line. That was something of a competition amongst the womenfolk.

Clara was eyeing the woodstove. "Aendi,

isn't your stove just like Rebecca's? Sure looks like it."

Ella Mae nodded. "I daresay it might even be the same make."

"Many of our womenfolk back home have gas ranges and ovens," Clara told them. "My Dat even bought one for my step-Mamm after they wed."

"Ain't that somethin'?" Rebecca said, her hazel eyes blinking to beat the band.

"Modern appliances are definitely inchin' their way into the People's lives," Clara said.

"Not so much here, they ain't," Ella Mae let it be known. "'Course, who's to tell what'll come down the road?"

Rebecca smiled mischievously. "I daresay you, the bishop's wife, Leona Ebersol, and I will be the last ones cookin' on woodstoves. And mighty happy 'bout it."

"No doubt on that," Ella Mae replied with a titter.

"Say, did ya know the bishop's wife has been ailin'?" Rebecca asked in low tones. "Sounds awful serious."

"I'm sorry to hear it," Ella Mae replied.

Rebecca shook her head. "She's been sickly ever since her last baby was born a year ago—little Jacob."

"Thought she was some better."

"Here lately, she's been strugglin' again, but she won't see a doctor."

"I'll remember her in prayer."

After they'd eaten and had their coffee, Rebecca and Ella Mae cleared the table and removed the green-checkered oilcloth. Then Rebecca excused herself to retrieve the quilt. In a few minutes, she returned with a bundle in unbleached muslin.

"You can assess the wear an' tear right now, if ya like," she said, unwrapping the cloth and then carefully spreading the quilt across the long table with Ella Mae and Clara's help.

Ella Mae leaned closely to look at the old piecework—the quilt had been pieced using a dark ginger background and twenty on-point nine-patch blocks made up of Miniature Variable Stars of brown, tan, and black alternating with squares of sky blue. The quilt's borders of sky blue and ginger set off the blocks to perfection, and intricately stitched designs covered each inch of fabric. Back when she was a girl, she'd thought it was the prettiest quilt ever made. The colors were terribly faded, worse now than a decade ago when Essie'd had it on her spare room bed.

Mamm was so careful with it, Ella Mae recalled. *Never left it folded for long and even had a quilt rack to store it on during the summer months.* Seeing the quilt after such a long time stirred up memories of her Mamm's rosy cheeks and big blue eyes, as well as the gentle voice that soothed Ella Mae and her brothers and sisters when they felt sick or sad. And all the times when, as a small girl, she'd found pleasure in tracing her pointer finger over the rows of four nine-patch blocks across and five down, counting in *Deitsch*.

Presently, from the end of the table, Ella Mae could hear Clara quietly counting the ragged pieces and those torn at the seams.

"A lot to do, ain't?" Rebecca remarked as Clara continued to move around the quilt, clearly intent on evaluating the work involved to restore it.

"Inch by inch, we'll get it done," Ella Mae said. She caught Clara's eye just then, hopeful the girl's father would permit her to stay on through the rest of the summer—if she wished to, of course. Not just to be a help with this major project, though. There was more to it than that for the both of them.

"It'll be many hours of work," Clara said, commenting on the beautiful, tiny stitches. "This quilting was definitely done by experts."

"From what Mamm told me, twelve women were at the frame. And every one of them vowed secrecy so as not to spoil the wedding gift surprise."

Clara seemed to perk up her ears. "Just look at the tiny piecework and the intricate quilting designs. . . . Amazing even by current standards."

Ella Mae replied, "This here quilt was considered a work of art back in the day."

Clara nodded, though there was clearly more on her mind. Yet all she said was "I can see why. What fabrics were used? Do ya know?"

"Well, a plain-weave cotton percale for the background, and chambray for the twenty blocks and the blue border," Ella Mae said, recalling what her Mamm told her. "Essie did some digging into the history some years ago. She'd always been keen on quilts, which is why she ended up with this one. I'm actually surprised she didn't try to restore it herself."

Clara leaned closer, examining the thin chambray border. "Would ya mind if I make a few suggestions about replacing the ripped pieces? Mamma enjoyed doin' this sort of quilt repair, and I helped her do it a number of times."

"Let's hear what ya have to say," Ella Mae replied, recalling a few of Lillian's letters sharing some of her experience.

"For one thing, it would be *wunnerbaar* to have vintage material to work with. Is there a shop that stocks it nearby? One in Shipshewana, Indiana, sells it, but that won't help us here."

Rebecca mentioned the Old Country Store in Intercourse Village. "You might check there."

"If they don't carry any, I know a little 'bout dyeing fabrics to make them look vintage," Clara said, her eyes sparkling. "My sister, Bertie, and I and our Mamma worked together to restore an old quilt that way several years ago."

"How'd it turn out?" Ella Mae asked, impressed with Clara's knowledge.

"Real nice, even though the replacement pieces didn't look quite as faded as the original parts."

Rebecca was intent on Clara, and a smile broke across her face. "Say, my sister-in-law Vera Lapp sells locally made quilts and other quilted items, as well as some sewing supplies, out of the back of her house. She's lookin' to hire someone. Would ya be interested, Clara?"

Ella Mae waited for Clara's response, secretly wishing she might consider it.

"Oh, *would* I!" Clara's eyes lit up.

"Then you'll wanna go an' talk to Vera just up the road," Rebecca said, urging her.

"I know she noticed ya at Preachin' yesterday, and I'll put in a *gut* word for ya."

"*Denki* for thinkin' of me, but I'm only here this week."

"Oh. Well . . ."

Surely we can remedy that, Ella Mae thought, hopeful as she was. *Such a timely visit.*

CHAPTER

Ten

As they rode toward home, Aendi looked over at Clara and drew a deep breath. "I've been wantin' to mention somethin' to ya, dear, but I haven't been sure when to ask since ya just got here two days ago. After our visit with Rebecca, though, talkin' 'bout restorin' the quilt and that job with Vera an' all, I think ya might guess what I'm gonna say."

"Well, I'm not sure, but no need bein' shy with *me*." Clara grinned, remembering how Aendi had said the same to her.

Ella Mae laughed softly. "I'd like ya to stay on longer, if ya want to. For the rest of the summer."

"But how would that go over with your family when they want ya to move and all?"

"What're they gonna do?" Aendi said,

a sudden catch in her voice. "Carry me out against my will?"

Clara felt plain sorry her aunt couldn't stay in the home where she and her husband had made decades of happy memories. "I'd love to visit longer, honestly. But I'd have to talk to my Dat 'bout it."

Aendi bobbed her head.

"Would your bishop mind ya letting me use the emergency phone in the shed?"

"Not if he doesn't know 'bout it." Aendi chuckled and directed Firefly onto the curvy lane that led to her house.

Clara held her breath so she wouldn't burst out laughing. Sometimes her aunt said the most surprising things.

While they unhitched the horse together, Clara kept thinking about the call to her father, hoping he'd take kindly to her asking about extending her time here.

When they were finished, Aendi pointed in the direction of the field across from the house.

"Do ya see the phone shanty stickin' up from the bushes not far from the northeast edge of the cornfield?"

Clara squinted into the sunlight. "I think so."

"I can walk over there with ya if you're not sure. Don't want ya gettin' lost."

Clara quickly shook her head. "*Nee*, I'll find it."

Aendi stepped into the house long enough to jot down a long-distance calling card code for her to use on the shared phone line.

All the way around the cornfield, Clara felt thankful for a chance to possibly work at Vera Lapp's quilt shop. And as she walked to the narrow wooden phone shed, she hoped Dat would be in the barn to answer her call so she wouldn't have to leave a message.

Turning the door handle, Clara stepped inside, then reached for the black receiver and dialed the long-distance code, followed by her Dat's phone number.

Ella Mae took her wicker laundry basket out to the clothesline to check on a few items while Clara made her phone call. Several were already dry, and she took them down and folded them right there in the yard, enjoying the sun's rays on her back. She could tell there was less humidity in the air than over the past few days. That would make the afternoon more comfortable.

"May Thy will, O Lord, be done for Clara," she prayed aloud.

She trudged back toward the house, carrying the basket with the folded clothing inside.

Once at the porch, she set the basket on one of the steps midway up, then gingerly walked up to that step before lifting the basket again to place it on the porch floor. She did the same thing when bringing freshly washed clothes up from the cellar into the kitchen, even more carefully, given their heavier weight.

There were plenty of ways to get around living alone while getting up in years. She'd had to learn when Joseph took sick. But she couldn't do everything herself. She was thankful for the granddaughters and their husbands who'd volunteered to plant the kitchen garden in the spring.

Ella Mae carried the basket to the screen door and managed to slip inside, then took it to her bedroom and began putting away the clothes. They smelled like fresh air and sunshine.

Even if Clara's father decides she can't stay, she thought, *I'll enjoy the remaining time with her.*

"There's one more thing, Dat," Clara said into the phone, pleased she'd reached her father. "A possible opportunity just came up for me to work at an Amish quilt shop here. I'm goin' to look into it tomorrow." She didn't want to sound too excited, but she was.

"A job . . . *there*?" Dat sounded taken aback.

"The Amishwoman who owns it sells local quilts, as well as a few other items tourists like to purchase. I'd use the money to help Aendi Ella Mae with groceries and whatnot."

"This is a surprise . . . and not at all what we agreed on, Clara."

She held her breath, wishing she could tell him how much she truly wanted the job. She wanted him to know more about the wonderfully welcoming youth she'd met, too, but she wasn't sure that was wise. "I know it's unexpected, but I'd really like to stay for the rest of the summer, Dat."

There was an exceptionally long silence as she again held her breath.

At last, Dat spoke. "I was reluctant to have ya travel all that way, and now ya want to extend your time there?"

"I'm havin' such a *gut* visit, Dat. And I—"

"Clara, listen, we had an agreement. You know what I think 'bout ya bein' exposed to a lower church *Ordnung* an' all. Besides, you're missin' out on the *gut* fellowship and biblical instruction here."

She disliked challenging him, but . . .

"What if I told ya things here really ain't much different, from what I can tell. I just mailed ya a letter sayin' I arrived all right, and also that the few differences I've seen ain't nothin' to worry 'bout."

"Remember, you're a baptized church member from *this* district, daughter. So if ya met someone there and fell in love . . ."

"Can't church memberships be transferred, though?"

"Can be mighty tetchy, dependin' on the districts—and the bishops. It was challenging to get the transfers when your Bruders met their mates out in Jamesport and decided to settle clear down there. 'Course, you weren't old enough to be aware of that."

"It won't hurt if I stay just for the summer, will it, Dat?"

He sighed. "*Ach*, Clara. I'm not happy 'bout this."

She felt awful tense, wanting his blessing.

There was an even longer pause, but finally he said, "If ya promise to come home right after Labor Day, and you're sure Ella Mae wants ya there that long, then I s'pose you can make your plans. Just be mindful of how you were raised in the faith."

A wave of relief washed over her. "*Denki*, Dat. I'll send home any money that's left over . . . *if* I get the job."

"Ain't necessary. You'll need to make a few new dresses."

He must think I should stop wearing my mourning clothes.

"I just might do that. *Denki* again!"

He seemed reluctant to say good-bye, which made her think he must miss her. Even so, once they'd hung up, she could hardly wait to tell Aendi the news.

Clara opened the shanty door and raised her face toward the sun. *I'm so thankful, Lord. Truly I am!*

It occurred to her that now she'd have time to get to know handsome Tom Glick, who might just be interested in more than casually dating her. And all the way back around the field to Aendi's, she felt like she was walking on a cloud.

CHAPTER

Eleven

The next morning, Clara woke before dawn. This was the day she planned to visit Vera Lapp at the quilt shop. First, though, she would pick more berries and then start the bread dough, both before breakfast.

Hearing the distinct sound of purple martins, Clara stretched in bed and thanked God for a good night's sleep and her father's permission to let her stay for the summer, though reluctantly given. And as often happened, she thought of Mamma, who loved the predawn hours. Sometimes she'd rise even before Dat to make coffee and have a little something ready for him to eat—just till he tended to the livestock and later returned for a hot breakfast with her and the family.

Mamma liked to pray during those hours,

Clara recalled, *and she often hummed a gospel song in worship while she worked.*

Ella Mae rolled over in bed and opened one eye, peering toward the pulled window shade to see if a crack of light had appeared. She didn't want to look at the wind-up clock on her bedside table just yet. She'd had a fitful night and a dream about Joseph. The dream had seemed so real, and she'd jerked awake with a start in the wee hours, expecting to see her husband lying next to her in bed.

Did all the talk of grieving trigger the dream? Although it wasn't uncommon for her to have a restless night. Her grief seemed to ebb and flow, and just when she thought the recurrence of sadness had lessened some, sorrow would splash over her again.

Yawning, she sat up and scooted to the edge of the bed, her feet fumbling about for her house slippers. *Clara meets Vera today,* she mused, reaching for her lightweight housecoat and pulling it on. *Glad I could get a message to Rebecca 'bout Clara staying on. Maybe she had time to tell Vera about her, too, like she offered.*

Smiling at the thought of having the agreeable young woman around for another two months or so, Ella Mae hoped this fact might bring an end to Jake and Mattie's insistence that she start packing up the house. Mattie had brought it up again after Preaching service, making it clear that Ella Mae should at least *start* sorting and discarding.

It won't be long before Mattie will be over here again to mention it, especially since no one in the family knows yet that Clara's staying on longer.

Aendi made scrambled eggs with ham and cheese while Clara set the table and waited for slices of the freshly baked bread to toast in the frying pan.

She was pleased when Aendi suggested she take Firefly and the carriage to Vera Lapp's. "It's quite a long walk," Aendi added.

"How far from Rebecca's?" Clara asked, flipping the bread with a spatula.

"I'll draw a rough sketch for ya." Aendi's eyes looked a little puffy, as though she hadn't slept well.

"*Gut*, then."

"Ain't too hard to find, really, since Vera's farmhouse is set right near the road. You won't miss the sign out front—'Vera's Quilts in Back.'"

Aendi was right. The place was fairly easy to find, Clara thought that afternoon as she tied Firefly to the hitching post behind Vera Lapp's house. The vet had recently told Aendi her other mare, Sparkles, required rest after a mild case of colic, so Firefly was getting a lot of outings.

The walkway leading to the shop in the back of the house passed through a bright array of pansies blooming on either side—white, red, pink, blue, and some multicolored. And a fenced-in area for the family's kitchen garden wasn't far away. Another sign gave the shop's hours, Tuesday through Friday, afternoons only. Clara surmised that Vera kept her mornings, Mondays, and Saturdays free to manage her household chores.

A woman opened the shop door, stepped outside, and waved a welcome as Clara approached. "Clara?" she said. "My sister-in-law let me know you planned to come this afternoon. It's *gut* of ya to stop by."

"You must be Vera, then," said Clara, smiling.

"I am, and I'm mighty happy to meet ya." Vera invited her inside, where the entire expanse of the single room was a display of quilts, many featuring patterns she knew and loved: Diamond in the Square, Log Cabin, Double Wedding Ring, Broken Star, and

Nine Patch and Heart. Some quilts hung on the walls, and others were spread over what looked like a queen-size bed. Bins of other quilted items were there, too, such as pot holders, oven mitts, toaster covers, and table runners. Some sewing supplies were organized against one wall.

"What a *wunnerbaar* place ya have," Clara said, gazing all around.

"My husband built this addition for me some years ago," Vera told her, all smiles. "But after a time, we were burstin' at the seams again."

"Well, it looks nice and orderly."

"Oh goodness, I'm glad ya think so. I tend to forget how it looks when customers first walk in." Vera motioned for her to join her behind the counter. "Let's get acquainted, okay?" She led her to two folding chairs next to a counter with two drinking glasses and a pitcher of iced tea filled to the brim. "Hope ya like meadow tea."

"I do. *Denki*." Clara accepted a glass once Vera had filled it, then settled into one of the chairs. "We make meadow tea back home, too. My Dat enjoys a tall tumbler of it at supper durin' summer."

Vera asked a few easy questions about her experience making and selling quilts and other quilted items, but after a while, they turned to talk of how she became so interested in quilting.

"I guess my Mamma's love for it spilled over onto me," Clara said. "Same with my sister, Bertie. We both enjoyed following in our mother's footsteps, and we sold quite a few of the quilts we made."

"Passin' down the Old Ways," Vera replied, looking mighty pleased.

A little bell over the door tinkled, and a pretty young girl came in with a woman most likely her mother. It took only a moment for Clara to recognize them. They'd been in the carriage that passed her and Aendi on the way to church last Sunday. And Clara had briefly met Aaron at the Singing.

Right away, Vera got up to welcome them, then brought them over to Clara. "I'd like ya to meet my neighbors, Leona Ebersol and her daughter Rosanna." Clara stood up. "Clara's from Indiana, visitin' her great-aunt Ella Mae Zook for the summer."

Leona glanced at her blond daughter, then with a big smile said, "Ella Mae's a dear friend of our family." She studied Clara. "So you must be Lillian's youngest, *jah*?"

Clara's heart sped up. "Did ya know my Mamma?"

"Only through Ella Mae, who always spoke so kindly of her." Leona stepped closer to the counter. "I'm awful sorry for your loss, Clara. And if there's anything we can do . . ."

Rosanna nodded slowly, eyes fixed on Clara.

"*Denki*," Clara replied, aware of how sweet Rosanna looked, waiting there so patiently as she held a small basket. And she couldn't help noticing a sympathetic tear on Leona's cheek. "Well, you're here to shop, I'm sure."

"So nice to meet ya," Rosanna said softly.

"You too."

Vera assisted them, and after they'd found their items and paid for them, Rosanna made a point of turning to wave at Clara as they headed for the door.

"Kindest people ya'll ever know," Vera said after they left.

"Aendi Ella Mae thinks so, too."

"Well, I've enjoyed getting to know ya, Clara. I'd love to have ya work for me."

"I'd be thrilled to . . . if you're sure it's okay that I'll be here only till Labor Day."

Vera offered her a job all four afternoons a week, Tuesday through Friday.

"That'll be ideal. *Ach*, ya don't know how happy I am about this," she replied, thanking Vera.

"Could ya start next Tuesday afternoon, then?" Vera asked. "That's the best day for me to start your trainin'."

"*Abselutt.*"

"I'll do that the first hour or so. Shouldn't take long."

"Sounds fine."

When they'd finished their iced tea and said warm farewells, Clara made her way back to Firefly. She heard someone calling her name, and when she looked up, Tom Glick was coming toward her.

What're the chances?

"Hullo again, Clara Bender." He hurried his step.

"Didn't expect to see you here," she said, smiling.

"My married sister twisted my arm to pick up some thread and whatnot for her." Tom glanced at the shop. "First time I've been here. Meetin' ya must've been meant to be."

She fought to suppress a smile at his smooth talk.

"So are *you* on an errand, too?" he asked.

"*Jah* . . . of sorts."

He winked at her. "Is it a secret?"

"Kinda."

"Well, now ya *have* to tell me."

She was amused and figured he'd find out soon enough, so she mentioned her new job and that she was staying for the rest of the summer.

Tom glanced toward a cornfield and ran his hand through his dark hair, a grin on his face. "What do ya know." He looked at her again. "I got my wish."

He likes me, she thought, unaccustomed to such forwardness. "Aendi Ella Mae suggested that I stay on."

Tom grinned. "Was hopin' maybe *I* had somethin' to do with it."

She blushed. "Did ya, now?"

"I'm just glad I ran into ya today, Clara."

Never had any fellow talked to her like this. "S'pose I should get back to Aendi's."

"Will I see ya at the youth cornhuskin' contest this Saturday?"

"I live one day at a time," she said, playing along. Besides, she didn't know what her aunt might have planned.

"It'll be fun," he said, his tone insistent. "And if ya go, I'll take ya out ridin' again."

"If I show up, you'll see me there. How's that?"

Tom guffawed, and she waved good-bye. *Goodness!*

After unhitching and then leading Firefly back to the stable, Clara pushed the carriage into the nearby shed and hurried into the house. "Vera offered me the job," she told Aendi, who began clapping her hands. "I start next Tuesday afternoon."

"*Gut* news!" Aendi was beaming.

"When I get my first pay, I'll be givin' ya some money."

"*Ach*, chust whatever ya want to contribute toward groceries, but no need to pay for anything else."

"Are ya sure?"

"Never more sure." Aendi straightened her apron. "How would ya like to make strawberry jam tomorrow?"

"Sure, and a pie or two if I get enough berries when I pick again." Clara could tell how happy Aendi was for her, and it made her day all the brighter.

Later, Clara managed to haul a large folding table up from the cellar and helped Aendi set it up in the front room, where they laid out the old quilt.

"We'll work on it whenever we can," Aendi said.

Clara agreed, then couldn't help looking over the faded piecework once more. Some of the task would be tedious, but working alongside her aunt would make even that part of the process pleasing.

Not long after, Aendi's daughter Mattie arrived, looking rather serious when she stepped through the back door with a casserole in a quilted carrier. Aendi accepted it, thanked her, and placed it on the kitchen counter. She also didn't waste a minute suggesting they head outdoors, so Clara assumed whatever was up wasn't her business.

She quickly got busy washing the floors on the main level, since doing chores made her feel useful. And considering Vera's eagerness to hire her, she felt an extra surge of energy.

Even so, Clara couldn't help but wonder why Mattie had looked so solemn. Had something upset her?

The minute Ella Mae was seated in her porch rocker, she told Mattie that Clara was staying the rest of the summer. "It's all set."

Mattie looked peeved. "When was this decided?"

"Ain't the end of the world. We're havin' us a special time together, an' I invited her to stay on, is all. And just this mornin', she got herself a job with Vera Lapp."

Mattie covered her face with her hands. "Mamm, you've gotta work *with* me, not against me."

"What's the difference if I live here till the *Dawdi Haus* is built or move in with you and David till then? Far as I can see, none a'tall."

Her daughter seemed to consider that. Then leaning forward in the brown wicker chair, she asked, "Mamm, would ya think 'bout putting Clara to work, helpin' sort out the attic and the second floor?"

Ella Mae shook her head. "Oh, now . . ."

"I'm serious, Mamm. If ya *have* to stay put here till the *Dawdi Haus* is built, might as well have Clara help organize things for the estate auction. The two of yous can work together."

Ella Mae frowned. "What auction? All but two of the upstairs bedrooms are empty and have been since your Dat an' I moved to the first floor. Have ya forgotten?"

"Still, those beds and dressers have to be sold or given away. Also, your big sewing room's up there, and that needs to be gone through."

"Well, I'll be takin' all of that with me when I *do* move."

Mattie nodded in agreement, or so it seemed. "What 'bout the furniture downstairs?"

After pausing a moment, Ella Mae said, "Your Dat made every last piece that's left, so I won't be partin' with any of it. Really, dear, there's no need for an auction."

Mattie grimaced. "Tell that to Jake."

Ignoring that comment, Ella Mae continued. "Oh, and no one's asked, but I'd really like two bedrooms and a smaller room for a sewin' room in the *Dawdi Haus*. Would that be possible?"

"S'pose you wanna help draw up the blueprint, too, Mamm?"

"Well, I wouldn't mind havin' a look-see before groundbreakin'." Mattie opened her mouth to speak, but Ella Mae had more to say. "Also, I won't be sellin' off my road horses and carriage. As long as I can hitch up on my own and drive anywhere I please, I want my team at the ready."

"Mamm, you're not getting any younger."

"That's the truth." Ella Mae reached down for the hem of her black apron and began to fan herself. "But neither are you, dear."

"You're getting all worked up."

"*Nee*, I'm just tellin' ya how things are gonna be while Clara's here and afterward."

Mattie sat there blinking, her lips all bunched up. "I sure hope I'm not like this with *my* children when I'm your age."

Ella Mae had to smile. "Think 'bout it, Mattie. Who'd ya get your spunk from?"

"*Schpank, jah*." Now Mattie was smiling, looking right at her. "For certain."

"*Gut* thing ya didn't know me when I was a teenager."

Mattie grimaced. "You've always said how outspoken you were back then."

"And plucky, too. Wasn't afraid of anything. My poor parents had a time keepin' me in line, 'specially in my midteen years. My Mamm's hair turned white in the space of one dreadful summer . . . and 'twas all my fault." Ella Mae sighed. "But that's water long since gone under the bridge."

At last, they began to talk more good-naturedly. Mattie mentioned that David—along with their middle son, Yonnie—and Jake would be over every other day like usual to clean out the horse stalls and freshen the straw, and that Lettie and her brother Judah would come and hoe the kitchen garden again, even though Ella Mae had just told her Clara had recently done it. Some of the other men in the family would come and chop wood for the cookstove.

Yet somehow the topic of an auction came up again. "You *do* have things in the attic and in the barn, as well, ain't so?" Mattie asked. "And the greenhouse, too."

"The fishin' gear and hunting rifles in the barn were divided up already, and whatever's left out there could be given away to others outside the family," Ella Mae told her, realizing she'd been too busy grieving to keep up with everything. "I'll just take one more look.

As for the attic, I haven't been up there in at least two decades. The few things added since then were taken up by your Dat."

Mattie was nodding like she'd somehow managed to win the battle. "At some point all the dusty whatnot up there will have to be sorted."

Ella Mae agreed.

"Several of the grandsons can come an' carry things down for ya. Don't you and Clara try to do it," Mattie urged, having clearly made some progress on the topic.

"Still, all of that can wait awhile. Clara an' I also have my parents' quilt to repair. We picked it up from Rebecca ourselves on Monday."

"*Ach*, Mamm." Mattie groaned now, pressing her lips together till they were pale.

"You're actin' like your Bruder Jake."

Mattie rose in a huff and went to stand at the banister for a moment, then turned around, red-faced. "Is something keepin' ya here, Mamm? Some unfinished business, maybe?"

Ella Mae's breath caught in her throat. "*Ach*, ya don't know it, but I still haven't disposed of the clothes."

"Dat's things?"

"All his clothes an' personal items." Tears stung her eyes. "I can't bear to part with 'em."

"I didn't know." Mattie's voice was soft now.

"Your father took his last breath in this ol' *Haus*. You an' all our babies were birthed here." Ella Mae stopped to wipe her eyes with a hankie from beneath her dress sleeve. "This *Haus* is a great comfort to me, daughter. I couldn't think of leavin' yet."

Mattie's gaze met hers, and then she slowly moved to kneel at her knee. "I wasn't thinkin'," she whispered. "I'm so sorry, Mamm." She bowed her head and was silent.

Ella Mae touched her daughter's shoulder. "It's still awful hard to reckon with. Truly 'tis." She paused to catch her breath. "For now, the memories made here are a shelter in my storm of sadness."

Mattie lifted her head as big tears rolled down her cheeks. "I miss Dat, too."

Ella Mae reached for her daughter's hands, clasping them and weeping along with her.

CHAPTER

Twelve

At six o'clock the next morning, Clara dressed quickly and swept her long hair into a thick bun, positioning it lower like the womenfolk here did. Then she tiptoed out of the house to pick strawberries, recalling that she and Mamma had often remarked how cool the dew on the grass beneath their bare feet felt.

How good it still feels.

She raised her face to a sky ever increasing in gold and pink tones as the sun rose over the green hills to the east. *I stayed up too late last night,* she thought, but she'd written letters to both Dat and Bertie, sharing her news about working at the quilt shop.

By now, Bertie probably knows from Dat

that I'm staying for the summer. I'll miss her, but I hope she's happy for me.

In her letter to her sister, she'd confided, *Even though it'll only be for two months or so, I'm delighted. Who knows, this may just be what I need to get past the worst of my grief.*

Now as she moved through the thick berry patch, she picked each glistening ripe red strawberry till she could find no more amidst the vines. A crow *caw-caw*ed high overhead, and she silently congratulated herself for getting there first.

Eventually, she walked toward the house with a partially filled basket of berries, then in the kitchen, she set her load on the counter and turned on the spigot, pooling cold water in the sink. With no sign of Aendi yet, she rinsed the strawberries for jam making, her mind wandering back to doing this chore with Mamma while standing on a kitchen chair pushed up next to the sink. *I was so little the first time we did it*, she recalled, picturing her mother's kitchen and enjoying the lovely memory.

But the joy began to fade as she suddenly envisioned Eva standing at Mamma's sink instead. And she felt the numbness toward Dat once again.

Not wanting to dwell on the image, she shook it away and started humming one of the gospel songs she'd learned at Singing last Sunday night. Very softly she did this, so no one could hear her but the dear Lord above.

A song of praise just for Him.

In the process, her sadness was replaced with a sense of peace, the kind her mother seemed to possess even on her weakest days. *The Prince of Peace, Mamma often referred to the Lord Jesus,* Clara recalled tenderly, clinging to that truth even now.

Later that morning Clara and Aendi worked together to make the jam and even had enough strawberries for two pies, just as Clara had hoped.

"We'll take one over to Leona Ebersol on our way to the Old Country Store today," Ella Mae said.

Clara nodded, happy to hear it. "I met Aaron Ebersol at Singing last Sunday, and Leona and her daughter Rosanna at Vera's yesterday. Leona said you're a dear friend."

"For many years now." Aendi went on to say Rosanna had turned sixteen back in January, but like a few other parents in the hollow with rather shy daughters, Leona and Adam had decided Rosanna should wait for six months before attending youth activities. "On July tenth, it'll be six months," she added.

"Not long now."

Aendi nodded. "I was hopin' ya might meet her. Rosanna also loves to quilt."

"If we become friends, we'll have that in common," Clara said, hoping so despite the three years between their ages. "So ya don't mind lookin' for vintage fabric today?"

"No time like the present."

"I wonder if Vera would know of a local place if the Old Country Store doesn't have it," Clara mused.

"Well, remember that Vera focuses on selling new quilts, but if need be, we'll ask around. There might only be reproductions of fabric available, but we'll see."

Clara assumed Aendi must be hesitant to buy new fabric and dye it in tea, so this time she didn't bring up that option.

Their stop to deliver the strawberry pie at the Ebersols' brought both Rosanna and Aaron hurrying across the barnyard. Aendi took the pie into the house, where she'd undoubtedly visit with Leona.

"Havin' a *gut* time here in the hollow?" Aaron asked, his light brown bangs noticeable beneath his straw hat.

"I am." Clara smiled, aware of the siblings' exchanged glances.

"Mamma says she's sure Ella Mae's thrilled you're stayin' all summer," Rosanna said softly, offering a sweet smile.

"*Jah*, thanks to Aendi's invitation. I'm also grateful to start workin' for Vera Lapp next week."

Rosanna nodded, most likely putting together why Clara had been talking with Vera that day. "She's real nice."

Aaron nodded as well, golden-brown eyes shining. "You'll enjoy bein' here."

"*Jah*, for sure," Rosanna said, looking surprised at her brother.

"It'll be nice getting to know everyone better, too," Clara replied.

Aendi was already coming this way, and Aaron and Rosanna waved to her.

"I would've gladly taken the pie in for ya," Aaron told her, protectively walking alongside Ella Mae.

"*Ach*, I'm chust fine, but *Denki*," Aendi said. "I wanted to speak with your Mamm. And it's nice to see ya both, too."

"Come again soon," Aaron said when Aendi was back in the buggy and picking up the driving lines.

I hope we do, Clara thought as she waved good-bye.

"Nicest young people, ain't?" Aendi said as she directed the horse to the turnaround.

"I can see why ya think so," Clara replied, glad they'd come.

"Aaron's already in partnership with his father in the harness shop behind their house," Aendi added. "Has a bright future, for certain."

Clara found it interesting she'd brought that up.

Clara and Aendi had carefully rewrapped the quilt in the unbleached muslin to bring it along, and as it turned out, the Old Country Store had only reproduction fabrics. Surprising Clara a little, Aendi described what they were hoping for to the helpful Amish clerk.

"Let's lay out the quilt and have a look," the clerk said in *Deitsch* as Clara placed the quilt on a large table.

Once they'd spread it out, the woman leaned over the quilt, pushing up her spectacles to examine it just as Clara had, moving from one end to the other. After a thorough inspection, she confirmed that they should be able to match fairly close to the original fabrics. "Let's look at the options we have here so yous can decide," she said, motioning them to follow her.

Much to Clara's amazement, the reproductions were available in a wide array of colors. "This is *wunnerbaar*," she told Aendi.

"No need to hesitate 'bout this approach," Aendi murmured.

"Take your time," the clerk said. "And let me know if there's somethin' ya don't find, all right? Or if ya need an opinion on how much fabric to purchase or whatnot."

Aendi was quick to thank her before they started searching first for the pale blue pieces they needed.

"Oh, look," Clara said, spotting a fabric that looked slightly faded and similar in tone to the torn ones. "This'll be perfect, *jah*?"

Agreeing, Aendi set that fabric aside, and the clerk came right over and carried it to the front, where the cash register was located.

Then she and Aendi searched for a variety of brown fabrics. Aendi eyed the worn, faded brown pieces on the quilt, comparing them to the reproduction options.

"We're findin' more than I expected," she told Clara.

They took the same approach for both the tan and black frayed pieces. Finally, when they'd accomplished their task, Aendi followed the clerk with their chosen fabrics to the checkout counter. Her aunt glanced over her shoulder at Clara, her little blue eyes twinkling.

She's so happy, Clara mused, lightly folding the quilt, then rewrapping it. *Now comes the time-consuming work.*

After purchasing the necessary amounts of fabric, she and Aendi thanked the clerk and headed toward the door. Clara enjoyed the sound of the old floorboards creaking as they walked over them, wishing Bertie could see this amazing historic store she'd learned was built way back in 1833.

Mamma would've loved it, too.

CHAPTER

Thirteen

Looking through the kitchen window after the breakfast dishes were washed and put away the next morning, Clara noticed Lettie and her brother Judah out weeding the vegetable garden. Eager to greet them, she opened the back door and stepped out. She'd met Judah at the Sunday picnic supper, along with other fellows Lettie had introduced her to, and she recalled how shy he was. He scarcely made eye contact with her now.

"Aendi Ella Mae says the vet's on his way to check on Sparkles," Clara said, making small talk.

"*Jah*, we saw him up at the neighbors' 'bout a mile away," Lettie told her. "Should be here fairly soon."

Not long after this, Mattie's husband,

David, and their son Yonnie arrived, and a few minutes later, Jake did, too. "Our family keeps close tabs on the farm-related things over here," Lettie said as she leaned on the hoe. "Mammi doesn't need to be thinking 'bout all that while she's grieving."

"*Jah*, that's what caring families do," Clara said, pleased they were all so attentive to her great-aunt.

An hour later, while Clara dusted and swept the floor, Ella Mae did some mending in the kitchen. Clara closed the front room windows since the outdoor temperature had risen significantly.

She could hear Lettie's voice across the house as she came in through the back door.

"The garden's tidied up for a few days," Lettie was telling her grandmother as Clara returned to the kitchen.

Aendi rose from the table, then stepped to the big cookie jar. "Yous were so quick! I have a little treat for ya both."

"That's okay, Mammi. We don't mind doin' it. Ya don't have to spoil us." But Lettie was grinning.

"Is that what your Mamma says? Or what *you* think?" Aendi clucked as she placed a handful of cookies in a plastic bag.

Lettie thanked her and accepted the treat. "Be sure an' share with Judah."

"Knowin' Judah, it'd be impossible not to." Lettie turned toward Clara. "Say, if you have time, Judah can drop us off at the house where your Mamma lived, then you an' I can walk back here. Judah will come for me later."

"That'd be nice," Clara replied, looking to Aendi for her consent.

"Then why not plan on stayin' for the noon meal, Lettie? I'm makin' corn dogs and baked beans." Her aunt's face lit up. "I love spendin' time *mit mei Kinskinner*."

Clara was delighted, looking forward to getting to know Lettie even better.

"It'll just be me," Lettie said, "since Judah has to get home. But he can let Mamm know where I am."

Aendi nodded. "All right, then."

"May I show Lettie the old quilt later?" Clara asked her.

"Of course. And while you're at it, see if ya can interest her in some quiltin' of her own, just maybe." She waved her hand in jest.

"Well, Judah's waitin', so I'll look at it when Clara and I return," Lettie said.

Clara headed for the back door with her new friend and shirttail cousin, eager to see the inside of the house where her Mamma had lived . . . and where Aendi said the heirloom quilt had been stitched.

By the time Clara and Lettie arrived at the three-story white clapboard house, the enclosed carriage Judah was driving had become quite warm. Clara was eager to get out for some fresh air. As she and Lettie made their way up the lane toward the house, Clara tried to picture Mamma and her siblings as children there, going to and from school together. Where Mamma learned to shell peas and sew and make her first nine-patch square. Where she ran to the phone shed to alert the midwife one dark night when her baby brother came early, a dramatic story Mamma had told often.

Approaching the back stoop, Clara noticed two wind chimes, their jingling sounds reminding her of the porch back home. *What would Mamma think of my coming here?*

Lettie led the way up the steps and knocked on the screen door. Clara hung back a little, thinking she was a stranger to the residents.

Lettie knocked again and waited. Then after a time, she said, "They must be away or busy upstairs."

Clara turned to look toward the barn and saw an older man coming their way, leaning heavily on his cane. He shielded his eyes from the sunlight.

"Lookin' for someone?" he called, cocking his head.

Lettie hurried down the steps to meet him, and Clara heard her telling him why they'd come. She felt embarrassed, not wanting to put the man out, hard as it was for him to walk and all.

Lettie returned to Clara. "He says for us to go in and look around on our own."

Clara nodded, excitement building as Lettie opened the door and they stepped inside.

They made their way through the kitchen and into the front room. Clara particularly wanted to see the latter, since her Aendi's Mamm's wedding quilt was made there. "Aendi said twelve women did the stitchin'," she told Lettie as they stood in the middle of the room.

"I'll have to see this quilt sometime. But as my grandmother probably told ya, given her teasing earlier, I'm not big on sewin' or quiltin'. Hard to believe for an Amish girl, *jah*?"

"Ya honestly don't care for it?"

"I much prefer to make fudge or sweets." Lettie grinned, patting her middle. "I wear my sweet tooth right here."

Laughing at Lettie's cute comment, Clara

looked around the large room. "It's easy to see how a big quilt frame could fit in here."

"*Jah,* and still have plenty of room for furniture and whatnot."

"Don't ya wonder what the womenfolk talked 'bout while they were stitchin' up that quilt?" Clara asked.

"You mean what stories they were tellin' out of school?" Lettie smiled.

"Gossip?"

Lettie clapped her hand over her mouth. "Did I say that?" She burst into laughter. "Many-a tale has been told at such gatherings, accordin' to my Mamma. Just ask your Aendi Ella Mae."

Clara thought again of the so-called unspeakable happening Tom Glick mentioned. *Lettie's too young to know about that,* she decided. Even so, she was still curious, especially considering the reaction she'd had from Aendi.

On the way back toward the kitchen, Lettie asked if she wanted to see the upstairs, but Clara didn't think that made sense since she had no idea which bedroom had been her mother's.

"We should prob'ly just head back, then. Mammi Ella Mae'll be ready for the noon meal."

"Okay." Clara fell in step with her.

They walked on the left side of the road, close to the dirt shoulder, where clusters of golden-yellow dandelions grew on the tall grassy slope. The sun beat hot against their backs as they went, and when Lettie mentioned Tom Glick's "obvious" interest in her, Clara was surprised.

"Is there somethin' more I should know?" she asked. "Other than Tom likes a lot of girls?"

"Honestly, if I were you, I wouldn't get tied down to one fella," Lettie said.

"Just be friendly with everyone, like Tom is?"

Lettie glanced at her. "Truth be told, I don't think he's ever dated anyone more than once or twice."

"Maybe he's just not ready to settle down." But since she really didn't know him, Clara felt awkward defending Tom.

"'Tween you and me, he seems much too restless for that. Just my opinion."

"That's fair."

Thankfully, their conversation turned to Lettie's excitement about taking a big batch of fudge to market tomorrow—her first attempt at selling peanut butter fudge, her own recipe.

"Sounds delicious," Clara said, wanting to encourage her. "I hope it sells well."

"You'll have to try it sometime."

"I'd love to."

As they approached Aendi's familiar lane, Clara noticed someone waving good-bye to her aunt from a carriage just turning onto the road in the opposite direction.

"*Kumme* again for tea sometime!" Aendi called.

"Looks like someone stopped by for some encouragement," Lettie said, sounding pleased about it. "My Dat said it's been much too long since folk outside the family have stopped by, most to cry on *Grememm*'s shoulder." She looked at Clara. "They call her the Wise Woman round here, ya know."

"She's a sage, all right . . . yet she can be comical, too."

"You can say that again."

Clara smiled, enjoying Lettie's banter.

Following the noon meal and Judah's return for Lettie, Clara considered Lettie's remark about Aendi imparting wisdom to folk over a cup of tea.

Is it time for me to finally share my greatest disappointment with someone? she mused as she and her aunt handwashed the newly purchased reproduction fabric.

But I don't want to burden Aendi.

CHAPTER

Fourteen

Following Bible reading and prayer together that evening, Clara and Ella Mae set to work on the nine-patch Miniature Variable Star heirloom quilt in the front room. The green shades were pulled up as far as they'd go to let in the light, as the sun was still fairly high in the sky. Clara had also opened all the windows, hoping for some cross-ventilation.

Sitting across the table from her aunt, she began to hand-stitch a small seam to cover a frayed piece at one end of the quilt. Aendi was intent on her work as well, making only a few comments now and then, mostly regarding the restoration process.

Feeling rather relaxed there in the stillness of the house, Clara decided to reveal what had happened to cause her and her beau to part ways—if Aendi seemed up to it.

"Aendi," she said, glancing over at her, "I've been wanting to tell someone 'bout my recent breakup with a serious beau . . . and the reason for it."

"*Jah?*" Aendi replied, a sweet expression on her crinkled face.

"I think it might help me to share it with you, but I don't want to add more to what you're already goin' through."

"Ain't a problem a'tall." Aendi pushed her needle through the fabric.

"All right, then." Clara drew a breath. "Wollie Lehman and I were friends for the longest time—seein' each other at school recess and at church gatherings through the years. The autumn we both turned sixteen, we started attending Singings and other youth activities, and before too long, he asked me to double-date with him and another couple. And for two years we casually dated that way, with several other young couples. But then a few weeks after Wollie's eighteenth birthday, he made it clear that he wanted to take me out, just the two of us."

She paused a moment, noticing Aendi had set down her sewing needle and was paying close attention. "This seemed like a serious step forward, and I welcomed it." Clara's voice wavered. "I was fallin' in love with him."

Aendi's soft eyes met Clara's.

"I still remember the moonlit night Wollie admitted he'd always felt a certain tug toward me—like a magnet was drawin' him. It sure didn't sound like a common line a fella might use to get a girl to court him. *Nee*, when Wollie shared that with me, it was a truly precious moment. One I cherished."

"Aww . . . of course ya did," Aendi murmured.

"Within six months' time, we were movin' toward betrothal, happily talking 'bout our future together, the Lord willin'. He said he felt sure I was the girl for him, and I felt the same way about him."

Stopping to gather her thoughts, Clara sighed, then went on. "One Sunday afternoon, though—not too long after losing Mamma—we were out walkin' in the dirt lanes round our field, and Wollie told me he'd recently discovered something startling 'bout himself. He was adopted, and his biological mother was a cousin to my father. Well, I looked at Wollie in disbelief. 'So we're blood kin?' I asked him, and then I started to cry. His eyes were welling up, too, and I couldn't speak further."

Clara couldn't go on for a moment *now*, remembering how she felt at such an astonishing revelation.

Aendi reached her hand across the table to touch Clara's. "You all right, dear?"

Clara nodded, quiet till she could go on at last.

"After Wollie's news seeped into my brain, I was relieved we'd never kissed on the lips, though I'd wanted to several times." Clara sighed again. "I mean, who'd wanna kiss their cousin?"

"*Gut* question," her aunt said gently.

"Honestly, at the time, I was downright embarrassed at the fact of our courtship, but I was also thankful to learn the truth before our relationship got any more serious."

For a time, Aendi was silent as sunbeams spotlighted the quilt. Then she said, "I daresay you're the pluckiest young woman I know, goin' through all that and comin' out of it with such a sensible outlook."

"There wasn't any other way to think 'bout it." Clara shook her head. "I was so mortified, I've never even told Dat or Bertie, although Bertie knew we'd broken up. It was enough that it ended privately, just 'tween Wollie and me. We really didn't want it known."

"Well, bless your heart." Aendi gave her a smile. "The Lord surely has another fella picked out for ya, Clara."

"It'd be *wunnerbaar* if he's not related to me. That's why I asked ya 'bout Tom Glick's mother's maiden name the other day. He's one of the young men I've met here."

"Oh. Well, I understand your worry, but none of your relatives live round here anymore, other than Joseph's and my children and their families, but it's quite clear who they are. Everyone else has either died, moved away, or already married."

"*Gut* to know."

Clara shared that Wollie's birth mother had come from somewhere in Pennsylvania, according to what his adoptive parents told him. "But honestly, it seems that we Amish are all so closely related, and more and more settlements are croppin' up round the country with the first few families originating from larger, well-established communities. It can be hard to know who's related to who."

"You're right." Aendi smoothed out the replaced fabric where she'd stitched a seam.

"I never, ever want to get myself into another relationship like that."

"Well, as your own dear Mamma understood, surrenderin' to the Lord's guidance is the path to peace."

Clara agreed. "God cares 'bout even the little things, she always said."

"Big or little, if they matter to you, dearie, they matter to Him." Aendi looked at her kindly.

"When I was a tiny girl, Mamma told me that when we trust in our Savior, we never have to fear."

Aendi nodded her little head, the white Kapp strings swaying.

Clara was glad she'd finally shared this, and with someone she could trust. Picking up her threaded needle and thimble, she returned to restoring the quilt. The sound of cheerful birdcalls floated in through the window screens, and she glanced at her aunt, now back at her work.

The elderly woman's affection for her was a true solace.

As the minutes passed and the repair work grew more exacting, Ella Mae turned on the gas lamp because the sun had set, and it occurred to Clara to bring up Tom again and what Lettie had said about him. Seeing how Aendi was absorbed in their task, though, she decided to dismiss it.

But as interested in her as Tom seemed to be, maybe he was the one God had planned for her.

Shouldn't I accept his invitations, then?

She considered again Lettie's suggestion not to get tied down to one fellow. And glancing again at her aunt, she couldn't help but wonder if she'd had any struggles during her courting years.

Dare I ask? Clara thought, trying to focus again on her stitching.

On the way out to the stable the next morning, Ella Mae asked Clara to take the reins for their trip to Friday market. It was the first time she'd suggested this, and it didn't take long to see that Clara was quite skilled at directing Firefly. *No worries there.*

As they approached Weaver's Creek a few miles into the journey, Ella Mae heard what sounded like guitar music coming from below the road, down near the creek on the right side. She looked over at Clara, who had a peculiar expression on her pretty face.

"Who'd be playin' a guitar round here?" Clara asked.

"No idea." Ella Mae leaned forward, gawking out Clara's open window. "Must be an *Englischer* down there a-strummin'."

"Sounds like two guitars," Clara said, still looking befuddled.

"Sure does."

"Tom said your present bishop ain't nearly as strict as the one ordained many years ago," Clara added, sounding hesitant to mention it.

How would young Tom know about that? From his father, I s'pose, but surely . . . Ella Mae fretted but tried not to react. She certainly didn't care to comment, not if what Tom Glick told Clara was linked in any way to what happened decades ago, when Ella Mae was courting age.

The dear Lord knows what a can of worms that would open!

CHAPTER

Fifteen

As Clara strolled toward the road the next day, the ground was still damp from early-morning rain showers. At least the sun had come out.

Having thought it over, she was happy to be going to the deacon's farm for *die Youngie*'s cornhusking contest. Aendi had encouraged her to go, remarking that she'd have a good time.

But she wished she'd made at least one new dress since deciding to stay in Hickory Hollow for the summer. She was growing tired of wearing dark mourning clothes.

As she walked, she was conscious of the rich green paddocks, white-painted horse fences, gold-tasseled cornstalks, and all the colors the Lord had created. *The sky is such a pretty blue when the sun's shining. And I'm very happy here, so maybe I ought to wear blue and other colors again.*

A half mile or so away from the deacon's, she rounded the bend and noticed two Amish girls strolling along, talking animatedly. Unable to identify who they were from that distance, Clara hurried to catch up with them.

"Hullo," she said, recognizing Mary Stoltzfus and her redheaded friend, Katie Lapp. "Yous headed to the youth cornhuskin' contest?"

"*Jah*," Mary spoke up. "I hope you are, too."

Katie smiled, looking nice in her long, bright green dress and matching apron. "I heard this contest is 'tween the guys and the girls again—to see which side can husk five baskets of corn first."

"Us girls won last year," Mary told Clara, her blue eyes beaming under her navy blue bandanna, the same color as her dress and apron.

"We're gonna beat 'em this time, too," Katie said, laughing. "But Daniel Fisher's determined the guys'll win."

Clara recalled that Daniel was the young man whose eyes had sparkled upon spotting Katie during the picnic last Sunday. "We'll see 'bout that!" she said.

Mary nodded. "I like the way ya think, Clara Bender."

"Glad ya caught up with us," Katie said. "Mamm told me you're stayin' for the rest of the summer now, and while you're here, you can always walk with us, okay?"

"*Denki.*" Clara smiled, so pleased.

Ten baskets were already set up in the deacon's big haymow when Clara arrived with Mary and Katie—five for the guys and five for the girls. Other young people were standing around talking, and several of the guys, including Tom Glick, were making a big show of rolling up their shirtsleeves, grins on their suntanned faces.

Aaron Ebersol was with Daniel Fisher and Judah Zook in one corner, all smiles like they were eager to get started. Clara was surprised when Aaron caught her eye and nodded discreetly. Judah, bashful as he still seemed, simply folded his arms, a determined look on his face.

When the youth had assembled, the deacon offered a welcome and invited them to help themselves to cold lemonade from large glass containers off to the side once the contest was over. Then, wasting no time, he asked *die Youngie* to line up alongside the baskets.

Once they had, he waved one hand and said in *Deitsch*, "On your mark, get set, go!"

Clara was no stranger to husking corn. She worked quickly, tossing each husked ear into one of the nearby baskets, silk strings and all, as the other girls were doing. A few of them were chattering, but most of them husked speedily in silence.

After the contest, Clara and Lettie headed for the homemade lemonade. "I'm not sure how us girls won last year," Lettie said, glancing over her shoulder at the triumphant fellows, who were giving one another high fives.

"It was lots of fun, all the same," Clara said. "And we husked a lot of corn for the deacon and his family."

"*Jah*." Lettie looked like there was more on her mind. "Say, I think Aaron Ebersol might have his eye on ya, Clara. And 'tween you and me, if he asks ya out, I hope you'll go."

Clara wasn't sure what to say to that. This was the third time Lettie had offered advice about fellows.

As they headed back to the other girls, Clara noticed Aaron smile at her, then step away from the guys, coming her way.

But at just that moment, out of the corner of her eye, she saw Tom coming her way, as well. He arrived first.

"I see ya decided to show up." Tom smirked

playfully when she turned her head to acknowledge him.

She nodded. "It was fun."

"Even though the guys won by a mile?"

"Half a basket's not a mile," she replied, noticing Aaron glancing her way from his place back with the group of guys. She actually felt a little sorry for him.

"Wanna go have some ice cream with me?" Tom's expression was one of expectancy. "It's an ideal day for a cold treat."

She took a sip of her lemonade. "Okay."

Ella Mae washed the two tumblers in her deep kitchen sink, placed them in the draining rack, and then wiped down the table. She'd had an unexpected visit from the newly widowed niece of Preacher Yoder. Thirty-eight-year-old Sylvia Riehl had poured out her heart, and Ella Mae let her talk as long as she needed to.

But now, thinking back on the conversation, Ella Mae wondered if she'd made a difference. Sure, she'd listened to tearful Sylvia and offered more iced peppermint tea and sweets, but she hadn't shared any of her own grief as a widow, nor let the woman know she wasn't alone in what she was feeling. It was one thing to open up and talk with Clara about sadness and the misery of losing a loved one, but she hadn't felt up to that with Sylvia.

I did promise to remember her in prayer, Ella Mae recalled, and she would, indeed. But poor Sylvia had seemed as gloomy when she left as when she'd arrived. Ella Mae was certain she'd failed in offering her empathy.

Is it too soon for anyone to come for a listening ear? Should I wait till I'm further along with my own mourning?

She dried the tumblers and placed them back in the cupboard, then turned her attention to making the noon meal, assuming Clara might not be back to eat with her. The thought made her surprisingly blue, and she realized yet again how good it was to have Clara staying with her. *She has such an openness about her that makes me feel ever so comfortable.*

In that moment, she realized people had said this very thing about *her* in the past. Yet losing Joseph had altered her, and she couldn't help wondering if she was any good to others now, especially those struggling with grief.

"Am I, Lord?" she whispered.

Tom was polite and asked Clara what flavor she wanted at the drive-through ice cream shop. She requested chocolate, and he ordered the same for himself, paying for both cones.

When the ice cream was ready, Tom directed the horse to pull over to a treed parking area, where they sat in the buggy and enjoyed the treat.

"Looks like we both like chocolate," Tom said before getting out and tying the horse to the hitching post while she held his cone.

Clara smiled. "Chocolate's only one of my favorites."

"What're the others?" he asked, eyes intent on her when he climbed back inside.

"Have ya ever eaten raspberry ice cream or pistachio? I like those, too."

"My Mamm has a *wunnerbaar-gut* pistachio ice cream recipe, *jah*."

"Does she mix the ingredients and then you or your Dat turn the hand crank?"

Tom laughed. "Exactly."

Instantly, Clara was transported in her memory to hot summer days when her mother was healthy and sometimes made several kinds of ice cream in the space of a week. The thought triggered a sudden melancholy mood.

"You all right? Ya look sad."

She shrugged, not really wanting to say. "Just thinkin'."

Tom's face softened. "Okay, then." He took another big bite of his ice cream.

"Ya know, I really should get home so I

can eat the noon meal with Aendi Ella Mae," she told him.

He glanced at the sky as if to check the time. "We could get some hot dogs or burgers if you're hungry. My treat."

She forced a smile. "*Denki*, but maybe another time."

"Okay, if that's what ya want." Tom finished his ice cream and stepped out of the buggy to untie his horse. "I can get ya there right quick," he said when he returned. Then without saying more, he picked up the driving lines, backed out of the space, and headed for the road.

Clara noticed how quickly the horse was trotting, nearly a gallop, and she felt uneasy on this narrow, ribbon-like road.

"Wanna see how fast my horse can go?" Tom asked, slapping the reins and hurrying the animal all the more. The horse nickered and snorted. "He's the fastest in Lancaster County!"

She quickly finished the last of her cone and looked around for something to hold on to. The buggy bumped and rattled as the horse raced ahead. Her heart was pounding, and her hands had clenched into fists. Never before had she ridden in a speeding carriage!

When at last they arrived at her aunt's, Tom having slowed the horse to a trot before turning into the lane, she could hardly wait to get out. But she remembered to thank Tom for the ice cream. He leaped down on his side and came around to help her down.

"I hope we can have lunch together sometime soon," he said, grinning.

She paused a moment before asking, "If ya could slow down your horse, maybe?"

He winked at her. "For you, anything, Clara."

They said good-bye, and then she made her way to the house as Tom took his place behind the reins again.

Despite that harrowing ride just now, a thought made her smile. Given what Lettie had told her about Tom moving on after dating a girl only once or twice, she might just be the only one in the hollow to have a third date with him.

CHAPTER

Sixteen

The rest of the day, Clara washed the raspberries she'd picked and then cooked and baked with Aendi ahead of the Lord's Day. She also harvested some of the sweet corn and many cherry tomatoes from the vegetable garden.

While baking several raspberry cream pies, Clara mentioned wanting to purchase some royal blue material for a dress and matching apron.

Her aunt's face brightened. "Why not some green or purple, too?"

Clara agreed and looked forward to going to the fabric shop on Monday after the washing was out on the line. And by the look on her aunt's face, she was happy that Clara wanted to wear dresses in colors now. She'd sew a longer hem for while she was here, as well.

When I write Dat again, I'll tell him about the new dresses. He'll probably be happy I'm making them, too.

The next day dawned a brilliant pink, thanks to wispy clouds near the eastern horizon. Clara rose from her bed to read the Good Book, then dressed and headed outside to pick more ripe berries. As she did, she prayed silently, thanking God for another Sunday in beautiful Hickory Hollow.

After breakfast, while Clara dried dishes and her aunt washed them, Aendi asked if she'd go with her to visit Leona Ebersol and her family that afternoon. "Hopefully, Rosanna will be there."

"I'd like that," Clara said.

"Since this is an off-Sunday for Preachin', I thought we might relax and read this morning—or write letters, maybe—then go to the Ebersols' after a light meal at noon. Take Leona one of the raspberry cream pies we made yesterday."

"A *gut* time to write to Dat."

"The morning's all yours." Aendi smiled. "I want you to feel completely at home here."

"Oh, I do." Clara couldn't begin to tell her just how much.

"I've been thinkin' 'bout what ya told me

'bout your beau, Wollie, the other evening. And I pray your disappointment will fade as you make new friends."

Clara thanked her. "I don't know why I waited so long to talk about it, but it feels *gut* to have that burden lifted. The Lord must've known it was *you* I needed to tell."

Her aunt gave her an endearing smile. "I'm grateful I could encourage ya, Clara. I don't think I'm so *gut* at it with others anymore, though."

This surprised Clara. She wanted to ask why Aendi felt that way, but she didn't want to pry. She waited for her to say more, and when she didn't, Clara said simply, "You're healing, too, remember. And you share the love of the Lord with everyone who comes for tea."

Tears filled Aendi's eyes, and she looked toward the window, silent for a long moment. "Chust s'pose I need to be more open, like I used to be."

Clara felt their roles had suddenly reversed, and she wanted to say something to boost her aunt's spirits. "Well, like ya told me 'bout wearin' colors again, you'll know when you're ready. The Lord will help ya."

This brought a thin smile and a nod of Aendi's head. "Bless ya for sayin' that, dear."

After a quiet time of reading from the Good Book, Clara wrote her letter to Dat, then one to Bertie, who'd already written once. *Her letter arrived in record time,* Clara thought. *You just never know about the mail. And Bertie also seemed to understand why I wanted to stay longer. I'm so grateful for that.*

She also wrote to two of her engaged girlfriends.

Later, Jake and his wife, Marta, dropped by for a visit. Marta was quite friendly, but Jake seemed focused on getting the house and barn ready for his mother's move. That, and he mentioned that her grandson, Clyde, and his wife, Susannah, currently residing in the Big Valley, were keenly interested in purchasing the farm and house here. He'd had a letter from his younger brother, Abe, telling him so.

By the pinched look on her aunt's face, it was apparent to Clara she was put off by this conversation. And though she felt awkward sitting there in the front room with Jake, she tried to be cordial. Sad to say, it was a relief when they left, though Clara would have liked to get better acquainted with Marta.

Why must Jake be so pushy? And Mattie, too? she wondered, thinking surely Aendi's other children weren't that way, living so far away. Weren't they all grieving their father's passing?

Following a delicious meal of warmed-up chicken and rice made yesterday, Clara and Ella Mae headed off to visit the Ebersol family. Since it was only a short distance, Aendi wanted Sparkles to get out on the road again, the horse having recovered from the mild case of colic. As before, she asked Clara to drive.

Thankfully, Jake and Marta's visit did not come up during the ride. Instead, they discussed repairing the heirloom quilt, and Clara shared how much she enjoyed working on it. Then Aendi brought up something Clara was quite interested in—her aunt's parents' love story.

"It's kind of remarkable how they ended up together," Aendi told her. "Ya see, they'd lost touch after dating only a few months, following my father's parents' move to New Wilmington in western Pennsylvania."

Clara's ears perked up.

"After that, Mamm no longer heard from her beau, convinced he'd found someone new where he and his family had settled. But then three years later, Mamm happened to take a hand-stitched quilt to an exhibit in Ephrata, where a Mennonite friend had asked her to display it. Unknown to Mamm, her former beau and his mother also brought a quilt to display, made by the exact same Mennonite quilter. She'd visited them in New Wilmington several months before and given it to them as a gift."

"How remarkable," Clara murmured.

"Well, listen to this," Aendi continued. "Looking at the quilt her former beau and his mother brought, Mamm noted the Mennonite woman's same crazy quilt pattern, just done in different colors, and her initials in a small red heart. And my Dat and his mother noticed the quilt Mamm brought had the same little heart and initials, too."

Aendi paused, smiling at Clara at the reins. "Can ya guess what happened?"

"S'pose they rediscovered each other that day?"

Aendi smiled. "Curiosity got the best of them when they realized the quilter had a connection to both of their families, and you're right—those quilts brought the two back together."

"An unexpected reunion," Clara said, loving this.

"You're exactly right."

"I wonder why your Dat didn't stay in touch with her after he and his family moved away."

"That's somethin' I wondered 'bout, too. But it seemed a little too personal to ask."

Clara understood. "They must've stayed in touch after that reunion, though."

"Dat courted her by letter and eventually moved back to Lancaster County to marry her and start their family here, where Mamm's perty wedding gift was pieced together and quilted—the very quilt we're slowly restoring."

Clara shook her head, grinning. "This makes me appreciate the quilt all the more."

"I thought ya'd enjoy this family story," her aunt said, grinning.

"It's a reminder that little things along the way can lead us, like stepping stones, to where we're s'posed to be, ain't so?"

"When we trust our heavenly Father, *jah*."

Now Aendi was pointing toward the turn-off to the Ebersol farm.

As Clara directed Sparkles into the driveway, she was eager to get back to repairing the beloved wedding quilt. Just not today. There was to be no sewing or mending on Sunday here or back home. She knew that for sure.

If Clara hadn't known better, she might have thought Rosanna and Aaron had somehow gotten word that she and Aendi planned to visit. While several younger children played in the yard, the two of them sat on the back porch steps as though they were waiting for visitors.

As Clara halted Sparkles, Aaron waved and hurried over to greet them before offering to tie their mare to the hitching post.

Rosanna came right behind him and smiled brightly at Clara. "What a nice surprise," she said.

"Hope yous ain't tired of berry pie," Aendi said, handing the raspberry cream pie to Clara before stepping down from the carriage.

"Not if *you* made it," Aaron spoke up, taking the pie from Clara and hurrying back toward the house with it.

"Would ya like some cold meadow tea?" Rosanna asked quietly.

"Sounds delicious," Clara said as she strolled beside her aunt.

"Indeed it does," Aendi added as they made their way to the back porch and then sat on two of the hickory chairs there.

Leona came right out and welcomed them, and shortly afterward Rosanna brought out a tray of the iced tea in pretty lime-colored glasses. "Adam took his father to visit a sick relative," Leona said, serving the tea. "Otherwise, they'd be happy to see yous, as well."

Aaron stayed around while the women talked. Shy as she was, Rosanna glanced at Clara now and then, but she didn't join in the conversation. The younger children scampered around the yard, playing hide-and-seek, and Clara's imagination bloomed again as she envisioned her mother and her siblings playing together quietly on a Sunday afternoon so long ago. She also thought about Aendi's parents and how they finally got together.

Little things can point us in the right direction.

After a time, Aaron excused himself, and in a soft voice Rosanna asked Clara, "Would ya like to take a walk with me?"

"I hoped we might," Clara said before sipping the last of her tea.

Rosanna took Clara's empty glass and her own and then excused herself to go inside. She returned quickly, and then the two strolled toward the meadow.

"It's a perfect day," Clara said as they headed toward the field lanes on the outskirts of the immense field of sweet corn.

Rosanna bobbed her head. "Mamma and I go walkin' a lot."

Clara enjoyed the light breeze on her face as they walked past enormous willow trees and wild daisies growing in clusters here and there. "Have ya ever repaired an old quilt?" she asked, remembering Aendi said the girl liked to sew and quilt.

"Not yet, but maybe someday."

Clara described how she and her aunt were replacing the now-shabby piecework in an heirloom quilt. "It was made in 1911, when Aendi Ella Mae's Mamm was wed."

"That *is* an heirloom."

"I just hope it turns out nice enough to use again—or at least display."

Rosanna nodded. "Mamma has a quilt she no longer uses, but she has it on a little wooden rack."

"Was it passed down through the family?"

"*Jah*, and Mamma took very *gut* care of it all these years."

"Do ya know how old it is?"

Rosanna's smile was faint. "It was made for Mamma's baby sister, who died before she was a year old."

"How very sad."

Rosanna nodded. "Mamma said I could have it when I marry since it was on my crib when I was a baby."

"That's precious."

"It's real perty, too." Rosanna fell quiet for a moment, then said more softly, "I guess I'll have to start goin' to activities and Singings with *die Youngie* if I'm ever to get married. Startin' next Sunday, I s'pose."

Clara heard her say *have to* and wondered. "So you're not so eager to go, then?"

"*Nee.*" Rosanna sighed. "My parents knew

I wasn't ready to start goin'—too bashful. So, I was relieved to be able to wait."

Clara knew of only a very few other girls who waited till they were a little older, but she didn't think it was necessarily because they were too shy. "That's all right. Go whenever you're ready."

"Aaron tells me how much I'll enjoy the activities, but I don't think I wanna go out ridin' with a fella just yet. Why, Aaron's been goin' to Singings for more than three years now, and he's only taken a few girls out. No serious courtin'."

"Well, then just enjoy the fellowship and fun. There's plenty-a time for exclusive dating. I'll be happy to sit with ya next Sunday night, if you'd like."

A smile spread across Rosanna's heart-shaped face. "*Denki*, Clara."

"Sure."

"Two of my older cousins offered the same thing. Like big sisters," Rosanna said, looking up at her.

"Havin' a big sister's a *wunnerbaar-gut* thing," Clara replied, realizing this was the most Rosanna had ever talked to her. *We're becoming friends.*

CHAPTER

Seventeen

Early Monday morning was taken up with the week's laundry, and Clara breathed in the fresh air as she hung out the linens and clothes, looking forward to fried eggs and waffles for breakfast.

Later, while Aendi put two loaves of bread in the oven to bake, Clara hitched up Firefly and left for the fabric shop in Intercourse Village on her own.

When she returned with material for several new dresses, Clara saw Aendi sitting out on the front porch, talking with a sad-looking woman. Was it Sylvia Riehl, the young widow her aunt recently mentioned?

Minding her own business, Clara took time to unhitch Firefly and stable her, then pushed the carriage into the shed nearby. She made her way into the house with the colorful new fabrics and washed them in warm water in the kitchen sink before rinsing and wringing them out. Then she pinned them to the clothesline.

Stepping back, she couldn't help admiring the pretty fabrics swaying in the breeze. *It's been a long time since I've worn anything but drab blacks and grays.* But now, thinking ahead to the pattern, she was unsure whether to make the new dresses in the style of the Lancaster County women or the style she'd always sewn for herself back home.

I'll see what Aendi says, Clara decided as she headed toward the house. Her thoughts circled back to her aunt's parents' courtship—how it had somehow ended when his family moved away.

What if Tom likes me a lot by the time I must return home in September? And what if I like him a lot, too? What then?

Clara swept the kitchen and washed the floor while Aendi was still with the woman out front. Then after the woman left, the mail carrier came up to the porch, and Clara could hear him talking with her aunt.

When Aendi finally came inside, Clara noticed her eyes were a little red. Sitting down at the kitchen table, her aunt sighed heavily, brushing fresh tears from her face. "I thought 'bout what ya said, and I opened up a bit to let Sylvia see into my sad heart," she told Clara. "It seemed to make a difference for her, and it did a world of *gut* for me, too."

Clara wanted to hug her, but instead she simply listened closely and smiled at her.

"You were right, dearie. Besides, no one should have to hurt alone. I'd honestly wondered what my purpose in life was, with Joseph gone. After takin' care of him for so long, it seemed like there was nothin' left for me." She pulled a hankie out of her pocket and dabbed at her eyes. "But I think I know what the Lord wants me to do with the rest of my days. Or should I say, I *remember*."

"Encourage others?" Clara asked, happy to see this breakthrough.

Aendi nodded. "Little by little, I just might be findin' my way back to that."

"Like slowly but steadily workin' on repairing your Mamm's wedding quilt?"

Smiling now, her aunt said, "S'pose ya could think of it thataway."

"Mamma used to say she felt like you saw her through the eyes of Jesus—the way you wrote to her in your letters all those years."

The older woman's expression turned serious. "Believe me, I had a special place in my heart for your Mamm." She glanced toward the window.

Clara knew that was true, having read her letters. "If Mamma were here, she would ask if you'd like some tea or coffee 'bout now."

"*Denki*, but I've had a-plenty." Then she said, "Speakin' of letters, I think there's a boxful of Lillian's letters in the attic somewhere if you'd like to read them sometime, wherever Joseph might have put them." She paused, her face scrunching up. "My daughter's like a dog on a bone, tryin' to get me to sort through whatever's up there."

"I could help with that." *And I'd love to read Mamma's letters.*

"*Ach*, we have other things to occupy our time together." Aendi shook her head. "Say, did ya find some dress material ya liked?"

"It's washed and hangin' on the clothesline. Fabric for several new dresses—blue, green, and purple."

"Well now. Looks like we're *both* turnin' over a new leaf—or tryin', ain't so?"

Clara nodded. "What would ya think if I make the new dresses in the longer style ya wear here?"

"Ya wanna fit in with the womenfolk?"

Clara didn't mention that the dresses would be impractical, really, once she left for home. "Since I'll be workin' at Vera's starting tomorrow, I thought it'd make sense . . . and when I'm round the other youth, too."

"Well, then I agree." Aendi was smiling now, the sadness gone, at least for now.

Clara could hardly wait to start making the first dress that afternoon. And for her head covering, she'd simply wear a bandanna over her hair bun at work and around her aunt. No sense making Lancaster County *Kapps* since she wasn't a church member here.

The next morning after breakfast, Clara stood on the kitchen bench while Aendi marked her hem with straight pins. Then she set to stitching right away, excited to start her job that afternoon. She wanted to look her best for Vera and the customers.

When the hemming was done, Clara pressed her new dress with her aunt's iron, heated on top of the woodstove. As she worked, she wondered if Aendi might have another visitor today, just maybe.

After she put away the ironing board, she hung her dress in the spare room and heard Aendi calling from her bedroom across the hall. She quickly slipped over there and stood in the doorway. "Do ya need somethin'?"

"If ya wouldn't mind, I left my father's

old Bible down cellar when we were doin' the washin' yesterday."

"I'll go get it." Clara hurried to the kitchen and opened the cellar door, very happy to help, considering how steep the stairs were.

She spotted the black leather Bible on the wooden table near the wringer washer and rinsing tub. Some of its pages were loose, and when she picked it up, a note fell out. Clara saw what looked like a prayer with a date on it—*September 1933*.

Curiosity overtook her, and she began to read.

> *O, heavenly Father, I beseech Thee for our precious daughter Ella Mae as she turns sixteen. May she be mindful of Thy loving-kindness and follow Thy ways all through her life, keeping her baptismal vow close to her heart. Earnestly, I entrust her into Thy care. Amen.*

Struck by the sincerity, and even urgency, of the prayer, Clara placed the note back in the Bible. As she did, another note fell out. She could see others sprinkled throughout the pages, as well. *Are these all from Aendi's father?*

Heading up the cellar stairs, Clara was amazed by the old Bible, still in her aunt's possession and certainly cherished all these years. *What a caring father she had, writing such earnest prayer notes!*

She found Aendi still in her room reading a devotional book, and handing her the Bible, Clara said, "Two notes fell out, and I read one of 'em . . . and saw others."

"Ah, that's chust fine," her aunt said, opening the Good Book. "This belonged to my father's mother 'afore it came to him." She mentioned that her Dat—and Mamm, too—had been worried about her during the teen years, especially. "And years later, my father told me he found comfort in writing his prayers for me and tucking them into his Bible. Obviously, he kept them in there long after God stopped me in my tracks and answered his prayers." She glanced toward the ceiling, a grateful look on her furrowed brow.

"It's hard to believe *you* gave them such concern," Clara replied, rather stunned.

"Oh, that wasn't the half of it." Aendi was shaking her head and sighing loudly. "I daresay they were at their wits' end."

Clara watched how gently, if not lovingly, Aendi turned the thin pages. "I've never heard of writing *out* a prayer," she said.

Her aunt glanced at her with a smile. "We learn new things each an' every day, don't we?"

Clara nodded, ever more curious about Aendi's teen years. *What did she mean about all that?*

The first customer at Vera's Quilts that afternoon was Rebecca Lapp, who seemed delighted when she saw Clara with Vera behind the cash register. "I'm glad it worked out for ya to work here," she said.

Clara agreed. "*Denki* again for recommending me."

Vera told her how nice she looked in her new dress, though she didn't point out the Lancaster County dress pattern.

"I talked it over with Aendi before I cut out the pattern." Clara smiled. "It was helpful to have her dresses and cape to look at."

"Ella Mae's a *gut* help to ya, I'm sure," Vera replied, then mentioned an upcoming canning bee at Mattie Beiler's, the morning of the fourteenth.

"Work frolics are *wunnerbaar*," Clara said.

Rebecca asked about the old quilt. "How's the repair comin'?"

"I'd say real *gut*, but it's slow goin' and takes time and care."

"I'm sure it'll be right perty when you're done."

Then after making her purchase, Rebecca said good-bye and left.

Between customers, Clara couldn't help thinking again about Aendi's strange remarks about her youth. Considering the prayer notes in her father's Bible, she must have been a handful.

When the time seems right, I'll ask her more about those years.

CHAPTER

Eighteen

Ella Mae figured it was past time to go have a look at the rough sketches for her future *Dawdi Haus*. So after she'd let Clara off at Vera's Quilts and picked up several items at the General Store, she'd headed over to David and Mattie's.

Mattie was out weeding her kitchen garden when Ella Mae pulled into the lane. Her daughter looked up and spotted her, then waved. *Ain't too miffed*, Ella Mae thought as she stepped out of the carriage and tied Firefly to the hitching post.

"Hullo, Mamm!" Mattie called, rubbing her hands together to remove the loose soil. "Didn't expect ya."

Ella Mae wandered across the walkway to where Mattie was down on her knees, close to rows of lettuce and radishes that ran along the edge of the large plot. "Need a hand to finish?"

"I'm done for today." As Mattie rose, she suggested Ella Mae have a seat on the back porch while she washed up at the well pump.

"I've been sittin' in the carriage awhile already, so I'll chust stand a bit." She mentioned taking Clara to work before stopping by here. "Then I thought I'd give my two cents on the *Dawdi Haus* sketches . . . if it ain't too late."

"David and Jake put their heads together after you an' I talked. I told 'em ya want a sewin' room and a second bedroom, so they made some changes," Mattie said as she headed for the well pump.

"Also, it'd be nice if my bedroom's on the first floor, along with the sewin' room," Ella Mae added, shielding her eyes from the sun. "Any company can sleep upstairs."

"That's what I figured, but what with all the field work and summer harvest, they won't be breakin' ground for a while yet."

"That'll suit me." Ella Mae was actually relieved. The longer she could stay in her farmhouse, the better.

"Ya might not be movin' into your new place till early December, then." Mattie primed the pump and held her left hand under the spout.

Ella Mae nodded, pleased she'd have that much time.

If only Clara wasn't leaving come September.

Once Mattie had washed her hands and dried them on her black apron, she invited Ella Mae into the house.

In the kitchen, Mattie went right to the table, removed the large bowl of bananas sitting there, and set it on the counter. Then she left, returned with a large sheet of roughed-out sketches, and placed it on the table. "Here's how your future home's shapin' up."

Ella Mae put on her glasses and leaned over to peer at the draft of the main entrance, where a small, square box of a porch would be. Inside, the small kitchen was to the right of the entrance and the hallway connecting the two homes. In comparison to her spacious farmhouse, the front room of the new build looked like a doll house, but of course hosting church wouldn't be a consideration there.

"Can ya think of anything ya'd like changed?" Mattie asked. "Anything at all?"

Ella Mae bit her tongue, nixing what first came to mind. *I'd like Joseph back from the dead.*

"While ya look, would ya like somethin' to drink?" Mattie asked, stepping away from the table.

"Cold lemonade's fine, if ya have it," Ella

Mae said as she again looked over every inch of the draft, trying hard to imagine living in such a wee house. *Less cleaning to do,* she thought. *But no memories there to cling to.*

She *was* pleased to see the placement of the kitchen windows, though. Spending time in a bright kitchen—cooking, baking, or having tea with a guest—had always brought her joy, and she hoped to continue doing so long into her twilight years.

Lord willing.

Mattie set a tumbler of lemonade on the table, the ice in it jiggling. Ella Mae sat down and took a long drink. "Right tasty," she said. "Plenty of sugar, *jah*?"

"It's *gut un siess*, the way ya like it," Mattie replied, returning with her own tumbler full and sitting on the opposite side of the table. "So how's everything look?"

"Aside from bein' much smaller than the farmhouse, I like it."

"All of us kids thought it was time for ya to have less house to keep up, Mamm. Some days I look forward to that myself."

Ella Mae took another drink. "For me, housework and cookin' are *gut* reasons to get up in the mornin'."

"But ya deserve an easier life now," Mattie replied, her right hand gripping the tumbler. "Time to slow down some."

The way she sounds, I'm being put out to pasture. "Seems to me I oughta keep workin' till God calls me home. Ain't that what Preacher Yoder said recently in his sermon?"

"*Ach,* ya know what I mean. You've worked hard your whole life. Time to do less of it is all."

Ella Mae still didn't much care for the implication.

Clara enjoyed working at the quilt shop the next three days. She liked assisting customers to find the ideal quilt for a guest room or their own bedroom, or some other quilted item. Vera even had a few faceless cloth dolls to sell. Clara had quickly observed that most of the customers were tourists looking for "a souvenir of Amish Country," as they would often say. This amused her. *They must think of us as quite unusual.*

Before closing time on Friday, Leona Ebersol dropped in to purchase a quilted table runner for a birthday gift. She said she would be mailing it to her cousin in Shipshewana, Indiana. Clara listened as Leona shared about the one time she'd traveled to visit out there by train, some years ago.

Suddenly, Leona frowned. "*Ach,* don't wanna make ya homesick."

"No need to worry. I'm real happy to be here."

After walking home from Vera's—as was her plan for most workdays—Clara found a letter from her father waiting on the kitchen counter. Quickly, she opened it and read that he and Eva were doing well. He'd written rather thoughtfully that he hoped she was having a pleasant summer there, and then he said he missed her, as did Eva . . . and all the family. *Looking forward to your return*, he'd written.

She refolded the letter, then went to her room to change clothes and take off her shoes. *I'm glad Dat's so nicely settled with Eva*, she thought, thankful for his letter.

Clara happily agreed to go to Saturday market with Aendi, who told her beforehand that she liked to walk around and visit with the various folks tending their wares. For Clara, it was more about seeing the lovely handiwork on display, like tatted doilies and embroidered tea towels and pillowcases. And of course the tempting goodies—homemade pastries and candies. But she stayed with Aendi as they moved from one market stand to another.

When they reached the snow cone stand at the far end of the building, Clara offered to treat her aunt, who resisted at first. But Clara won out and ordered a cherry-flavored cone for Aendi and a root beer cone for herself.

They continued their walk as they sipped the cold syrup in crushed ice, and Clara couldn't remember having such a lovely time with an older relative. *Aendi's just the way Mamma always said she was.*

As they strolled past the creamery, Clara heard her name. And turning, she saw Tom Glick waving at her.

Aendi quickly said, "I'll be fine on my own if ya'd like to talk to him."

So Clara wandered over to say hello to Tom, who smiled big like always. He even offered to buy her a soft pretzel to go along with her snow cone, and she thanked him politely.

"It's not really lunch, but we can do that another time," he said.

They walked around together, stopping at two of his relatives' market stands, and Clara felt like they were being viewed as a couple.

She wasn't too sure how she felt about that.

CHAPTER

Nineteen

After returning home from Preaching and the fellowship meal on Sunday, Clara felt queasy and went to her room to rest. She tried to write a letter to Dat but felt too sick. By the time she would have started getting ready for Singing, she was still too ill to leave the house. Disappointed because she'd offered to sit with Rosanna Ebersol, Clara remained in bed.

Aendi peeked in, indicating her concern, and offered to bring her some warm peppermint tea. But even that didn't sound like a good idea, and Clara stayed put, hoping Rosanna would understand.

Ella Mae twiddled her thumbs at the kitchen table, a light supper of tuna sandwich and half an apple in front of her. She hated to think of Clara suffering alone in her room and wished she could help her. Apple cider vinegar mixed with water was known to aid with stomach upsets, and so was tea from burdock root, but if the poor girl couldn't keep anything down, it was best to just wait.

Her thoughts flitted back to the only time her father had ever had tea with her. She was just a wee girl, no more than four, and she'd been in bed with an upset stomach. Quietly, her father had come up to her room, carrying one of Mamm's trays with a teapot and cups and saucers for the two of them, as well as honey in a small glass jar with the tiniest spoon.

He set the tray on her and Essie's shared dresser before pouring tea into each of the two cups, then pulled a chair over to her bedside and sat there sipping tea with her in his work clothes. Before he left to return to the barn, he sang "Jesus Loves Me" in *Deitsch*, his bass voice so soft and low. The sweet memory had lingered all these years.

Such a tenderhearted father, she thought, lifting a slice of the apple and taking a bite.

After she'd finished eating and had washed and dried the few dishes, she walked down the hallway and into her room, then sat on the bed, staring at Joseph's clothes. She felt at a loss to do anything with them. But what was keeping her from discarding them?

Stepping to her dresser, she lifted her father's old *Biewel* and opened to a page in Isaiah, where one of his written prayers was pressed between the pages.

> *Most gracious and loving heavenly Father, discerner of our hearts, if fear stands between our Ella Mae and obeying Thy commands, open her heart to trust wholly in Thee. May she yearn to walk the narrow way that leads to life everlasting and seek it with all of her heart, soul, and mind. I pray this in the name of Jesus Christ our Lord.*

Ella Mae's eyes fell on the word *fear* in Dat's handwriting, and it was as though his prayer reached her across the years.

Am I fearful of letting go?

The possibility startled her. She'd experienced this before, long ago when she was in a courting relationship with a young fellow who wasn't sure he wanted to be baptized and join church. It had been such an exciting yet conflicted time for her, keeping that secret from her family. Until . . .

She gritted her teeth and pushed away the memory, then scanned each of the verses on the page where her father's prayer had been. Especially Isaiah forty-one, verse thirteen— *For I the L<small>ORD</small> thy God will hold thy right hand, saying unto thee, Fear not; I will help thee.*

Ella Mae believed that the Lord was with her, for certain, and she cherished that. Even so, she wondered, did she trust Him to help her move past her husband's death? To help her *want* to?

Sighing deeply, she looked again at Joseph's church clothes hanging on the wooden pegs—a familiar if not comforting sight right then. *How would I feel if I cleared out his things?* The thought was a fright to her heart. *Ach, I am afraid. In all these years the Lord's given me life, why must it hurt to have loved so deeply?*

She fought back tears. *Can I give the memory of those years to God and move forward? And if so, what's next for me?*

Hours later, Ella Mae sat on the back porch, her Bible and reading glasses in her lap, ready for reading and prayer. She admired the green row of hanging ferns, a peaceful image making the porch a private haven of sorts. She could see her little garden shed out yonder and admired the colorful dahlias and other flowers. It was Joseph's idea to plant them after he and their sons constructed the small but picturesque place. She'd always enjoyed taking care of the plants, deadheading them when the blooms were finished so more would come.

"Plant flowers wherever ya can," her dear Mamm had often said when Ella Mae was young. *"It'll make people happier when they see them . . . and hopeful, too."*

The screen door opened and Clara appeared, looking much better.

"It's *gut* to see ya up an' around, dearie."

"Probably just somethin' I ate at noon that didn't set well." Clara sat next to her. "Unfortunately, the Singing's over by now."

"Well, there's some nice cold peppermint tea in the fridge, if you'd like."

"*Denki.* Do ya want some, too?"

"It's all for you, but sip only a little at a time."

Clara nodded, then headed into the house.

While she was gone, a siren began to wail in the distance. As she always did, Ella Mae cringed at the eerie sound also fixed in her memory. She immediately bowed her head and prayed for whoever was in need of help.

Clara returned with a tumbler of the tea and sat down again. "I heard a siren just now. Hope no one's hurt."

"*Jah*. Might be a fire truck, but I always pray for anyone who might be sick or injured." A tic trembled her lips. She opened her Bible to Psalm 119. "Would ya like to read the Scripture tonight?"

Clara began to read where Ella Mae pointed to verse forty-seven. "'I will delight myself in thy commandments, which I have loved. My hands also will I lift up unto thy commandments, which I have loved; and I will meditate in thy statutes. Remember the word unto thy servant, upon which thou hast caused me to hope. This is my comfort in my affliction: for thy word hath quickened me.'"

Clara glanced at her. "Verse fifty—'my comfort in my affliction'—helped me so much when Mamma was sufferin' toward the end."

Ella Mae nodded. "When we stumble into a rough patch, God's Word is the truest guide. The best help."

"I'm learnin' that, too." Clara smiled.

Ella Mae reached to clasp her hand. "Why don't we have our evening prayers right here tonight . . . with the song of birds all around?"

"All right."

Clara folded her hands and bowed her head, and Ella Mae thanked God aloud for His great blessings and for bringing Clara to her for this special summer together. She also asked for divine comfort in Clara's affliction of grief over the loss of her mother and for wisdom to guide her.

As they raised their heads, another siren rang out in the stillness, and Ella Mae trembled.

CHAPTER

Twenty

Clara rose before Aendi did the next day, hoping to get the washing hung on the line by daybreak. The Scripture passage her aunt had asked her to read had given Clara an abundance of calm for the rest of the evening and into the night.

Just what I needed.

When the *Lancaster New Era* newspaper arrived that afternoon, Clara noticed one of the headlines on the front page—about a serious accident involving two Amish buggies. "Near Hickory Hollow," she murmured, recalling the sirens they'd heard.

Reading the report, she learned that two Amishmen had been racing their carriages when one sideswiped the other, causing it to flip over. A young female passenger and the driver were both injured and taken to the Lancaster hospital. None of the people in the carriages were named, but the article did say the other buggy driver and his female passenger—as well as their buggy and horse—weren't hurt.

Clara shuddered, wondering if any of the Hickory Hollow youth had been involved. She took the paper outside to show Aendi, who was taking down a few last pieces of clothing.

Her face turned pale as she read the paper. "Land a-mighty," she said. "Can't for the life of me imagine any of *our* youth racin' like that. Although," she added, her voice softer, "buggy racin's been around for a long time."

Considering her wild ride with Tom Glick that once, Clara wondered if he might have gotten caught up in a contest with another fellow, maybe. But Tom wouldn't race like that with a girl in his carriage, would he?

Besides, he'd suggested they have lunch sometime soon. *And Lettie never said he'd date two girls at the same time, did she?*

The remainder of the afternoon was spent rather quietly, and neither Clara nor Aendi brought up the news article. They kept busy putting away their clothing, and Clara helped redd up the little garden greenhouse. Later, she made stuffed peppers for supper, as well as a side dish of baked asparagus smothered with cheese. She also picked lettuce, cucumbers, and tomatoes from the garden.

After Bible reading and prayers, she wrote a pleasant letter to Dat, not mentioning the accident. *It's best he doesn't hear anything like that from me.*

When Clara stepped into Vera's shop the next day, she knew something was wrong right away. The woman was wiping tears from her cheeks. "Vera?" Clara rushed to the checkout counter, where her employer sat on the other side. "Are ya all right?"

"I'm so upset. Rosanna Ebersol's in the Lancaster hospital." Vera wiped her nose with a hankie. "Did ya hear 'bout the buggy racin' accident?"

Clara nodded, bracing herself.

"She was in the one that flipped over."

Clara caught her breath. "How terrible! Aendi Ella Mae and I read 'bout it in the paper yesterday afternoon, but no names were given, so we had no idea who was involved."

"The poor girl's in awful shape—cracked ribs and a fractured right arm, a concussion, and bruises everywhere."

Clara clenched her jaw, just sick at this news. To think sweet Rosanna had been injured following her very first Singing. *She'd been so worried about going, too!*

"The People are helpin' with the livestock and the younger children an' all at the farm so her parents and Aaron can be with her."

Fighting back tears, Clara wondered who on earth would so recklessly race a buggy with Rosanna or anyone else as a passenger. Surely not any of the fellows Clara had met at the youth activities, but why would Rosanna be riding with anyone else?

"Do ya know who was drivin' the buggy, Vera?"

"*Nee*, I don't. I don't know who either driver was."

Aendi will want to go to the hospital to see Rosanna and her parents, thought Clara, surprised they hadn't heard this news from their neighbors.

The afternoon was demanding, with eager tourists coming off a large tour bus. A number of the women wanted to purchase a finished quilt or order one in a different color. Yet all the while, Clara's thoughts were with Rosanna.

That evening, Clara and Aendi headed to Helen Ranck's home, several miles away. She was a Mennonite friend of Aendi's, and they paid her for a car ride to Lancaster General Hospital. Once they arrived, Helen kindly offered to wait for them in the parking area, urging them to take their time.

When the elevator doors opened on the fourth floor, Clara wasn't surprised to see a number of Hickory Hollow Amish gathering in the waiting area, especially Rosanna's family and other relatives. This sort of thing happened frequently in Indiana, too, though primarily womenfolk waited at the hospital with the family of the ill person. The younger men were more inclined to stay behind and look after the farm for the injured person or do whatever else was needed.

Once they were welcomed, Clara stood in the hall away from the crowd, allowing her aunt space to sit with the others. She saw a nurse slip into what they'd been told was Rosanna's room, then reappear in a few minutes. As the door opened, she caught a glimpse of Rosanna's parents sitting near the hospital bed. Silently, Clara prayed for her young friend.

Not long after, Clara noticed Aaron Ebersol coming up the hallway, carrying food on a large tray. When he spotted her, he came to greet her.

"Rosanna will be glad to know you're here," he said, eyes serious. Then, glancing down at the tray, he said he'd be right back. "I need to get this to my parents while the food's still hot."

"Of course," Clara replied, wishing there was something she could do to help.

When Aaron returned, he suggested they move down the hall, where a window overlooked the city. "My sister's first Singing didn't end well, as ya must know."

"How could she have been in a buggy race?"

He looked surprised. "You don't know?"

"Aendi Ella Mae and I read about the accident in the paper, but there weren't many details. Then today, Vera Lapp told me Rosanna was hurt, but she didn't know much else."

Aaron looked at the floor, shaking his head. "She was out riding with Tom Glick. I don't know what possessed him and his cousin Gideon to race their buggies with girls along. They know better."

She trembled. "Tom?"

Aaron nodded and ran his hand through one side of his hair. "*Jah*, Tom was racin' in the buggy that flipped over, and he and Rosanna were both thrown out. But Tom isn't hurt nearly as bad as Rosanna—just bruises and a busted ankle. Even so, his buggy is damaged beyond repair. Thankfully, the horse is okay."

Clara stood there in silent disbelief. *Tom took Rosanna out riding?* She felt befuddled. Had he just decided to move on when she didn't show up at Singing that night?

"The bishop is so put out that he's forbidden Tom's father to replace the wrecked buggy," Aaron continued. "Wants to call *die Youngie*'s attention to their misbehavior."

Clara shuddered to think of what could have happened, her heart tender toward dear Rosanna. What had Tom said to get her to go out with him?

"I'm so sorry this happened," Clara said softly, not wanting to keep Aaron from his family yet dying to know more. "I wish I could've been there for Rosanna."

"The attending doctor said she was in bad shape when the ambulance brought her here. She could scarcely breathe from the pain in her cracked ribs and broken arm. She also struck her head when she flew out of the buggy, so they had it iced for a time." He shook his head again. "She's never taken anything stronger than aspirin, and now she's on strong medication, which makes her groggy. But she needed somethin' for the terrible pain."

Clara sighed, feeling sad . . . and betrayed. She still couldn't believe what had happened. *Poor Rosanna!*

"If I'd known Tom was a buggy racer,"

Aaron added, "I would've taken Rosanna home with me after Singing."

Clara didn't reveal how fast Tom had pushed his horse the last time she'd ridden with him. She felt terrible for Rosanna and struggled to know what else to say. At last, she told Aaron, "Rosanna's fortunate to have such a caring big Bruder."

Aaron shrugged, his eyes meeting hers. "Any fella oughta use his noggin and think of the girl first." Then, glancing behind him, he said, "I s'pose I should get back to my family."

They turned to walk toward Rosanna's room.

"Will ya tell her I'm prayin' for her?"

"I will . . . and that ya were here."

Aaron gave her a quick smile before heading into his sister's room.

During the ride back to Hickory Hollow with Helen Ranck and Aendi, Clara considered the startling things Aaron had shared. Even though it wasn't her fault this accident had happened, she felt somehow responsible. *If I hadn't been ill, I would've gone to Singing, and maybe Rosanna wouldn't have suffered this terrible accident.*

CHAPTER

Twenty-One

Since she had a hard time seeing well after nightfall, Aendi had asked Clara if she'd take the reins on their way home from Helen's. Clara directed the mare to a slow but steady trot as she shared that she'd momentarily seen Rosanna's parents' solemn faces through the doorway when a nurse left the room. And she told her aunt how very concerned Aaron had been for his sister when they'd talked.

"Rosanna's kinfolk were horrified at what happened," Aendi said softly.

"Well, that accident never should've happened!" Clara blurted, keeping her eyes on the road ahead and wishing there was something she could have done to keep Tom from racing. "I feel just numb."

Aendi was quiet for a moment. "Ain't

s'posed to be any buggy racin' goin' on in the hollow." She said it so ardently that Clara glanced at her.

"The fellas back home in Indiana have been instructed not to race, too."

"It makes no sense to take such a risk, let alone with young women in open buggies—or any buggy. Such thoughtless drivers they were." Again, Aendi spoke emphatically. "Was anyone else hurt besides the driver?"

"*Nee*. Aaron said Tom Glick was the one drivin' with Rosanna and has a broken ankle. Tom's cousin Gideon was the other racer, but neither he nor his date was hurt."

"Tom Glick?" Aendi said, and Clara looked over once more to see her raising a brow.

Clara nodded, recalling Tom's charming manner and smooth words . . . and how she'd allowed herself to be fooled into thinking he might be genuinely interested in her. *Lettie warned me.*

When they arrived home, Clara walked with Aendi into the house, then went back out to unhitch Firefly and lead her to the stable. There, she offered the mare fresh water and feed, and like Dat always did with his horses, she gave her a good grooming.

I need some time to ponder things. And to pray for Rosanna.

As Clara contemplated what had happened, she worked all the more quickly, her heart heavy. When the task was completed, she placed the curry and mane combs, brushes, and hoof pick into the grooming box and walked back outside to push the carriage into its shed. She closed the door behind her, then, heartbroken for Rosanna, she plodded back to the house.

"Gracious Father," Ella Mae whispered in the privacy of her room, "help Rosanna fully recover. Let Thy spirit hover near her this night and each and every day till she's well. Surround Leona and Adam and all their family with Thy loving care."

She paused, still shaken by what Clara had told her about the identity of one of the irresponsible drivers, a young man with whom she now assumed Clara herself had gone riding. *Racing takes dreadful risks*, she thought. *Life-threatening ones.*

Continuing with her prayer, she asked God for wisdom when she talked to Clara more about the dangers. *When the time is right*, she thought, thankful her grandniece had not gone to Singing Sunday night. *She's in my care while she's here.*

Ella Mae sighed deeply. To think Lillian's

daughter might have been the one thrown from that buggy!

Fairly early the next day, Clara was surprised when, from the kitchen, Aendi announced that the deacon had arrived and was coming up the back walkway. Curious, Clara hurried to the kitchen doorway, where she could see and hear her aunt inviting him in. But he, in turn, asked Aendi to step onto the porch, and then as she moved away from the closed screen door, Clara could hear no more.

Is this about the buggy accident? Clara wondered as she moved to the counter to finish kneading her aunt's bread dough. Her shoulders and neck tensed as she hoped Rosanna hadn't made a turn for the worse.

After leaving the dough for its second rest, she dropped to her knees beside the wooden bench, folded her hands, and began to pray in earnest for her friend.

Ella Mae followed the deacon as he removed his straw hat and held it in both hands. He motioned for her to sit on one of the rockers, then said, "Bishop John is clampin' down on all the youth, both the fellas and the girls. Doesn't want to lose control. And since ya have a young person visitin', he wanted me to drop by here, too."

"Clara hasn't given me any reason to think she needs reining in," Ella Mae spoke up.

"Well, considering the racing accident, Bishop wants not even a speck of the fancy creepin' in further . . . not in the width of the young men's hat brims nor in the length of young women's hems. No more boom boxes or carpet in courting carriages or fancy consoles. None of that." Deacon went on to say there would now also be more parental supervision at every youth gathering, as well as no music from any instruments. "Absolutely none. Only human voices at Singings."

His stern, pinched face made Ella Mae feel like she was the one being scolded. Even so, she folded her hands in her lap and kept quiet, but it wasn't easy. Hadn't anyone pointed out to the brethren that most of these new rules made no sense? It was as if they were trying to make a connection between the outside world sneaking up on the youth and a buggy-race-turned-perilous, yet none of these changes would stop worldly influence.

Deacon continued. "Since you're overseein' your grandniece this summer, I expect you to share these rules with her. And we want *die Youngie* to report anyone who breaks 'em," he added.

At this, Ella Mae felt growing dismay. *Reporting could turn the youth against one another. Such a stress on our little community!*

Still standing at near attention, the deacon put his straw hat back on his head and waited a moment, as though he expected Ella Mae to speak up again.

Oh, did she ever want to, but over the years, she'd learned it was far better to bypass the brethren and take her concerns directly to the Lord.

"Well, I'll be on my way," Deacon said, still scowling.

Ella Mae didn't say thank you for coming. She *did* say, "May God be with our youth." She waited till the deacon had gone down the steps and was heading to his carriage before rising to return inside.

They'll confiscate all the courting buggies next, she thought sarcastically, mulling the bishop's drastic and immediate response to the buggy racing. Even so, she was still shaken by the awful accident last Sunday.

By Aendi's glum expression when she came into the house, Clara could tell she was quite upset.

"I kneaded the dough for ya," she said.

Her aunt leaned against the long counter,

her gaze on her. "You're a *gut* girl, Clara. Your Mamma and Dat brought ya up right."

Why was she saying this?

Aendi placed her hand on her chest and breathed deeply. "The deacon's letting folks know 'bout some new guidelines for the youth," she said quietly. "Wanted me to pass them along to ya."

Clara listened, surprised at the new requirements. The restrictions on courting buggies stood out to her as she recalled Tom's carpeted carriage, as well as the extra buttons and whatnot on his dashboard. So was she supposed to report that to the ministers?

But Aaron had said Tom's buggy was irreparable, so what did it matter now?

When Aendi was finished, offering no judgment on this news, she divided her dough in half before placing each portion into one of two already-greased loaf pans to let the dough rise again.

Meanwhile, Clara headed outdoors with a wicker basket to harvest cucumbers. It was obvious the deacon's visit was troubling to her aunt. Clara had never seen her frown so deeply in the two and a half weeks she'd been there.

Making her way to the row of hardy cucumber vines, Clara could hear Mattie's husband, David, and his son Yonnie calling back and forth in the stable across the way. *They must've arrived before the deacon.*

As she wondered how the youth would respond to the new rules, her thoughts turned to Tom, who was surely carrying an incredible weight on his shoulders, knowing his irresponsible actions had caused such suffering for Rosanna. And now prompted the bishop's harsh response to the accident.

Carefully, Clara placed each cucumber in the basket, her bare feet pressing into the fertile soil. When she finished picking, she made her way back to the house, remembering what Aaron said about the bishop forbidding Tom's father to replace the wrecked courting carriage.

He'll have no way to buggy race again . . . or to court.

CHAPTER

Twenty-Two

Midmorning, Mattie stopped by with a batch of snap beans, and Aendi gladly shared some cucumbers with her. Clara wasn't too surprised when Mattie made a point of mentioning the canning frolic at her house tomorrow, asking right out if they were coming.

Her aunt was quick to say she didn't think so, but Clara wanted to be there for at least a few hours before working at the quilt shop in the afternoon. She recalled Vera indicating she'd be at the frolic, and likely several young women would be there, too. Just not Rosanna, but maybe Lettie or Mary or Katie. Still, she kept mum and let Aendi decide, and Mattie left the house looking a bit glum as her mother followed her out the back door.

Is there still tension between them over the move?

The two of them stood outside for a while, and Clara started to pinch off the ends of the snap beans, getting them ready to cook.

"You can certainly go to the canning bee on your own," Aendi said when Mattie had left and she'd come back indoors.

"Oh . . . it's okay."

"Really, you could go on your own."

Aendi seemed convincing enough, Clara thought. "Well, then. I'll go for a while."

"Mattie just told me Rosanna's home from the hospital. Still resting a lot." Aendi shook her head. "Poor thing."

"She is?" Clara was relieved to hear it.

"*Jah*, my daughter seems to know everything 'bout everyone." Aendi grimaced. "*Ach*, I shouldn't talk so."

"I'd like to visit Rosanna." Clara paused, then blurted, "I wonder if Mattie knows 'bout the new, stricter rules for the youth."

"She didn't mention it, but all her children are grown."

The grapevine will surely spread that news around, Clara assumed.

Later that morning, Aendi suggested Clara take the carriage and visit Rosanna right away. Clara thanked her aunt for suggesting it. She could have easily walked, but this way, she could spend more time with Rosanna before returning home in time for the noon meal, if she was up to more than just a quick hello.

When Clara arrived at the Ebersols' farm, Aaron again spotted her, this time as he was coming out of the harness shop. He tied her horse to the hitching post as he said, "Rosanna'll be happy to see ya. She was sad when I told her ya came with Ella Mae to the hospital last night."

"I'm just glad she's on the mend."

Aaron nodded, then walked with her toward the house. "Just so ya know, she's not s'posed to laugh and has to try not to sneeze, too." He sighed. "Kinda hard to control a sneeze, though."

"That's for sure."

He accompanied her into the big kitchen, where Leona was rolling out pie dough. "Clara's here to see Rosanna," he told her.

"Ain't that nice!" Leona straightened and welcomed her. "We've got her situated in the spare room down the hall till her ribs heal. Every little step takes her breath away." She wiped her hands on her white work apron. "*Kumme*, I'll take ya to her."

Aaron excused himself, and Clara followed Leona through a large sitting room and into a hallway.

"Someone's here to see ya, Rosanna," Leona said, poking her head through the spare room doorway. "It's your friend Clara Bender." She motioned Clara in.

The room was on the same side of the house Clara's was at Aendi's, and interestingly enough, the bed with Rosanna in it was in the same spot. She stepped lightly toward her friend. "Hi."

Rosanna smiled weakly from her pillowed perch, propped up with cold packs across her ribs on both sides and her right arm in a splint. The right side of her face and neck were terribly bruised.

"Hullo, Clara. I was thinking 'bout ya." Rosanna's voice was breathy. "And feelin' sorry you and Ella Mae couldn't visit me in the hospital after ya came all that way. I just wasn't ready for visitors."

"That's okay, really," Clara told her. "Everyone's concerned 'bout ya, I'm sure ya know."

Rosanna smiled sweetly. "Prayin', too, I hope."

"For certain."

"Can ya stay awhile?" she asked, offering Clara the cane-back chair near her writing desk.

"Just so I don't tire ya out." Clara pulled the chair close to the bed and sat down.

"Mamma will prob'ly let ya know. She's been protective since the accident. So has Aaron."

"I can understand. I just wish . . ." Clara didn't know how to continue, and she struggled with a lump in her throat. *She could've been killed.*

"Don't know why I went with him," Rosanna mused. "He was just so friendly, asking if I wanted a quick ride home. What a *Dummkopp* I was. Didn't know what he meant by *quick.*"

There was a catch in Rosanna's voice. It was obvious that reliving that night upset her.

"Don't be hard on yourself," Clara replied, pushing down the ire she felt toward Tom.

"He *did* come to visit me in the hospital, but the nurses wouldn't let anyone in but immediate family." Rosanna paused, glancing out the window. "I don't know what got into him, but he sure tricked me into ridin' home after Singing."

"What did he do?" Clara asked. She'd wondered this from the start.

"Just insisted I shouldn't walk home after no fellas had offered me a ride." Rosanna blinked back tears. "Now I get the feelin' he was just eager to show off his fast horse."

Clara understood.

"Aaron thinks he wanted to apologize when he came to the hospital," Rosanna said softly.

"I should hope he did."

Rosanna continued to talk, like she needed to get it off her mind, saying the fellow wouldn't be taking anyone out riding for a long, long time. "Not till he's permitted to get another buggy."

"Hopefully, whenever that happens, he'll have learned his lesson and will drive safely."

Rosanna nodded. "But who'd ever trust goin' with him?"

Clara agreed. "Tom's cooked his goose."

Rosanna's eyes widened. "So . . . ya know him?"

"*Jah.*" And that's all Clara wanted to say about it.

At that moment, Leona appeared in the doorway, just as Rosanna had said she might, and Clara knew it was time to end her visit.

"Will ya come again?" Rosanna asked, looking almost sad.

"Sure. But I'll say good-bye for now." Then Clara followed her friend's mother out of the room and into the kitchen.

"Our girl's shy, so your visit means a lot

to her," Leona said once they were out of Rosanna's earshot.

Now Clara felt shy. "*Denki* for letting me see her. And I'm glad if it helped."

"*Kumme* again," Leona said, then walked with her to the back door.

Clara stepped outside, pondering many things.

Very little was said at the supper table that evening, and Clara could practically feel the tension in the air. Aendi seemed distant or possibly distracted, so unlike her. *Is she still preoccupied with the deacon's visit? Is that why she doesn't want to go to the canning bee tomorrow?*

After the kitchen was redded up, Clara excused herself to read a letter newly arrived from Bertie that afternoon. She felt ever so alone in her room, and just when things had been going so well here.

CHAPTER

Twenty-Three

As she drove Aendi's enclosed carriage to Mattie's the next morning, Clara noticed how beautifully kept each farmhouse she passed was, just like her aunt's own.

When she arrived at the Beilers' place, the shining white clapboard house with its ivy on one side caught her eye. Clara pulled into the long driveway and took in the lovely petunia-lined walkways, profuse with white, pink, yellow, and burgundy blooms. Along the side yard, several gray buggies were already parked, and Yonnie was coming down the driveway toward her, waving.

"I'm happy to unhitch your horse for ya," he told her. "And I'll hitch up for ya, too, since you're leavin' early afternoon for work."

"*Denki*," she said, surprised he knew her schedule.

In the backyard, Katie Lapp and Mary Stoltzfus were sitting in the creeping shade of a tall maple, husking sweet corn and wearing matching plum-colored dresses and capes and long black aprons. They glanced up to see Clara, who quickened her pace toward them.

Mary greeted her with a sweet-sounding "Hullo!"

Waving her over, Katie smiled. "*Kumme* and join us."

"Okay, but first I want to say hullo to Mattie." Clara veered toward the house and stepped into the kitchen. Two older women stood near the sink with Mattie, who turned and grinned when she saw her.

"Hullo there, Clara. Is my Mamm with ya?"

"*Nee*, she's not."

"Oh. I was hopin' . . . Well, make yourself at home, ya hear? We're just waitin' for the water to boil." She pointed to the large pots on the cookstove.

"*Denki* for including me."

"Oh, anytime. You're always *Willkumm*." Mattie turned toward the women and said, "These are two of my friends, sisters Nell Miller and Molly Blank. They both live over yonder on Cattail Road, east side after the fork."

"Real nice to meet ya," Clara said, noticing their resemblance to each other.

"We've heard *gut* things 'bout ya," Molly, a brunette, said.

"Will ya tell Ella Mae we missed her?" Nell asked, then glanced at the pots of water.

"I will." Feeling a bit awkward, Clara excused herself and returned to the backyard to join Mary and Katie, where she reached into the galvanized tub for a bunch of corn and began husking.

A few more women and girls arrived, and soon they had an assembly line from the yard to the kitchen.

"Did ya know Rosanna's home from the hospital?" Mary asked Clara.

Clara mentioned having visited Rosanna yesterday. "She was hurt somethin' awful."

"I wanna go over an' see her soon," Katie said, pulling silk off the cob.

"Me too," Mary added. Then in a softer voice, she said, "Some are sayin' Rosanna's fortunate to be alive . . . and Tom, too."

"I can't imagine what she went through," Katie said, shaking her head and frowning. "Wonder if Tom'll show his face at the next Singing. He must know everyone's talking 'bout him."

Mary shook her head. "Hard to imagine. And now because of his and Gideon's foolishness, all the youth must pay. I'm sure ya heard 'bout this, Clara," she said, lowering her voice all the more.

"Aendi Ella Mae told me what the deacon said when he dropped by. Some of the new rules make it seem like *die Youngie* can't be trusted."

Mary glanced at Katie. "It's a shame for all of us, really."

"The worst of it? No accompanied music's allowed. None at all." Katie suddenly looked aghast, like she'd said something she shouldn't have.

"Well," Mary went on, "Bishop John is worried that worldly ways are startin' to influence us."

Katie sighed loudly. "Are *die Youngie* in your church back home allowed to sing in harmony at Singings . . . or play instruments, Clara?"

"Sure. Just no radios or boom boxes."

"But guitars are okay?" Katie asked quietly.

"Occasionally, at a barn Singing. But not when we gather in homes." Clara wondered why she'd asked. "Harmonicas are fine, too."

Katie and Mary husked silently after that, and the three of them made quick work of the first large tub of corn. David and Yonnie carried another big tubful over, set it down near them, and removed the empty one.

At ten o'clock, Mattie stepped outside and announced it was time for refreshments. She welcomed several arriving stragglers and asked for everyone to gather in the kitchen, where they all bowed their heads for a silent blessing.

Then Mattie said, "Amen," ending the prayer.

Out loud, like Aendi does, Clara thought.

In an adjoining room sat a large folding table with a variety of delicious treats for everyone—glazed and cream-filled donuts, lemon bars, sugar cookies, raw vegetables with a creamy dip, and meadow tea and coffee.

The womenfolk all made their way back through the kitchen to take their goodies to the back porch. The last to go, Clara could hear Mattie talking with Nell and Molly near the food table, saying she still couldn't get her mother going on clearing out the farmhouse, especially the attic, while Clara was there to help.

"That so?" Molly replied.

"Well, Mamm says it's hard with Dat gone. So many memories. And I understand that, but it has to be done. Before we know it, the *Dawdi Haus* will be ready for her."

Mattie must not realize how truly brokenhearted her mother still is.

After supper that evening, Clara made a card to mail to Rosanna the next day. That finished, she stuck her neck out and once again offered to help Aendi start sorting through the contents of her attic. "Whenever you're ready, of course."

Her aunt grimaced from her kitchen rocker, where she was mending an apron. "No tellin' what all you'd find up there. Besides, we have a quilt to repair."

"Maybe we can do both . . . depending on how much is in the attic." *And I'd love to find Mamma's letters . . . if they're up there.*

With a quizzical look, Aendi asked, "Did Mattie talk to ya?"

"Not 'bout that." Clara wasn't going to add fuel to the fire.

"Well, I s'pose ya could look round an' let me know what you find."

"All right, then. I'll go now."

Aendi added, "Take a trash bag with ya and discard everything that looks useless. If I haven't needed it in more than twenty years, best to just throw it out." She chuckled, and Clara smiled at her remark.

"Oh, and take the flashlight, too, so ya

can see on the way up there," Aendi told her. "It's stored in the closet off the sitting room."

Hoping she hadn't pushed her aunt into this, but excited at the prospect of looking for Mamma's letters, Clara grabbed the flashlight and then headed upstairs. She made her way down the hallway toward the front of the house, past the vacant bedrooms and a large sewing room. At the end of the hallway on the left, she saw the door leading to the attic staircase and opened it.

Glad for the flashlight, she reached the top of the stairs, then spotted the hatch overhead and pushed it up. Stepping into the attic, she noticed the two dormer windows she'd seen from the outside on the day she arrived. She walked over and noticed a cloud of cobwebs across the top of the rain-streaked windowpanes.

Looking around, she also saw a tall stack of *Lancaster Farming* newspapers on an old wooden chair, as well as a large number of boxes marked with either the words *Farmers' Almanac* or *The Budget*. She also spotted a charcoal-gray, barrel-top trunk with four brown cross slats on it.

"Not too awful much here," she murmured, unsure what to discard, really. The periodicals might be useful to someone, for instance.

She lifted the lid on the interesting trunk, its lock missing, then pointed the flashlight inside. A blue dress and white organdy cape and apron lay wrapped in clear plastic. Lifting that bundle, she found a yellowing tablecloth and some old books with faded covers beneath it.

Reaching inside the trunk again, she felt something hard. Removing it, she discovered a wooden box about the size of a hardcover book, and since it had been kept in the trunk, it wasn't dusty at all. There was no latch on the lid, and she gently lifted the box from its place.

Inside, she found the prettiest tinwork art, then held it up to the light from the windows, the image of a heart encircling a rose quite clear. On the stem, amidst leaves and a few thorns, the name Isaac Smucker was etched as part of the artistic rendering. *So beautiful*, she thought as she moved closer to the windows, curious to see if a name or date might be on the back. But she didn't see any.

Some paper artwork sat in the bottom of the box, but she decided she'd better take her discovery to her aunt before looking further. Once downstairs, however, she realized she'd neglected to thoroughly sort through the contents of the trunk.

Now in the front room working on the heirloom quilt, Aendi asked her if she'd found the letters. "*Nee.* Not yet anyway. I'll have to look again." Then she told her about the blue dress encased in plastic.

"'Twas my weddin' dress," her aunt said humbly. "I'll wear it for my viewing and burial, when the Lord calls me Home."

"Thought maybe."

"I was willowy back then. 'Bout your size, honey-girl. But the years and the pies have added a few extra pounds. They'll have to cut a seam down the back of the dress, which won't be seen, of course. That's how we do things here in the hollow."

Clara nodded. "Same as back home," she said, holding up the tinwork art.

"What's that ya got?"

"It's awful perty." Clara handed it to her along with the wooden box.

Aendi stared at the tin, eyes wide. "I displayed this on my dresser for years."

"Was it a gift?"

"My first beau made it for me." She paused as if the years were passing in reverse. "Isaac was a right *gut* artist." Setting the tinwork aside, she opened the wooden box and pulled out quite a few small squares of paper with pencil drawings on them. "He could draw anything, and he loved to do tinwork. Gave it all to friends or family, never wanted to sell it," she said softly.

Holding up an image of a young woman, she added, "I had to sit very still for this one."

"He drew your face?" Clara couldn't believe how good it was, and despite the passage of years, she could see the striking resemblance to the woman sitting before her.

Clara sat down opposite her and picked up her needle.

"*Jah*. I was sixteen. Isaac gave me the tin art two months before I was baptized that September."

"You must've been so pleased," Clara said, glancing at her and hoping to hear more.

One at a time, her aunt placed the small drawings on the quilt, where Clara could see them. A Labrador's sweet face. A clump of black-eyed Susans near a fence post. A close-up of a girl's bare foot. An apple with teeth marks in it. The front porch of a house with a cat lying near the door.

"These are *wunnerbaar*," Clara said, stunned at such talent.

"Isaac did his art in his spare time, like some boys might whittle or go fishin'. He also took apart clocks—all sorts of timepieces, really, and put 'em back together. No one had to teach him how. He just knew." Aendi picked up the tinwork art again and traced the outline of the rose with her pointer finger.

"He was a kind fella, and so attentive to me, but there was another side to him."

Clara braced herself, wondering what was next.

Placing the tinwork on a nearby table, her aunt took a deep breath. "It's strange that ya found this, 'cause I've been thinkin', even prayin', 'bout telling ya what things I experienced during my courtin' years. And I wonder if now might be the time, 'specially on the heels of this terrible racin' accident here in the hollow."

Clara looked again at the delicate rose surrounded by a heart on the piece of tin, hungry to know more about her aunt's youth.

"The summer I turned sixteen, the days were sultry and the nights ever so warm, just like now," Aendi began.

CHAPTER

Twenty-Four

SUMMER 1933

Hickory Hollow was replete with lush green meadows and flourishing cornfields, and the dirt roads, far off the beaten path, were dotted with vegetable and fruit stands up and down the hollow.

Ella Mae moved back and forth between the house and her family's roadside stand every day but Sunday. The locals and folks from other areas of Lancaster County were enthusiastic about purchasing freshly picked lettuce, lima beans, onions, cucumbers, snap beans, tomatoes, and sweet corn. Occasionally someone requested eggplant or rutabaga, but her Mamm didn't much care for them, so they'd never grown those. Wanting to help, Ella Mae would simply point down the road, directing those customers to their neighbors' vegetable stand.

"Just three farms over, the Smuckers sell 'em," she'd say, grinning at saying the Smucker name. One day she might end up married to their son Isaac, who'd turned eighteen a few months back. Here lately, he'd been waving at her whenever he passed by.

She wasn't one to flirt, but she did her best to let Isaac know she liked him by smiling when he sought her out after her first two Sunday Singings back in April. And it didn't take long before he asked her to go walking with him, an invitation she happily accepted.

Isaac had an artist's temperament. She'd learned this from his older sister, Amanda, who'd said, *"My Bruder keeps his nose in his tinwork . . . once chores are done."*

After Ella Mae had four walking dates with him, Isaac began to share about his lifelong dream of owning a clock repair shop. It was surprising, because all the clock shops round Lancaster County were owned by Mennonite folk. That made her wonder if he might be leaning toward not joining church.

As they got to know each other, she also found it odd that he walked everywhere and asked to borrow his Dat's buggy for their dates. But as mid-June led into ever-warmer July, one night Isaac asked her if she'd like to see his recent purchase.

"Sure," she'd said, curious about why his eyes lit up so.

"Can ya keep a secret?" he asked as they walked by the light of the moon after Singing.

She almost said, *"It depends on the secret,"* but as much as she liked Isaac, she decided to just agree. "*Jah*, I'll keep mum."

He grinned and said they'd have to walk out of their way to get to his Mennonite cousins' place over on Hershey Church Road.

"What for?" she asked, feeling a little uncomfortable now.

"You'll see." He reached for her hand as they picked up their pace.

His secret turned out to be a green 1927 Model-T Coupe with inflated tires and two big headlights, which Isaac delighted in pointing out to her. It was the first time she'd ever gotten into a car with an Amish driver at the wheel, but Isaac seemed to know what he was doing. He even showed off his driver's license in his wallet before turning the switch on the dashboard, then pressing the pedal in front of the seat.

They headed up toward Old Philadelphia Pike, and very quickly, she realized how much she was enjoying the ride—and sitting close to Isaac, like she would've if he owned a courting carriage. It crossed her mind to ask why he'd bought himself a car, but she actually liked going this speed, quicker than the snail's pace of a buggy. And with the windows down, oh, the breeze on her face!

That wasn't the last time Ella Mae agreed to go driving with Isaac. They started seeing each other nearly every weekend, either on a Saturday night or after Sunday Singings. Sometimes he'd come to the house after his work and help her at the roadside stand, or if it was a Sunday afternoon, just to visit. Other times he'd bring his knapsack with paper and pencils inside, then take her out to the high meadow, where the grass was tall and warm. They'd sit under a tree while he drew whatever captured his attention—typically her.

All the while, Ella Mae was delighted to be in the presence of someone so different from all the other fellows. She, of course, always had homemade cookies or other tasty treats to share while they sat in the grass or walked together.

On one of those afternoons, while Isaac was intent on drawing a close-up of her face, she got the nerve to ask what made him want to own a car.

"Ya mean instead of a courtin' carriage?"

He smiled. "Hope you're not sayin' ya don't like getting to places faster."

"Oh, I didn't mean *that*." The tender way he looked at her made her heart nearly melt. "Maybe what I should've said is how long will ya keep your car?"

Isaac looked puzzled—and a bit frustrated, too. "I just bought it, so I'd like to get my money's worth."

Now she felt right silly, because that went without saying. But what she really wanted to ask was locked up in her throat.

"What're ya worried 'bout, Ella Mae?"

She paused, hoping she wasn't speaking out of turn. "Do ya plan to be baptized?"

"Not just yet. I do know *you're* takin' baptism classes, though."

"*Jah*, joinin' church come fall."

He set down his pencil and straightened, looking deep into her eyes. "I want to take my time with all that, honestly."

Her heart pounded. If Isaac didn't join church, they could never move into a serious courtship. Never be wed. All the same, she was glad he'd been frank with her.

"I want to be absolutely certain before I make my vow to God and the church." Isaac looked mighty solemn, so much so that Ella Mae was almost sorry she'd brought this up.

"I keep askin' myself if I want to be Amish for life," he added.

Ella Mae's breath caught in her throat. "You'd leave the People?" she asked softly.

"Well, I can't have a car *and* be Amish."

She nodded, feeling dazed at the unexpected turn their conversation had taken. "It *is* a real nice car," she replied. *But not worth walking away from God.*

"If ya'd rather not, ya don't have to ride with me anymore," he said matter-of-factly. "I'd hate to be a bad influence on ya."

She felt like all the blood was draining from her head. Was their relationship going to fall apart?

Isaac returned to drawing her face, and she sat as still as could be, hoping she hadn't ruined their afternoon. And long after they'd walked back to her house and said good-bye, she struggled to know what to do about all he'd shared with her.

If he cares enough for me, surely I can change his mind.

The next time Ella Mae saw Isaac, they walked to his cousins' house for cookies and ice cream after supper and didn't end up riding in his car. She was secretly relieved, considering what they'd talked about before.

Maybe, just maybe he was beginning to lean toward her way of thinking.

After eating their dessert, they sat on the comfortable sofa in his cousins' basement, and Isaac reached into his knapsack and pulled out something flat wrapped in a soft cloth. "I made this for you," he said, handing it to her.

Curious, she carefully opened the cloth and discovered a piece of tinwork art large enough to frame. Its beauty took her breath away, and she held it up to the gas lamp next to them on a small table, so pleased she simply stared at it.

"The rose represents beauty," Isaac said, slipping his arm around her.

She smiled at the heart surrounding the rose. "*Denki*, Isaac."

"And the heart . . . well, that's obvious, ain't?" He winked at her.

Drawn to him, she leaned her head on his shoulder.

"Will ya be my sweetheart-girl?" He touched her cheek lightly.

Isaac's saying he loves me, she thought, straightening to look into his handsome face.

So many thoughts turned over in her mind. What would happen to their relationship after she was baptized in two short months? Wouldn't she be in trouble with the bishop if she continued to see Isaac?

With all her heart, Ella Mae wanted to agree. And without thinking it through further, she nodded and said, "*Jah*," hoping Isaac didn't detect her concerns on such a lovely night.

Looking at the tin art, Isaac asked, "Would ya like to put this where you can see it first thing in the morning and the last thing at night? As a reminder," he added.

He must really care for me. She couldn't stop looking at it. "*Jah*. This is so beautiful."

"*You* are, Ella Mae." He kissed her cheek, and she fought back joyful tears.

CHAPTER

Twenty-Five

Clara couldn't help thinking Aendi must have gotten herself in over her head that long-ago summer. "Did Isaac keep the car for much longer?" she asked hesitantly.

"*Ach*, he was so proud of it, but the pride clouded his thinkin'," her aunt replied, stitching one edge of a replacement piece on the heirloom quilt. "After all, he was brought up in the Old Ways, so he knew better." She glanced over at the tinwork on the table. "But he was havin' too much fun to settle down."

"Well, there *is* more freedom durin' the teen years."

"Both then an' now." Aendi paused. "Actually, not as much at the present, since the bishop has placed more restrictions on the youth."

Clara hoped she might continue with her story, but for the longest time they worked on the quilt without Aendi talking further about Isaac Smucker and his uncertainty about joining church.

Will I ever learn about the unspeakable happening? she wondered.

After a good hour or so, Aendi ceased working. It was time for prayer and Bible reading, so Clara stopped, too. They moved to the settee, and Clara listened intently as her aunt read from Isaiah, chapter thirty.

When Aendi came to verse twenty-one, she read more slowly. "'And thine ears shall hear a word behind thee, saying, This is the way, walk ye in it, when ye turn to the right hand, and when ye turn to the left.'"

As they knelt together during prayer time, Clara continued to ponder the words *This is the way, walk ye in it.*

She prayed for Rosanna, then for her Dat and Eva and all the family back home. And she was mindful to ask for God's will to be made known in her life, and for God to help her be obedient to it, whatever that might mean for her future.

The next morning, Aendi and Clara were making a breakfast of pancakes and sausages when Clara politely asked her aunt if she'd share more of her story. Aendi picked up where she'd left off.

"It was several weeks before Isaac invited me to ride in his car again," she said while the sausages sizzled in the black skillet and Clara flipped the first pancake. "I hoped he might not be as interested in drivin' it, but it turned out I was wrong." She tested the sausages for doneness.

Clara's eyebrows lifted. "Did ya go with him again?"

"*Jah.* And 'twasn't the smartest thing I ever did."

The situation was becoming more muddled to Ella Mae. Sometimes being around Isaac made her downright fuzzy-headed, like she couldn't think clearly. Then when she was away from him, she'd feel disgusted with herself. She remained enamored with him despite the fact he was straddling the fence between the world and the People, yet she hoped her influence might somehow bring him around, back to the faith. She also tried to gently share the importance of staying Amish.

When his cards and notes started arriving in the mailbox every few days, always accompanied by drawings, she figured Isaac was still wooing her despite her attempts to influence him. So romantic! And each morning, upon first waking, she purposely directed her gaze toward the dresser to lay eyes on Isaac's lovely tin art with the heart around the pretty rose.

All the while, along with eight other baptismal candidates, she faithfully attended classes every other Sunday before Preaching service, enthusiastic during the instruction yet losing that fervency when she was with Isaac. Torn and struggling, she didn't quite know what was happening inside her—a tug-of-war, to be sure.

One Preaching Sunday afternoon, she took off walking through her father's large pastureland, ducking beneath willow trees and talking to the cows as she rimmed the field. "Should I wait for Isaac to join church, too?" she asked them. "Or should I go ahead with baptism in hopes he'll join me later?"

A big black crow circled the cows, and Ella Mae clapped her hands, shooing him away. "Perturbing bird," she murmured, remembering that when she was little, Dat had told her crows were smart.

But her twin sister, Essie, had said a crow landing on an animal's head—or a person's for that matter—was a bad sign. Ella Mae had brushed that aside, thinking it was silly. Sure, there was a generous amount of superstitious talk amongst the People, but she'd never been one to take any of it to heart. Even as a girl, she'd been wary of such talk, and she'd told her sister so. *"A crow ain't the devil, ya know,"* Ella Mae had retorted.

At the next Singing, Isaac was absent. His sister Amanda told Ella Mae he'd gone to another youth gathering over in Stumptown, but that's all she knew. Ella Mae felt sick in the pit of her stomach as she walked home with Essie, who was so full of questions about Isaac's absence it was downright annoying.

Then Isaac stopped sending her cards and letters and drawings. *What's happened between us?* she asked herself as the days passed, recalling their former conversations, looking for an answer.

As they hung laundry together the next day, Essie—of course sensing Isaac was hesitant about joining church—pointed out he might be stepping back because Ella Mae was getting close to her baptism. "He might be thinkin' that'll help ya not be confused about your decision to follow the Lord and join church. Don't ya think that could explain it?"

"I'd rather not talk 'bout Isaac," Ella Mae replied, deep in thought trying to figure out what to do about the constant pain in her heart. She missed Isaac. Truth be known, she thought about him morning, noon, and night.

Doesn't he know I care deeply for him?

She contemplated writing Isaac a letter, but what could she say that hadn't already been said to his face? Yet another part of her wanted to be his girl, just as she'd agreed to be.

When the next Sunday Singing came around, Ella Mae stayed home despite Essie's protest that Isaac might be there and then she'd be sorry. But Essie's pleas fell on deaf ears, and Ella Mae sat on the back porch steps watching her sister ride off with Dat at the reins.

She's hoping Henry Mast will ask her out riding tonight.

Handsome, blue-eyed Henry was jovial and charming, and Essie had recently dropped his name to her more than once.

Fighting back tears, Ella Mae didn't want Mamm to see her like this. So she walked to the springhouse and dipped one foot in the cool water.

I won't pursue Isaac, she decided, sitting on the ground to dangle both feet in the pooled water. *I'll wait for him to decide about joining church . . . and seek God's guidance.*

Days passed, and still no word came from Isaac. Ella Mae tried her best to keep a cheerful expression around her Mamm as they worked together making pies, but there was a moment when her mother noticed her sad countenance and asked what was bothering her. Ella Mae shrugged it off, saying she wasn't feeling so well, which was the truth. If she'd had her way, she would have spent the day in bed brooding.

Never before had she cared so much for a fellow, and Isaac's silence was worrisome. She also suspected he continued to flounder about church baptism. But the longer she didn't hear from him, the harder it was for her to stick to her resolve not to pursue him.

Now sitting at the kitchen table, Ella Mae poured coffee for herself, then offered some to Clara, who was leaning forward across from her, wholly absorbed.

"You must've fallen hard for Isaac," Clara said with wide eyes as she accepted the hot coffee.

"I daresay there's a fine line between love and foolishness." Ella Mae used the small spoon to place a cube of sugar in her black coffee. "After my baptism, weeks later, I did something that got me put off church for six weeks."

"*Nee.*" Clara's jaw dropped. "Ya didn't chase after Isaac, did ya?"

"S'pose I should finish tellin' the story."

Clara nodded emphatically. "Don't leave me hangin', Aendi. I won't be able to think straight all day."

"All right, then. But just know things took a terrible turn."

Ella Mae began to share how she encountered Isaac again. "I was walkin' home from my Dawdi's up the road one evening, and here came Isaac in his car, waving at me. He stopped, rolled down his window, and leaned his head out. Then he rather comically asked if I needed a ride."

Ella Mae's heart was on her sleeve, and Isaac's smile drew her across the road to talk to him. The first thing on her mind was how wonderful it was to see him, but before she could get a word out, he said he'd been missing her like crazy but hadn't wanted to interfere or get her in trouble with the church since she was newly baptized.

Essie was right.

Ella Mae looked fondly at the empty space beside him there in his car, where she'd always sat. Yet she was hesitant to admit she'd been pining for him.

"What if I picked ya up right here some evening, after sunset?" he said. "I could park over there beneath the trees with the headlights off and wait."

"So no one'll see me with ya?" Her heart raced at the tempting thought.

Isaac's eyes held such expectation . . . and longing. "I'd like to spend time with ya again."

She could not refuse, she was so drawn to him, and immediately, their plan was set into motion. Next Sunday, he'd attend Hickory Hollow's Singing, and afterward, they'd each leave separately. Then he'd walk to his cousins' house and pick up his car before meeting her here.

When Ella Mae returned home, she had a terrible time keeping a straight face, thinking ahead to her secret meeting with Isaac come Sunday night.

CHAPTER

Twenty-Six

1933

The fellowshipping after the Singing had lasted longer than usual. Talk of a party at Henry Mast's brother's place extended the time. But as soon as she could, Ella Mae slipped out of the barn, walking leisurely, knowing Isaac had a much longer trek to get to his car.

Mindful to stay close to the right side of the road, she wished she'd brought a flashlight. But her excitement overshadowed that. Several couples slowed up to offer her a ride, but she graciously declined. Henry Mast and his date, Mary Anna Fisher, were one of the couples, and recalling her twin's growing fondness for Henry, Ella Mae felt a little sad for Essie. *Hopefully someone else asked her to the party*, she thought, aware of the tree branches moving overhead. The breezes were anything but gentle.

Accustomed to walking briskly, Ella Mae had to remind herself to slow down lest she arrive at the appointed spot too early, raising suspicions with anyone who might come by and see her there.

Finding Isaac parked beneath the trees as planned, she opened the door on the passenger side and quickly got in. Then off they went driving around the back roads, once again talking and enjoying each other's company.

After a while, Isaac said he'd like to drive past Henry's brother's farm to see how many of the youth had gathered there. "We won't stop, of course."

Curious, Ella Mae agreed, then quickly learned that Isaac had overheard some of the fellows talking about buggy racing after the Singing. "That's forbidden," she said.

"And so is ownin' a car," Isaac replied, chuckling a little.

"But not for the unbaptized—the youth still in *Rumschpringe*—which you are."

"*Jah*, but still I've kept my car a secret as best I can."

"Your family doesn't know?"

"Not unless my cousin spilled the beans."

Ella Mae didn't know what to think. Surely the longer Isaac drove his car, even after dark, the more likely someone who knew him would spot him and tell his parents. But the last thing she wanted to do was ruin their evening by continuing this conversation.

In no time, they arrived at the farm where many of *die Youngie* had assembled near a large bonfire in the side yard. "Today must be Henry's birthday," she said.

"*Jah*. He's eighteen." Isaac slowed the car even more, inching along and gawking. "Hey, looks like the deacon came for the party," he said, pointing out the spring wagon at the back of the line-up of courting carriages.

"Ya sure it's his?"

"See that extra board on the back? That's how I know."

"Well then, I doubt there'll be any buggy racin' tonight." She hoped not.

"Deacon must've gotten word of it."

Isaac accelerated, taking the highway for a while. He drove to Bird-in-Hand and down to Lincoln Highway, then back around to the less-traveled roads.

The nighttime chorus of crickets and katydids made for a soothing backdrop as Isaac drove with one hand on the wheel and the other holding hers. Every so often, he glanced at her and smiled, lifting her formerly sad heart.

A few minutes after they'd turned onto a quieter road, Ella Mae noticed two open courting buggies side by side and moving at a fast clip. Isaac kept pace with them for a while, and then the buggy on the left suddenly pulled ahead, leaving the one on the right behind.

Isaac sped up some to pass the slower carriage, staring. "Looks like Henry Mast and his date, skippin' out on his own party," he said.

"That's odd."

"*Jah*, but knowin' Henry, I would've thought he'd push his horse harder."

She shuddered, knowing her sister was interested in Henry. "Ain't safe on such a narrow road. Anybody knows that, rules or no rules."

"And on such a dark night, too," Isaac said, sounding more reasonable as they headed toward Route 722 and turned west. She could see moths in the occasional headlights coming this way, and then a raccoon ran across the road and Isaac swerved to avoid it.

Eventually, they headed south on a connecting road that led toward Lincoln Highway again. Aimlessly, they continued onward, and Ella Mae wondered if Isaac just liked driving for the sake of it, with no destination in mind.

Close to Lancaster, they stopped for some ice-cold root beer, and Ella Mae noticed the breezes had calmed. As a baptized church member, she shouldn't be going anywhere for food on a Sunday, or out with a fellow still in *Rumschpringe*, but she pushed all that aside, thrilled to be with her beau again. She sipped the cold drink with her straw, savoring the sweet flavor of store-bought fizzy root beer, so different from Mamma's homemade.

"I hate to think 'bout it, but I s'pose it's time to get ya home, love," Isaac said, smiling at her. "It's been *wunnerbaar-gut* seein' ya."

Love. She nodded, suddenly speechless.

They headed east on the highway with not a car in sight at this late hour. Only one courting carriage was ahead of them, moving along at quite a clip.

"He's goin' mighty fast," Isaac said, and just then the young driver's straw hat blew off and skimmed Isaac's windshield. "Wonder what's his hurry."

Ella Mae squinted into the darkness, hoping this wasn't Henry Mast being so reckless. "Whoever it is, he's got someone with him."

She could hear the shrill sound of a train whistle not far away. *Must be close to midnight.*

"Why's he rushin' *holler-boller* like that?"

Isaac said, watching the buggy make haste toward the railroad crossing. "He ain't racin' that train, is he?"

Ella Mae's heart leaped. "Wh-what?"

"It's nuts. *Dummheit!*"

"Oh, Isaac, I can't bear to watch." But she did all the same, eyes glued to the fast-moving horse and buggy still pressing on toward the tracks. The horse pulled the courting carriage past the crossbuck sign and into the railroad crossing. Yet instead of going on, the horse reared up, as if spooked by the thunderous sound of the coming train and the second piercing warning whistle.

The horse reared again, the buggy frozen perilously on the tracks. Ella Mae felt like she might faint in terror. She heard herself scream as the train thundered forward and struck the buggy.

"*Lieber Gott im Himmel*," Isaac murmured under his breath. Immediately, he pulled the car over and leaped out, running toward the wreckage as the train slowly came to a stop farther up the tracks.

Petrified and dazed, Ella Mae wept inconsolably. Then an idea came to mind, and though it was alarming, she scooted over to sit behind the steering wheel, the engine still idling. *I must try to get help*, she thought, having seen Isaac drive plenty of times. His left foot pressed and then eased up on what he called the clutch, and his right foot alternated with the left. But when she tried to move forward, the car's engine sputtered and quit.

Turning the switch on the dashboard and pressing the pedal in front of the seat, she tried to start the engine again and failed, desperately wanting to get help. *O Lord God, please make this car start!* she prayed, realizing in that moment the absurdity of such a prayer, breaking the *Ordnung* as she was.

Once the engine did start, it took countless tries before she managed to get the rhythmic pattern correct between her left foot and her right. Driving jerkily to the nearest farmhouse a mile or so away, where power lines stretched from the utility pole to the house, she turned into a dirt lane and stopped the car. Trembling, she could see lights on toward the back of the house.

Rushing to the back door, she knocked several times and held her breath, not knowing what to expect at this late hour. Before long, a sleepy-looking middle-aged man came to the door in his pajamas and bathrobe, eyes widening at the sight of her.

"Awful sorry to bother ya," she said, her words tumbling out. "But there's been an accident at the railroad crossing. A buggy . . . got hit by a train."

"Dear Lord," the man blurted. Then, snatching some keys off a nearby shelf, he said, "I'll go alert the fire station."

She thanked him, then hurried back to Isaac's car while the man ran to a free-standing garage and lifted the door, still in his nightclothes and slippers.

Later, after she'd somehow managed to drive back to the tracks and Isaac had dropped her off at the end of her family's lane, it was impossible to fall asleep. The tragic images repeated over and over in Ella Mae's mind. Mamm, having heard her come into the house crying, tried to soothe her, sitting beside her on the bed and stroking her hair, reciting the Lord's Prayer quietly in German. Essie, with whom Ella Mae shared a room, fought back sobs nearby.

All the while, Ella Mae could still hear the sharp train whistle, then the crash . . . and the awful sirens.

By now the coffee in the bottom of Clara's cup was lukewarm, and staring at it, she could scarcely breathe, let alone speak.

Aendi wiped her eyes with a hankie. "Henry Mast died instantly that night, and Mary Anna Fisher succumbed to her devastating injuries in the hospital not many hours later. Even the poor road horse died." She shook her head. "It was the most shocking railroad accident in Lancaster County . . . and 'twas the unspeakable happening you once asked about."

Clara's mind raced. She couldn't imagine witnessing anything so terrible. *I'd never be the same.*

"What're ya thinkin', dear?"

"Many things, really, but I'm wonderin' what happened to Isaac. Did he get back on the straight and narrow?"

"Well, the accident shook him up, that's for certain. And later I confessed to the deacon that I'd been seein' a boy who wasn't baptized . . . and had even driven his car. Because of that, I was put under the *Bann* for six weeks, and my father urged me not to do such a thing again. So I sent Isaac a note saying I wouldn't be seeing him anymore. That was ever so difficult. Yet I knew I must do the right thing.

"Meanwhile, the youth had to mind stricter boundaries because of Henry's recklessness and his and Mary Anna's untimely deaths— just like 'tis happenin' now. So not only did the young people grieve the loss of their friends, and in many cases kin, but they felt the bishop's thumb resting heavily on them."

She continued, "The bishop's severity

with the youth lasted for many years, and that was one of the reasons your grandparents moved away from the hollow when your Mamma was at an age to join *die Youngie*. I would have told ya when ya asked why they left Hickory Hollow, but it wasn't the right time to tell ya this story."

"So they didn't agree with the strict rules."

"*Nee*. Your Dawdi wanted his teenage children to freely choose to join church and not be put in a box, so to speak."

"Makes sense." Clara was slowly putting the pieces together. She recalled her father years ago saying Mamma's parents thought the Hickory Hollow church district was too strict about the wrong things, focusing on rule following instead of grace. *No wonder Indiana's Amish settlement was more appealing to them*. She wished she'd known more about all of that prior to her mother's passing.

So many questions and no way to get answers now.

"That railroad accident must've made ya stop and think 'bout what was most important," Clara said softly.

"Well, that and bein' severely excommunicated for a time—put off church and sittin' alone at mealtimes in my own home—brought me to my senses right quick." Aendi sighed. "Other *gut* things came out of that time, too. My *Bann* played a part in Isaac's return to his upbringing and faith. He was baptized the following year. We even talked 'bout getting back together."

She stopped speaking for the longest moment. Then ever so quietly, she looked into Clara's eyes and said, "I never told a soul I witnessed that horrible accident, 'cept Mamm and Essie. And I'm sure Isaac never told anyone I was there."

Deeply moved that her aunt had entrusted her with this hard secret, Clara touched her wrinkled hand. *"Denki* for sharin' with me. It won't be for naught, I promise."

Aendi sighed. "Seein' that train crash into Henry's buggy made me realize that the path *I* was on might also lead to destruction."

Clara's pulse was still pounding from the heartbreaking story. "You met Joseph Zook a while later, and that changed everything, *jah?"*

Her aunt's eyes were suddenly misty. "It surely did."

CHAPTER

Twenty-Seven

The rest of the day and far into the night, Clara could not shake off her imagined visions of that long-ago accident. And in the days that followed, talk of clearing out the attic faded completely as she did as much cleaning and cooking as Aendi would let her.

Around midmorning the following Tuesday, Lettie and Judah came to hoe the kitchen garden, and afterward, Clara asked if Lettie would like to go with her to visit Rosanna. Lettie was all for it, and Aendi dropped them off at the Ebersols' on her way to visit a friend.

As they stepped out of the carriage, Clara and Lettie spotted Leona sweeping the front walkway. They were quickly invited inside, where Rosanna sat with a book in a straight-backed chair in the front room. Her face brightened at seeing them, just like when Clara visited her the first time.

Interestingly, Rosanna's talk turned almost immediately to Tom Glick. "He's goin' to Yoder, Kansas, to work for his Dat's cousin who runs an Amish furniture store there. His sister told me about it when she visited me the other day. She thinks Tom'll be gone at least a year."

Lettie nodded rather dramatically. "Sounds like a *gut* thing—and not just for Tom."

Clara wasn't sure what she meant, but she could guess. Tom was likely being sent away to grow up and learn a lesson because he'd been a poor example to other young men in the church district. And that meant she'd never see him again. She'd be leaving Hickory Hollow well before his return. Would there ever be another fellow to show such keen interest in her?

"'Tween you two and me," Rosanna said more softly now, glancing toward the kitchen, "I think Tom needs a new beginning."

Lettie replied, "I think you're right."

But Clara only nodded and stayed out of it.

Ever since telling Clara about the tragic railroad accident, Ella Mae had experienced a strong nudge to pay a visit to Sylvia Riehl.

Ella Mae couldn't ignore the tremendous relief she'd felt at sharing the past with Clara—a burden and a secret she'd carried for six decades. And though recounting it had shaken her deeply, her grandniece's knowing about it was somehow satisfying. Even so, the parallels between then and now—especially in two different bishops clamping down on the youth after a buggy-racing tragedy—were uncanny.

How many times had she shivered at the thought of her sister Essie possibly riding with Henry Mast that terrible night? And just what had caused Henry to race a train, for pity's sake? Was he angry over losing the earlier buggy race, or were other factors involved?

As far as Ella Mae knew, those questions had never been answered. But one thing was sure: During those weeks of her temporary *Bann*, she'd made time to kneel beside her bed and plead with God to give her a softer heart, one that listened to His leading and will.

And a listening heart that encouraged others.

Walking up to Sylvia's back porch, Ella Mae was conscious of the spring in her own step. As she knocked before opening the door, she called to the younger woman, "I've come for a visit, dear."

Sylvia came to meet her, eyes wide. "So glad to see ya!" She welcomed her into the kitchen, where her youngest, two-year-old Zeke, was playing with blocks under the table. "The older boys are helpin' their Dawdi Yoder this mornin', so we can sit and talk awhile."

Ella Mae placed a wrapped loaf of zucchini bread on the table, then sat across from Sylvia, mindful of the young one below. "Brought ya some sweet bread. Thought we could have some together if ya have the time."

"You don't know how glad I am you're here." Sylvia sighed as she wiped her face with the hem of her black apron, then retrieved a knife from a drawer. "I'd just set out this cold meadow tea an' was gonna drink some by myself, wishin' for someone to talk to." She reached to pour a glass for Ella Mae.

"*Gut* timing, then, I daresay." Ella Mae studied the fatigued woman, stretched thin with all she had to do alone to keep her family running with three young sons. "May I ask the blessing?" she asked when her friend sat down.

Sylvia looked befuddled, but as her frown mixed with a smile, she nodded.

Ella Mae bowed her head and folded her

bony hands. "Our gracious heavenly Father," she began, "I thank Thee for Thy precious child, Sylvia, and her family. Be ever near in her daytime chores, her nighttime uncertainties, and all her comings and goings. We're also grateful for this tasty bread and nice, cold tea. In the name of our Savior and Lord, Jesus Christ, amen."

Now Sylvia looked not just baffled but a little stunned. "Where'd ya learn to pray like *that*?"

"Years of practice." Ella Mae sliced through the loaf of zucchini bread, then offered some to Sylvia on a paper napkin from the table. "Since the Lord has so many of us prayin', why not help Him out some and pray aloud?"

Now Sylvia was grinning. "I'm not sure if I should laugh or not."

"That's all right. And I hope ya don't think I have a special corner on the Lord's attention, 'cause He hears your every prayer, too. Unspoken or otherwise."

"Just never heard anyone pray out loud like that, but I didn't mind it one bit."

Ella Mae recalled when Clara said this, too. "Remember how the psalmist said he cried out to the Lord with his mouth, and his praise was on his tongue? Sure doesn't seem like a silent prayer, now, does it?"

"Since ya brought that up, I can think of

other verses in the Bible where cryin' out to God is mentioned." Sylvia took a sip of the meadow tea, smiling again. "*Denki* for sharin' this, Ella Mae. You've been such a help to me whenever we visit."

"I'll be comin' to see ya once a week for a time. And bringin' something sweet for us to have with your meadow tea, if that's all right."

Sylvia's eyes glimmered. "I know you're grievin', too," she said, her voice breaking. "So I don't expect ya to put yourself out for me."

"Well, I'm a little further along than you are. Sorrowin' takes time . . . and energy."

"What if we help each other, then?" Sylvia brushed a tear away.

Nodding, Ella Mae reached over to clasp her friend's hand.

Clara and Lettie said their good-byes to Rosanna and thanked Leona for the iced tea she'd brought to the front room during their visit. As they headed down the back walkway toward the road, they noticed Aaron turning into the driveway with a hay-filled wagon. He stopped and waved his straw hat at them, smiling.

"Hullo, Lettie and Clara."

"We just had a nice visit with Rosanna," Lettie told him.

"She needs the company. Still can't move round much without pain."

"She should be havin' even more visitors soon," Lettie replied.

Clara nodded. "Lots of the other girls want to help cheer her up."

He put his straw hat back on his head. "Say, are yous goin' to the volleyball game Saturday afternoon at Samuel and Rebecca Lapp's?"

Clara had to smile at his invitation. "Don't see why not."

Lettie looked at her, then said, "We'll *both* be there."

Aaron bobbed his head, said good-bye, then signaled the horse to pull the wagon forward.

"Ya must be lookin' forward to the game," Lettie commented once they were on their way.

"Why do ya ask?"

"Well, you were quick to answer." Lettie glanced at her. "Besides, it was obvious he intended the question for *you*."

Clara remembered Aaron's attempt to talk to her at the cornhusking contest weeks ago. "He's nice, don't ya think?"

"No question 'bout that. But he's not Tom Glick."

"I'm no longer interested in Tom."

Lettie started to swing her arms, hurrying the pace.

"Have *you* ever gone out with Aaron?" Clara asked, feeling a bit nosy.

Lettie shook her head. "*Nee*, and not Tom Glick, either."

Smiling, Clara asked, "Are ya interested in someone?"

"Well . . ."

Clara quickly added, "Just thought it might be fun to double-date sometime is all—if I ever get asked out again, that is."

"Maybe." Lettie shrugged. "But ya won't be here all that much longer, will ya?"

"Honestly, I'm tryin' not to think 'bout that." Dat had been so hesitant about her staying longer than a week. Surely he'd put his foot down if she asked to extend her visit beyond summer.

"Couldn't ya stay on indefinitely?"

"It's only July nineteenth, so there's still plenty of time," Clara said, looking on the bright side. Truth be told, she loved working alongside Aendi at her house, and she enjoyed working for Vera, but she'd also hoped to meet someone who might change the course of her future. Could that still happen?

"I can always *hope* you'll stay longer," Lettie told her. "You're such a *gut* friend."

"You are, too."

Finding a beau or not, Clara couldn't bear to think of leaving the hollow. But she'd told her father she would.

As they turned into the lane leading up to Aendi's house, Clara noticed the buggy was still gone. So she decided to invite Lettie to have some more iced tea, this time with lemon cookies. They headed inside for their goodies, then took them out to the bench near the rose arbor and enjoyed the fragrance of the flowers.

A light breeze came up, and several rose petals fell lightly on Lettie's shoulders.

"Well, look at that," Clara said, reaching for the delicate pink beauties to show her. "Maybe the fella you're interested in will ask ya out soon."

Lettie grinned, waving a honeybee away. "How do ya get *that* from rose petals?"

"Just made it up." Clara laughed, wishing Lettie would tell her the name of the young man she liked.

Lettie leaned over to put her nose in the middle of a trailing blossom. "Nothin' quite like that sweet fragrance."

Clara smiled. "There's a verse 'bout the sweet aroma of those who live for the Lord," she said. "It's found in Second Corinthians, chapter two. 'For we are unto God a sweet savour of Christ . . .'"

Tilting her head, Lettie didn't respond right away. "You memorize Scripture?"

"Without really tryin'."

"Well, we don't recite verses from memory," Lettie replied.

Clara recalled what her father said about the differences between the two districts' beliefs and *Ordnungs*. "Guess the more I read God's Word, the more it settles into my heart." She hoped she wasn't sticking her neck out, but this was what she believed, and she believed it with all her heart. "My Dat always told us kids growin' up that the *Ordnung* is a revelation of our need for a Savior. I mean, it's impossible to follow all the rules perfectly."

Lettie was suddenly quiet, like she was pondering this.

After a time, Clara asked, "Would ya like to see the quilt I'm workin' to repair with Aendi Ella Mae now? I know you're not very interested in quilting, but ya said you prob'ly should be. And ya might enjoy seein' what we've done so far."

Lettie agreed. They took the tumblers inside and set them in the kitchen sink, then washed their hands and stepped into the front room. Clara showed her how they were restoring the quilt with reproductions of the original fabric, and she was pleased to see her friend study the new piecework.

"It's hard to tell where the old pieces were covered over with the new," Lettie said, touching several places. "You're *gut* at this, Clara. I can see how tiny the stitches are—I'd never have known they weren't sewn on a machine."

"Well, confidentially, I'd love to have my own quilt shop someday. Not that I don't like workin' for Vera."

"I understand. Everyone has a special talent, Mamm says. For some, it's makin' the best fudge." Lettie grinned.

"Having a family of my own—after losin' Mamma, and Dat remarryin' and all—well, that's my *first* desire. But somewhere further down the road, I'd like to keep my hand in quilt-makin', like Mamma and I enjoyed doin' together. And now Aendi and I are enjoying this." She gestured at the quilt.

"If ya want a family, Clara, then I'm thinkin' ya really need to keep goin' to the youth activities."

Clara nodded. *That's my plan.*

CHAPTER

Twenty-Eight

On her way home, Ella Mae couldn't get over how good she felt after visiting Sylvia and praying with her before leaving. The younger woman had also taken obvious delight in showing her a colorful summer-weight crazy quilt upstairs. Interestingly, she mentioned that her husband hadn't cared for the busy pattern on their bed, but here recently she'd brought the quilt out of the blanket chest and was enjoying it, remembering the fun she'd had making it with her Mammi years ago.

This got Ella Mae thinking about Joseph, and while she didn't want to stare around Sylvia's bedroom, she had noticed that none of her deceased husband's clothing or personal effects were visible.

Now she caught herself brooding.

By a peculiar turn of events, Clara ran into Tom Glick's mother at the General Store that evening. Although Clara had never met her, Lettie had pointed her out at the last fellowship meal, so she knew who she was.

Wanting to be polite, Clara engaged briefly in small talk, then left the store carrying the bag of items she'd offered to pick up for Aendi. Her aunt had seemed tired after supper. *Tired and pensive*, she thought, hurrying toward the waiting horse and carriage.

Just as she opened the buggy's passenger door to place the grocery bag inside, someone called her name. Turning, she saw Tom himself sitting in an enclosed family carriage next to hers with the passenger door open, the white cast on his ankle visible.

"What a coincidence," he said, looking embarrassed.

She hadn't expected to see him and had no idea what to say. She closed her buggy's door and walked around to untie Sparkles from the hitching post.

"Got a minute, Clara?" he asked, glancing toward the General Store. "Was hopin' I might see ya before I leave for Kansas."

She gathered up the lead line and stroked Sparkles's neck. Truth be told, she wanted to lash out at Tom, tell him how awful he was to race his buggy, especially with dear Rosanna along. But she said calmly, "What is it?"

"I'm sure ya heard what happened."

She nodded. "*Gut* thing yous weren't killed that night."

Tom said he wanted to explain. "Since I hadn't seen ya at Singing, and no one had asked Rosanna out ridin', I offered to give her a lift home. I was just bein' kind." He paused. "I know it was a mistake when you and I were startin' to see each other."

"Not for long, really. But what was a mistake was the racin', Tom." It was all she could do not to say more.

Tom lowered his head for the longest time. "I wasn't thinkin'." He sighed, lifting his head to meet her gaze. "It was wrong. I know that."

She drew a breath, eager to be on her way.

"I'd like to write to ya." His voice was softer now.

For a while, she'd thought Tom might be her chance to court and marry, settling down here near Aendi and Lettie, too. But she saw him in a different light now.

"It'd prob'ly be best if ya didn't." Rounding her buggy, Clara slid into the driver's seat, then reached for the driving lines. She had nothing more to say to him.

Quickly, she directed the horse to move

forward. She wished she'd been wiser and not fallen for Tom's flirtatious ways.

Six girls stood on Clara's side of the volleyball net that Saturday afternoon at the Lapps' farm, and six fellows stood on the opposite side. The same number of girls and guys were already playing at a second volleyball net farther over on the yard.

Several times, Clara noticed Aaron's strong serve and spikes. *He's very good,* she thought, smiling at the memory of his asking her and Lettie about coming today. Wanting to play her best, too, she focused on the teamwork required to win against not only Aaron and his cousin Josiah, but Daniel Fisher, Judah Zook, and Elam and Benjamin Lapp.

The girls kept the volleyball high, making leaps into the air and some great offensive spikes. Clara quickly realized volleyball was taken as seriously here as it was back home.

When the guys won the first set, then switched sides with the girls, the sun was now in the fellows' eyes. Aaron smiled at Clara, and she smiled back.

After winning two of the three sets in the match, the fellows high-fived each other. The girls, being good sports, walked to the net and cordially shook hands, congratulating them on a great game.

Rebecca had set out sliced watermelon, whoopie pies, and cold soda pop on a table in the backyard under a shady tree. The guys hung back and let the girls get their refreshments first. Clara chose a slice of seedless watermelon, then leaned over her paper plate to bite into it.

When she finished, she carried the rind and plate to a trash bin Samuel had placed nearby. As she did, Aaron joined her.

"You have a powerful serve, Clara," he said, holding a can of soda. "Have ya been playin' long?"

"My parents played with us kids growin' up. And Dat and my uncles taught me to play confidently, guess ya could say."

"That's obvious." Aaron's bangs fluttered in the breeze. "My family and I played together, too."

She appreciated Aaron's friendly, straightforward manner. And his smiles were different from Tom's flirtatious ones.

Aaron took a swig of his soda, then asked, "Was wonderin', would ya like to go with me to my *Onkel* Mark's farm to play Ping-Pong after Singing tomorrow night?"

"Are you as quick at Ping-Pong as ya are at volleyball?" she asked, laughing.

"You'll have to see for yourself." This was the closest he'd come to a coy answer.

"Okay, then."

"I think you'll enjoy yourself, Clara," he said, his eyes alight. He then excused himself to join the group of guys who'd been on his team.

That quick, Lettie appeared. "So did Aaron ask ya out?"

Nodding, Clara couldn't help but smile.

"Honestly, I couldn't be happier to hear it," Lettie said, slipping her arm through Clara's.

Ella Mae was pleased to see Clara already home and cooking spaghetti for supper. The sight of her standing there at the cookstove stirring the pot reminded her of another long-ago evening when Joseph was the one helping with preparations for their meal while she tended to their little ones. Jake and his younger brother, Abe, had been fussy all day, both cutting teeth—one a molar and the other a front tooth—and they needed her attention. Joseph had even tied on one of her white half aprons, prompting her spontaneous spurt of laughter.

Smiling now at the memory, she was once again comforted by Clara's presence. *The time is hastening away. She'll return home before we know it.*

Clara glanced at her, the wooden spoon in her hand. "I forgot to tell ya I saw Tom Glick at the General Store the other evening."

Ella Mae let out a little gasp. "Oh dear."

Clara filled her in on their conversation, making it clear that she'd put the kibosh on their friendship.

Greatly relieved, Ella Mae nodded. "You're *schmaert*."

Then, surprising her, Clara said, "May I ask what all ya know 'bout the Adam Ebersol family?"

"Ya don't let any grass grow under your bare feet, do ya, dearie? Like I've said before, Adam, Leona, and *all* their family are mighty *gut* people."

Blushing bright red, Clara nodded with a quick smile.

Ella Mae knew better than to ask more, but she was delighted if Aaron Ebersol was indeed paying some attention to her grandniece.

As Clara worked on the repair of the heirloom quilt that evening, she asked Aendi why she'd kept Isaac Smucker's tin art and pencil drawings all these years.

The older woman smiled. "I wondered if

ya might ask that," she said, explaining that she'd wanted to return his art after Joseph began courting her. "But Joseph insisted the art was so well done that it was worth keepin'. So I did.

"Now you've found it, it seems that Isaac's art opened the door for me to share a glimpse into my past with ya." Aendi paused, looking wistful.

Clara wondered if she would have ever known about that troubling time if she hadn't found the old wooden box. "I'm glad it opened that door."

Her aunt nodded. "Here lately, I've considered givin' some of the drawings to Isaac's grandchildren."

"Are they here in the hollow?"

"Oh *jah*. In fact, Isaac's oldest grandson, Jonas, is one of our two preachers."

Clara pondered this. "So when you encouraged Isaac to be baptized and he did, it paved the way for generations after him to follow the Lord. And for one to be ordained for ministry."

Aendi's eyes welled up, and she set down her sewing needle and thimble. "Never thought of it thataway."

Clara added, "Seems to me your decision to join church made a big difference for Isaac's descendants."

CHAPTER

Twenty-Nine

In accordance with Bishop Beiler's new rules, two sets of parents oversaw the next Sunday Singing. Clara also noticed at least four fellows missing, and later Lettie told her they'd gone to another youth gathering, one not as strict.

"They're prob'ly chafing under the bishop's changes," Lettie whispered.

Later, playing Ping-Pong in Aaron's aunt and uncle's basement made for a much lighter atmosphere after the somewhat solemn Singing. Clara was having fun and realized how competitive Aaron's Onkel Mark and Aendi Frieda were. Fortunately, it didn't take long for Clara to partner fairly well with Aaron on their side of the net. After several practice games, they were ready to play in earnest.

Doubles Ping-Pong was so fast-moving,

especially with such skilled opponents, that Clara was literally kept on her toes. She marveled at how well Aaron and his uncle and aunt played.

Later, the four of them sat on the back porch, overlooking the meadow teeming with lightning bugs, eating Frieda's strawberry-rhubarb pie and homemade vanilla ice cream. Clara learned that Mark had been playing Ping-Pong since he was a young boy. And when he'd first started dating Frieda, the two of them played a lot at *his* uncle's home.

"Frieda picked up most of my tricks right quick," Mark said, turning to wink at his wife.

No wonder they're such a good team, Clara thought, delighted to have met them.

Frieda looked her way and said, "I daresay Aaron and Clara make excellent partners, too."

Clara couldn't help but notice the twinkle in Frieda's big brown eyes.

During the ride home, Clara could tell they were taking the roundabout way back to Aendi's. She didn't mind, though, because she was so caught up in her conversation with Aaron. He'd started by mentioning how much Rosanna had enjoyed receiving Clara's thoughtful card and note.

"I'll be sendin' her more."

Aaron glanced at her. "She's fond of ya, Clara."

"I like her, too."

Aaron was quiet for a moment, then admitted how upset he still was with Tom for driving recklessly with Rosanna along. "I cannot understand what on earth he was thinkin'."

Clara agreed as she recalled Tom telling her he knew it was wrong to race.

"His cousin Gideon is mortified that he got caught up in racin'," Aaron said. "He's since told me he'd never raced before that night." He paused. "And when Tom's buggy flipped, Gideon pulled over and he and his date leaped out to help Tom and Rosanna."

Clara had wondered about that, but she really didn't want to continue on this topic. "Do ya mind if we talk 'bout somethin' else?"

"Not at all." He smiled at her.

"I'm curious 'bout your hobbies."

"Well, I'm busy in the harness shop all day, so I really have only one hobby of sorts." Aaron told her he'd recently become a scribe for *The Budget*, the weekly newspaper serving Plain communities. But he didn't make much of it, really. "I just thought it was somethin' I could do for the Hickory Hollow community since our former scribe—my father's eldest brother, Caleb—can no longer write the column."

Aaron paused. "His Parkinson's disease makes it mighty hard to hold a pen, so I offered to take it over for him."

That's so kind, she thought. "When will your first column be published?"

"August tenth, according to my editor."

"I'll be sure to look for it."

Aaron nodded. "Not many folks know I'll be takin' Onkel Caleb's place," he said quietly. "S'pose the word'll get around soon enough."

Clara respected his humility.

"What do *you* like to do in your spare time?" Aaron asked.

"Since I was little, quiltin's been a special joy." She told him about the repair process on Aendi's heirloom quilt, then about all the years she'd created quilts from scraps of fabric with her Mamma back home.

"It's *gut*, then, you're workin' for Vera Lapp, *jah*?"

"I like to think God opened that door for me."

Aaron was quiet for a moment before saying, "Do ya feel that way 'bout comin' to Hickory Hollow, too?"

"It's odd the way that all came about, really."

Holding the driving lines steady, Aaron looked at her. "Mind tellin' me more?"

"It might take a while," she said.

"I have the time if you do." He gave her another smile.

Warming to his interest, she described her father's request to clear out her mother's desk and the many letters she'd discovered there from her great-aunt Ella Mae. "Their close bond was unusual because they lived so many miles apart," Clara told him. "It was the dearest thing, and it made me want to come to Hickory Hollow to meet Aendi."

By the time Clara finished telling him how she'd traveled by train to get here, the road they were on was completely empty of courting buggies, and the bush crickets' song filled the moonlit night.

"Hearing that story, I tend to think you were led here, Clara." He slowed the horse to a walk. "Providentially, I mean."

She perked up her ears. *Did he really say that?* Blushing now, she was thankful for the covering of night.

"I'd like to see ya again soon," Aaron added.

"That'd be nice," she replied, thinking he was nothing at all like Tom Glick—and that was a good thing.

Aaron's words stayed with her long after

he'd walked her to the back door and said good-night.

Wednesday afternoon after work, Clara found a card from Aaron in the mail inviting her for ice cream after supper on Saturday. The memory of eating ice cream with Tom—and what happened afterward—reared up, but then quickly disappeared.

She gathered supper ingredients for cornmeal muffins and two green tomato pies, then set to work. She had a strong feeling her aunt would wholeheartedly approve of her going out with Aaron, considering how Aendi had responded to her question about the Ebersol family.

That evening, Clara jotted a short note to Aaron, then with Aendi's permission, went to the General Store. She wanted to mail it right away so he'd be sure to receive it before their date.

At Vera's shop Thursday, Clara was tasked with showing numerous quilts to a rather vivacious woman. Taking her to the queen-size bed with many quilts laid out on it, Clara asked what colors or patterns she was looking for.

The brunette woman grimaced. "I really don't know, but sometimes you just have to see it to know it's the right one."

"Well, we have all types of Amish patterns, and anything ya see here can be custom-made in a different set of colors." She thought of asking the lady what color scheme she had in the room where she hoped to use the quilt, but the woman was already marveling aloud about the Log Cabin pattern in several blue hues with yellows.

Clara waited as the customer stepped back, clearly studying the quilt. Eventually, though, she shook her head and asked to see the next one. So Clara carefully folded back the first quilt to reveal one with a lovely Broken Star pattern in purple, some red, and gray. "This is more in keepin' with the colors some of our People prefer," Clara told her.

"I can see why. Those red splashes really make the whole color scheme pop."

Clara nodded. "Ya'd think deep purple and red would clash, but I think they're real perty together."

Just then, Vera's petite seven-year-old granddaughter, Becky, who was visiting for the afternoon, wandered over. "It's so perty!" the blond girl piped up, pointing to the Broken Star quilt before grinning up at Clara.

The customer turned and chuckled. "I

suppose you'll be a quilter when you grow up," she said, apparently taken by the child.

Becky bobbed her head. "Mammi Mast is already teachin' me to make a Nine Patch sampler."

Clara smiled, enjoying the unexpected encounter. She glanced over her shoulder to see Vera at the cash register with another customer. Becky must have slipped away without her grandmother's knowledge.

"If I practice a lot, Mammi says I'll be a *gut* quilter," Becky added, leaning forward to look more closely at the quilt in question.

The customer turned to Clara and asked, "Do you make quilts, too?"

Clara said she had in the past. "Some of the happiest days of my life were spent quiltin' with my Mamma." *Ach*, she'd mentioned her mother to a stranger.

"Are ya gonna buy this quilt?" Becky asked the brunette.

"I do like it," the woman replied. "And I already know which bedroom it'll go in."

"It's *my* favorite pattern," Becky declared, blue eyes wide.

"So that settles it, since it's your favorite."

Becky nodded. "But don't worry. My Mammi Mast can have another one just like it made for someone else."

The woman's face burst into a big smile. "Aren't you the sweetest little salesperson!"

Clara motioned to Vera, whose customer was just leaving. She came over and helped remove the beautiful Broken Star quilt from beneath the other quilts on the bed. Then the two of them packaged it in protective plastic for the delighted woman.

Later, when Becky returned to her spot on the floor behind the counter to play with her faceless cloth dolls, Clara thought about how many times her own Mamma had her sit next to her while working on a quilt or in the sewing room. And in that moment, she truly dreaded the thought of leaving Hickory Hollow for First Light, where there was the very real chance she'd end up a *Maidel* with no family of her own.

But again, she'd promised her father she would be home right after Labor Day. And that meant it was only right to tell Aaron she couldn't see him again after their date Saturday evening. As tempting as it was to get to know Aaron, a long-distance courtship would just be too challenging.

Clara was happy Aaron took her to a different ice cream stand than the one she and Tom had visited. They slipped out of the buggy and walked up to the window to order together, then with their order number, they sat at one of the several little café tables with wrought-iron chairs as other customers milled about the well-lit area.

While they waited, Aaron rather tentatively told Clara he'd noticed she'd begun wearing Lancaster County–style dresses and capes soon after deciding to stay the summer. "Kinda surprised me," he said.

She was a little surprised he'd mention it. "I talked it over with my Aendi just before I started workin' at Vera's shop. All I brought with me were mourning dresses, ya see. And since I was makin' new dresses anyway, I thought it might be better to look like I was from round here. Ya know, not to confuse customers, who might ask questions."

He nodded. "And ya wanted to fit in?"

She almost expected him to wink at her, his smile was so endearing. "That was part of the reason."

"I understand why you'd want to. And 'specially now with the bishop's new rules and all, it's a *gut* thing."

"Hadn't thought of that, but you're right. The dresses I brought from home have shorter hems, and the style has more long block pleats and whatnot." *Fancier*, she thought he might think.

Aaron told her several fellows had already been reported to the ministerial brethren for violating the new rules, or so he'd heard through the grapevine. "Some by their own girlfriends for fancy dashboards and whatnot. Makes ya wonder how those relationships will last."

Clara again recalled the modern interior of Tom's buggy.

Aaron continued. "One of the guys was even caught playin' a guitar somewhere near the outskirts of town." He didn't mention a name.

Clara remembered hearing what had sounded like guitar music when she and Aendi were on the way to Friday market a few weeks ago. "Does it bother ya that *die Youngie* are bein' restricted more now?" She was thinking of how her grandparents had left Hickory Hollow because of similar strict rules.

"I've thought about that," Aaron said. "I s'pose there's two ways to look at it. One, if you're followin' the rules already in place, what's the concern if more boundaries are set? On the other hand, if you're pushin' the limits, maybe lookin' to jump the fence and go fancy, well, I can see why a person would duck away from the bishop's new wishes."

Had her grandparents wanted to push limits here? Or just move to where they wouldn't have to?

When their order number was called, Aaron walked up to the window and paid for their cones—butter pecan for him and raspberry for her—then suggested they stay right where they'd been sitting and enjoy the evening breeze.

While brushing her long hair at bedtime, Clara realized she'd been having such a pleasant time with Aaron that she'd completely forgotten her resolve to explain she couldn't go out with him again. And Aaron had already asked to see her after next Sunday's Singing and even hinted they might see each other when she visited Rosanna again this coming Monday afternoon, on Clara's day off.

Not knowing what to do about it now, she prayed her silent rote prayers and then about her growing friendship with Aaron. It was difficult to know what to say about the special connection that seemed to be developing between them—to the Lord, and even to herself.

And knowing how strict the bishop here had become, she wondered if Aaron would be in hot water if, after she left Hickory Hollow, he continued dating an out-of-state girl from a more progressive community.

If word got out, that is.

CHAPTER

Thirty

After a tasty noon meal of cold cuts, macaroni salad, pickled beet slices, and peanut butter spread on homemade bread, Aendi suggested they do some visiting. It was the last day of July, and Clara could tell her aunt was itching to get out of the house on this between-Sunday from Preaching.

"Would ya like to get better acquainted with my daughter Mattie and her family this afternoon?" Aendi asked. "I'll be living in their *Dawdi Haus* in a few months."

"Sure. I'll go wherever ya like."

Not long after they arrived at Beilers, Mattie offered to show Clara the completed blueprints of the *Dawdi Haus*, and glancing at her smiling aunt, Clara agreed. David spread the draft out on the long kitchen table and pointed out the location of each room Aendi had evidently requested. She seemed the most excited about the sewing room on the main level next to her proposed bedroom.

Then David brought up an idea he said he'd had recently. "What if we got some of the menfolk to help load your greenhouse on a wide-bed wagon and brought it over here once the *Dawdi Haus* is constructed?" He had an engaging smile on his ruddy face.

Aendi's eyes widened. "You'd wanna *do* that?"

"Shouldn't be too difficult." David leaned over to show her where the small structure could be placed in the side yard.

Clara was touched by his kindness and felt that maybe something about all this talk of Aendi's moving had changed. Maybe Mattie had come to realize her mother had just needed time—and no pushing.

"That'd be right nice," Aendi said, looking at Clara, then back at David. "Could ya bring over my rose arbor, too?"

David chuckled.

"I'm serious," she said, keeping a straight face . . . but not for long.

"We'll plant ya another rose garden,

Mamm," Mattie said. "And bring along the old bench ya love, too."

Aendi turned to Clara, looking a bit sad. "I sure wish you could see the *Haus* when it's built . . . and I'm settled in."

Clara nodded, thinking the same thing. "I'll be long gone by then, sorry to say."

Mattie smiled. "You could always come visit again." She pointed to the upstairs second bedroom on the blueprint. "See there? The spare room'll be waitin' for ya."

Aendi bobbed her little head. "You'll always be *Willkumm in mei Haus.*"

Clara's eyes met her aunt's, and she felt nearly as close to the older woman as she had to her own Mamma.

Early the next morning, Clara got her washing pinned to the clothesline right after Aendi put her laundry in the wringer washer. She was eager to start her day and to visit Rosanna after breakfast. Since it was three weeks past the accident, and Rosanna was halfway through the six weeks the doctor said it would take her ribs to heal, Clara hoped to encourage her friend to walk with her outdoors.

Clara arrived in Aendi's carriage and could see Rosanna walking slowly on the back porch, her right arm still in its splint. Quickly, Clara tied up Firefly and made her way up the walkway bedecked with red and white petunias. "Well, look at you," she said, heading up the steps and smiling.

"I've been movin' round more lately," Rosanna told her, the bruises on her face and neck now turned pink and blue. "But a couple of days ago, I had sudden pain in my ribs, and that set me back a bit. The doctor said that sometimes happens after a rib injury."

"Are ya feelin' better now?" Clara asked, concerned.

Rosanna said she was. "Maybe we can do some walkin' together."

"I was hopin' we could!"

Leona poked her head around the screen door just then. "Hullo there, Clara."

Clara smiled. "Is it okay if we slowly walk around the yard?"

"Why, sure." Leona stepped onto the porch. "Rosanna's been wantin' to show ya around a little."

Rosanna gingerly walked to the steps, then grasped the wood railing on the left as she navigated each one. "I don't wanna fall, so I'll go carefully and not move my upper body too much. Mamma says that'll come in due time." She grimaced a little as they turned to walk through the yard. "It's strange that I feel every step I take all the way up in my ribs."

"Our body is knit together, the Good Book says. When one part suffers, it all does."

Rosanna smiled. "I hadn't thought of those verses, but you're right."

"Well, I think the suffering is more about the body of Christ—the church—than our natural bodies."

"Have ya studied that passage?"

"Not really, but my Dat always tried to explain Scripture verses to us kids when we were growin' up."

"That's interesting," Rosanna said, looking a little surprised.

Clara didn't ask, but from Rosanna's reaction, she assumed her father didn't do that.

They walked slowly to the herb garden, where white stepping stones lay here and there in the dark soil.

"Looks like you've got quite a selection of herbs," Clara observed.

"Can ya name any of them?"

"Let's see. I see some sage, thyme, chives, and dill weed." Clara pointed at each plant as she named it.

"*Jah*, and what 'bout basil and oregano?"

"Is that the basil over in the far-right corner?"

Rosanna nodded. "You must've grown these herbs before."

"Well, my Mamma had a big herb garden, and I loved to help her weed it. Now, which plant is the oregano?" She scanned the area. "If I could smell it, I'd know for sure. Its scent is a bit minty, right?"

Rosanna smiled. "True."

"I'm guessin' that's the oregano, then." Clara pointed to the clump of small dark green leaves of a plant about a foot high.

"*Jah.*" Rosanna walked with her farther. "Does Ella Mae grow herbs? I've seen her perty flowers round the greenhouse."

"She grows peppermint and lemon balm for her teas."

"My Mamm has enjoyed peppermint tea with her, 'specially in the wintertime." Rosanna said her mother had often visited the "Wise Woman" several years ago. "Not anymore. I think she's moved past whatever was troubling her. Ella Mae must've helped her look at certain things in a different way, maybe."

"She has a listening heart."

"Mamm says she prays right out loud, too, which is ever so peculiar. Does she do that with you?"

"I've actually come to appreciate it."

Rosanna didn't reply to that.

"How far would ya like to walk?" Clara asked, changing the subject.

"Let's go an' sit near Mamm's butterfly garden. I think you'll like it."

"All right." Clara fell into step with her friend.

The butterfly garden was a sanctuary set apart from the main house, reminding Clara of her aunt's rose arbor, where she and Lettie had sat the other day. Here there were many different varieties of perennials, though, including white and purple asters, pink dianthus, sky blue dwarf lobelia, yellow goldenrod, and bright purple phlox. A white wooden bench sat perched on one side not far from a cement birdbath.

"Mamm sits out here in the cool of the evening an' writes letters to her out-of-state relatives," Rosanna said as she sat down carefully.

"It's so peaceful here."

"See those monarch butterflies over there?" Rosanna said, pointing gently with her left arm before adjusting her right arm with a sigh. "Sometimes dozens are out here—and more."

"Butterflies represent hope," Clara commented softly.

"*Jah*, and rebirth, too, Dat says."

Clara looked at her friend, so sincere. "They struggle hard in the darkness, then emerge ever so beautiful."

Rosanna nodded. "Since the accident, I've stared a lot at this garden through the front room windows. Seein' the butterflies encouraged me not to give up."

"And now you can come out here and watch them more closely."

"Aaron once told me this garden is a *gut* place to pray. That was quite a while ago, when Onkel Caleb first got sick."

Clara didn't mention she knew Aaron had taken over their uncle's column for *The Budget*. "My Mamma used to say that havin' her hands in the soil was the best feeling of all. Workin' in the garden made her think 'bout God."

"I wish I'd known her."

"I wish so, too." Clara smiled, observing many more butterflies just then—copper and brown brush-footed, brilliant yellow dainty sulphur, and red-spotted purple, along with various monarchs. She felt so tranquil there with Rosanna that she wished she could stay all day.

About the time Rosanna said she was growing tired and wanted to return to the house, Aaron arrived and greeted Clara. Standing near the tall blue lobelia, he removed his straw hat and fanned his face with it.

"Did ya tell Clara why we decided to plant this garden years ago?" he asked, looking at his sister.

"Why don't *you*?" Rosanna suggested, smiling at him.

Aaron put his hat back on his head. "Well, when I was just a little boy, a yellow butterfly landed on my shoulder and stayed there for the longest time. Dat saw it happen more than once that summer and suggested we dig up a nice, large plot and plant flowers that would attract even more of 'em."

Rosanna was grinning. "Keep goin'. There's more to the story, Bruder."

"*Jah.*" Aaron looked at the flowers, where many kinds of butterflies fluttered about. "Our Mammi Ebersol had passed away a few weeks before this, and I was sad. But Dat thought the cloudless sulphur butterfly might be a sign from heaven somehow, and bein' so young, I wanted to agree."

Clara had heard of yellow butterflies appearing after the passing of a loved one, but she hadn't seen one after her own mother died. She'd never put too much stock in such superstitions. Even so, she was impressed by Aaron's gentle way of sharing about this one.

"Once we planted all these flowers, more yellow butterflies began comin'," he said. "It was downright heartening."

Rosanna smiled. "We don't really know what brought that first yellow butterfly, or why it sat on Aaron's shoulder that summer. But like ya said earlier, Clara, it brought hope."

By now, Aaron looked self-conscious, so Clara didn't comment further. Still, she was happy to see him again.

When Clara returned to Aendi's, a family carriage was parked in the lane. She unhitched Firefly, led her to the stable, and then took the time to do a thorough grooming as she relived the lovely visit with Rosanna.

It was still hard to think of how her friend had been hurt so badly when the buggy flipped. Thankfully, Tom was nowhere around now, and hopefully he would straighten up and get some wisdom, perhaps from his relatives out there in Kansas.

Finished with the grooming, she walked across the backyard to the porch, and once near the screen door, she could hear a woman's voice coming from inside the house. She sounded sad, making Clara wonder if Sylvia Riehl might be visiting again. *"Grievin' takes time,"* Aendi had said.

Not wanting to disturb whoever it was, Clara headed to the rose arbor and sat on the pretty bench. Even from there, she could still hear the woman's voice and occasionally Aendi's reassuring one.

They must be in the front room.

Clara rose and walked around to the back again, this time heading for the greenhouse. Once inside, she closed its door. It was rather stifling in there, but she sat down on the wooden stool and looked around, thinking it wouldn't take much time to sort through the items so Aendi could take what she needed to David and Mattie's.

But all the windows of the structure, and the skylights, too . . . How would they hold up in a move? Clara hoped David's plan would work out, though. The place would be wonderful on a cooler day.

After a while, Clara spotted a middle-aged woman she didn't recognize walk down the back steps, then head to the waiting horse and carriage. Clara smiled at the thought of someone new coming for tea . . . and for some gentle, caring words. *The purpose Aendi feared she'd lost.*

While eating supper with her aunt later that evening, Clara relayed her conversation with Rosanna at the edge of that special butterfly garden. "Seems to me the girl's open-hearted to the Lord and His creation, like you must have been around her age, Aendi."

"Well, after that one terrible summer,

maybe. But not much before then, even though I often sat at my Mamm's knee hearin' the Word of God read—like Timothy of old. But Rosanna's always enjoyed readin' her Bible." Aendi paused. "Readin' and ponderin' Scripture, takin' it to heart—that can make any young person wise." She rose and began clearing the table. "Say, would ya like to work on the old quilt again tonight? Shouldn't be more than a few evenings till we're finished."

"I'm ready whenever you are," Clara replied, looking forward to it.

"Once the repairs are done, we'll have more time to sort and discard things round here," Aendi said, surprising Clara a little.

"That'll be just fine." She stood to help clean the kitchen, her thoughts still on Rosanna and her tender heart . . . and on Aaron's sweet story about the yellow butterfly.

CHAPTER

Thirty-One

Wednesday after work, Clara noticed a spring wagon parked in her aunt's lane. Not wanting to interrupt in case another person needed some time alone with Aendi and a cup of sweet peppermint iced tea, Clara took more time than usual grooming Firefly.

A short while later, David and Yonnie Beiler came into the stable to clean out the horse stalls. Clara was glad about that, since that wasn't a task she cared to do.

"How're things?" David asked as she put away the grooming tools.

"Just fine," she said, suspecting he had more to say.

"Glad ya got to see Ella Mae's *Haus* plans Sunday," he said, bringing over the shovels and handing one to Yonnie. "We're lookin' forward to havin' her closer to us."

Clara nodded. "You'll take *gut* care of her."

"Well, you've been *wunnerbaar* yourself, Clara."

His compliment took her off guard. "I've learned so much from her this summer. She's a wise woman for sure."

Now Yonnie was nodding, walking toward the first stall to take Firefly out to pasture.

David glanced out the window toward the house. "Looks like Ella Mae's gettin' her stride back."

"Oh?"

"*Jah*, the deacon's son's in the *Haus* talkin' to her. I recognized his horse when we pulled in. Womenfolk ain't the only ones needin' a soothing word and a glass of nice, cold tea from time to time." David chuckled and headed for the first stall to start shoveling manure.

Clara was glad to hear it and smiled as she made her way to the stable door.

As Preacher Jonas Smucker gave the second sermon of the morning, stressing the importance of baptism and following the Lord throughout one's life, Clara recalled the wondrous Sunday two years ago when she'd knelt before her bishop and promised her life to God and the church. Remembering Aendi's account of Isaac Smucker's struggle to come to a place of surrender, she was again thankful her aunt had shared that redemptive story. *It helped me move past my experience with Tom and realize how one's choices can affect a family for generations.*

While the youth waited outside for their turn to be seated for the common meal, Lettie told Clara the bishop's wife's health had taken a sudden turn for the worse, and that's why she wasn't able to help today. Without delay, Clara hurried inside to offer her assistance to Nell Miller, Mattie's good friend. Nell seemed relieved to have someone wash dishes after the first seating for the older adults, and she was talkative, too. She asked how Clara liked staying with her aunt.

"I'm havin' the best summer," Clara said.

"Mattie says you're Aendi's right arm."

That was the last thing Clara would have expected to hear. She'd always had the feeling Mattie wasn't all that happy Clara had extended her stay. "Aendi Ella Mae was a *wunnerbaar* support to my Mamma when she was sufferin' . . . before she died. So it's the least I can do for her, though I've come to love her just as Mamma did."

"Well, ain't ya sweet," Nell said right out, a white flour-sack towel draped over her arm.

Embarrassed, Clara simply shrugged and rinsed the next plate.

After that batch of dishes was washed and dried, then placed on the table, which had been recently wiped off for the upcoming second serving, Clara enjoyed talking with the other womenfolk who were helping today. That included Tom Glick's Mamm, who mentioned he'd already made a couple of friends out in Kansas.

Clara was pleased to be so accepted here, even though everyone knew she was leaving for Indiana soon.

Right before Clara left on foot that evening for the Singing to be held in Nell's two-story bank barn, Yonnie, his wife, Annie, and their two little ones arrived to visit Aendi. Clara was delighted her aunt wouldn't be alone this evening.

Since Nell was a widow, her married nephew Ivan was there to help host the youth gathering. And Daniel Fisher's parents were present, along with the deacon and his wife, who sat facing the guys' side of the table. The several girls who Lettie said had reported the fellows with fancy courting buggies looked rather glum.

Ivan welcomed *die Youngie* and asked who had an August birthday. Two hands were raised. Reaching into his pocket, he took out a small pitch pipe and blew it to start the birthday song. After that, Ivan blew another note for the beginning of "Shall We Gather at the River."

Clara enjoyed sitting with Lettie, Katie, and Mary while singing. But it was sad to think of Rosanna at home, still too fragile to be involved. As soon as her young friend was able, though, Clara would sit with her and make her feel comfortable. She certainly hoped that might happen before she left for home.

Several times during the first song, Aaron caught her eye, and she could scarcely wait to go out with him again. What would they talk about this time? Would he mind her asking about his childhood?

All these thoughts and more scurried across her mind, and she regretted having such a short time left with him.

After her grandson and his family left for home, Ella Mae poured more iced peppermint tea for herself. Sitting there in her kitchen, she couldn't help but recall the visits from the two folks who'd recently come with a burden to share. Right then, she kept her promise by bowing her head and praying for them both. Out loud, she asked the Lord to help them forgive the faults of the people around them, and for His spirit to be with them as they endeavored to do that.

Even though both had come with heavy hearts, she'd felt uplifted by their visits. Knowing they'd entrusted her with their troubles and believed she could help them gave her a wonderful, warm feeling.

The bishop's wife suddenly came to mind. *I must visit her soon*, she thought, having heard how gravely ill she'd become. *So young to be dying.*

Eyeing the cookie jar, she stepped over to lift the lid and removed an oatmeal cookie. Then, missing Clara, she made her way outside to sit on the back porch with her tumbler of tea. She enjoyed the birdcalls as the daylight began to fade. The sky had a soft gleam to it, as if to remind her that the dawn would come again tomorrow. Very soon, a wood thrush began to sing its evening song, its timing linked to the sunset.

"O Father in heaven," she began to pray again, "use me to lift the spirits of the brokenhearted and suffering. Help me reach where they hurt and point them to Thee." She opened her eyes and saw the soft dappled sunlight on the flowers rimming her beloved greenhouse.

To think my son-in-law would move it to their place just to please me! she thought, thankful for his unexpected suggestion and thoughtfulness. And David and Mattie's son Yonnie and Annie had been kind tonight, too, bringing their toddlers over, which brought her such joy.

We raised some wonderful children together, Joseph. . . .

In that golden hour as the sun sank gently over the meadow beyond the barn, the idea of moving from this lovely old place with hundreds of happy memories suddenly seemed far less repugnant.

Perhaps I've acted like a stubborn mule.

Clara was surprised yet delighted when Aaron told her they'd be double-dating with his cousin Josiah Ebersol and Lettie after Singing. And Lettie seemed delighted, too.

So Lettie has a crush on Josiah. She smiled recalling what she'd said about those rose petals falling onto her friend's shoulder.

Both Aaron and Josiah had dressed in church clothes, even slipping on their black suit coats before walking out of the barn with Clara and Lettie, then helping them into the carriage, where Josiah and Lettie took the second seat. Clara was glad she'd worn her best blue dress from Preaching service, although of course she'd changed her organdy apron to a matching blue apron she'd recently made.

Clara enjoyed the chatter in Aaron's father's enclosed buggy. After a time, Aaron asked if they'd like to have some homemade root beer at his parents' house. Clara waited, letting Josiah speak up first and thinking she'd go along with whatever the fellows decided. But it struck her that Aaron didn't seem to mind that his parents would know he was seeing her—though as friendly as Leona had been, maybe she and Adam already suspected as much.

If so, how do they feel about Aaron seeing someone from a church district like mine in First Light?

"This way, Rosanna'll get to enjoy some *gut* fellowship tonight, too," Aaron was saying.

Clara glanced at Aaron at the reins and felt a great sense of respect for him. "You're a thoughtful Bruder," she said quietly.

Aaron smiled. "It'll be a nice surprise for her."

The rest of the evening was spent around

Leona's kitchen table, where Rosanna joined them, sitting beside Clara. And Leona didn't just provide the ice-cold root beer Aaron had promised. She brought out a three-layer chocolate fudge cake and offered a bowl of nuts, too.

Clara couldn't think of a better way to spend the evening than by cheering up Rosanna. And not once did it dawn on her that only one month was left till she'd be leaving for home.

It did later, though—as she was changing into her nightclothes—but she couldn't bear to think about it. She much preferred the memory of Aaron walking her slowly from the carriage toward Aendi's back porch at the end of the evening, just the two of them. As they strolled up the walkway, he'd even reached for her hand.

How she loved the feel of their fingers entwined! Then he'd asked to take her out for supper next Saturday evening. The way her heart fluttered, she wanted to remember it for always.

But how could this possibly work? Would their friendship be reduced to letters? And if she and Aaron actually fell in love, would they be doomed to wait years before they could be together, like Aendi's parents had? Besides, what could change to even allow them a life together, given Dat's assessment of the Hickory Hollow district's beliefs?

She reached to outen the gas lamp, and gazing into the darkness, she realized how very much she already cared for Aaron Ebersol. More than she'd expected. And this wasn't just about Dat. Would she be willing to live in such a strict church district even if her father weren't set on her returning home?

The new moon was not visible through her open widow, but in that moment, she yearned for its pearly light.

CHAPTER

Thirty-Two

Monday afternoon, Ella Mae saw Mattie pull into the lane, then watched as she came rushing up the walkway to the back door with a sad face. Was there bad news?

"Bishop John's wife died an hour ago," Mattie said breathlessly, her face flushed as she came into the kitchen. "The children, 'specially Hickory John and Nancy, are in shock, as is the bishop."

"Seems so sudden, *jah*?"

Mattie nodded. "I knew you'd wanna know right away so you could be prayin' . . . and maybe bake a casserole to take over there."

"Clara an' I will do that for sure." Ella Mae shook her head, feeling so sorry for the bishop, who was only thirty-seven and had five young children to take care of.

He'll need good help, O Lord, she prayed.

The following Wednesday after work, Aendi asked Clara to check the mailbox. She delivered her aunt's mail to her, then decided to sit by the rose arbor to read the latest letter from Bertie.

> *Dear Clara,*
> *How are you? I think of you so often and look forward to your return. We're counting the days now. I've never seen Dat so eager about anything. He says he'll be sending you money for your train fare soon.*

Clara read the rest of the letter—descriptions of the boys' summer activities and Bertie's days busily keeping up with the fresh produce and all the canning. But then Bertie mentioned this: *Eva has been asking about you, Clara. Ain't that sweet?* Bertie went on to say that she'd become better acquainted with Eva and surely Clara would, too, once she was home again and more settled.

More settled there? How could that be, when Aendi's here and has become so dear to me?

Clara clenched her jaw. Dat wasn't even asking if she was ready to come home, giving her no say in the matter at all. *Like I'm still a child.*

As for getting *better* acquainted with her step-Mamm eventually, Eva had seemingly cared little about her all this time. It surprised Clara that Eva had bothered to ask about her.

Frustrated, Clara plodded toward the house. But then she slowed, accepting reality, her heart sinking with every step.

From her kitchen window, Ella Mae could see something had upset Clara—terribly. And when the young woman came in the back door and forced a smile, Ella Mae knew her true emotions did not match that pasted-on expression one iota.

"What is it, dearie?"

Clara sighed and leaned against the counter, then removed her blue bandanna, revealing her hair bun. "Feelin' a little down, I guess." She sighed. "I'd really like to just stay here longer."

Ella Mae was thrilled. "Of course ya can, Clara. As long as ya want!" She studied her, wondering why she was so upset.

"*Denki.* But Dat would never agree," she said, looking ever so glum. "I wish I could say he'd understand why I want to stay. And I *do* want to, despite the differences and rigid rules on the youth."

Ella Mae felt sorry for her. "Have ya thought of writin' to your Dat 'bout your feelings?"

Clara shook her head. "If he wants me home, it's pointless to argue."

Ella Mae didn't want to jump ahead of herself, so she empathized silently.

"I don't know what to think. If I go home, I'll surely end up bein' a *Maidel*. There aren't any available young men my age in First Light—not who aren't kin." Clara stared at the floor for a moment, then straightened and said, "But I'm an adult, nearly twenty."

"That ya are."

"So I should be the one decidin' where I live," Clara said, tears brimming. "Truth be told, I've had such a *wunnerbaar-gut* time here, I'd rather not go home at all."

Ella Mae was aware that she'd made a number of friends, too. "Remember, dear, you're *Willkumm* here, even after I move. Ya heard Mattie say you can stay in the second bedroom upstairs in the new *Dawdi Haus*." She hoped she wasn't pressing too hard, but oh, her heart was right there with Clara's.

"I hadn't thought of that, but you're very kind, Aendi."

"With every ounce in me, I mean it."

Clara seemed to consider that, glancing at the ceiling, then back at Ella Mae. "I've got a job here with Vera, who really needs my help, and . . ." She paused, seeming to gather herself. "Well, there's somethin' else, too."

"Oh?" Ella Mae thought she might know where this was going.

Clara's face softened. "Maybe ya can guess what I'm about to say."

"I can hope, ain't so?" Ella Mae didn't want to broach the subject before Clara did.

"Aaron Ebersol asked me out for supper this Saturday evening, and I accepted. Ain't the first time we've gone out. I know it hasn't been long, but . . ."

Ella Mae slipped an arm around her waist. "A young woman your age who's seein' someone *wunnerbaar* has the right to tell her family she's changed her mind and wants to stay—if for no other reason, to see where things might lead with her young man."

"But what Dat wants me to do and what I want is all jumbled up. I mean, I'd never want to disobey him."

"I daresay if ya pray about what's in your heart and sleep on it, you'll know better what to do in the mornin'." Ella Mae walked to the stove to fill her teakettle. "Maybe some hot tea'll help, too."

This brought a fleeting smile.

"Do ya want honey in it or chust plain?" she asked Clara.

"Honey's fine. *Denki.*" Clara went to sit at the table, then leaned her face into her hands.

"*Ach*, don't try an' think too hard," Ella Mae said gently, wishing she could erase her sadness. "The Lord will walk with ya through this."

Clara looked at her. "I'll just sit here awhile, then help with supper after we have tea."

"Well, the roast is already in the oven, so ya can relax."

Clara straightened. "I can't believe I didn't smell the aroma when I came in. Must've been in a daze."

"Well, sure ya were, an' who wouldn't be? Everything ya seem to want is right here in the hollow, honey-girl."

"Everything 'cept my family. And my church membership, which might prove to be difficult if I decide to transfer."

Ella Mae kept her thoughts to herself on that. From what she could tell, Clara viewed her as a close friend, not just a great-aunt. But she was right. Her immediate family was a mighty long way from here. As for transferring membership, that was another looming question.

Clara has a big decision ahead of her.

Clara contemplated Bertie's letter—and Aendi's advice—as she baked a batch of snickerdoodle cookies, trying to focus her attention on the coming weekend. But that was a challenge. She was still chafing against Dat's no-discussion expectation that she return home. Of course, she hadn't told him she wanted to stay, giving him a chance to understand her point of view. It probably never occurred to him that she might.

While Clara baked, Aendi watered her many flowers. Clara glanced out the window from time to time and hated the thought of not seeing her aunt anymore.

She's like a dear Mammi to me.

Once the cookies were cooling on a rack, she opened all the windows to get a cross draft while the woodstove cooled down some. Then she headed out to the kitchen garden to pick zucchini squash, sweet corn, and more tomatoes than they could possibly eat. *Looks like we'll be canning homemade tomato soup and spaghetti sauce soon*, she thought, thankful to work alongside Aendi while she could.

Carrying the produce into the house, Clara again recalled Aendi's remark about sleeping on her decision. And not just sleeping on it but talking to God. *Will I really know what to do when I wake up tomorrow?*

And should I pray aloud this time? she wondered, knowing how confident yet humble her aunt sounded when she talked to the Lord about whatever was on her mind . . . and in her heart.

Will it make a difference?

CHAPTER

Thirty-Three

Clara awoke the next day with a strong sense of peace. She knew what to do, and it was a settled kind of feeling, as though the book of her life was turning to a new chapter.

Aendi had been right about opening her heart in prayer last night. Clara had spent time on her knees talking aloud to the Lord, trusting in Him and not in herself.

At breakfast, she told her aunt she looked forward to writing a letter to her father after prayer and Bible reading this evening, buoyed by this amazing peace and wanting to share with him what was truly on her heart.

While Clara had been working at Vera's and Aendi had been attending the funeral for the bishop's wife, the weekly publication of *The Budget* arrived in the porch mailbox. Clara brought it into the house with the letters for her aunt, then quickly looked for Aaron's column by scanning the index listing Lancaster County Amish communities.

When she found it, she read every word, impressed by Aaron's writing ability. Farther down the column, she was surprised to see a mention of the recent buggy race and accident, although it was discreetly written, with no names mentioned. *Interesting*, she thought, eager to tell Aaron she'd enjoyed reading his very first publication.

That evening, Clara and Aendi worked together on the last few spots of frayed piecework on the quilt. Her aunt was quite subdued, the funeral surely on her mind.

Carefully, Clara checked the seams on every inch of the border. "It's lookin' perty," she said, satisfied they had accomplished what they'd set out to do.

"Only a quilter knows the *wunnerbaargut* feelin' we have right now—conquerin' the challenge and persevering." Aendi's solemn face suddenly lit up. "Just think who might come across this quilt years from now and look at it with a happy heart."

Clara nodded. "There's love in every repair stitch, not to mention all the original stitches made so long ago."

Aendi suggested Clara hang it on a quilt rack in the spare room. "So you can admire it."

"Are ya sure?" Clara said, delighted yet surprised.

Aendi grinned, her eyes squinting shut a little. "Well now, if it wasn't for your help, this heirloom prob'ly wouldn't've been repaired by now."

Together they carried the quilt into Clara's room, where they placed it tenderly on the bed till Clara could run up and get the wooden quilt rack from the sewing room.

Once they'd arranged the quilt, Clara stepped back to take in the lovely heirloom. The dark ginger background with twenty nine-patch blocks of alternating Miniature Variable Stars and sky blue squares had been fully restored. She felt honored to have partnered with her aunt on this challenging project.

"Such a *gut* feelin'," Aendi murmured, standing there with her. "My dear Mamm would be so pleased."

Spontaneously, they reached to embrace each other.

Their Bible reading and prayer time was poignant to Clara that evening. Aendi opened to the book of Isaiah, chapter fifty-eight, and began to read. Then at verse eleven, she slowed down. "'And the LORD shall guide thee continually, and satisfy thy soul in drought, and make fat thy bones: and thou shalt be like a watered garden, and like a spring of water, whose waters fail not.'" She stopped reading to ask Clara if she understood the verse.

Clara could envision Aendi watering her beloved dahlias and all the flower beds on days when rain showers didn't last long. "Well, doesn't it mean that God's leading never stops? He guides us through *all* the days of our lives."

"That's right, and not just durin' certain times or when we're falterin', *nee*. He takes our hand and makes the way before us ever so clear. I pray that for Bishop John now, too." There was a catch in her voice. "The poor, dear man's all alone . . . and with young ones to raise."

Clara nodded, awful sorry the bishop had lost his wife at such a young age. She slowly turned the conversation to the letter she was about to write, deciding to share more details.

"Aendi, I wholeheartedly believe I'm s'posed to ask my Dat to ship my clothing and other personal items here, an expense I'll pay for." She sighed with relief as the words fell from her own lips. "I'll tell him that, after prayin' 'bout it, I believe God wants me here in Hickory Hollow. I hope when he thinks it through, he'll understand."

She also shared that it was only fair for her father to hear from her that she'd met a kind and God-fearing young man who seemed interested in her. "I don't think he'd want me to miss an opportunity to possibly find love and have a family."

"All that sounds like a *gut* idea," Aendi said, her little head bobbing up and down. "I'll pray your father accepts your decision without further stress for either of you."

Clara's heart warmed. "*Denki*, Aendi."

After Clara headed to the kitchen to write her letter, Ella Mae made her way to her own room. There she thanked God for touching Clara's precious heart and giving her the courage to send her father such a challenging message. "Continue to be near Clara durin' this time, O Lord, I pray." She tucked in a prayer for the grieving bishop and his young family, as well.

Looking around the bedroom, her eyes fell on Joseph's house robe, still hanging on the door. She sighed deeply, stepped to the small closet, and found Joseph's hardly worn house slippers on the floor. Maybe it had something to do with attending the funeral today, but she picked them up and carried them across the room, where she set them beside the door. In the morning, she wanted to remember what she now felt she ought to do.

It's a start, she thought, taking a deep breath.

During breakfast the next morning, Ella Mae told Clara what she'd decided to do with Joseph's almost-new slippers and the house robe she'd made for him the Christmas before he passed. "Samuel Lapp's older brother's long been a widower an' looks to be 'bout the same size as my Joseph."

"You must feel it's the right time," Clara replied, pouring maple syrup on her buttermilk pancakes.

"Ain't sure, really, but gonna try. Hopin' I won't break down and realize I can't give 'em up."

Clara looked at her with a concerned expression. "Years ago, Mamma told my Mammi Bender that she wasn't discarding her memories by givin' away Dawdi's clothing and whatnot."

"'Tis interesting." Ella Mae pondered the wisdom behind what Lillian had said. "I need to get that in my noggin." She sighed, stirring sugar into her coffee. "I daresay I know why I clung to Joseph's things for this long." Then she nodded. "*Denki* for sharin' that. The Lord surely knew I needed to hear it."

Clara smiled so sweetly, such a comforting gesture.

Right after dishes were redded up and put away, she placed Joseph's nice slippers and his house robe into a large paper bag. Clara hitched up for her, and soon Ella Mae was off to test her resolve. It occurred to her that Mattie, being the bishop's wife's sister-in-law, might soon be dealing with the same issues of clothing and personal effects, as well.

Ella Mae removed Joseph's belongings from the brown grocery bag in the front room of Mose Lapp's *Dawdi Haus*, where he lived next to his married son and family. "These were Joseph's," she told Mose. "The slippers were worn only once or twice."

"I've been in need of a house robe, since mine wore out," Mose replied.

"May's well put this one to *gut* use, then." But she felt ever so reticent now that she was here.

Mose stood and took the robe, eyeing it. "I s'pect ya made this?"

She nodded. She'd wondered how she'd feel with someone other than Joseph handling his robe. It was the thing she'd buried her face in and sobbed in for so many weeks after the funeral . . . the robe that had brought her such comfort.

But now she was surprised to feel a measure of enjoyment seeing Mose make over the robe, then try on the slippers—keeping his socks on, he said, in case they didn't fit.

"I appreciate this kindly," Mose said, tugging on his long gray beard, so like Joseph's. All married men were required to grow a beard, of course, and they kept them even after their wives passed.

"Then I'm glad." She stepped back, toward the door.

"Some womenfolk would've used this to make a quilt, ya know," Mose added.

Goodness, she could never have brought herself to cut it up. "Seems ya needed it more than I needed another quilt."

Mose chuckled at that, keeping the slippers on and carefully folding the robe.

"Well, I'll be gettin' on with my day." She said good-bye, then let herself out the back screen door.

But as she took the first steps toward her buggy, she heard Mose call out, "If there's anything else of Joseph's . . ."

She kept on walking, not ready to commit to that yet. *In God's good time*, she thought, untying her horse.

Ella Mae looked forward to canning some homemade tomato soup from the abundance of tomatoes ripening in her kitchen garden. And when she arrived home, she and Clara began preparing a big batch. While they worked, she told Clara about her errand. "Mose seemed happy to have them."

"How do ya feel 'bout it now?" Clara asked, looking sympathetic.

"Hasn't hit me yet, I don't think."

"Might not right away."

This was a bigger step than she'd realized, but on the other hand, she'd seen how thankful Mose Lapp was to receive the robe and slippers. "Step by step, ya know," Ella Mae said, curious to see how such a task felt going forward, especially when it came to Joseph's church clothing. Was she ready to take an even bigger step?

CHAPTER
Thirty-Four

Clara sensed an air of expectancy as she entered the Amish-owned restaurant with Aaron Saturday evening. She quickly realized they had the place mostly to themselves, likely because they'd arrived before five o'clock. *Aaron must prefer it to be quieter*, she thought as they were seated.

Her date was dressed almost like he was going to church, in a long-sleeved white shirt and black broadfall trousers, only his black suit coat missing. Clara had worn her purple dress and matching apron, feeling more relaxed now that she'd sent off her letter to Dat.

Aaron's gaze met hers across the table for two, his expression filled with curiosity. She could tell by the look in his golden-brown eyes and the smile on his handsome face. Of course, there was no way he could possibly know she'd decided to stay on in Hickory Hollow. No one else knew but Aendi, and it wasn't her news to tell.

"You seem mighty happy tonight," Aaron said, handing her a menu.

She nodded.

"I'm happy, too," he said. "Can ya guess why?"

Any number of reasons floated through her mind, but she shook her head.

"I'm enjoying spending as many evenings with ya as I possibly can before . . ." Despite his smile, he looked a little sad. But then he quickly changed the topic. "Feel free to order anything ya like."

"*Denki.*" She smiled back at him. "Do ya have a favorite?"

"I've only eaten here twice before, both times with my parents. Once was for Rosanna's sixteenth birthday, and the other was for my twentieth." Aaron went on to say what he'd ordered those times, then added, "But I want you to choose something *you'll* enjoy, Clara."

She scanned the offerings, the homestyle pork roast catching her eye. The list of side dish options was long, and she ran her finger all the way down before choosing scalloped potatoes and buttered lima beans.

A waitress took their order, and Clara reached for her white linen napkin and unfolded it. Then, feeling Aaron's eyes on her, she placed it in her lap and raised her head.

"I hope this doesn't seem too sudden," Aaron said quietly. "But I've been praying 'bout somethin'."

Clara folded her hands in her lap lest she tremble.

"We've had only a few dates," he continued, "but I'd like you to be my steady girl."

Clara's heart sped up.

"Would ya consider letting me court ya till ya leave . . . and then by letter afterward?" His eyes were soft, his smile sweet. "I don't wanna lose ya, Clara."

She fought back happy tears, her eyes fixed on his. "I'd like that, but—"

An instant frown appeared on his brow.

"What I mean is, I've decided to stay in Hickory Hollow."

Aaron's face relaxed into a most pleasing smile. "All the better." He reached across the table, and she was about to bring her hand up from her lap when the waitress returned with a pitcher of water and began to fill their glasses.

Once they were alone again, Clara told him about Bertie's letter. "I prayed earnestly and slept on it, like Aendi Ella Mae suggested, and in the mornin', I knew I was s'posed to stay here."

Aaron's eyes shone, his face in a perpetual grin. "Since you're baptized, I've already talked with my father, who I greatly trust, 'bout the differences between our church districts. 'Specially the ordinances. It impressed him that on your own accord you made your dresses and capes to fit in here."

Back when she'd made that decision, she'd had no idea how important it would be to Aaron and his father. Maybe to Bishop Beiler, too?

"Dat says he and Mamm want to get better acquainted with ya. I realize this approach to courtin' is different from how most couples do things round here, but I don't mind bending the old tradition a little if spending some time with ya makes my parents feel more comfortable."

They're nervous because I'm from a less traditional church. Clara's eyes met his. "If that's what you and your family want, of course I'll come over."

"Will tomorrow evening suit for supper?" he asked. "I can stop by for ya round four-thirty." She assumed she'd been invited then because tomorrow was an off-Sunday, an ideal time with no Singing.

"I'll let Aendi Ella Mae know not to plan for me."

Aaron asked about the courting traditions in Indiana.

"They're actually similar to what you're suggesting. We interact a lot with each other's families, including them in our time together. And since I'm close to Aendi Ella Mae, maybe she won't mind if I invite ya for a meal sometime, too." She paused, still catching her breath at how quickly he'd become serious about her. "I mean, if you've never tasted her crispy fried chicken, you'll be glad ya came for supper."

Aaron chuckled. "Sounds like we have a *gut* plan, ain't?"

Nodding, Clara agreed. Even so, she wondered how this courtship would work with both fathers seemingly concerned—and for the selfsame reasons.

At four-thirty the next afternoon, the scent from summersweet shrubs hung in the air as Clara stepped outside to meet Aaron. He was pulling up to the back walkway in his black courting buggy.

"My Mamm wants us to eat on the porch," Aaron said after they'd greeted each other. "My younger siblings are excited 'bout it." He grinned. "They're also lookin' forward to Mamm's peach cream pie."

Clara wanted to pinch herself at how handsome her beau looked in his crisp white shirt and black trousers. He also wore tan suspenders, which went nicely with his straw hat.

She would be the guest of honor this evening, or so it sounded. "I love anything with peaches," she said.

She was still wondering what his father would have to say.

"Rosanna requested a seat next to ya," Aaron said, smiling brightly. "She's liked ya since the first day yous met at Vera's Quilts."

"She told ya that?"

"She volunteered it when I confided that we're courtin' now," he said, eyes twinkling. "I really trust her opinion."

Right away when they arrived, Clara spotted a long table laid with a tablecloth on the back porch, a glass fruit bowl in the center. "Hope your Mamm didn't go to a lot of trouble."

"Oh, you just wait. She wanted to do somethin' special, and fun, too, for this first supper with ya." He got out and came around for her, then walked her up the porch steps, where his Mamm was just coming out the back door, face glistening with perspiration.

"'Twas much too hot inside," Leona said, welcoming her with a big smile. "The girls are 'bout done setting the table."

Clara could see Rosanna and her next younger sister, as well as another girl of about eight, setting out the utensils. They whispered to each other as they worked.

Aaron excused himself to unhitch the horse, which made Clara think she'd be spending the whole evening there.

She noticed the nice spread of food coming out dish by dish. Between them, Leona and her three daughters carried two large platters of chicken salad sandwiches and several serving bowls of sides—Jell-O salad that looked like it might be strawberry, pea salad, three-bean salad, and applesauce with cinnamon.

I'm so grateful to be welcomed so warmly, Clara thought, offering to help. But Leona shook her head. "We're nearly ready to sit down. As soon as Adam and the boys wash up."

Once the whole family had gathered at the table, Aaron's father greeted Clara, then introduced her to his younger children, also mentioning their ages—golden-blond Arie, twelve; wiry Reuben, ten; freckle-faced Leta, eight; and towheaded Lucas, seven. Then it was time for the blessing over the food, and heads bowed for the silent prayer.

As the serving dishes were passed first to Aaron's father, Leona mentioned what a lovely evening it was, although Clara wasn't sure if she meant the weather or their gathering. All the children bobbed their heads, though, including Aaron, who sat directly across from Clara. His eyes again twinkled as he looked at her. Rosanna, sitting between Clara and Leona, reached for her lemonade as Clara tried to enjoy the relaxed atmosphere and Aaron's family.

She noticed Leta look first at Aaron and then at her, then back at Aaron again. Clara was pretty sure she was the mischief of the family. Reuben was the most serious of the younger four, Clara assumed by his overly polite demeanor and the way he rarely spoke when passing the food to his jabbering sisters.

But their eldest brother, Aaron, was obviously the one they looked up to. That was how it had always been at home with her brother Calvin, too, Clara recalled.

The family banter calmed once the food was on each plate and the eating commenced.

Clara's eyes were drawn to Aaron as she ate, and when he met her gaze, she felt his encouragement. Did he know what was ahead, what was on his father's mind?

Adam did most of the talking, especially later when Leona, Rosanna, and Arie rose to clear the table. He seemed particularly interested in her hometown, but his questions didn't indicate any sort of judgment. He had a more curious tone, if anything.

When he inquired about tractors, she told him they used them only for filling silo, and he said they did the same there. She also mentioned they had motorized lawnmowers and rototillers, and Adam leaned back in his chair at the head of the table, his arms folded as if he was contemplating that fact.

"Here, we only have push mowers, and I doubt that'll ever change," he finally said, picking a bread crumb off the table. "What 'bout Bible studies and Sunday school? Do ya have those out there?"

Now he sounded concerned, though his tone was still congenial. Clara was fairly sure her father would speak the same way if she were old-style Amish and her beau was more progressive.

"Some of the younger couples have monthly Bible studies, and others do, as well," Clara told him, deciding it was best to be forthright. "But there's no Sunday school. My Dat always leads us in family worship, though, and when we were little, he'd teach us a verse every week or so. He said God's Word is essential for godly livin', and that if we hid it away in our hearts, we'd be able to stand strong against the temptation to sin."

"Committing verses to memory?" Adam asked, leaning forward now.

"He wanted us to keep certain ones close

to our hearts . . . the wisdom for growin' up in God's ways, he would say."

Nodding, Adam ran his fingers through his untrimmed brown beard, clearly pondering all she'd said.

Clara didn't mention it, but her father and brothers trimmed their beards some, which by the looks of all the older men she'd seen in Hickory Hollow wasn't happening here. She figured if she and Aaron ever traveled to Indiana, he'd find out about the beard trimming then. But if Adam knew about it now, would even something small like that be a hindrance to his approving of their courtship?

After Leona's delicious peach cream pie and coffee, Clara, Aaron, and his parents remained around the table long after Rosanna and the younger children left, the girls to do the dishes and the boys to resume their barn chores. But now the conversation had less to do with her growing up out of state than about the Hickory Hollow church's beliefs and *Ordnung*.

Again, Adam was easygoing in the way he spoke, though the information he was sharing with Clara was significant and something she could tell he wanted her to know.

Does Aaron's father worry the bishop will think I'll bring practices from my background that could alter what happens here? Is there actually a chance I'd do that without being aware of it? And if so, will it keep me from being accepted as a member here?

All these questions raced through her mind.

On the ride back to Aendi's, Clara assumed Aaron might comment on this first family meal together. As fond of him as she was, she certainly hoped she'd measured up in his father's estimation.

"That was quite an evening for ya," Aaron said when they were settled in his open buggy and on their way.

"I enjoyed getting to know your family."

"You were so gracious to answer Dat's questions, Clara." He looked over at her. "That means a lot to me."

She was taken by his thoughtful attempt to put her at ease. "I didn't mind."

"As ya know, our bishop wants to protect the way our church district is—quite traditional compared to other districts. There won't be any Bible studies takin' place here."

"I understand."

"Have ya attended them?" he asked.

She shook her head. "*Nee.*"

"So ya wouldn't miss that, then."

"I enjoy reading my Bible on my own."

He nodded. "I do, too. Both the German and the King James Bibles." He paused, then said, "On another subject, I'd like to take ya to meet my Onkel Caleb, the scribe for *The Budget* I told you about. Would ya like to do that next Saturday? I can pick you up after supper. Say, around six-thirty?"

She agreed, looking forward to it. *I love spending time with Aaron*, she thought, hoping his father wouldn't ponder the things she'd told him and then put the nix on their courtship. *Could that happen?*

CHAPTER

Thirty-Five

While they washed and dried the breakfast dishes the next morning, Clara asked her aunt what she thought of inviting Aaron over for a meal sometime. "It doesn't have to be soon, but since his family had me over there for supper, I wondered what you'd think of returnin' the favor?"

"Honey-girl, if ya want to do that, it's all right with me."

"Would ya be willin' to make your crispy fried chicken?"

Aendi gave a little titter. "Better yet, why don't *you* make my recipe? Show off your cookin' skills, *jah*?"

"*Gut* idea." Clara dried the second coffee mug. "I think you'll like havin' Aaron over. I know I will."

Clara looked forward to a nice supper here. There'd be no grilling of Aaron from Aendi Ella Mae, that was certain.

A letter from Clara's father arrived on Friday, much sooner than she'd expected. *Dat must have written back the same day and managed to catch an early mail pickup.*

Clara was still very glad she'd written him about her decision to remain in Hickory Hollow, an opportunity to choose her words extra carefully rather than speaking to him by phone. And because she was certain this was what she was supposed to do, she was actually looking forward to reading his response. Surely he'd support her after hearing all the reasons for her to stay, especially finding a beau, and about what peace she'd found.

Reading his letter on the front porch, though, she quickly discovered her father was determined to make a dissenting point.

I wonder if you have forgotten that I already extended your initial week's visit there and agreed for you to stay through the summer. And now you're indicating you don't want to come home at all!

Clara hadn't expected him to mention their past agreement. Clearly, he was upset.

> *Let me remind you, daughter, that you made your baptismal vow in the church here.*

This struck a blow, as she'd hoped this might not be a concern. Others had been able to transfer their church memberships in the past, her brothers included.

> *One other thing, Clara. I have no way of knowing the dedication of the young man you're seeing. If he's only focused on following the Ordnung, you might be tempted to go backward in your own faith and upbringing. Remember, we can't save ourselves by following rules. Does your beau understand that?*

Clara sighed when she finished reading, then refolded the letter. *Dat's as concerned about Aaron as Aaron's father was about me. But Dat's more pointed about his concerns.* These were significant issues to her father—and to her, too—yet nothing she'd gathered at Preaching services here had set off alarm bells.

As for what Aaron thought about the local *Ordnung*, he'd never openly shared that with her, but his life definitely indicated his devotion to Christ. And he'd been baptized, giving his whole life to God.

She stared down at the letter, saddened and upset by her father's displeasure.

On their trip to Saturday market in Bird-in-Hand the following afternoon, Ella Mae noticed Clara's gloomy demeanor, which lingered from yesterday evening, when Clara hadn't seemed interested in eating much supper despite Ella Mae's tasty cabbage rolls on a platter in front of her. But not wanting to pry, Ella Mae said nothing.

Then Ella Mae remembered seeing Clara bring an opened envelope into the house yesterday and carry it to her room. Could it be she'd already received a response from her father?

"I hope you're up to goin' today," she said as Clara held the driving lines.

"I'll be okay." Clara's voice sounded lower than usual . . . and flat.

Ella Mae let it be, hoping the market atmosphere might help lift the dear girl's spirits—get her mind off whatever was troubling her.

Clara was glad for the chance to be with Aendi. Dat's comments were still troubling, and the best way to put them behind her for a few hours was to occupy herself with other things.

At the farmers market in Bird-in-Hand,

they stopped to look at rows and rows of homemade canned goods. Aendi talked to the woman managing the stand for a while, and Clara heard them chattering about the young new scribe who'd written the Hickory Hollow column for *The Budget*. She smiled, hearing Aaron's name mentioned so favorably.

Later, when they came upon the vendor for the pretzel-wrapped hot dogs, her aunt suggested they purchase two to eat while strolling along. Clara didn't feel hungry, but she waited while Aendi paid for hers.

They wandered past the crafts and quilts, her aunt pointing out the color arrangements of several she liked as she nibbled on her hot dog. Clara especially enjoyed seeing the lavish display of silk flowers in so many colors.

After a while, Aendi wanted something to drink and offered to pay for a lemonade or apple cider for them both. Clara accepted and chose the cider.

"Won't be long now till apples are in season an' we'll have us a cider-makin' frolic," she told Clara, obviously trying to cheer her up. "I'll invite my children, grandchildren, an' greats in the Big Valley to come. I'd love for ya to meet them, 'specially my grandson Clyde and his wife, Susannah. They're chust itchin' to buy *mei Haus* and move here."

Clara nodded, wondering if Dat might

show up before apple harvest in an attempt to haul her home. *He sounded that miffed.*

Clara could not hold back her emotions at supper. She'd kept them tucked away for as long as she could all day, but while Aendi was praying aloud for the meal, the floodgates opened. Sniffling, Clara pulled a hankie from her pocket and wiped her eyes.

Lord Jesus, help me do Thy will and Thine alone.

"What's-a matter, dearie?" her aunt asked when she raised her head. "Can ya talk 'bout it?"

Clara told her about Dat's letter, struggling not to cry. "He's even questioning Aaron's faith."

"Let's take this to the Lord in prayer." Aendi reached for Clara's hand, and when she bowed her head again, Clara did, as well. "Most gracious Father in heaven," her aunt began, "we come to Thee with young Clara's concerns."

Clara managed to gather her wits while she washed her face and freshened her hair bun in preparation for her date with Aaron. And by the time he arrived, her eyes weren't puffy anymore. She even asked her aunt if she looked okay.

Aendi opened her arms to embrace her and said she was the "pertiest little thing ever. And I mean that."

Clara was heartened. Aendi had a special way of making her feel that everything would be all right, even while she had such apprehension over her father's letter.

The ride to Aaron's uncle's place was pleasant, and Aaron seemed exceptionally happy to see her. He talked animatedly about introducing her to his Onkel Caleb. "I've always looked up to him," he said. "I think you'll like him, too."

Clara was delighted to sit with Aaron in his courting carriage, still amazed at how they'd ended up together in such a short time.

The minute they walked onto Caleb Ebersol's back porch and he shuffled slowly to the screen door to greet them with a warm welcome, Clara knew there was something intriguing about the man. His gentle spirit shone through his countenance, reminding her in some ways of Aendi.

Caleb opened the door, then put out his trembling hand to shake hers and invited them inside. Stiffly, he made his way to a chair in the front room and eased himself into it with a grunt.

Aaron carried most of the conversation at first, sharing some of the interesting back-and-forth he'd experienced with his editor in Sugarcreek for his first column in *The Budget*.

"*Ach*, things'll get easier as ya continue workin' together," Caleb assured Aaron as he nodded, his thin gray beard long enough to reach his knees when seated.

Clara enjoyed the friendly interaction between the two men, content to fold her hands in her lap and simply observe.

After a while Caleb asked her how it was she'd come to visit Hickory Hollow.

"It started with my Mamma's old desk and the many letters Ella Mae Zook wrote to her over the years."

"Ya don't say?" Caleb's head wavered gently, never stopping—a symptom of his disease.

She explained that the thoughtful and caring way the letters were written had stirred up a desire to meet her mother's favorite relative.

"And now Ella Mae's your favorite, too, ain't she?" Caleb's lips parted in a lovely smile.

Clara was quick to reply. "She's very dear to me."

"Dozens of womenfolk—and some men, too—would have to agree. And that peppermint tea of hers!"

"Ya mean you've tasted it?" Clara asked.

"Once or twice, *jah*." He nodded. "So ya say Ella Mae's letters brought ya here?"

Before Clara could answer, Aaron looked at her with a winning smile and said, "Thanks to Ella Mae's letter-writin' skills, I met my Clara."

My Clara. She couldn't believe he'd said that!

"Well, those letters and the Good Lord, too, don't forget." Caleb's eyes sparkled. "I'm pleased ya brought her over to meet me."

Aaron leaned his shoulder lightly against hers as they sat there on the sofa. "You'll be seein' a lot more of her, I hope."

"Ya hope?" Caleb looked puzzled.

Aaron merely nodded, and Clara wondered if his father had perhaps talked more with him about her. "Courtship takes time," he said flatly.

"But not too long once ya've found the girl." Caleb's hands shook as he managed to clasp them, then raise them in silent applause.

"Sometime, maybe you can show me some of the columns you wrote," Clara said, changing the subject.

Caleb's eyes softened. "Oh, I s'pect they're round here somewheres."

Then she remembered. "Come to think of it, Aendi Ella Mae's attic is full of old copies of *The Budget*—boxes of 'em."

"Well, I wrote the Hickory Hollow columns for fifty-some years. There were times I felt like preachin' a little in them columns, but I tried to stick with the way the editors wanted the community news presented."

Clara's ears perked up. "What sorta preachin'?"

"Oh, just things 'bout God's presence bein' seen and felt daily. I mean, if we pay close attention and observe with an open heart, we know He's with us as plain as the dawn." Here, Caleb patted his heart.

Clara understood why Caleb had been such an influence on Aaron through the years. "Were ya ever nominated for minister?" she asked.

"Several times. But my name was never found in the lot." He glanced toward the ceiling. "The Good Lord had other plans. I *have* shared His love with all my children, grandchildren, and greats, though. Never missed an opportunity. A lovin' father and Dawdi must do all he can to pass on the faith."

Clara smiled, appreciating that Caleb seemed to share Ella Mae's sincere beliefs.

She got through the visit without thinking much about Dat, but while she and Aaron rode back to Aendi's, she told him about her father's letter.

"Have you written him back?" Aaron asked, glancing at her.

"*Nee*, not yet. I'm still thinkin' and prayin' 'bout how to respond this time." She paused. "He's interested in knowin' what *you* believe, Aaron." She'd really hesitated to bring this up, considering it was such a personal matter.

Aaron held the driving lines with his right hand and reached for hers with his left. "I can assure ya I've given my life over to the Lord Jesus. Also, I'm in good standin' with the church here." He squeezed her hand gently. "Is there anything I can do to make this easier for you . . . and your father? It seems challenging for ya right now."

What Aaron had just said confirmed what she already believed about him—that he belonged to the Lord. "*Denki*. Just pray that all will go well. I really love livin' here, so I want my father to agree on that, too."

"We'll convince him together." He smiled so sweetly.

I really hope so.

But did Aaron's own father also still need convincing? Based on what Aaron said about courtship taking time, she wondered.

CHAPTER
Thirty-Six

Returning from buying some nonperishable items for Aendi at the General Store, Clara noticed the little red flag was finally down on the mailbox. Making her way to the front porch after putting her purchases away, she lifted the lid, reached in for the mail, and carried it inside before placing it on the kitchen counter.

Sorting through the stack, she spotted a letter addressed to her in her father's handwriting. Another one so soon? The last one had come a mere three days ago, and she hadn't even answered it yet.

Both worry and trepidation immediately filled her heart as she headed back to the front room, then sat down to open the envelope.

> *Dear Clara,*
>
> *After reading about a rather alarming buggy-racing incident in* The Budget, *I'm quite worried about what is going on with the youth there in Hickory Hollow. So I'm sending the enclosed money order for your train fare home, hoping you'll change your mind after my last letter.*
>
> *I'll keep this short, Clara, but please, for your own safety, consider returning home as soon as possible.*
>
> *Yours, Dat*

Clara sighed. Despite understanding her father's concern, she was terribly frustrated—and stressed. He'd read Aaron's column, and her beau's report of the accident had caused him to fret enough to want her home directly.

Taking several deep breaths, she carried the letter to her room, where she placed the money order on the dresser. "What should I do *now*, Lord?" she whispered. "Please help me know how to reply. And give Dat an understanding heart."

She began to weep, unable to hold back the tears.

After a time, a gentle knock came at her door, then Aendi's soft voice. "Are ya cryin', dearie?"

Clara brushed her tears away and rose to open the door. "*Kumme en*," she said. "I need to talk to ya."

Aendi sat on the one chair while Clara sat on the bed and told her about Dat's latest letter. "He really wants me to come home now, worried as he is." Clara noticed how calm her aunt looked, sitting there with the late-afternoon light coming through the window.

"Far as I can tell, not much is different from the last letter to this one, really," Aendi said slowly. "He chust wants his daughter safe . . . in every way."

"He's clearly worried."

"Well, seems there's some wiggle room there, dear. He wants ya to *consider* goin' home, ain't so?"

Aendi was as measured as usual. "*Jah*. But I think he means right away instead of waiting till after Labor Day."

"Still, your Dat's reacting like a caring father," Aendi said. Then she added, "Yet one full of fear."

"And *I'm* afraid—that I have no say now."

Her aunt shook her head thoughtfully, eyes on Clara. "Over the years, I've found the voice of fear ain't always to be trusted."

Clara should have expected this kind of reaction from her wise aunt. "While I've been prayin', I thought of writin' a letter to my bishop back home, asking about a church transfer."

The older woman smiled. "Prob'ly a *gut* idea."

"But what 'bout Dat's concerns 'bout the youth here?"

Her aunt scrunched up her face. "I daresay you're bein' courted by the cream of the crop, so maybe start your letter to your father with that?"

Clara understood—and she wasn't a bit surprised Aendi recognized that she and Aaron were already to that stage in their relationship.

"And should I tell him the bishop's come down hard on any reckless drivin' amongst *die Youngie*, too?" Clara asked. "And that the fellas know the consequences will be severe if they do?"

Nodding repeatedly, Aendi smiled. "See there? Ya know the answers. Don't need me to tell ya."

Clara felt some better. "And we didn't even have tea!"

Now her aunt was grinning. "Speakin' of that, let's have us some iced tea and a cookie or two. Sweets have a way of helpin' sometimes, *jah*?" She rose and made her way into the hall.

Clara followed her to the kitchen, glad

she'd expressed her qualms to God and then to Aendi. *I mustn't hold back anymore.*

On the edge of dusk that evening, Clara finally wrote to Dat, telling him she'd received both his letters and had carefully considered her response.

First she let him know that her beau, Aaron, was a safe driver. *You don't have to worry at all.* She also shared that Bishop Beiler had put a quick halt to any further racing. *Hickory Hollow is a beautiful and safe community.*

Then she brought up her desire to contact the bishop back home to explain why she wanted to transfer her membership to this church district. She hoped this would satisfy some of the concern her father had expressed in his first letter on the subject.

You wondered about my beau's piety, but I've observed nothing but goodness and kindness in his life—and patience, too. He has a deep and abiding faith in the Lord, and he reads both his Bibles daily. I'm also getting to know his family. Interestingly, Aaron's father is curious about my spiritual standing, too, as well as the differences between our churches' ordinances. It's obvious that you and Adam Ebersol both care about your children and want God's will for us . . . just as Aaron and I do.

Clara felt much calmer as she signed off—*With love, your daughter, Clara*—enclosing the money order.

Oh, how she hoped this letter might help her father see into her heart on these important matters and why she felt led to stay in Hickory Hollow despite his concerns.

May it be so, dear Lord.

The next morning, Ella Mae headed out to visit Sylvia Riehl while Clara ironed her clothes. It was also a good time to drop off Joseph's church clothes at Mose Lapp's, since he'd been so pleased with the slippers and house robe.

It's time someone else wears them, she thought, still appreciating Clara's comment about how giving Joseph's clothes away didn't mean also getting rid of the memories.

Up the road, Ella Mae noticed the neighbors' cattle wandering under the willows near the creek bank. *A pleasant sight,* she thought, never taking for granted nature's beauty. She'd loved bringing in the cows for afternoon milking starting when she was only five years old, talking low and sweet to them like Mamm taught her. Such happy days. Those memories were still vivid.

She thanked God right then for her clear mind. *Something not everyone my age enjoys.*

Insects tapped against the windshield as she drove, a reminder to clean the outside of the entire carriage. Thankful each day for Clara's dependable help, she realized the young woman would undoubtedly want to do that for her, too. Ever so many times she'd come into the kitchen to find Clara prepping a meal, washing each leaf of newly cut lettuce two or three times before placing them on paper towels, then slicing other garden-fresh veggies for a colorful salad.

Lillian taught her daughter well. If only she could see Clara here with me now.

She wondered if writing to Clara's father to tell him how well she was doing and what a tremendous help she was around the house might help in some small way.

I'll talk this over with Clara.

The kitchen seemed too quiet with Aendi gone from the house, but Clara had enjoyed making and eating breakfast together. And there'd been no need to discuss her father's letter further—a relief.

As she ironed, she planned the letter to her home bishop. She actually looked forward to writing to him and wanted to start as soon as she folded the ironing board and put it away. The iron would take awhile to cool, so she'd let it stand on the counter.

Later, sitting at the kitchen table to write, she knew she must get the wording right the first time. There'd be no opportunity for a second letter to make her important request. And once she was satisfied with what she'd written, she'd send the letter off with a prayer.

It was possible that her father would let the bishop know her letter was coming, even try to dissuade him from granting the transfer, but the bishop always looked to God for wisdom. *Shouldn't Dat be happy that I've met someone like Aaron, especially now that I've explained he can be trusted?*

As for her bishop, Clara recalled how kind he'd always been toward her family, especially after Mamma's passing. But she'd never talked with him alone, much less needed to write a letter to him. She also knew some bishops disliked losing their devout youth to another church district, especially if theirs was a very small district like First Light's. Years ago, their bishop had been disappointed when her older brothers moved to Jamesport after working at a construction site there for weeks, meeting their sweethearts, and deciding to settle there in Missouri.

Maybe that's an underlying reason Dat's so reluctant for me to stay here, she thought suddenly. *He lost Calvin and Harley, then Mamma . . . and now me.*

Ella Mae headed straight to her room after her visits with Sylvia and Mose, still unsure how she felt with most of Joseph's clothing gone. Closing the door behind her, she sat on the edge of the bed and looked at the wooden pegs on the wall where his for-good clothes had hung.

Sighing, she got up and moved some of her best dresses and capes to those pegs, giving her clothes more space. Then she hung her own bathrobe on the hook on the back of the door. "There," she murmured, stepping back to take in that side of the room.

Then, moving to the window, she looked out at the dahlias, blooming beautifully, and recalled the day Joseph had planted them for her—just where she wanted them, encircling the little cottage greenhouse in the garden. He'd stopped working halfway through to tell her what a *wunnerbaar-gut* idea this had been and kissed her right then and there.

"The memories are still strong," she whispered, grateful.

Turning, she headed down the hallway to the kitchen, only a wee bit blue.

Clara cleaned her room Wednesday morning, then swept and mopped all the main-level floors. When she'd finished, her aunt surprised her by asking, "What would ya think if I were to write to your father on your behalf?"

"Aw, Aendi, that's awful kind of ya."

"Just thought since I've known Aaron's family for a long time, I could stand up for him."

Clara didn't care much for the idea, really. "Honestly, I think Aaron will eventually win Dat's heart on his own. That's my hope and prayer, anyway."

"All right, then. I'll hope right along with ya."

Clara asked if she could take the carriage over to visit Rosanna, and Aendi quickly agreed.

Clara discovered Rosanna walking freely, without pain. Her right arm was out of the splint, too, but Rosanna said she still had to wear the compression wrap for another week.

"I hoped ya might've been at Singing last Sunday," Clara told her as they walked through the meadow.

"I wanted to be safe and wait for the next one in two weeks." Rosanna looked nice in her blue bandanna. "I hated to miss it, since you'll be leavin' real soon."

Should I tell her? Clara wondered, not sure if Aaron had mentioned her staying to anyone in his family yet.

"I know Aaron confided in ya that we're courtin', but I don't know if ya heard I've decided to stay in Hickory Hollow," she said tentatively.

Rosanna gave a little shriek and reached up to hug Clara's neck with her good arm. "Aaron didn't tell me that, but oh, I'm so happy, Clara!"

"Me too." Clara told her a little of what made her decide—besides the courtship with Aaron, of course. "I love my job at the quilt shop, as well as the many friends I've made here . . . and then there's Aendi Ella Mae."

Rosanna's smile spread across her face. "So you'll ask to transfer your membership to our district, then?"

"That's what I've requested." She paused. "My letter was sincere."

"Does your bishop know anything 'bout Hickory Hollow?"

"I'm not sure." Clara felt worried a little. "My father read 'bout the racin' accident here, though."

"*Ach*. Prob'ly not *gut*. If he's anything like my Dat, he's protective. He never would've wanted me to ride with Tom Glick if he'd known how reckless Tom was. I wouldn't've gone with him, either."

Clara had never felt her father was overly protective with her or Bertie, but now was a different story. "Rosanna, I never told anyone this, but Tom galloped his horse faster than I've ever experienced after he took me out for ice cream one day. Tom's gone, so I s'pose it's not somethin' I need to report to the deacon, but I want you to know. I mean, maybe if I'd spoken up to someone, the racin' he did with you in the buggy wouldn't've happened."

She sighed deeply, feeling the old pang of guilt.

"Ain't your fault how Tom drove." Rosanna's eyes met hers. "Please don't feel bad about it."

"It's somethin' I still think 'bout," Clara said softly. "Ain't a secret, though. I'm sure we're not the only girls he drove with fast and reckless."

Aaron caught up with Clara after Rosanna headed back into the house, asking if he could talk to her.

"Sure," she said, glad to see him.

They strolled down the driveway, deciding to walk along the road for a bit.

"How've ya been?" He looked at her with concern.

"Since we saw each other Saturday night, I received a second letter from Dat." She told Aaron what her father wrote after reading his account of the buggy-racing accident in *The Budget*.

"Oh," he groaned.

Clara explained she'd already written back, assuring her father all was well. She also told Aaron she'd mailed a letter to the bishop in Indiana requesting a transfer of membership to the Hickory Hollow church.

For a while, he was quiet, as though contemplating something. Then he asked, "Say, your Dat's turnin' sixty this fall, ain't?"

For the life of her, she couldn't remember telling him her father's age specifically, but maybe when they were first getting acquainted . . . when she'd shared that her stepmother was seven years younger than her father. "*Jah*. Dat's birthday is October fifth."

"I'd really like to meet him."

This astonished her.

"You've met *my* parents," he added. "And ya know my sister Rosanna very well, too."

"True." *But I didn't have to go out of my way.*

"What if you and I go to Indiana together to celebrate his landmark birthday?" Aaron suggested, smiling.

"Honestly, Dat's not one for doin' much, if anything."

"Celebration or not, I want to get acquainted with him—and your sister, Bertie, too." He paused, running his thumbs under his black suspenders. "And if your brothers lived closer, it'd be nice to meet them, as well."

Clara couldn't help smiling as they turned back toward his house. "I'll check with Bertie and see if anything's bein' planned. And if not, I'll let her know we want to come anyway."

"I could help with your Dat's last cutting of alfalfa hay durin' our visit if it's time." Aaron touched her elbow, carefully guiding her away from several rocks scattered on the road.

Flabbergasted, Clara studied him. *What will Dat make of all this?*

CHAPTER

Thirty-Seven

Upon arriving home Friday afternoon, Clara noticed Jake's wife, Marta, using the push mower on the front lawn. She hurried into the house to get some cold meadow tea, then took it out to her.

Aendi was talking with yet another visitor over near the rose arbor, so Clara visited with Marta and said if she ever needed help with the mowing, she'd be glad to do that.

Marta thanked her. "I got a late start today, but I might take you up on that offer if I ever run into a snag." Then, out of the blue, she added, "I'm so glad to hear you're not going home after all."

Clara nodded. "I've even requested a transfer of membership from my home bishop."

"Then it'll be up to the two bishops to

decide before fall communion in mid-October. If they don't meet in person, they'll exchange letters about your standing as a member out there. You won't need to meet with Bishop Beiler at all, and ya won't hear from your home bishop, either, till all is decided. That's how it's done."

According to Marta, then, Clara wouldn't be involved at all. But since she'd never caused trouble as a church member back home, always carefully following the *Ordnung*, the decision just depended on how the two bishops felt led.

After visiting with Marta, Clara sat in the kitchen and wrote a letter to Bertie, saying she and her beau wanted to visit for Dat's sixtieth birthday in October. *Is anything planned?*

Clara twiddled her pen, thinking it was rather absurd to ask about a celebration. Dat certainly wouldn't want a fuss, although maybe Eva was planning a gathering of some sort.

She finished the last half of the letter by describing her recent meal with Aaron's family. She didn't share about his father questioning her, though.

I think you'll really like Aaron—and his family. His parents have six delightful children, including Aaron, who's the oldest. I can hardly wait for you to meet him this fall if it works out for us to come.

By now, I assume Dat has told you I've decided to stay here in the hollow. I've sent him two letters about it. I wish you could see this place, Bertie. No wonder Mamma hated to leave when she was young.

When she signed off, Clara hoped Bertie wouldn't think she was selfish in choosing to remain in Hickory Hollow. No matter where she lived, she would want to stay in close touch with her only sister.

A loud clap of thunder and then a rain squall ended Ella Mae's time with Rachel Stoltzfus, Mary's mother. Ella Mae quickened her pace toward the front porch, waving to Rachel as she headed off in her enclosed carriage. The dear woman had come with a sad heart regarding one of her older sons' eagerness to dip his foot into the world.

Hope I encouraged her to give her boy into God's safekeeping.

As warm as it had been, the cool raindrops felt good on her shoulders, neck, and face. And from the look of the heavy clouds to the south, this could be making down for quite a while.

In the kitchen, she found Clara sitting at the foot of the table, addressing an envelope. "What would ya say if we start organizing my sewin' room upstairs this evening?" Ella Mae asked.

"Might be an ideal project for a night like this." Clara looked out the rain-streaked windowpane. "I'll bring up a pitcher of cold tea and two tumblers. How's that?"

Ella Mae smiled, nodding. What a thoughtful young woman!

The next morning, Ella Mae was surprised when Clara suggested they sort through the two bedrooms upstairs instead of going to Saturday market, but she actually liked the idea. So they spent a little time going through the blanket chests in each of those rooms, and Ella Mae pared down the number of bed linens she had, since she'd have only one spare room at the *Dawdi Haus*.

Clara insisted on carrying the items Ella Mae wanted to give away downstairs to place them on the small table in the utility room. The few items left in the dresser drawers were mostly bath towels and washcloths Mattie's grown children might want. *But there really isn't enough for a full-blown auction*, Ella Mae thought.

Of course, she still had to look around in the barn and sort through things in her little haven away from it all—the cottage greenhouse. *That'll be last*, she thought, sure she'd need most everything out there.

"What 'bout the attic?" Clara asked when she returned upstairs.

"*Ach*, I forgot."

Clara recited the items she'd seen there besides the wooden box with the tin art and drawings, mostly stacks of periodicals and Ella Mae's wedding attire.

"I'm not sure why Mattie was so anxious for me to get goin' on the sorting when there's not a whole lot of it to do." Ella Mae sighed, glad for what she and Clara had accomplished last evening and so far today.

Clara smiled. "Maybe she wanted to be sure you're actually gonna move."

"I daresay ya know my daughter well." Ella Mae had to laugh. "*Nee*, I'm committed to movin', and the whole family knows it now."

"I think you'll be more excited once ya see the *Dawdi Haus* goin' up."

Ella Mae didn't voice it, but since Clara's decision to stay here, she'd had a much happier outlook all around. "I believe ya may be right, dear. And we'll get to the attic next."

Two weeks had passed since Clara had written to her home bishop and to Dat in response to his two letters. Of course, after talking with Marta, she didn't expect to hear anything about her request for a transfer of church membership, but not hearing from her father was nerve-racking.

Now it was September sixth, the day after Labor Day, and tourists were flocking into Vera's shop, bus tour after bus tour. Very good for business, but with just Clara and Vera, they were shorthanded.

Around midafternoon, Leona and Rosanna stopped by, and Vera put them right to work. Clara especially loved working alongside Rosanna.

After giving Rosanna her happy news two weeks ago, Clara had told Vera she planned to continue on in Hickory Hollow, as well. "I won't be goin' home to live," she'd said.

Vera had grinned and clasped her hand. "I'm ever so glad. I need ya here."

"Was hopin' you'd feel that way," Clara told her, then smiled the rest of the day.

After work, Clara hurried to check the mailbox, since Aendi was away for the afternoon. Even Aaron had recently asked if she'd heard anything back about their going to Indiana for Dat's birthday. But nothing had arrived from Bertie so far.

Still nothing from her father, either.

No doubt they're both busy with the summer harvest, Clara thought, wanting to give them the benefit of the doubt.

CHAPTER

Thirty-Eight

Clara felt both anxious and unsettled as she and Aendi ate together at noon three days later. Halfway through the meal, she confessed she was running out of patience with her sister. "Even a short note from Bertie about Dat's birthday would be nice. We're already well into September."

Aendi spoke up, suggesting Bertie might be yearning for Clara to return home to stay, too, but didn't quite know how to express her feelings.

Clara sighed. "S'pose that could be. I've never known her to be standoffish. But I need to hear from her, and as for Dat not writing back..."

"Aw, now, dearie."

"I feel just *ferhoodled*—I get knots in my stomach every day before the mail arrives."

Aendi's reassuring smile gave her a smidgen of hope. "Keep prayin' 'bout what's on your heart, giving it to our heavenly Father. He's listening. Knows your every care and need."

Nodding, Clara said she'd try not to give up hope.

Several hours after Clara arrived at Vera's Quilts, Katie Lapp and Mary Stoltzfus came in looking for a gift to give Mary's cousin, who was turning sixteen soon. The girls were excited about giving a gift together, and Clara planned to show them options among the many smaller quilted items. Vera had even more in stock now that the fall tourist season had begun.

"It's for her hope chest," Katie said, her autumn-brown eyes dancing.

"Somethin' practical, maybe?" asked Clara, leading them over to see the quilted oven mitts and pot holders to match.

Mary picked up a black mitt. "This would go with my aunt's cookstove, but I doubt my cousin'll still be cookin' with wood by the time she's married."

Katie reached for a dark green mitt and a pot holder, the outline of an apple stitched into the fabric of each one. "What 'bout these?"

Mary stepped back and smiled. "Much better." She reached into her shoulder bag and took out her wallet.

Katie did the same, mentioning this was the first they'd had the opportunity to do any shopping for a gift. "What with all the studyin' we've been doin' for our baptism comin' up next Preachin' service on the eighteenth."

The glow on Katie's face was impossible to miss.

"We've almost memorized the Dordrecht Confession of Faith, ain't so?" Mary added.

"My Dat says it's a *gut* thing to remember forever." Katie bobbed her head as she carried the mitt and pot holder to the cash register.

"Now that I've decided to live here, I look forward to your baptism," Clara said, ringing up their purchase.

Smiling at her friend, Mary said, "I can hardly wait."

"It's somethin' we always wanted to do together," Katie said softly.

That's sweet, Clara thought, recalling again the sacred moment of her own baptism and how the bishop's cupped hands had let the water fall lightly over her head.

Saturday evening, Clara welcomed Aaron for the planned supper at Aendi's. She'd practiced making her aunt's wonderful fried chicken recipe earlier in the week. Now she felt confident enough to prepare the chicken for Aaron herself. She would also serve creamy mashed potatoes, brown chicken gravy the way Mamma made it—starting with lard in the frying pan—and buttered snow peas and chow chow.

Aaron was dressed up for the occasion when he arrived. He quickly removed his straw hat as he stepped into the house, sniffing the air and remarking how wonderful the kitchen smelled.

Clara welcomed him, and Aendi smiled. "Hope you're hungry," her aunt said.

"Never more so," Aaron replied.

Once they were all seated, Aendi asked the blessing aloud, and Clara wondered what Aaron thought of that. Of course, Rosanna had told her that Leona knew Aendi often prayed out loud, so Aaron probably knew about it, too. He certainly didn't react unusually just now.

She enjoyed seeing her beau sitting at the head of the table with Aendi across from Clara on his right. With all her heart, she hoped someday she and Aaron would sit at their own kitchen table just like this. *Surely Adam wants his eldest son to be happy.*

And surely her own father wanted her to marry. He'd sounded so sorry when she told him that she and Wollie Lehman had broken up, though she hadn't given him her former beau's name. But that was before she left home to visit Hickory Hollow. So much had changed for them both since then.

Aaron broke the silence. "You were right, Clara. This *is* the best crispy fried chicken."

Aendi's eyes brightened, but she said nary a word.

"There's plenty more, so help yourself," Clara simply replied.

"*Denki.*" He smacked his lips in appreciation like Clara's brothers and father always did when Mamma cooked for the family.

It tickled her to see Aaron enjoying what she'd made for this special meal. She hoped there might be more meals together here at Aendi's and at the Ebersols', too. It was homier and more comfortable than eating in a restaurant.

Just before Clara served her chocolate mocha pie, Aaron asked if she'd heard anything back from Bertie about her father's birthday. Truth be known, she wished he hadn't brought that up, but she politely told him her sister was likely tied up with summertime chores and would write when she could.

He didn't ask about her father, but he knew she was still hoping to hear from him.

Later, when Aendi insisted on washing the dishes on her own, Clara and Aaron strolled to the bench near the rose arbor and watched the sky turn from shades of light to dusk. Such a quiet and lovely place at this time of day in September.

Eventually, the moon was visible on the western horizon, a waxing crescent. Aaron reached to hold her hand as she quietly mentioned not knowing where things stood with the transfer of her church membership.

"You'll know on Communion Sunday," he told her, gazing at her in the dim light.

"It's just that my brothers each received letters from our home bishop only a week or so after they requested their transfers of membership to Jamesport, Missouri. I remember how pleased they were."

"Well, the bishops in Lancaster County correspond only with the men in the church over such matters. That's the way it was when my Dat's unmarried sister moved to Somerset from here years ago."

Clara also thought of Aendi's children in the Big Valley area. They would have had to get their memberships transferred, as well.

Aaron added, "Keep in mind, though, my aunt was moving to a church district very similar to ours. Makes for less deliberation on the bishop's part, I'm guessin'."

"And that was long before Bishop Beiler set down stricter measures on the youth here," Clara said, wondering if that would make a difference for her membership transfer. *Since he doesn't want any of the fancy to creep in here.*

Aaron lifted her hand to his lips and kissed it. "You've been a faithful church member since your baptism, Clara. Can ya trust that all will go well?"

She had no inkling of what was to come. "I'll keep prayin' about it."

Aaron was quiet for a time. Then he said almost reverently, "Prayin's the best thing we can do." He released her hand and slipped his arm around her shoulders.

Pray more, worry less, Mamma always said.

CHAPTER

Thirty-Nine

Ella Mae wanted to use up the rest of her jam from last summer, so the following Tuesday, she served buttered biscuits and raspberry jam for breakfast along with scrambled eggs.

"I've been thinkin' of makin' several *Kapps* in the style ya wear here," Clara said, "hopin' my membership transfer goes through. I'm trustin' even when I can't see the end result."

"That's a *wunnerbaar-gut* idea." Ella Mae was so pleased.

"I just hope my father's not so unbending that he comes to bodily carry me away...."

Ella Mae lowered her spectacles. "Sounds like you're a bit annoyed." *Or angry.*

"It's been bubblin' up in me here lately—'specially since I haven't heard from him."

"Honestly, 'tis healthier than pushin' it down." Ella Mae had to say it. "Doin' that might keep ya from givin' in and walkin' away from what ya really want." She paused, hoping she wasn't stepping on Clara's toes. "Pray for God's will to be made clear to ya."

"I have, and so has Aaron," Clara replied, eyes glimmering. "You're prob'ly right, and a while ago ya said the anger might come later. And it has."

She stopped to sip some coffee, then added, "Dat doesn't seem to care much 'bout my future—whether I have someone to love— yet he didn't even wait a full year to remarry after Mamma died. Makes me downright sad . . . and, *jah*, mad, too, if I'm bein' honest."

Ella Mae nodded, relieved these emotions had finally come to the surface.

When the mail came shortly after Clara returned from Vera's, Aendi seemed surprised to learn her grandson Clyde had written. He and Susannah were coming from Big Valley with their eight-month-old son to see the house and take a look around the farm.

"Now you'll get to meet them," Aendi said, waving the letter around like a flag.

Clara smiled at seeing her aunt so happy.

"They'll arrive Saturday afternoon and

stay with us upstairs, whichever bedroom they choose." Ella Mae set the letter down and folded her hands. "'Tis always *gut* to have room for company . . . well, family." She went on to say she hadn't seen Clyde and Susannah for at least two years, which meant she'd never laid eyes on their baby. "He's my Joseph's namesake, ain't that nice?"

Clara grinned this time. "It'll be fun havin' a baby in the house."

"*Jah*, an' you'll like Clyde! He's easygoin' and chust plain fun."

"I'll do the cookin' so you're free to visit with them."

"*Ach*, that ain't necessary."

Clara insisted. "I *want* to, Aendi. After all you've done for me."

"We'll just see 'bout that." Aendi tittered like she did when she wanted the final say.

While Clara groomed Firefly and Sparkles in the stable, Ella Mae took herself off on a walk through the meadow. She needed time alone after Clyde's letter, though she wasn't upset they wanted to see the farm. It was just happening sooner than she'd expected.

She slowed her pace near the row of honeysuckle bushes that were finished blooming, a place where hummingbirds and bees had gathered in the spring and summer. Butterflies too. As girls, she and Essie liked to pull off the spirals of honeysuckle, place them between their lips, and draw out the delicious sweetness. *The carefree days*, she thought, enjoying the sunshine and milder temperatures as summer wound down.

She would especially miss certain spots around the farm, and this section of the meadow was one of them. She halted and stood there taking in its beauty, abundant clusters of purple clover growing not far away. She and Joseph had often brought their children out here when they were little to romp and play, picking wildflowers and leading the ponies around, catching lightning bugs at twilight and putting them in glass jars with holes punched in the lids.

She reminded herself that the beauty of nature was also ever present at David and Mattie's farm. But while the scenery was similar, it wouldn't be home.

Sighing, she walked to the edge of her property. *Change will be a challenge, but I'll try to remember the past, enjoy those memories, and make new ones.*

"At last!" Clara announced to no one but herself Thursday afternoon as she spotted a letter from Bertie in the mail. Quickly, she went to one of the oak rockers on the front porch to read it.

Dear Clara,
　How are you?
　I'm sorry for not writing sooner, but we had two batches of company—family on Peter's side from out of town—and then ten days ago, Peter lost his balance, fell off the market wagon, and broke his left shoulder. It's been one thing after another, seems, as well as the usual summertime work. Now that school's back in session for the boys, though, I feel like I might have the chance to get caught up some.
　Peter's two brothers have been helping round the farm, so that's a blessing. I've been trying to help outside, too, but putting up food for the winter takes a lot of time, as you know.
　I wasn't aware of any special plans for Dat's birthday, but I talked privately with Eva about it and was pleasantly surprised when she said she'd been thinking of having family over for cake and ice cream. I mentioned that you and your beau want to come visit for the occasion, and she smiled. Then she

decided to invite our brothers and their families to come from Missouri, too, as a surprise.

Will you let Aaron know he's welcome to stay with Peter and me when you come?

On another topic, Peter told me Dat asked him if we thought you might be unhappy with him for remarrying, and if that might be the reason you don't want to come back home to live. Peter reminded him you have a beau in Hickory Hollow, so there's that. Since I wasn't present when they spoke, I don't know how Dat took that, really.

Later, Dat told me about the buggy racing, but I think what bothers him most are the teachings of the Hickory Hollow church compared to ours here. He also said that, after you sent the money order back, he talked to our bishop about your request for a transfer of membership. But he didn't say what transpired between them.

So maybe when you come, things can be aired out between you and Dat. He wants what's best for you, Clara. So do I, though it's hard for me to have you so far away. But in his view, what's best is for you to be a part of this church *district, even if it means you remain single.*

Clara had to stop reading after that last sentence. *He doesn't mind if I never marry and have a family?*

Eventually, she finished reading Bertie's letter and headed inside to help Aendi make supper. Thinking about how Dat said he wondered if she was unhappy because he'd remarried pulled at her heartstrings, and she blinked back tears. But it was also true that she'd been suppressing anger toward him for his treating her like a child . . . and his attitude toward her heartfelt desires.

Till now, anyway.

Even so, it sounded like her father missed her and didn't want her to think poorly of him. And she did look forward to seeing all her family again, including her brothers. Aaron would be pleased, too.

Just maybe, she thought, *Aaron's presence will impress Dat that he is, indeed, a good choice for a mate.*

Feeling good about all the sorting she and Clara had done recently, the next afternoon, Ella Mae headed over to Preacher Jonas Smucker's farm with the old pencil drawings from his Dawdi Isaac. The preacher's wife, Deborah, should be home from any errands by now, so it would surely be an appropriate time to stop by.

As she pulled into the driveway, Ella Mae noticed Bishop Beiler talking with Preacher Jonas near the stable door and wondered if she ought to simply wait in the carriage. But Deborah—in the side yard watering her flower beds while her youngest daughter played with a gray barn cat nearby—waved her over. So Ella Mae got down from the carriage, tied Firefly to the hitching post, and made her way over there, out of earshot of the ministers.

Ella Mae stood next to Deborah as she hosed down the shrubs and thick ground cover on the side of the house, talking about the weather and school back in session. When she was finished with her task, Deborah invited Ella Mae to sit up on the back porch.

"Won't stay long," Ella Mae said as she lowered herself into a wicker chair. "Chust thought your family might like to have these drawings." She opened her purse, then handed them to Deborah—all but the one she'd left at home. "Your husband's Dawdi Isaac drew these many years ago."

"Is that right?" Deborah looked at each one, shaking her head in wonderment.

Ella Mae didn't reveal her connection to

Isaac, since that wasn't the point. And she doubted Deborah would ask how the drawings came to be in her possession even if she wanted to, not one to pry.

"I've been clearin' out things, what with my movin' to my daughter's farm in a few months, and I thought Isaac's descendants oughta have these drawin's. I 'spect Isaac wouldn't want anyone to make over them, though, but they *are* worth keepin'."

"I'm glad ya thought to bring them over," Deborah said, shuffling through them again and remarking on Isaac's talent. "He's an excellent clockmaker, but I never realized he could do art like this." Then she paused, frowning. "Hope having these won't be a problem since Bishop John's gotten . . . well, much stricter. At least with *die Youngie*."

"Are ya worried it might encourage your children to become artists?" Ella Mae hadn't thought this through. "If so, I can take 'em back."

"*Nee*, I'll have my husband decide about that."

Ella Mae hoped Jonas Smucker wouldn't dispose of them, but it was time for her to let them go.

They talked awhile longer, and Ella Mae noticed the two men were still out there talking, their heads together. It wasn't her place to know, but she hoped to goodness their discussion didn't indicate a problem with Clara's membership transfer.

The dear girl will need to be a member here if she's to marry!

When Clara arrived home from work that afternoon after getting a ride from Vera's cousin, she nibbled on a chocolate chip cookie from the big jar on Aendi's kitchen counter, then made her way to her room to change clothes.

Removing her bandanna, Clara set it on the dresser, then noticed Isaac Smucker's pencil drawing of Aendi's profile lying there. "My favorite," she murmured, picking it up.

Curious where her aunt might be so she could thank her, Clara stepped out of her room and saw the door across the hall ajar. But when she checked, the room was empty. She walked to the kitchen and looked out the back window. The carriage shed was empty, too.

I'll get supper started, she decided, then gathered ingredients for a baked meal Mamma always referred to as dinner in a dish. It had layers of lean ground beef, cut corn, minced onions and green peppers, and tomato slices, all topped with buttered bread crumbs.

As Clara worked, she remembered Vera saying Bishop Beiler's sister, who'd dropped by the shop briefly, mentioned her brother had important business over at Preacher Smucker's that afternoon. At the time, Clara hadn't paid much attention. Now that she was home, though, she hoped it didn't have anything to do with the youth, some of whom were attending less strict gatherings in other church districts, causing the ministers concern.

If so, Aaron would know, but he's not one to gossip.

CHAPTER

Forty

The sky was overcast by the time Aendi's grandson, his wife, and their baby arrived Saturday afternoon. The taxi driver removed a suitcase from the trunk and Clyde took out a playpen, as well. Aendi greeted Susannah and made over the smiling little boy while Clara hung back a little, wanting her aunt to have this special time.

As the taxi pulled away, Clyde placed the folded playpen on the walkway next to the suitcase, then offered to shake Clara's hand when he saw her there. "We must be related somehow," he said with a grin. "I'm Clyde Zook, and this is my wife, Susannah, and our son, Joseph."

Clara remembered what Aendi had said about how easygoing the man was. "Your grandfather was my Mamma's uncle."

"So my Grememm's your great-aunt by marriage, then."

Clara nodded. "*Jah.*"

Aendi came over and stood with Clara. "She's definitely family," she said, smiling at them both.

The baby rubbed his eyes with his chubby little fists. He was so cute wiggling about in Susannah's arms, like he wanted to get down and explore the yard.

"He's sure tired of travelin'," Susannah said, nodding a greeting to Clara.

As Aendi led the way to the back porch, Clyde brought their belongings. "I've got fruit and sweets set out," she told them. "Whatever ya want."

"*Denki,*" Susannah said as she carried little Joseph up the porch steps.

"I'd be happy to watch him for ya while yous look at the house," Clara mentioned as they walked.

Susannah thanked her warmly. "He likes sitting on the floor or in the playpen, and he's starting to crawl. I brought along a few of his favorite toys." She mentioned that Clyde had them stuffed in a bag in the playpen.

Clara waited until they'd had their snack around Aendi's kitchen table, where they talked about the train trip from Big Valley. But before Aendi took them to see the front room, Susannah placed Joseph on Clara's lap, kissed the top of his head, and headed off.

"Hullo, little one," Clara whispered in *Deitsch*. He was so cuddly, with deep dimples on his cheeks and elbows. She'd wondered if he'd fuss when his parents left the room, but he didn't. Instead, he studied her with his blue and very serious eyes.

Rising from her chair, Clara walked to the window and pointed to Sparkles and Firefly in the meadow, saying their names softly, her face close to his little ear. Joseph started babbling then, and she hugged him close, longing to have her own babies one day.

And wouldn't Aaron be a wonderful father, kind and patient as he was? He'd sent her a note in the mail, saying he was looking forward to taking her out riding after Singing tomorrow evening. Just the thought of being with him again made her heart swell with happiness.

"Let's find some toys for ya," she said, taking Joseph to his now-open playpen in the corner of the kitchen. She put him inside, and when she emptied out the contents of the bag, he immediately reached for a cloth book with felt farm animals sewn on it. She thought of trying to make a book like this and then maybe selling several at market for a little extra money. She had more than enough saved for a round-trip train ticket to visit First Light next month, but she also wanted to start collecting more linens and things, as serious about her as Aaron seemed to be.

Unfortunately, her hope chest was back home, and there was no inexpensive way to get it here. But she could ship its contents to Aendi's house while she and Aaron were in First Light. She'd never asked Dat to send her belongings as she had planned. She'd just have to do it herself.

In her room that evening, Clara looked fondly at the restored heirloom quilt, considering again what Aendi's parents had gone through before they could be together. *All those years apart before they found each other again!*

She couldn't bear the thought of being away from Aaron for months at a time, let alone years. *I must convince Dat I won't fall back in the faith by living here. If Ella Mae can be a silent believer in some less traditional ways, so can I.*

When the baptismal candidates walked forward to take their seats near the bishop the next morning, Clara spotted Katie Lapp and

Mary Stoltzfus among the other teens she'd come to know these past months. Seeing the girls in their lovely white church capes and aprons reminded her once more of her own baptism and catching Mamma's eye afterward, seeing the tears on her dear face.

A day never to be forgotten.

She felt sure her mother would have written to Aendi Ella Mae about it, before she became so ill. And just maybe Aendi still had that letter somewhere in the attic with all Mamma's letters she thought she'd kept.

Yearning for another connection to her mother, Clara could hardly wait to ask Aendi about it. But she'd wait till after Clyde and his family left for home tomorrow morning.

Early Monday, an hour or so before dawn, Clara rolled over in bed and thought back to last night's date with Aaron after Singing—mainly his reaction to Bertie's invitation for him to stay with them during their October visit. Aaron had remarked how eager he was to meet her family, her father included.

I'm getting excited, she thought, slipping her hand beneath her pillow and snuggling down, hoping to sleep a little while longer. *I just hope Dat doesn't expect me to stay home once I get there.*

Later that morning, after Clyde and his family had left for Big Valley and the washing was on the line, Clara asked Aendi if she still thought she'd saved any of her mother's letters.

"I do, and I daresay quite a few." Aendi was kneading the dough for two loaves of bread.

"And might they be in the attic, maybe?" Clara asked.

"*Jah*, I believe so."

Clara told her what she was hoping for especially, then explained how deeply touched her Mamma had been on the day of Clara's baptism.

"Now that ya say this, it seems there *was* a letter from Lillian right afterward." Aendi squinted as if trying to remember. "As I recall, she wrote about a handful of youth joining church that day. More than usual."

"Yes, there were several of us." Clara was happy to know such a letter existed.

"Well, feel free to go up there again and bring all the letters down if ya find 'em."

While the loaves of bread baked, Ella Mae slowly made her way up the stairs, then to the bedroom where Clyde and Susannah and their baby had stayed. Clara had very helpfully stripped the sheets and pillowcases for washing after Clyde and Susannah came downstairs for breakfast. But Ella Mae wanted to make sure they hadn't left anything behind, still marveling at how happy they were with the house and the entire property.

Clyde had made an offer for the house and farm, and she was just fine with the amount. The thing was, he'd hoped to move in sooner than early December and even suggested they move in upstairs and pay rent till she vacated the house. But Ella Mae needed to ponder that.

She gingerly peered under the bed, then checked the dresser drawers, but found nothing that belonged to them. Turning from the dresser, she noticed something on the windowsill—a note in Susannah's lovely hand.

Dear Mammi Ella Mae,
    Clyde and I and our little Joseph loved being here with you and your grandniece Clara this weekend. We believe God's hand is in our plan to purchase your beautiful house and farm, keeping it in the Zook family. Clyde says the Lord led

us in this decision. Denki once again for your hospitality, as always.

  With love, Clyde, Susannah, and Baby Joseph

"So thoughtful," Ella Mae murmured, swallowing the lump in her throat. "The Lord led them." She didn't hear that stated round here very often.

Clara remembered to take the flashlight along to see where to unlatch the overhead door at the top of the stairs leading to the attic. Returning to the old trunk, she opened it and carefully lifted the plastic wrapping with Aendi's wedding dress, cape, and apron inside, as well as the old tablecloth beneath it.

Sure enough, when she rooted around some more, she found not one but three bundles of letters in thick rubber bands. All from her Mamma. She removed the bundles, then set them on the floor before lowering the trunk's lid.

I'll be back up here soon. Still have to clear out this attic.

Back downstairs, she placed the letters on the kitchen counter for Aendi to sort through. She could see Mattie Beiler had arrived, and

Aendi was outside talking with her now. So Clara headed upstairs to dust and dry mop the bedroom where Clyde and his family had stayed.

Ella Mae was surprised to see Mattie visit on washday, but her daughter had made a fresh batch of apple Danish to share.

"One of my favorites," Ella Mae said. "*Denki*, dear." She led Mattie into the house while carrying several items of clothing from the line outside over her arm.

"I've been thinkin' we could get together and make applesauce soon," Mattie said, glancing at Clara, who'd just come into the kitchen and made a beeline for the Danish on the counter.

"'Tis getting to be that time," Ella Mae replied. "Have ya picked apples already or are ya plannin' to?"

"Early next week, David and I will go over to Kauffman's. We'll get extra and share with ya, Mamm."

Ella Mae thanked her, and Clara nodded, indicating she'd help with the applesauce-making, too.

"Just a couple of weeks now till Clara and her beau go out to Indiana," Ella Mae told

Mattie. "'Twas Aaron's idea . . . wants to meet Clara's family."

"Ah, sounds serious," Mattie said, smiling at Clara.

"*Jah*, but there're some hurdles ahead of us," Clara said, her eyes still on Mattie's treat.

"S'pose we could slice some Danish and have us a cup of coffee while the rest of the clothes dry," Ella Mae said. She set the items she'd brought in on the wooden bench, then stepped away to find a knife.

"Sounds *wunnerbaar*." Clara spoke right up.

"Well, why don't yous enjoy it while I run my errands," Mattie said, scooting toward the back door.

"*Ach*, stay, daughter. Errands can wait. Besides, it's Clara's day off from work."

Mattie nodded, then moved to a cupboard and took out three of the small yellow-and-white plates before placing them on the counter. Then, eyeing the stacks of old letters, she said, "Say, what're all these?"

"Oh, Clara's lookin' for a specific letter from her Mamma." Ella Mae made coffee, then cut into the apple Danish while Clara held each plate.

Mattie looked surprised. "Didn't realize ya'd kept so many, Mamm."

"I'm hopin' to find the letter she wrote 'bout my baptism," Clara told her.

Once she was settled at the table, Ella Mae asked the blessing before taking a bite of the moist and delicious treat. "Coffee'll be ready soon enough," she said.

During their conversation, Mattie mentioned that Tom Glick's father told her husband he was concerned about his son working out in Kansas. "Thinks it was a mistake for the brethren to have urged it."

"Why's that?" Ella Mae asked, wondering what Clara thought of this.

"The Yoder Amish are broad-minded," Mattie replied, grimacing. "They use tractors for field work, even have rototillers. And because of the heat come summer, they're allowed to have air-conditioned tractor cabs. Can ya imagine?" She frowned severely.

"Could it be our ministers didn't know how progressive they are?" Ella Mae asked.

"That might just be," Mattie replied, then took a bite of her Danish.

Clara looked befuddled as she rose from her chair, then poured three cups of coffee before bringing them to the table one by one.

"How a person's brought up—the kind of *Ordnung* their church has—can make a difference in how they think and how they raise their children," Mattie was saying.

By Clara's solemn expression, Ella Mae could tell she was contemplating all this.

After Mattie left, Clara told Ella Mae she was going for a walk. Watching as she headed outdoors and then down the walkway, Ella Mae mused, "Poor girl. She's a-ponderin' many things."

Then she turned to take her clean, dry clothing into the bedroom, still pondering some things of her own.

Hearing Tom Glick being discussed at the table hadn't bothered Clara one iota. If anything, it made her appreciate what she had with Aaron. But what *had* upset her was hearing how Tom's father felt about his son living and working around such liberal folk in Kansas. It got her to thinking, for certain.

No wonder Aaron's father asked me all those questions. Is that why Aaron wants to meet my father? So he can find out just how liberal the First Light community is? Is Adam Ebersol behind this?

CHAPTER

Forty-One

Clara had almost forgotten how long the train ride was last June, but the hours seemed to pass more quickly with Aaron by her side. They'd talked quietly and enjoyed the delicious snacks both Aendi and Leona had packed for them, and Aaron had even taken forty winks while Clara worked a crossword puzzle. She loved traveling with him, holding hands between their seats so as not to call attention to their affection. She still worried how the visit home would go.

Presently, she looked out at the scenic rural landscape—all the beauty of the green and rolling countryside—the motion of the train relaxing her. She needed this time of respite before seeing her father again. It was hard not to think ahead to what he might say about her bringing Aaron home, even to celebrate his birthday tomorrow.

If only Dat had written, I'd know more what he's thinking by now.

Bertie had suggested they simply show up and surprise him, as her brothers were planning to do. That way, there'd be no chance for resistance of any kind.

She looked down at her dark dress, one of her home-style dresses and capes she wore out of respect for her family despite the fact it would indicate she was still mourning Mamma. Wearing the Indiana-style attire while visiting there was the right thing to do, she'd told Aendi before she left the house that morning. Her aunt looked somewhat pensive when they said their good-byes, but she said she was praying for traveling mercies, which was a true blessing.

As the train finally slowed to approach the First Light station, Clara wondered how Eva could keep such a birthday surprise from Dat. She groaned inwardly, hoping she and Bertie knew what they were doing, especially keeping the secret that Aaron was coming, too.

Ella Mae had been so caught up with making applesauce the last week of September, and then managing a rather steady stream of visitors the first few days of October, she'd overlooked the stacks of Lillian's letters now stored in her dresser. Clara had been taken up with her beau and their plans to travel, so she must've forgotten about them, too.

Eager to search them now, Ella Mae placed the letters on her bed and sat there to check the dated postmarks on the envelopes. Mid-September 1992 was the approximate time when Lillian would have written about Clara's baptism.

"*Gut* thing I kept these in somewhat chronological order," she murmured.

She wondered how Clara and Aaron were managing on the trip. *Won't be long till they arrive,* she thought, hoping Clara would indeed return to the hollow. *Once she's faced her father...*

At last she located the letter Clara most wanted to see. She opened it, feeling tenderhearted toward Lillian, as she always had when reading the dear woman's words.

"Oh my," she said at her niece's inspiring description of Clara's baptismal vows. She stopped to wipe her eyes, deeply touched. Then, sighing, she read through the entire letter again, reassured that Clara's lifelong vow to God and the church was heartfelt and true. *And more important, the dear girl lives out her faith every day.*

Setting the letter aside, Ella Mae gathered the others, bundled them up again, and placed them back in the dresser. Glad to have found the one Clara wanted, she took it across the hall and placed it on Clara's dresser to see first thing when she returned.

Satisfied, she made her way to the kitchen, opened the fridge, and removed the pitcher of peppermint tea she'd made last evening. She poured some for herself, then sat at the table, sipping it—and missing Clara.

A half hour or so later, she saw Mattie coming up the lane in her family buggy. *I wonder what she's up to.* She recalled the apple Danish her daughter brought the last time she visited, but Mattie didn't always bring goodies along. Sometimes she brought more gossip than anything.

It turned out Mattie was thirsty for some ice-cold tea and was quite talkative, asking what was to be done with the blankets and linens she'd spotted in the utility room. After they'd settled that question, she mentioned an unexpected visit from Bishop Beiler the day before.

"He came to borrow some tools, so he and David headed out to the barn together. And they were gone a long time," Mattie said, holding the tumbler of peppermint tea, its ice jiggling against the sides.

Ella Mae took a sip of her tea, listening.

"When all was said and done, David must've felt okay tellin' me what they discussed—one Bruder to another—after Bishop left." Then Mattie shared that Bishop Beiler and Clara's Indiana bishop had been trading letters regarding Clara's transfer of membership. "Thing is, our bishop is concerned she might not be able to blend her upbringin' with our *Ordnung* and beliefs."

For goodness' sake, Ella Mae disliked that this part of the process rested on a difference of opinion. Although, truth be told, she'd wondered how rigid Bishop John might be on the matter. *Especially now.*

Continuing, Mattie said, "Since Clara's been in the hollow only since late June, Bishop's not certain she's ready to be a member here. From what David said, he talked 'bout having her wait for a period of time, till she proves herself."

"A provin', when she's already baptized Amish?" Ella Mae tried not to shake her head in dismay, but she did inhale loudly. "That's unheard of, ain't so?"

"Well, ya can't argue with the man of God."

"True, but what if she and Aaron want to marry durin' this wedding season?"

"Well, that can't happen unless Bishop accepts her membership transfer."

"It'd be a shame to hold up their wedding if Aaron's as serious as I s'pect he might be."

"I understand, Mamm. But David made it clear to me that it's rare for a church member who grew up in a higher church district to even *want* to move to one with stricter ordinances like ours. It's uncharted waters for round here."

Ella Mae said softly, "Some of Clara's folk back home might think she's goin' backward."

Mattie ignored that, saying it was too bad someone couldn't vouch for Clara's ability to be submissive to the local *Ordnung*.

"Well, keep in mind she *did* make her new dresses and capes to fit in with our womenfolk. Even has been doin' up her hair bun lower at the neck. She doesn't seek to call attention to herself."

"*Jah*, I noticed that right away, and I reminded David of it, too."

Ella Mae contemplated Clara's decision to do that. Seemed like a long time ago now.

"Not sure I should say this, but Bishop heard through the grapevine that Clara went out with Tom Glick several times," Mattie said. "So that's likely a problem."

"*Puh!* I'm sure other young women made that mistake, too, before poor Rosanna was hurt." Now Ella Mae felt really upset and added, "All I know is everything rests on Bishop John's decision."

Mattie seemed to sense Ella Mae's growing frustration. Yet Ella Mae kept her mouth closed now, lest she say too much.

Just then, Lillian's glowing letter about Clara's baptism crossed her mind. "*Ach*, wait here chust a minute."

She got up and headed to Clara's room, and when she returned, she placed the letter on the table. "Not sure if this'll help."

"What is it?" Mattie picked up the envelope.

Ella Mae told her about Lillian's beautiful letter written on the day of Clara's baptism.

Mattie's right eyebrow arched. "How could this possibly make a difference?"

"Ain't it worth a try?"

Mattie shifted in her chair. "Ah, so ya want me to give it to David to pass along to his bishop brother."

"Chust read the letter and see what ya think." Ella Mae didn't care to argue with Mattie. There was no need to, really. Whatever happened was in the Lord's hands.

It was close to sunset as Clara and Aaron rode in the back seat of their taxi. Clara fidgeted when one familiar sight after another came into view, and Aaron reached over to touch her hand.

"Can ya trust that all will go well?" he whispered with a reassuring smile. He'd asked her that once before, when they talked about her church transfer.

"I'm tryin'." She breathed deeply, hoping her father would at least be cordial when he met Aaron. *Surely* . . .

Her feet felt pinched since she wasn't used to wearing shoes for this many hours in a day. She looked forward to getting comfortable and going barefoot once they arrived. But first, they had to get past the initial greeting.

When Clara's stepmother opened the back door, Clara immediately introduced her to Aaron. He offered to shake her hand, and Eva responded politely in kind. Then she welcomed them inside and invited them to have something to eat. Though it was well past suppertime, there was indeed an array of items set out, for which Clara was thankful.

"Your Dat's over at the smithy's," Eva said as they sat down together. "He still has no idea about your comin'." She glanced at Aaron. "Or you either, Aaron."

"Bertie wrote that Calvin and Harley and

their families are arrivin' for the surprise, too," Clara said.

"*Jah*. Tomorrow afternoon."

Later, after they'd enjoyed Eva's reheated roast beef, mashed potatoes, and buttered carrots—without much conversation—Aaron left to retrieve Clara's suitcase.

When he returned, Clara asked Eva if it was all right for her to take it to her old bedroom, and her stepmother said it was, almost looking surprised Clara would ask.

Briefly leaving Aaron and Eva together in the kitchen, Clara headed toward the stairs, glad the gas lamps in the hall were lit. She tried to manage her old feelings about not being able to connect with her stepmother, but it was hard.

Clara turned on the gas lamp on the dresser in her former room and looked around. She marveled that Eva hadn't changed one thing. *She dusted and cleaned in here but didn't even change the calendar from last June?*

After setting her suitcase on the floor, she stepped to her mother's desk, recalling the day she'd sorted through its drawers. *The day I really understood how close Ella Mae was to Mamma.* Clara touched the desk fondly, so grateful.

She removed her shoes and dark hosiery, then quickly made her way downstairs to the kitchen barefoot. Aaron was telling Eva about their train trip.

Standing, he asked, "Is it too late to show me round the farm, Clara? Eva says your brother-in-law won't be here to pick me up for a while yet."

"It's still a little light out," she replied, glad they could be alone together before Peter arrived—and her father.

Clara offered to clear the table, but Eva encouraged them to go and enjoy themselves, like she always had when Clara lived here. So they left the house and headed to the field lanes, where Aaron could get a view of the vast acres of corn and alfalfa hay.

"Looks like it's 'bout time for another cutting of hay," he said as they strolled along.

"*Jah.* Dat knows just when."

Aaron reached down to pull up a tall blade of grass and put it in his mouth, the end hanging out.

She laughed. "My brother Harley does that, too."

"Eva was tellin' me 'bout him, Calvin, and their families all comin' tomorrow. Said she guessed the children might end up sleepin' on blankets on the floor, maybe in the hallway upstairs." Aaron chuckled. "I think she's a little uncertain 'bout this all bein' a secret from your Dat, though."

Clara looked at him. "Goodness. Seems like she talked to you more than she's ever talked to me."

Aaron shook his head. "That can't be."

"It's always been awkward 'tween us." She shrugged.

"I think she'll come round."

"But what 'bout Dat? The question is, will he?"

CHAPTER
Forty-Two

When Peter arrived in his buggy to pick up Aaron, Clara and Aaron were strolling across the yard toward the house, after their walk. Clara noticed her brother-in-law's left shoulder and arm were still in a sling from his fall.

"Hullo!" Clara called to him as he stepped onto the driveway. She was eager to introduce Peter to her beau.

"*Willkumm* to Indiana," Peter said, pushing his right hand into Aaron's.

"How's your shoulder these days?" Aaron asked. "Heard 'bout your accident."

"Pain's mostly gone, but the orthopedic doc wants me to wear the sling for another ten days or so."

Clara wondered if Aaron noticed Peter's

well-groomed beard. Of course, she didn't want to point it out, but it was definitely in contrast to the men's beards in Hickory Hollow.

At that moment, Dat pulled into the driveway behind Peter's buggy, and Clara felt tense as he stepped down from his own. "*Ach*, Dat's home," she said, her throat turning dry.

"Ya haven't seen him yet?" Peter asked quietly.

"*Nee*, he's been at the smithy's."

Peter nodded. "Well, let's get ya introduced, Aaron," he said, waving to Dat.

Her father wandered over, then spotted Clara there. "Daughter?" His mouth gaped open.

"I'm home for a visit, Dat," she said, mixed feelings bubbling up.

"Just a . . . a visit?" He looked crestfallen.

"It's so *gut* to see ya," she said, trying to find the right words.

"Clara brought her beau along," Peter interjected. "This here's Aaron Ebersol, and he's gonna stay with Bertie and me."

"I've been wantin' to meet ya," Aaron said, not wasting any time.

"Well, how 'bout that." Dat shook his hand but still eyed Clara before offering Aaron a "*Gut* to meet ya."

Peter immediately suggested Clara and

Dat go inside while he and Aaron unhitched Dat's horse.

"I must say you're full of surprises, Clara," Dat said, turning his head to look at her as they walked toward the house. "Never expected ya'd just show up."

"Aaron wanted to come and get acquainted with ya. Of course, I wanted to visit, too."

Dat was quiet, then said, "Wish I'd known ahead of time."

She couldn't explain about the birthday gathering tomorrow. That would spoil things. "I'm real glad to be home for now."

He stopped walking. "Did Eva give ya supper?"

"We had a nice meal, *jah*."

"All right, then." He opened the back door for her, and they stepped inside.

It felt like they were almost strangers.

Much later, after Aaron left with Peter, and Eva had served apple crisp and whipped cream to Clara and Dat, they headed into the front room for family worship.

It seemed odd to be back listening to her father read from the Bible instead of Aendi Ella Mae. She missed her aunt's way of doing things—especially praying aloud—but her focus must be here now. So when she knelt for silent prayer with Dat and Eva, she asked God for wisdom.

When Clara awoke the next morning, it took her a few moments to realize she was back in her old room. Stretching, she looked around, and spotting Mamma's desk, she sighed. "How will things go today, Lord?" she prayed, trying to follow Aaron's advice and trust all would go well.

She rose and meandered to the window, wishing she had the same hope he seemed to have. The sun's golden rays shot high into the sky as it rose over the horizon. Standing there, she thanked her heavenly Father for His faithfulness and love, as she did first thing every morning, not wanting to let the looming conversations interfere with her peace.

Downstairs at breakfast, she wished Dat a happy birthday. He smiled faintly, humbly downplaying the occasion, seeming surprised she'd remembered. She wondered how he'd react when her brothers and their families arrived later to celebrate. Surely he'd be happy to see them, no matter the occasion.

When Eva sat down to his right, Dat mentioned that he planned to cut hay this morning. Clara cringed a little, hoping he wouldn't still be out there when Calvin and Harley arrived.

That afternoon, back from Peter and Bertie's after lunch, Aaron brought folding tables and extra chairs up from the basement and helped Eva set them up. Clara was sweeping the back porch following some food preparation Eva had surprisingly allowed her to do.

When she heard what sounded like cars approaching, Clara turned to see her brothers getting out of two taxi cabs. Then she turned again to see her father coming back from the hayfields.

"Look who's here!" she said, eager to witness her father's expression.

"What the world," Dat murmured, heading down the walkway toward his sons as they paid their drivers.

"Happy birthday!" Calvin called, then rushed around the cab before his wife, Chrisann, and their three children even got out. Calvin hugged Dat tight and then held him at arm's length, looking him over. "Ya don't look a day older than last time I saw ya."

Clara grinned, happy to see her big brother again, and then Harley came over to greet their father, too.

When her brothers spotted her, they motioned her over. "You're all grown up, little sis," Harley said, his two-year-old son running over to hang on his arm. *Have I changed that much since Mamma's funeral?*

Chrisann and Harley's wife, Fanny, joined them. Then after the guys grabbed the luggage, the whole group of them headed inside. Clara looked forward to sitting next to Aaron at the table during the birthday supper—and, hopefully, Bertie, too.

When her sister and her family arrived and the meal began, it all seemed like a murky kind of dream—though not because she wasn't having a good time. But with Dat's cool greeting toward her, she felt nearly lost in the midst of it all.

Thankfully, Bertie's presence gave her some moral support, as did Aaron's. Now and then, Dat glanced over at her, but she couldn't tell what he was thinking.

Looking back on the birthday gathering later that evening, with the three-layer fudge cake, ice cream, and other goodies Eva had made, Clara was encouraged by her siblings' warm interactions with Aaron. And when Aaron slipped away with Peter, Bertie, and their boys for the second night, Clara was surrounded by her brothers and their families during Bible reading and prayers, all of them together with Dat and Eva in the front room.

It was wonderful to spend time with them again, yet she felt as if she were holding her breath till she could return to Hickory Hollow.

Next morning, Clara was delighted to see Aaron arrive with Peter after breakfast. Her father went out to finish crushing the hay to dry it more quickly for baling tomorrow, and after a quick hello, Aaron joined Calvin and Harley to help muck out the horse and mule stalls and tend to other outdoor chores.

Once Clara's sisters-in-law and nephews and nieces left for a walk, Clara told Eva what a wonderful birthday get-together yesterday had been. "Do ya think Dat suspected anything?"

"*Nee.*" Eva shook her head as she filled the sink with hot, sudsy water. "He was focused on bringin' in the last cuttin' of hay."

"He has plenty of help this time."

"It's awful kind of Aaron to pitch in," Eva replied.

"He really wants to get to know Dat," Clara said, picking up a tea towel instead of asking if she could help.

"Maybe they'll talk tomorrow while they

work baling the hay," Eva said, smiling. "I heard Aaron say he wanted to help with that, too."

Clara nodded, finding it interesting that Eva had actually exchanged information with her.

When Bertie came over later that morning, Clara was happy to see her. But right away, her sister asked if they could speak privately. Wondering what was on her mind, Clara led the way to her room.

"Let's close the door," Bertie said once they were there.

Clara motioned for her to sit on the chair at Mamma's writing desk, then perched on the edge of the bed. "Everything all right?"

Bertie straightened her black apron and drew a long breath. Then looking at Clara, she said, "Has Aaron talked with ya this morning?"

"He's been helpin' with chores. Why?"

"I doubt ya know this yet, but accordin' to Peter, while Aaron and Dat were talking last evening, Aaron asked for Dat's blessing on marryin' you."

Startled that Aaron would have had the confidence to ask—and so soon—Clara asked, "How'd Dat respond?"

Bertie placed her hand on her heart. "Evidently Dat told Aaron he's sorry, but he can't give his blessing on your union since he hasn't known him long enough. And he doesn't see how livin' in a church district with such a fixation on rule followin' is *gut* for raisin' a family in faith." Bertie shook her head.

Tears sprang to Clara's eyes. "But I love him, Bertie."

Bertie came to sit beside her on the bed. Clara welcomed her sister's arm around her, and the two of them sat there, silent.

What'll happen now? Clara fretted, tears threatening. "Mamma never would've let it come to this," she said.

"Do ya want me to talk to Dat? I'd be glad to, not that it'd make any difference, maybe."

"*Nee*, the blessing should be given freely." Clara coughed, trying not to cry. "I can only imagine how Aaron must be feelin'."

"Peter talked to him quite a while last night, I know that much."

Clara raised her head to look at Bertie. "Have ya ever heard of a couple marryin' without a father's blessing?"

Bertie sighed again. "*Jah*, but not having the support of family is a rough way to start married life."

Clara wondered who she was thinking of,

but she let it be. "Even though it hurts terribly to learn this, I'm glad ya told me."

"I wanted to soften the blow, if that's possible, even though Aaron will surely tell ya at some point. He won't know I told ya."

Clara nodded, determined to find a way to show her father how wonderful Aaron was while at the same time wanting to respect his opinion.

But would that make any difference if Dat was so set against her building a life in Hickory Hollow?

CHAPTER

Forty-Three

In her bedroom at nightfall, Ella Mae removed her hairpins, unwound her hair bun, and set her tresses free. Then, stepping outside, she sat on the back porch in her nightgown and warm bathrobe. A chilly breeze rippled through her flowing hair—just what she needed, strange as it seemed.

Earlier that afternoon, she'd run into Mattie at the fabric store, where in whispering tones she was told David said the bishop wanted to talk with Clara when she returned.

A bishop asking to see a young woman seeking a church membership transfer was highly unusual as far as Ella Mae knew. The way Mattie put it, this sounded quite worrisome, and she doubted Clara would be instated as a member anytime soon.

If at all.

Now sitting there with one of the barn cats curled up on her slippered feet, Ella Mae had no idea what to think. She recalled the various times she'd felt oppressed under their strict *Ordnung*, as well as other expectations that really had nothing to do with church ordinances. Certain things were hard to make heads or tails of, like the bishop's strictness with *all* the youth when only Tom Glick and his cousin were racing buggies.

Other things didn't add up, either, hard as she'd tried to understand the reasoning behind them. Such as the use of push mowers for lawns instead of the power mowers like the Amish in the next district over were permitted to own. Yet despite all that, she'd been faithful to the Lord and drawn closer to Him, wholly embracing the grace He so generously offered.

I can't go wrong if I follow in His footsteps, she thought, recalling what Lillian had written in her letter about Clara's baptism. On that holy day, the dear girl had told her mother, "It's my joy to live for God and to obey His commandments."

Ella Mae hoped the letter had found its way to the bishop, and if so, that he'd taken it to heart. For the life of her, she would have a very hard time grasping it if Clara's transfer of church membership was denied, earnest as she was.

The stars began to appear one by one, and Ella Mae pulled her robe closer. If Joseph were alive, he'd tell her to come in now, out of the chilly air. But her heart wasn't where it ought to be. What with fall Communion Sunday just ten short days away, she must deal with these feelings by way of fasting and prayer. *I don't want to be out of harmony with the People and unable to share in the communion service and foot washing.*

So there she sat, surrounded by the sounds of crickets nearby and frogs over yonder in the neighbors' pond, beneath the night's dark sky, where no one could see her but the Lord above, her precious Savior, who knew her heart and loved her . . . and understood.

While it was still dark the next morning, hours before dawn according to the clock on her nightstand, Clara awakened out of a strange and unnerving dream—though now that she was conscious, she could no longer remember it. Only the fragments of uneasiness lingered.

Try as she might, it was impossible to return to slumber. Rising from her bed, she slipped on her bathrobe and tiptoed down the stairs to sit on the sofa in the front room. There, she peered through the window and saw the moon, scarcely visible, a mere silvery slice against the black sky.

On top of the startling dream, she'd slept terribly—and in her own bed, too. Unnerved and worn-out, she whispered a prayer asking God to mend her broken heart. *First Wollie and now Aaron.*

Knowing her father was opposed to her marrying Aaron felt like a shattered dream, perhaps like the one that had awakened her.

"O Lord, please help me know what to say to Dat," she murmured into the darkness.

But deep in her heart, she knew she could never defy him.

Stirring from unexpected sleep, Clara heard someone in the kitchen. She sat up and yawned, thinking she ought to return to her room before anyone caught her wandering in her robe in the dark.

Eva came to stand in the doorway just as Clara crept toward the stairs, a glow from the kitchen behind her. "Is that you, Clara?"

"I was restless, so I came downstairs a while ago."

"Would ya like some hot cocoa?" Eva

asked, already dressed for the day. "There's plenty to share."

Still a little hazy, Clara said, "That would be nice," then followed Eva into the kitchen, where milk was warming in a saucepan on the gas range.

"Restless, ya say?" Eva turned to look at her while slowly stirring the milk.

Nodding, Clara sat at the foot of the table, staring at her hands in her lap for the longest time.

"Ya seem awful sad."

Clara was taken aback by Eva's comment. *Surely she knows what Dat told Aaron.* "It's the worst thing, really."

"*Ach*, and durin' a nice family reunion, too?"

Clara's lip trembled, and she covered her face with her hands.

"What is it, Clara?" Eva left the stove and came to stand near her.

"I might as well stay here since Dat won't give his blessing for Aaron to marry me," she said between sniffles. "I'm all *ferhoodled*."

Eva pulled out the wooden bench and quietly sat down. She reached into the pocket of her dress and handed Clara a clean hankie.

"Sorry," Clara murmured, wiping her eyes.

"Sheddin' tears can help sometimes. Ain't *gut* to keep such sadness bottled up."

Clara looked at her, blinking her eyes at Eva's sympathetic remark. She hadn't expected this.

"You must care for Aaron very much," Eva said softly.

Clara nodded. "I can't imagine not bein' with him for the rest of my life." She sighed and dabbed at her eyes. "By the way he treats me, I know he loves me, too. But none of that matters if we can't be together."

Eva listened, eyes wide.

"I know Dat's worried that I'd have to line up with the Hickory Hollow church, but I can't lose my salvation just 'cause I'm part of a church that's different from ours here. The Bible's clear on that—Jesus died to save us, and that's far more powerful than any *Ordnung*."

Eva sighed. "Your Dat's strong on a personal relationship with Christ."

"And he thinks the church I want to transfer to isn't. But rules and requirements don't change the truth of salvation through grace. I'm choosin' to follow God in all that I do. Where I live won't change that."

Nodding, Eva said softly, "I believe you, Clara."

Clara glanced at the saucepan on the stove. "*Ach*, don't let the milk scald."

"Oh goodness." Eva jumped up to stir the

hot milk, then poured it into two mugs before scooping homemade cocoa mix into each one. "Do ya want marshmallows, too?"

Clara said she did, trying to get used to this new Eva. *"Denki."*

As they sipped on their hot drinks, Clara opened up and told her about Aaron's devotion and love for the Lord. "He's the kind of man who might just be nominated for preacher one day, that's how sincere he is 'bout his faith."

"Almost immediately, I could tell he's earnest," Eva replied. "Thoughtful too."

"Seems there's no doubt in anyone's mind . . . 'cept Dat's."

Out the window, Clara saw the first tendrils of dawn reach over the horizon. Just having someone with her at this moment helped her not feel so alone with this piercing heartache—especially since she had no idea how to tell Aaron she must stay here and not return to Lancaster County with him.

We have no future together now.

CHAPTER

Forty-Four

Before lunchtime, Ella Mae rolled out dough for a cheesy ham and potato quiche, filling up the hours till she'd think about Clara getting back on the train with Aaron the next day. *Hopefully so* . . .

As she leaned on the rolling pin, smoothing out the dough, it crossed her mind that she might just be part of the hold-up of Clara's transfer of church membership. She hated the thought, if there was any truth in it.

Joseph's siblings were the ones who left Hickory Hollow for First Light. But I'm the relative Clara's been staying with these past months, and I'm not the most yielding church member ever.

Even so, she mused as she lifted the flattened dough into a glass baking dish, *Bishop Beiler is a rigid bishop.*

Chrisann and Fanny insisted on making the noon meal, giving Eva a chance to spend time with the two youngest children, little Felty and his tiny, curly-haired cousin Lucy. To Clara's surprise, Eva had willingly stepped aside and let the women take over making egg noodles for lasagna.

Eva invited Clara to go outside with her and the towheaded toddlers, where Clara hitched up one of the horses to the small, two-wheeled cart she and her siblings had ridden in when they were children. She and Eva walked along with the horse to give smiling Felty and teething Lucy a ride around the farm. Clara liked Eva's idea, and the children babbled happily, enjoying the warm fall day.

The weight of the sun seemed to fall more lightly than even a week or so ago, and clouds like cotton pulled apart over near the western horizon, revealing strips of blue sky. The turning leaves received the lingering light, which dappled the soon-to-be shades of russet that would come with autumn's peak. Behind the trees, the white horse fence divided the pastureland from the roadside's grassy slant, and Clara remembered walking this way with Dat when she was a little girl.

Now she scarcely felt related to her father,

even as, strangely enough, her once-distant stepmother seemed to be warming to her.

They continued to stroll beside the horse, and Clara told Eva about the friends she'd made back east and how she was going to miss them, as well as dear Aendi Ella Mae.

"Your Dat has mentioned how close Ella Mae and your Mamm were," Eva said, directing the horse to make a slow, easy turn.

"I never realized how close till I read her letters to Mamma back in June." Sighing, Clara thought how wonderful it had been getting to know Aendi. She dreaded having to write her to say she wasn't coming back. The thought made her gasp a little.

Eva looked at her. "Ya feelin' all right?"

"Honestly, I can't put into words what Aendi Ella Mae has come to mean to me," Clara said, hoping she wasn't stepping on Eva's toes.

"I can imagine. Your Dat says you're a lot like your Mamma."

Clara soaked up that remark. "I hope so, in all the ways that matter."

Eva nodded, then glanced back at the children.

All the while, Aaron, who'd been helping with hay baling all morning, remained in the forefront of Clara's mind. She longed to spend time with him, missing him already.

She couldn't bear to think of walking away from him. Out of the blue, she thought of the harness shop he and his father owned and managed. Aaron was set to take it over when his father was ready to retire.

He'll be a wunnerbaar-gut husband and provider for someone else, she thought miserably.

The noon lasagna dinner was delicious, but Aaron got seated across from Clara instead of next to her. That was okay, and maybe even better so they could see each other. But Clara had to put on a smile though her heart was breaking, and she felt sure Aaron's was, too, quiet as he was. At least neither of them had to join in the conversation since her brothers and Peter were chewing the fat about the coming corn harvest here, as well as in Missouri.

She couldn't help noticing that Dat never once looked her way like he had during the birthday supper, yet he was fully engaged with Calvin, Harley, and Peter.

Thankfully, Bertie had come for the meal, too, and was sitting next to her. When Eva and Chrisann rose to bring the dessert to the table—sweet pumpkin nut bread and freshly whipped cream—Bertie whispered that Aaron wanted to see her tonight. "Peter will let him use our buggy so yous can be alone."

Nodding her agreement, Clara fought back tears.

Eva and Chrisann took over the kitchen clean-up while Clara helped Fanny put the youngest children down for afternoon naps. The older three had already gone outside to play.

Later, when Clara had a chance to slip away to her own room, she opened her hope chest and knelt beside it, locating the list she'd made of all the lovely items inside, including the dates she'd received them as gifts or made them with Mamma or on her own. Just as Aendi had when she'd sorted through the drawers in her upstairs bedrooms, Clara thought about just giving away some of her household items. *Since I'm staying here, I'll only need them if I should fall for a widower or if someone moves into the area here in the future, maybe.*

But she trembled at the thought of not being with Aaron, the man she dearly loved.

David and Mattie were hosting a wiener roast in their vacant field behind the barn, and the bonfire twinkled in the darkness as Ella Mae directed her horse into the lane. After days of feeling restless, she was glad to be occupied with family the evening before Clara's expected return. Mattie greeted her and tied up Sparkles, then walked toward the bonfire with her, carrying a folding chair.

"The *Kinskinner* are already here," Mattie told her. "Their parents dropped them off for the evening. They're lookin' forward to seeing ya."

"It's been a while since all your grands were in one place," Ella Mae said, glad for Mattie's big flashlight lighting the way.

"They'll be singin', I'm sure, 'specially the youth."

"Singin's always a joy." Anticipating a nice time, Ella Mae chuckled. "Wish Clara was back to enjoy this."

"Would be nice," Mattie said—but with a doubtful tone.

This made Ella Mae shudder. Did her daughter know more about the bishop's decision regarding Clara's church membership? And would a denial be enough to keep her in First Light to stay?

Oddly, the leaves on the trees seemed more brilliant as the sun began to set that evening. Clara's heart rose to see Aaron arrive in Peter's black buggy, the V-shape back so different from the boxy Lancaster County carriages. Aaron offered his hand when she stepped inside, and sadness descended as she realized this was the last time they'd be alone together. Tomorrow she'd say good-bye before he left for the train station, but tonight she wanted to put on a happy face for him, at least while it was still light.

The temperature had dropped as the sun lowered, and she was glad for the warm knit sweater she'd found in her closet. In fact, most of her Indiana dresses and capes were still here, and she planned to have Aendi give her newer dresses to Rosanna.

Fewer things for Aendi to fuss with, Clara thought as the carriage rumbled over a rutted section of the narrow road. *My mourning clothes can be boxed up and mailed to me.*

She could see a few stars now, shiny dots against the dimming sky. Her hand safely in Aaron's, she wished he would say something.

"Have ya enjoyed your time with Peter and Bertie and their boys?" she eked out.

"Real nice family, *jah*." He glanced at her. "What 'bout you? How's the visit with your Dat and Eva?"

Now she wished she'd kept quiet. She didn't care to talk about Dat unless she had to. "It's been much different from what I imagined."

Aaron squeezed her hand. "Hope you're not sorry we came."

She struggled with what Bertie had told her. *Should I bring it up before Aaron does?* she thought.

"What is it, Clara?"

"Well, I s'pose it's all right to tell ya." She sighed, willing herself not to cry. "My sister wanted to soften the blow for me, so she let me know 'bout what Dat told ya." Tears still threatened, but she was determined not to make this any harder than it already was. "Given his decision, I've decided to stay in First Light."

"*Ach*, Clara, I wish you hadn't found out that way," Aaron blurted. "Why won't ya return with me to Hickory Hollow, though?"

"I want to, but I can't go against my Dat's wishes, and it would be too hard for me to live in Hickory Hollow if we can't be together."

Aaron slowed the horse, pulled over onto the dirt shoulder, and stopped. Turning toward her, he said, "I'm not leavin' without ya, Clara."

Astonished at how firmly he'd said it, she frowned. "But—"

"We're *adults*. And I *love* you."

She couldn't believe what he was implying. "But to go against my Dat?" Much as she wanted to be happy at Aaron's declaration of love, she remembered what Bertie had said. "Don't ya think it's a terrible way to start our life together?"

Aaron looked at her, his eyes ever so serious. "I've been praying, askin' God for wisdom ever since your Dat's refusal."

She held her breath.

"I understand your father's opposition, I do," Aaron said.

"*Jah*, but while things might be a lot more conservative in Hickory Hollow, Dat's forgetting that my faith isn't based on where I go to church, but on my relationship with Jesus. Have you talked to him at all about what you believe?"

Aaron shook his head. "*Nee*, I didn't even get a chance, unfortunately—he wanted to talk more about my bishop's severe restrictions on the Hickory Hollow youth and how he didn't want you to have to live in fear of overstepping the boundaries. But it's important for him to know that I'm a believer, too—I know that it's not what I do that makes me acceptable to God, but I still choose to honor my church's *Ordnung* out of respect."

She sighed. "Maybe I could get Dat to see that way of thinkin' in time if he knew of your faith. Either way, I really think I should stay home, Aaron, at least till Dat and I can come to terms . . . if that's even possible." She had a hard time getting the words out.

"Well, remember what I said." Aaron picked up the driving lines and signaled the horse to move back onto the road. "I'm not leaving."

"You can't stay here indefinitely, Aaron."

"I'm a man of my word, and I won't go without ya. I also pledge to help convince your Dat we should marry."

Clara drew a deep breath, and with all her heart, she wished Aaron would hold her hand again—or even slip his arm around her.

Maybe Dat would come to trust Aaron if he got to know him over a period of time, she thought.

CHAPTER

Forty-Five

While it was still dark the next morning, Clara helped with the children amidst her brothers' and their wives' packing. They planned to leave for the train station immediately following a predawn breakfast.

After good-byes and hugs were exchanged and the taxis had pulled away, Dat and Eva went out to the barn, and Clara returned indoors to redd up the kitchen.

Dat has Eva, Bertie has Peter, and I have no one, she thought, letting tears fall into the sudsy dishwater. Her determination to remain at home would undoubtedly complicate things for Aaron if he didn't return on the train today. His father was expecting him back to work at the harness shop on Monday, just as Aendi was expecting *her* today. Sadly, she thought, too, of Vera Mast and how she'd manage without the necessary help going forward.

I'll write to her, as well as dear Aendi.

Contemplating all this made Clara feel worse. All the same, under God, she couldn't defy her father's wishes when it came to marrying. Deciding to live in Hickory Hollow was one thing, but a marriage Dat would not bless was quite another.

After the dishes were washed, dried, and put away, she took her time wiping the oilcloth on the table, then swept the floor. Anything to keep her mind off this trying day.

Then she made her way upstairs to the rooms where Calvin and Harley and their families had stayed and stripped the beds. *Such a special time with them, yet a painful one for Aaron and me,* she thought, folding blankets where the children had slept on the floor.

Ella Mae glanced at the clock, thankful this day had finally come. *Clara will be home late tonight,* she thought, planning to make fudge for the occasion. *She might enjoy a treat before bedtime.*

Then, indulging herself, she made a large buttermilk pancake and fried up two strips of bacon to celebrate.

After washing the dishes, she sat at the table to write a letter to Clyde and Susannah, giving her answer to their request to settle in prior to her own projected December move. She'd decided it would be most helpful to them, and since she and Clara had their bedrooms on the main level, that plan should work just fine.

After she'd signed off, she walked out to the front porch to place the letter in the mailbox, then pushed up the little red flag. Leaning against the banister, she looked across the road to the field corn, nearly ready for harvesting. Her gaze drifted over to the old beech trees along the lane, the leaves beginning to change from green to golden-bronze, and she gave praise to God for this lovely autumn day.

Clara washed the first set of sheets and pillowcases, not wanting to wait till Monday washday. She'd have quite a few clothes to wash or freshen up then, including those hanging here in her closet the past months.

Then she walked up the basement steps and across the house to the front room. There, she began the arduous task of writing to Aendi and Vera, relieved to still have the house to herself, gloomy as she felt.

A while later, she heard Eva come in the back door and walk upstairs. Clara was glad she'd chosen to write in the front room so she didn't have to encounter her. Although soon she'd have to tell Eva of her decision not to return to Hickory Hollow.

Once the letters were written, Clara picked up a Bible on the table near the sofa and read several chapters from the book of Romans, one of Dat's favorite New Testament epistles.

If only my own father would trust me . . .

After a time, she heard a horse and carriage come into the lane, and through the window, she saw Peter dropping Aaron off.

Aaron had his suitcase!

Her heart dropped at the sight. She hurried to the utility room, pulled a sweater off the hook, and made her way out the back door to meet him. Peter waved from the buggy, then headed toward the stable and turned around to return to the road.

"Have ya come to say good-bye?" she asked Aaron softly, his solemn gaze meeting hers.

"*Nee*, want to spend time with ya before I look for a place to stay. I can't put Bertie and Peter out." He moved toward the walkway lined with golden mums, suitcase in tow.

"Can we sit on the sunny side of the porch for a while? It's a perty day."

Aaron set his suitcase near the back door, and they walked to the far end of the porch, where the wind chimes jingled softly overheard. "Of course, I'm all packed to go if you change your mind," he said as they sat down.

She couldn't speak for the powerful emotions overflowing.

"You're my girl . . . for always," he said, reaching for her hand. "Never forget it, Clara."

She nodded, biting her lip. *He truly loves me.*

Silently, they sat holding hands in the privacy of the porch beautified by clay pots of purple and orange mums. Over in the grazing land, two horses nuzzled each other's long necks, and a mule brayed loudly.

Clara noticed her father coming their way and stiffened. *Now what?*

"Does your Dat know you're stayin' home to honor him?" Aaron asked quietly, releasing her hand.

"I'll tell him now."

Aaron inhaled deeply but said nothing more.

One of the barn cats trailed behind Dat as he moseyed this way, and Clara stood. "Got a minute, Dat?"

Pushing his big hands into his black trouser pockets, her father ambled up the porch steps, eyeing Aaron's suitcase. "*Guder Mariye,*" he said, leaning against the porch's white handrail.

Aaron said it back as he stood up as well, then glanced at Clara.

"Dat," she said quickly, "I've made a hard decision."

"All right." Her father removed his straw hat and placed it on the railing.

"You and Mamma always taught me to submit to your guidance." Her breath felt jagged, but she willed herself to continue. "So since you won't bless my courtship with Aaron, I'll be stayin' here, much as I want to go back to Lancaster County with him."

"I won't be leavin', either," Aaron said firmly, still standing. "Not without Clara."

The lines on Dat's brow knit together. "But ya have work to get back to, don't ya?"

"I'll do whatever I must to be with the woman I love." Aaron kept his eyes on Dat. "I believe the Lord brought us together—without a doubt."

At that moment, the back door opened, and Eva stepped out, carrying Clara's suitcase. She set it down next to Aaron's with aplomb. "I took the liberty of packin' up your things, Clara," she said. "Don't want yous to miss your train."

Dat's eyebrows fluttered.

Eva turned her focus on him. "Vernon, your daughter here made a promise before the Lord God and all the People to follow her Savior all the days of her life. She's not gonna back down on that vow . . . and neither will Aaron."

An ensuing silence fell over them, her father looking a bit stunned.

Then Clara said softly, "Eva's right, Dat." She looked at her darling beau, whose eyes were glistening. "My faith's essential to me no matter where I live. Just like it is for Aaron."

Clara's father straightened, his arms limp at his sides.

Aaron turned to face her. "And if Clara will have me as her husband, I'll support her in her faith . . . and our children, too. She has my word on that."

Breaking into a smile, Clara couldn't keep from joyfully accepting his marriage proposal.

Eva walked over to stand before Dat. "So all Aaron needs now is the blessin'. Ain't so, dear?" She looked up at him with shining eyes.

Dat folded his arms and looked out at the meadow for the longest time. Was he upset with Eva? Did he feel cornered?

At last, he stepped forward, and Clara held her breath. "I daresay I've never done things quite so backward," he said, pushing his hands through his trimmed beard. "Never needed to. But I'll trust the Lord above for His grace to cover my daughter Clara . . . and her husband-to-be, Aaron. Though I can't say I'm not goin' to miss ya, bein' so far away," he said with a glint in his eye.

Clara folded her hands tightly, looking toward the sky, then at her father. "*Denki*, Dat. Ever so much," she said, her voice breaking.

"You won't regret this," Aaron said, reaching to shake Dat's hand.

The wind chimes pealed as if to emphasize the poignancy of the moment, and Clara realized what had just taken place. They had her father's blessing . . . and Aaron had actually proposed to her in front of him and Eva!

Clara followed Eva into the house, where they quickly made sandwiches and gathered snacks for the long traveling day. "I appreciate what ya did for Aaron and me just now. More than ya know."

"'Tis obvious the Lord's hand is on the two of yous," Eva said, smiling sweetly. "I hope ya'll come visit again after the wedding. We'll have a nice, big doin' with the People and your friends here."

Clara smiled. "I couldn't be happier. And I'm sure we'll come see you and Dat as husband and wife, whenever that might be."

Later that evening, Clara felt elated at the sight of Ella Mae's grand stone house. The taxicab pulled into the lane, and she rushed to the walkway, where Aendi stood smiling in the twilight as Aaron removed Clara's suitcase from the trunk.

"I'm engaged," she whispered.

Aendi clasped her hand, briefly grinning away her smile lines. "Praise be!"

"I'll tell ya 'bout it later." Clara paused, glancing back at Aaron as he carried her suitcase to the back porch. "Now I just have to become a member of this church district," she said softly.

Aendi's smile faded. "Bishop Beiler wants to see ya as soon as you're settled."

Clara's breath caught. "I wish Aaron could go with me."

"Honestly, I don't know if that's possible, but I'll ask Mattie's husband. He'll ask the bishop."

"I'd feel better 'bout it," Clara said.

"Can't blame ya, dearie."

Clara felt the old apprehension churning as Aaron came their way.

"I'll see ya again real soon, Clara," he told her, then greeted Aendi. "Will ya take *gut* care of my bride-to-be?"

Aendi's smile returned. "That, you can count on."

Once Aaron was heading for home in the taxi, Aendi asked, "Have yous discussed a wedding date?"

"*Nee.* It was enough of a challenge to get my father's blessing."

"Well, thankfully, ya have it now."

"I'll need to know if I'm permitted to join church here before we can plan."

"*Jah,*" Aendi said, suddenly subdued again.

Clara slowly walked to the house arm in arm with dearest Aendi, wondering what would come of the visit with Bishop Beiler. *The final obstacle.*

CHAPTER

Forty-Six

The next day, Mattie stopped by early to bring sticky buns she'd made the day before. Clara greeted her at the door this no-Preaching Sunday, and Aendi asked Mattie to find out if Clara could bring Aaron to the meeting with Bishop Beiler, hopefully later today. She really wanted to know where she stood with the church as soon as possible.

Eager to help, Mattie headed right back home to talk to David. Midmorning, she returned with the answer from the bishop: Aaron was allowed to accompany her. Clara was greatly relieved as Mattie left, and she and Aendi sat down at the table with another cup of coffee.

The outdoor temperature was summer-like, not unusual for some early Octobers in

Lancaster County, according to Aendi. Yet Clara pressed one hand to her forehead and asked Aendi if she looked feverish.

"Here, let's see." Aendi reached over to touch her cheek with the back of her hand. "*Nee*, you're prob'ly nervous . . . and who wouldn't be?"

Clara nodded. "For some reason, Mamma's on my mind. I try to think what she would do in certain situations, openhearted as she was to the Lord."

"Like *you* are, Clara." Aendi's eyes sparkled. "You've been in my prayers ever since ya left for Indiana with Aaron, and now, too, since you're home again."

"*Home*," Clara repeated. "Such a *wunnerbaar* word."

"I couldn't agree more."

Clara set down her coffee cup. "I'd love to know what Mamma would say if she knew my future with Aaron depends on what happens today with Bishop Beiler."

Aendi shook her head. "I think she'd say to be honest with him and then trust God for the outcome."

Clara took that in, wishing she could know right now what the man of God would say. But like Aendi said, her role was to be truthful, just as she'd been with Aaron's father. "Very little rattles Aaron, it seems," Clara said. "I wish ya could've heard him speak up to Dat, sayin' he wasn't leavin' there without me. It was the dearest thing, really. And scary, too, considering I didn't know what Dat would think . . . or do."

"Sounds like God honored Aaron's *Mut*."

Clara nodded. "*Jah*, his courage, for sure. I think Dat was impressed, but we can't always know ahead of time what will happen when we take a stand."

Aendi smiled. "That's the beauty of puttin' every ounce of trust in our heavenly Father. We know He'll do what's best for us, opening the right doors and closing the others."

"I'm glad we talked 'bout this." Clara smiled.

"While you're visitin' with the bishop this evening, I'll be on my knees talkin' to the Lord."

"*Denki*, Aendi." Clara felt less flushed and more confident.

The young bishop immediately came to the door when Aaron knocked, then showed them into the kitchen. Like Aaron, he was dressed as if to go to Preaching. Clara had worn her Lancaster County–style blue dress and matching apron, since it was customary to wear a white organdy apron only to church.

But she'd had to don her Indiana *Kapp* since she hadn't yet made the heart-shaped one so distinctive of this area.

The familiar aroma of coffee filled the bright room, and she and Aaron were invited to sit at the long table. As expected, the bishop sat at the head. He asked Aaron to take a seat to his left and Clara next to Aaron on the same side of the table, both of them facing the large windows.

"It's mighty *gut* this visit could take place today," Bishop Beiler began, looking first at Aaron, then Clara, his blue-gray eyes serious. "Your home bishop and I've been discussin' your request for membership transfer for some time, exchanging letters."

Clara had to remind herself to relax and remember what Aendi told her.

"I've felt strongly that a period of time should pass—months, possibly a year—before considering accepting your transfer of membership," Bishop continued. "A proving of sorts."

Aaron looked her way, and she took it as concern that they wouldn't be getting married this wedding season.

Bishop Beiler squinted into the light pouring in from the windows, emphasizing his ruddy complexion, so like his brother's. "But your Mamm's words spoke volumes to me, Clara."

Her arms prickled. *Mamma's?*

Reaching into his black suit coat pocket, Bishop brought out what looked like a letter. "This is what she wrote to Ella Mae two years ago." He unfolded the letter and read, "'Following my daughter Clara's baptism, she told me with tears brimming that it was her joy to live for God and to obey His commandments all the days of her life. Vernon and I are so thankful to hear it. She is submissive to the Lord and to His ways, and has been since she was a young girl.'"

Bishop Beiler handed the letter to Clara. She accepted it, her gaze on the bishop.

"Your Mamm's letter, which came to me from your Aendi Ella Mae, got me thinkin' that, since you were raised to be obedient to the Lord and the church ordinance there in Indiana, then, just maybe, you could more easily settle in with the People here in the hollow. Even with our stricter *Ordnung*."

Aaron leaned forward. "If I might add somethin', Bishop. Clara is so compliant that she was actually willin' to stay home to honor her father's wishes when he initially withheld his blessing on our possible union, even though she longed to marry." Then he revealed what had ultimately come to pass.

"Is that so?" Bishop asked him, then looked kindly at Clara.

"Her father was deeply moved by her heart toward him. And her commitment to her faith was made even more clear to him."

Clara felt calmer now, pleased Aaron had spoken up on her behalf and glad Aendi had found this letter in the batch of many others and somehow gotten it to the bishop.

"Then, knowin' all this, Clara," Bishop said, "I will welcome ya into the congregation next Sunday before communion."

Aaron gave her the biggest smile, and she inhaled deeply. "I'm ever so grateful," she said meekly. "I truly am."

Nodding emphatically, Aaron reached out his hand to Bishop Beiler, still smiling.

On the ride home, Aaron took the long way. Near Weaver's Creek, he pulled over and halted his horse. "What would ya think about a late November or early December wedding?" he asked.

"This year?" she asked, again hearing guitar music rising from the creek below.

He nodded. "I can get everything ready if you can."

"*Jah*," she said. "I can."

Leaning closer, he kissed her cheek lightly. "God answered my every prayer for you, love, and then some."

The guitar playing continued, and now a man was singing, too. This music was not a hymn from the *Ausbund*. Not at all. It sounded more like a love song.

"What on earth?" Aaron slipped his arm around Clara.

"Aendi and I heard guitar music right in this same spot some months ago, too."

Aaron kissed her cheek again. "Not exactly the kind of music ya'd expect to hear round here."

She looked in the direction of the forbidden music.

Aaron shook his head and reached for the driving lines. "I best be gettin' ya home."

Clara agreed but soon forgot the mysterious music and turned her thoughts to their wedding. "Where do ya want to have our marriage ceremony?"

"Will your father and sister be disappointed if we wed here in the hollow instead of First Light? After all, Bishop John would have to oversee it."

"They'll understand, I'm sure. Eva did when the two of us talked about the wedding just before we left. Also, Ella Mae's like a second Mamm to me, and I want her to be present."

Aaron agreed. "This morning I took the liberty of talkin' to my Dat 'bout building a small house on some of his land. He's offered us a nice-sized plot for a wedding gift in hopes the bishop would accept your membership transfer. After all the time he took deliberating, I prayed he would come round, but Ella Mae certainly helped that along with your Mamma's letter."

Clara briefly leaned her head against Aaron's shoulder. "The Lord opened the door for us."

"He did. And thankfully, I've been able to answer Dat's questions and concerns about our union. He's supportive of us, dear."

"It'll be so nice to meet everyone in your extended family at the ceremony . . . and afterward."

"Trust me, I have oodles of kinsfolk." Aaron chuckled. "Visiting them every weekend, stayin' with my parents or wherever the Lord makes a way, will give us plenty of time to get our house built."

"Eva hopes we'll visit them again, too."

"Most definitely."

Thinking of her step-Mamm, Clara had to smile. *Things sure have a way of turning round*, she thought as she saw Aendi's house come into view. She was overjoyed at the thought of telling her aunt the good news.

Aaron walked with her up the driveway.

He slowed as they approached the back porch. "*Ich liebe dich,* Clara," he said.

"I love you, too," she replied, looking into his handsome face. "*Denki* for goin' with me to the bishop."

He grinned. "*Wunnerbaar* how it all worked out."

She opened the screen door, nearly bursting with delight in so many ways. Then she thanked her heavenly Father for Bishop Beiler's astonishing decision before hurrying to find Aendi.

Epilogue

J ust imagine how I felt when my sweet Aendi Ella Mae suggested having the wedding at her big farmhouse right after I told her what had taken place with the bishop. I didn't want the wedding preparations to be a burden to Aendi, but she reminded me Clyde and Susannah would be moved in by then and would be happy to help redd up the house. Not only that, but she showed me the pattern for her Lancaster County *Kapp* and taught me how to make the center seam on top to create the familiar heart shape. After all, I had to be ready for Communion Sunday the following week. I was soon becoming a member of the Hickory Hollow Amish church!

As for Aaron's and my wedding, I already knew I wanted Rosanna to be one of my two attendants and Lettie the other. And as for my friends Katie Lapp and Mary Stoltzfus, I needed to ponder which one I'd ask to help Ella Mae and Mattie with all the cooking. Maybe both. Aendi suggested Mary, but she didn't say why.

Dat generously boxed up all the items in my hope chest back home and shipped them to me a few weeks later. He also offered to send the wooden chest, but Aendi had an extra blanket chest she wanted me to have. That, and she surprised me by declaring the wedding quilt we'd restored to be mine.

"Oh, Aendi, are ya sure?" I asked as we admired it in the spare room.

"Wouldn't have said it if I wasn't." She nodded her little head. "This heirloom—and its story—brought the two of us closer together than I ever thought possible, dearie."

"I still think of all the special evening hours we spent working on it." I smiled, then for fun, I found several of the many places where the replacement fabric had been stitched over the worn-out vintage pieces. "It's an heirloom, all right."

I turned to look at Aendi with all the love I held for the dear woman, thinking, *She is the true heirloom treasure.* And she was, considering all the wisdom of her years and how God had given her a listening and understanding heart following her teenage rebellion.

She's led many to the path of peace, pointing them to the Savior, I thought, giving her a gentle hug.

Bertie and Peter came to represent my family at our late-November wedding, which was the nicest surprise. And like Dat and Eva, my brothers and their wives sent sizeable checks with their pretty cards.

The day was chilly but sunny, with no hint of rain or snow. Aaron later said that it was a blessing on our new beginning as husband and wife.

Two weeks later, we helped Aendi's family move her into the lovely new *Dawdi Haus*. It wasn't nearly the sad day she'd anticipated or even dreaded. "'Twas a very *gut* day, for certain," she admitted to me, even smiling about it.

"We've both come such a long way, ain't so?" I said, sipping warm peppermint tea at her little table in the much smaller but sunny kitchen the next day.

"I'll say." Aendi tittered. "An' your comin' was a big part of that for me, dearie."

I felt the very same way toward her, and I told her so. "God has a way of puttin' people together, allowin' their paths to cross for His glory and honor."

"That's chust what your Mamm would've said."

Then Aendi brought up the idea of making some quilts together this winter to sell at Vera's. "Chust think 'bout it."

"I'd love that," I told her. "And Aaron's talked of building me a little shop where I can sell quilts, if Vera won't mind the competition. Of course, it would never be as big a shop as hers or have the same variety of items. But this could be a dream come true for me. I could even give quilting lessons and advise others on how to repair their own heirloom quilts while we display some of our creations to sell."

"Well, I'll be. That Aaron's a gem of a husband."

"Absolutely."

"Ain't it somethin' how the Lord arranges our lives when we're willin' to let Him?"

I couldn't help but smile, refusing even happy tears.

Aendi reached for her round yellow teapot and offered more of her delicious peppermint tea. Feeling loved and content, I held up my yellow-and-white saucer and matching cup as she poured.

Author's Note

For at least two decades, I considered writing a prequel to *The Shunning*—the shocking backstory of why Katie Lapp's excommunication was so severe. Then because of readers' pleas for more about Ella Mae Zook's life, it became evident to me that the time had finally come to write this novel, *The Heirloom*.

Many people generously assisted my research on this particular story journey. And several quiltmakers took time to describe the meticulous process of restoring a vintage quilt, for which I am thankful.

My paternal great-grandfather, Will Jones, created beautiful tin art, which caught my attention when I was a young girl. His unusual talent continues to stand out in my memory, so I included this art form in the story of Ella Mae's own youth.

The following individuals and resources

also facilitated my inquiries regarding the transfer of membership from one Amish church district to another, among other important issues: Erik Wesner of Amish America, my consultant for many years; Cousin Bonnie Fortuna, who shared with me the tragic railroad event in Paradise, Pennsylvania, in 1896, which altered our young grandmother Ada Ranck's Mennonite church district; Dodie Robbin, collections manager for research at Railroad Museum of Pennsylvania; Donald Kraybill's books *The Amish* as well as *The Amish and the State* and his other writings; *I Hear the Reaper's Song* by Sara Stambaugh; Eve Wheatcroft Granick's book *The Amish Quilt*; and the book titled *Quilts (The Fabric of Friendship)*, published by Schiffer Publishing Ltd.

Greatest appreciation to Rochelle Gloege, my editor of thirty years, who directs my wonderful editorial team, which includes David Horton, Charlene Patterson, Jean Bloom, Hannah Ahlfield, and Cheri Hanson.

Enormous thanks to Bethany House's amazing fiction marketing and publicity team, with Michele Misiak, Raela Schoenherr, Karen Steele, and Anne Van Solkema, as well as Rachael Betz, Joyce Perez, and Lindsay Schubert. And Jennifer Parker, senior art director, fiction.

Dave Lewis, my dear husband, cheered me on not only with his encouraging words, as he's done from early in my writing journey, but with countless acts of kindness (healthy meals, anyone?). My sister, Barbara Birch, can always be counted on to proofread final pages with a keen eye for typos that may have slipped by unnoticed. Each member of my precious family offers enduring inspiration and cheer—thank you!

You, my ever-devoted reader, continue to be a source of great joy to my heart. I am grateful beyond words.

To our heavenly Father, I give all the glory and honor, trusting and praying that the words on the pages of my books will always resonate with divine truth and light.

Soli Deo Gloria!

Beverly Lewis, born in the heart of Pennsylvania Dutch country, is the *New York Times* bestselling author of more than one hundred books. Her stories have been published in twelve languages worldwide. A keen interest in her mother's Plain heritage has inspired Beverly to write many Amish-related novels, beginning with *The Shunning*, which has sold more than one million copies and is an Original Hallmark Channel movie. In 2007, *The Brethren* was honored with a Christy Award.

Beverly has been interviewed by both national and international media, including *Time* magazine, the Associated Press, and the BBC. She lives with her husband, David, in Colorado.

Visit her website at www.beverlylewis.com or www.facebook.com/officialbeverlylewis for more information.

The Beverly Lewis Amish Heritage Cookbook

20th Anniversary Edition

More than 200 favorite, time-tested recipes collected and passed down by Beverly Lewis from Amish and Plain family and friends and updated for the benefit of cooks with less time to spend in the kitchen. Perfect for gift giving, this updated volume also contains a new foreword, as well as a trove of Amish sayings, household tips, story excerpts, and personal glimpses from beloved bestselling author Beverly Lewis.

Available Fall 2024

For more Ella Mae Zook and the story of Katie Lapp, read on for an excerpt from the groundbreaking bestseller that launched a genre.

The
SHUNNING

by BEVERLY LEWIS

All her life, Katie Lapp has longed for the forbidden things, but will her dreams come at a price too dear to pay?

AVAILABLE WHEREVER BOOKS ARE SOLD

Prologue: Katie

If the truth be known, I was more conniving than all three of my brothers put together. Hardheaded, too.

All in all, *Dat* must've given me his "whatcha-do-today-you'll-sleep-with-tonight" lecture every other day while I was growing up. But I wasn't proud of it, and by the time I turned nineteen, I was ready to put my wicked ways behind me and walk the "straight and narrow." So with a heart filled with good intentions, I had my kneeling baptism right after the two-hour Preaching on a bright September Sunday.

The barn was filled with my Amish kinfolk and friends that day three years ago when five girls and six boys were baptized. One of the girls was Mary Stoltzfus—as close as any real sister could be. She was only seventeen then, younger than most Plain girls receiving the ordinance, but as honest and sweet as they come. She saw no need in putting off what she'd always intended to do.

After the third hymn, there was the sound of sniffling. I, being the youngest member of my family and the only daughter, shouldn't have been too surprised to find that it was Mamma.

When the deacon's wife untied my *kapp*, some pigeons flapped their wings in the barn rafters overhead. I wondered if it might be some sort of sign.

Then it came time for the bishop's familiar words: "Upon your faith, which you have confessed before God and these many witnesses, you are baptized in the name of the Father, the Son, and the Holy Spirit. Amen." He cupped his hands over my head as the deacon poured water from a tin cup. I remained motionless as the water ran down my hair and over my face.

After being greeted by the bishop, I was told to "rise up." A Holy Kiss was given me by the deacon's wife, and with renewed hope, I believed this public act of submission would turn me into an honest-to-goodness Amishwoman. Just like Mamma.

Dear *Mam*.

Her hazel eyes held all the light of heaven. Heavenly hazel, I always called them. And they were, especially when she was in the midst of one of her hilarious stories. We'd be out snapping peas or husking corn, and in a blink, her stories would come rolling off her tongue.

They were always the same—no stretching the truth with Mam, as far as I could tell. She was a stickler for honesty; fairness, too, right down to the way she never overcharged tourists for the mouth-watering jellies and jams she loved to make. Her stories, *ach*, how she loved to tell them—for the telling's sake. And the womenfolk—gathered for a quilting frolic or a canning bee—always hung on every word, no matter how often they were repeated.

There were stories from her childhood and after—how the horses ran off with her one day, how clumsy she was at needlework, and how it was raising three rambunctious boys, one after another. Soon her voice would grow soft as velvet and she'd say, "That was all back before little Katie came along"—as though my coming was a wondrous thing. And it seemed to me, listening to her weave her stories for all the rest of the women, that this must be how it'd be when the Lord God above welcomed you into His Kingdom. Mamma's love was heavenly, all right. It just seemed to pour right out of her and into me.

Then long after the women had hitched

their horses to the family buggies and headed home, I'd trudge out to the barn and sit in the hayloft, thinking. Thinking long and hard about the way Mamma always put things. There was probably nothing to ponder, really, about the way she spoke of me—at least that's what Mary Stoltzfus always said. And she should know.

From my earliest memories, Mary was usually right. I was never one to lean hard on her opinion, though. Still, we did everything together. Even liked the same boys sometimes. She was very bright, got the highest marks through all eight grades at the one-room schoolhouse where all us Amish kids attended.

After eighth grade, Mary finished up with book learning and turned her attention toward becoming a wife and mother someday. Being older by two years, I had a head start on her. So we turned our backs on childhood, leaving it all behind—staying home with our mammas, making soap and cleaning house, tending charity gardens, and going to Singing every other Sunday night. Always together. That was how things had been with us, and I hoped always would be.

Mary and Katie.

Sometimes my brother Eli would tease us. "*Torment* is more like it," Mary would say, which was the honest truth. Eli would be out in the barn scrubbing down the cows, getting ready for milking. Hollering to get our attention, he'd run the words together as if we shared a single name. "Mary 'n Katie, get yourselves in here and help! Mary 'n Katie!"

We never complained about it; people knew we weren't just alike. *Jah*, we liked to wear our good purple dresses to suppers and Singing, but when it came right down to it, Mary and I were as different as a potato and a sugar pea.

Even Mamma said so. Thing is, she never put Mary in any of her storytelling. Guess you had to be family to hear your name mentioned in the stories Mam told, because family meant the world to her.

Still, no girl should have been made over the way Mamma carried on about me. Being Mam's favorite was both a blessing and a curse, I decided.

In their younger years, my brothers—Elam, Eli, and Benjamin—were more ornery than all the wicked kings in the Bible combined—a regular trio of tricksters. Especially Eli and Benjamin. Elam got himself straightened out some last year around Thanksgiving, about the time he married Annie Fisher down Hickory Lane. The responsibilities of farming and caring for a wife, and a baby here before long, would settle most any fellow down.

If ever I had to pick a favorite brother, though, most likely Benjamin would've been it. Which isn't saying much, except that he was the least of my troubles. He and that softhearted way he has about him sometimes.

Take last Sunday, for instance—the way he sat looking so forlorn at dinner after the Preaching, when Bishop Beiler and all five of his children came over to eat with us. The bishop had announced our upcoming wedding—his and mine—that day right after service. So now we were officially published. Our courting secret was out, and the People could start spreading the news in our church district, the way things had been done for three hundred years.

The rumors about all the celery Mamma and I had planted last May would stop. I'd be marrying John Beiler on Thursday, November twenty-first, and become stepmother to his five young children. And, jah, we'd have hundreds of celery sticks at my wedding feast—enough for two-hundred-some guests.

Days after the wedding was announced, Benjamin put on his softer face. Today, he'd even helped hoist me up to the attic to look for Mam's wedding dress, which I just had to see for myself before I finished stitching up my own. Ben stayed there, hovering over me like I was a little child, while I pulled the long dress out of the big black trunk. Deep blue, with a white apron and cape for purity, the dress was as pretty as an Amish wedding dress could be.

Without warning, Ben's words came at me—tumbled right out into the musty, cold air. "Didja ever think twice about marrying a widower with a ready-made family?"

I stared at him. "Well, Benjamin Lapp, that's the most ridiculous thing I've ever heard."

He nodded his head in short little jerks. "It's because of Daniel Fisher, ain't?" His voice grew softer. "Because Daniel went and got himself drowned."

The way he said it—gentle-like—made me want to cry. Maybe he was right. Maybe I was marrying John because Dan Fisher was dead—because there could never be another love for me like Dan. Still, I was stunned that Ben had brought it up.

Here was the brother who'd sat behind me in school, yanking my hair every chance he got, making me clean out the barn more times than I could count . . . and siding against me the night Dat caught me playing Daniel's old guitar in the haymow.

But now Ben's eyes were full of questions. He was worrying out loud about my future happiness, of all things.

I reached up and touched his ruddy face. "You don't have to worry, brother," I whispered. "Not one little bit."

"Katie . . . for certain?" His voice echoed in the stillness.

I turned away and reached into the trunk, avoiding his gaze. "John's a *gut* man," I said firmly. "He'll make a right fine husband."

I felt Ben's eyes boring a hole into the back of my head, and for a long, awkward moment he was silent. Then he replied, "Jah, right fine he'll be."

The subject was dropped. My brother and everyone else would just have to keep their thoughts to themselves about me and the forty-year-old man I was soon to marry. I knew well and good that John Beiler had one important thing on his mind: He needed a mamma for his children. And I, having been blessed with lavish mother-love, was just the person to give it.

Respect for a husband, after all, was honorable. In time, perhaps something more would come of our union—John's and mine. Perhaps even . . . love.

I could only hope and pray that my Dan had gone to his eternal reward, and that someday I'd be found worthy to join him there.

Sign Up for Beverly's Newsletter

Keep up to date with Beverly's latest news on book releases and events by signing up for her email list at the link below.

FOLLOW BEVERLY ON SOCIAL MEDIA

Beverly Lewis

BeverlyLewis.com

More from Beverly Lewis

For generations, Ellie Hostetler's family has tended their orchard, a tradition her twin brother, Evan, will someday continue. But when Evan is drafted for the Vietnam War, the family is shocked to learn he has not sought conscientious objector status. Can Ellie, with the support of a new beau, find the courage to face a future unlike the one she imagined?

The Orchard

Susie Mast's Old Order life has been shaped more by tragedy than by her own choices. But when she decides to stop waiting on her childhood friend and accept another young man's invitation, she soon realizes her mistake. Will family secrets and missed opportunities dim Susie's hopes for the future? Or is what seems like the end only the beginning?

The Beginning

BETHANYHOUSE

Bethany House Fiction   @bethanyhousefiction   @bethany_house   @bethanyhousefiction

 Free exclusive resources for your book group at bethanyhouseopenbook.com

 Sign up for our fiction newsletter today at bethanyhouse.com

SEP 2023